THE BETRAYAL

THE
BETRAYAL

THE LOST LIFE OF JESUS

KATHLEEN O'NEAL GEAR
AND
W. MICHAEL GEAR

A TOM DOHERTY ASSOCIATES BOOK
NEW YORK

THE BETRAYAL

Copyright © 2008 by Kathleen O'Neal Gear and W. Michael Gear

Map and illustrations by David Cain

A Forge Book
Published by Tom Doherty Associates, LLC
175 Fifth Avenue
New York, NY 10010

www.tor-forge.com

Forge® is a registered trademark of Tom Doherty Associates, LLC.

Library of Congress Cataloging-in-Publication Data

Gear, Kathleen O'Neal.
   The betrayal : the lost life of Jesus : a novel / Kathleen O'Neal Gear, W. Michael Gear.—1st hardcover ed.
      p. cm.
   "A Tom Doherty Associates book."
   ISBN-13: 978-0-7653-1546-5
   ISBN-10: 0-7653-1546-7
   1. Jesus Christ—Fiction.   2. Apocryphal Gospels—Fiction.   I. Gear, W. Michael.
II. Title.
   PS3557.E18B38 2008
   813'.54—dc22

                                                                              2008005865

First Edition: June 2008

Printed in the United States of America

0   9   8   7   6   5   4   3   2   1

In Memory of

WANDA LILLIE BUCKNER O'NEAL

October 5, 1925, to June 23, 2007

Her search for Truth led her on a long journey of scriptural study. As a child, I remember watching her ponder the Tibetan and Egyptian books of the dead, and sat beside her as she patiently learned to read Mayan codices. Later, when I was studying New Testament Greek, she made me teach her. For the rest of her life, she struggled through a multitude of ancient texts seeking the smallest biblical insights.

   She was a true Renaissance Woman. . . . A powerful force of nature . . . She will be deeply missed.

Kathleen O'Neal Gear
September 24, 2007

ACKNOWLEDGMENTS

We would like to offer our sincere gratitude to the following scholars for the many lessons in religious studies and philosophy that they tried to get through our thick skulls: Bruce W. Jones, Gary E. Kessler, L. Stafford Betty, Jacqueline Kegley, Norman Prigge, John Bash, Shigeo Kanda, and Donald Heinz. And though he can no longer hear us in this world, we also offer our heartfelt thanks to Dr. Charles W. Kegley. No more hiding the light under the bushel, Charles.

We appreciate all of you.

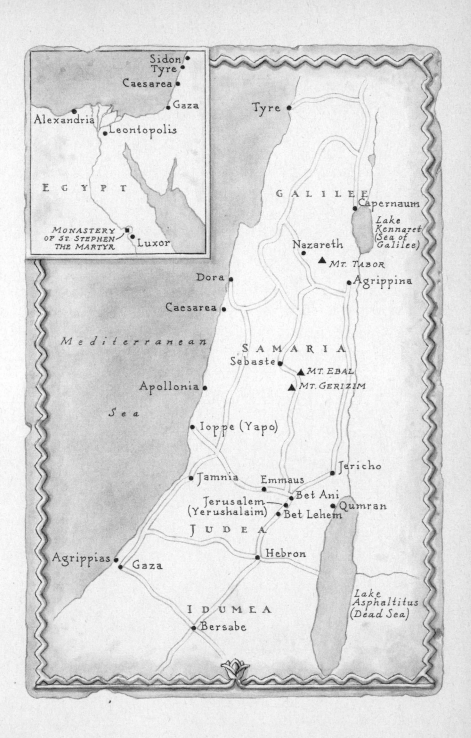

Sidon
Tyre
Caesarea
Gaza
Alexandria
Leontopolis
EGYPT
MONASTERY
OF ST. STEPHEN
THE MARTYR
Luxor

Tyre

GALILEE
Capernaum
Lake
Kennaret
(Sea of
Galilee)
Nazareth
▲ MT. TABOR
Dora
Agrippina
Caesarea

Mediterranean

SAMARIA
Sebaste
▲ MT. EBAL
▲ MT. GERIZIM
Apollonia

Sea

Ioppe (Yapo)

Jericho
Jamnia
Emmaus
Bet Ani
Jerusalem
(Yerushalaim)
Bet Lehem
Qumran
JUDEA

Agrippias
Gaza
Hebron

IDUMEA
Lake
Asphaltitus
(Dead Sea)
Bersabe

INTRODUCTION

There is an alternate story of the life of Jesus. It is a very *human* story, one that has been suppressed for nineteen centuries. Those of you who are not familiar with this story may find it disturbing. If so, you are not alone. The early Church fathers found the books that chronicled this story so menacing that they outlawed them, ordered them burned, and threatened with death anyone found copying them.

Remember that what follows is based on actual documents recovered from archaeological sites in the Middle East, or respected repositories of ancient literature, like the Vatican library.

Yeshua ben Miriam's story, that is, the story of Jesus, the son of Mary, as told in these books, is brilliant and tragic. It is the story of a man whose own family thought he was mad (Mark 3:21). It is the story of a man who met a violent end at the hands of Roman authorities. Nearly all of the ancient texts verify that Yeshua was crucified as the "King of the Jews." He was not, as many movies and books would have us believe, a meek man who spent his time spinning parables and healing the sick. Such a Jesus would have been a threat to no one. The historical Jesus *did* threaten and enrage people, from the priestly aristocracy in the Jerusalem temple to the Roman prefect who finally condemned him to be crucified.

He was a controversial figure. For many of you, this will be a controversial book.

Keep in mind that during the first and second centuries an immense variety of Christian beliefs and practices existed. There were numerous gospels.[1] It took three hundred years before the Church decided to organize an ecumenical council—the Council of Nicea in 325 C.E.—to dictate uniformity and outlaw all gospels that did not meet its narrow criteria of Truth.

The New Testament as we know it today was not finally settled on in the West until around the year 400.

Because the ancient accounts of the life of Jesus often conflict, we have used the archaeological record and the earliest documentary evidence to piece together this story. The documents include the traditional New Testament books, the Qumran and Nag Hammadi codices, as well as other literature that dates from roughly 50 C.E. to 250 C.E. These early documents are probably closer to the truth than the later, and much more spectacular, documents written in the late third and fourth centuries, or even later. We have footnoted the sources of the major events, especially those that are dramatically different from the traditional story of Jesus' life and the lives of those around him. There is a bibliography in the back of this book for those who want to see the sources with their own eyes. *We urge you to read the notes, as they provide detailed information on the historical events surrounding the life of Jesus, and those closest to him.*

Some of you will consider these documents to be a threat to your faith. We especially encourage those who do to press on and read them. Knowledge does not destroy faith. It does not take Jesus away. In fact, we believe it can give back the profound meaning to his life that has been lost over centuries of revisionism.

GLOSSARY

With one exception, *Jerusalem,* we use the correct historical names for biblical places and characters like Jesus, Mary, Joseph, and John—which means we use the names they would actually have been called by at the time. Many of the names are obvious. For example, *Markos* and *Loukas* were clearly the figures we know as "Mark" and "Luke." *Bet Lehem* and *Bet Ani* are "Bethlehem" and "Bethany." Other proper names, however, are not so obvious. Hopefully, this glossary will alleviate some of the confusion associated with the more unfamiliar names.

Please keep in mind that though scholars suspect some of the original gospels may have been written in Hebrew or Aramaic, the extant New Testament documents were written in the Greek language, which means the original Hebrew or Aramaic names of people like *Yeshua* (Jesus) and *Yakob* (James) were translated into Greek as *Iesous* and *Iakobos.*

Lastly, in Greek there is no *sh* sound, and in Hebrew and Aramaic there is no *j* sound. As well, Hebrew and Aramaic are written almost entirely without vowels. These unique features of the languages have led to many spelling variations over time, as can be seen in the following.

Galilee
In Hebrew it was referred to as the *Galil.* In the original Greek New Testament it was called the *Galilaian.*

James

In Hebrew and Aramaic his name was *Ya'akov,* or *Yakob* (Jacob). In Greek it was *Iakobos,* and in Latin, *Iacomus,* which when translated into the Germanic spelling became *Jacomus,* then in Spanish *Jaime.* Finally, because the King James version translated it as *James* in 1611, it has remained *James* ever since in English translations.

Jerusalem

Hebrew: *Yerushalaim.* Greek: *Ierosoluma.* We mention the Greek here only for the sake of historicity. From this point on, in the chapters set in the fourth century, you will read "Jerusalem." We have made this concession because we think the English name helps to better anchor English readers to the place and time.

Jesus

His name was *Yeshua* in Hebrew, or in more formal situations—for example, in the Jerusalem Temple—*Yehoshua.* However, because the first-century dialect of Galilee dropped the final letter (*ayin*), Yeshua's Galilean friends, or those who were very close to him, probably called him by the name *Yeshu.* As well, early rabbinic sources largely use *Yeshu* for "Jesus of Nazareth," and the Talmud *only* uses *Yeshu* for "Jesus of Nazareth."

In Greek his name was *Iesous,* or *Iesous Christos,* which we translate into English as "Jesus" or "Jesus Christ."

Jews

Hebrew: *Yehudim.* Greek: *Ioudaiosoi.*

John

The Hebrew is *Yohanan.* Greek: *Ioannes.*

Joseph

Hebrew: *Yosep, Yosef,* or in more formal situations, *Yehosef.* In the Greek manuscripts there is a great deal of variance: *Ioses, Iose, Iosetos, Ioseph.* Many scholars believe that the form *Ioses* follows the Galilean pronunciation of the Hebrew *Yosep.*

Mary

    Miriam in Hebrew. In Aramaic it became *Maryam,* and in Coptic it was *Mariham.* The New Testament Greek gospels call her *Maria* or *Mariam.*

Matthew

    In Hebrew it is *Matthias, Mattiyahu,* or *Matya.* The Greek is *Maththaios.*

THE
BETRAYAL

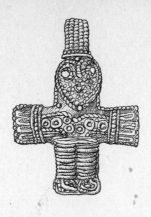

ONE

NISAN THE 9TH, THE JEWISH YEAR 3771

Misty rain had been falling for two days and the dark mountaintop was cold and sweet with the fragrance of damp pine needles and wet earth.

Maryam drew her himation, a large square garment cut from white linen, over her head for warmth and stared down at the holy city of Yerushalaim. From up here, high on the Mount of Olives, the view was stunning. Starlight gilded the ancient stone walls and painted the wide streets. All was quiet and still. Even the tendrils of smoke that rose from the houses lay unmoving, like a dead black filigree spread upon the windless heavens.

Her gaze drifted to the Temple Mount. The trapezoidal platform of the Temple, supported by massive retaining walls that towered more than 50 cubits above the roadways, covered over 344,000 square cubits.[2] It was twice as large as the monumental Forum Romanum, and more than three and a half times bigger than the combined temples of Jupiter and Astarte-Venus at Baalbek. The grandeur of the entire complex of buildings, baths, mosaic courts, magnificently columned porticoes, and exquisite arches was unmatched in the world. And the Temple itself, the place where God lived, was awe-inspiring. The surface was covered with so much gold that when sunlight kissed it, it virtually blinded. Tonight, in the starlight, it was a shining silver bastion of light and dreams.

Maryam turned to the man seated on the angular limestone boulder to her left. Slender, with muscular shoulders, he was of medium height, and had shoulder-length black curly hair. The white himation over his head framed his bearded face and contrasted sharply with his dark glistening eyes. "This is dangerous, Yeshu. They are violent men."

"We are all violent men," he softly responded.

She stood for a time, deciding what to say, then sank down upon the rock beside him. The Mount of Olives was composed of limestone with a chalklike top layer. Despite the inhospitable soil, extensive olive groves covered its slopes, and pine trees dotted the high points. After several anxious heartbeats, she whispered, "If word gets back to the praefectus, he will think you are conspiring—"

"I *must* speak with Dysmas."

His tone silenced her. She looked away and ground her teeth beneath the tanned skin of her jaw. The knot of fear in her belly was pulling tighter, hindering her breathing.

"Maryam, please trust me. I know how this may appear to the Roman authorities, but it's necessary."

He leaned over and gently kissed her cheek, for it was by a kiss that the perfect, or those striving for perfection, conceived and gave birth. They received conception from the grace that lived in one another.[3]

She fought to keep her voice from shaking when she answered, "It's the Zealots I don't trust."

"They are from the Galil, as I am. They are friends of my friends, people I grew up with. That is enough justification for me to agree to speak with them."

"But, why now?" She lifted her hands in exasperation. "After Yohanan's murder they tried to take you by force and make you a king. You ordered us to avoid the crowds because you feared they would ambush and capture you. What if they do it tonight?"[4]

"They won't."

She lowered her hands and clenched them to fists. Only yesterday he had ordered his followers to buy swords.[5] Though Yeshu taught that God, not humans, should exact vengeance, he was taking no chances with the Zealots, who hated the Romans and wanted to cleanse the land with their blood.

Or perhaps it is the Romans he fears . . . or the Temple priests, or the screaming crowds begging for a single glance from him. These days, we are surrounded by enemies.

Involuntarily, her gaze drifted to the north. Outside the city walls, she could see the fenced area that had been set up for the pilgrims who flooded Yerushalaim during the holy days. Thousands of tents had already been pitched. In all, there were three pilgrim camps around Yerushalaim: the one to the north, another to the west of the city, and a third south of the Siloam pool, in the Kidron valley.

Yeshu gave her an apologetic glance. "Forgive me for sounding stern. It's just that I promised the Zealots I would meet them here at the ninth hour of night, Maryam, and I must keep my word. They *are* violent men, but they are also powerful men. With the two holy days coming, it is critical that we all understand each other."

"Yes. Of course. I—I understand."

In the valley below, a few oil lamps gleamed. She studied them longingly. After the killing exhaustion of the past few days, the press of the crowds, the shouts and cries, she yearned to be lying next to him, rolled in blankets, somewhere far out in the desert, safe and warm.

She mustered the courage to ask the question that had been plaguing her. "Yeshu, if . . . if you are still free to do so . . . will you enter Yerushalaim?"

He smiled and bowed his head to stare at the damp ground. "You are the first to ask me directly. The others are either too frightened, or assume they already know the answer. The truth is I haven't decided yet. I must speak with Yosef Haramati first."

Yosef Haramati, whose name literally meant "Yosef of the highlands," was a member of the sacred Council of Seventy-one, and a secret friend. More and more of the Temple leaders had been expressing anxiety about Yeshu and his teachings. Yosef, despite the danger to himself and his family, would tell them what was being said behind closed doors.

"Are you worried about what the Seventy-one are planning?"

"I am more worried about Rome, but the Council concerns me, yes."

"They are wicked old men, full of spite. I don't understand why they hate you so." She pulled her white himation tightly around her shoulders and shivered.

"Are you cold?" He removed his own himation and started to drape it around her.

"No." She held up a hand to stop him. "Keep it. I didn't shiver because of the night air."

Compassion filled his dark starlit eyes. He hesitated a few long moments before saying, "We are all afraid, Maryam. Fear is the grist of the mill."

As he slipped his himation over his shoulders again, he watched the light play in the olive trees that filled the Kidron valley. When the breeze shifted, the leaves shimmered, and the scent of freshly plowed fields came to them.

"The holy days may embolden them to take action against us," Maryam whispered. Desperately, she added, "We could leave and return after Pesach.[6] We have friends in Samaria. You and Shimon both studied with Yohanan. Perhaps he would—"

"Maryam"—he reached over to stroke her hair—"do you remember, thirty-four years ago, when Praefectus Varus ordered two thousand men, underground fighters leading the rebellion against Rome, to be crucified in the mountains outside Yerushalaim?"

She hesitated. "I recall hearing about it. Why?"

The lowing of a cow drew her attention to the rolling hills north of Bet Ani where silver-bellied thunderclouds drifted across the sky.

"I was two years old," Yeshu said, "but I saw them die, as did every other person in Yerushalaim that month. Rome wanted to make certain that we understood the price of rebellion." He exhaled a breath that fogged in the cool air. "Then there was Yudah of the Galil. I was twelve when he was killed."

Yudah had formed a sect called the Fourth Philosophy, comparing themselves with the Pharisees, Sadducees, and Essenes. They believed that Jews were required to submit to the will of God alone. When Quirinius, governor of Syria, ordered that a census be taken, Yudah proclaimed that only God had the right to number his people, and said that to submit to the census was to deny His Lordship.[7]

Sadly, Yeshu said, "I remember Yudah standing on the shore of the Jordan, shouting that God would deliver His people only when they rose up in armed rebellion against Rome. It took Yudah two days to die. It was terrible, not just for me, but for everyone in the Galil. He had been one of our great-est heroes."

A whisper of pine-sharp wind meandered across the mountaintop. He pulled his himation more tightly around his shoulders.

Maryam studied his troubled expression. "Why did you ask me about Yudah and the two thousand?"

"Because Zealots have paid terribly in the past for their unwavering faith in God. The least they deserve from me is to be heard."

"But, Master, please consider waiting. You can talk with them later, after—"

He put a hand on her wrist to quiet her.

Footsteps, soft and carefully placed, sounded on the slope below them.

Ten heartbeats later she saw the black silhouettes of two men. One was tall and thin, the other short, but very muscular.

Yeshu rose to his feet, preparing himself for the confrontation.

When they came to within three paces, Yeshu called, "Dysmas, Gestas, welcome. Please sit with me." He gestured to the rocks that thrust up from the hillside to his right.

Dysmas stopped two paces away, but remained standing. His brown himation hung around his skinny frame in tattered, dirty folds. He had a lean face with dark pits for eyes, and long black hair hung over his shoul-ders. "Magician, you surprise me. I didn't expect you to be here."[8]

Yeshu dipped his head. "How may I serve you?"

Dysmas had the distinctive accent of a man born and raised in the Galil, as Yeshu did. He had often been accused of being a Zealot because of his accent. The Zealot movement had started in the Galil with Yudah and most of its members continued to come from there.

Gestas stopped beside Dysmas and spread his feet as though bracing himself for a long night. He had a pockmarked face with a squashed nose, probably broken in one too many brawls, and brown hair.

Dysmas looked at Maryam. "Why is she here?"

"Maryam is my companion and adviser."

Dysmas looked her up and down, clearly disturbed that a woman would dare to attend a political meeting, but he wisely turned to Yeshu. "That leper spread the news far and wide, didn't he?"

Yeshu smiled, but cocked his head. "Is that why you're here? To discuss my healings?"

"We're here because we've seen the thousands who gather to hear you preach every day. We know that before you arrived here, so many followed you that you couldn't even enter a town, but had to remain in the country-side for safety. Even then, the sick and those possessed by demons ran to you from every corner. It is said that some came from as far away as Sidon."

Yeshu answered simply, "As you have come. Are you also in need of healing?"

The Zealots' unblinking eyes reflected the starlight like silver shields, and Maryam could tell from their stony expressions that they were irritated by his question.

Dysmas said, "I don't need any of your magic potions or spells. We're here to learn your plans for Pesach." He took a step forward and leaned toward Yeshu to whisper, "Do you truly wish to destroy the Temple and sweep away the corruption? I've heard you say it. If you mean to try to fulfill the prophecies, let us help you."

The man's face resembled a weasel's, predatory, waiting for the slightest hint of weakness to leap.

"I would welcome your help, Dysmas, if I thought our goals were the same. I'm not sure they are."

"You preach loudly against the corruption and immorality that infects the priests like a deadly rot. We agree with you. It must be stopped."

Yeshu quietly frowned at the ground. "Dysmas, it is true that many members of the priesthood, as well as the ruling class, have adopted evil, licentious ways. They tax the poor until they cannot afford to buy bread and spend the spoils for silk sashes to bind their waists. Injustice is rampant. It sickens me, but violence is not the solution."

"We *must* cast off the yoke of Rome and get our nation back! The holy books say that the *mashiah* will conquer the enemies of Yisrael and restore our nation. Are you the promised redeemer or not?"

Yeshu hesitated.

Maryam's eyes jerked to him. He had never said it. At least, not aloud.

Gestas, for the first time, spoke up: "Magician, we have five thousand men ready to attack. With you as our leader, the general populace will flock behind our soldiers with whatever weapons they can grab from their fields or labors. God is sure to see our hearts and rush to our aid. Not even the Romans can withstand—"

"Who is your leader?"

Dysmas and Gestas exchanged a glance, then Dysmas replied, "He calls himself the 'Son of the Father,'[9] in much the same way you call yourself the 'Son of Man.' You are both God's prophets who, if you work together, will conquer our enemies and lead Yisrael back to its glory."

Yeshu took a deep breath and let it out slowly. He must have been thinking, as Maryam was, that they had gotten down to their true reasons for the meeting much more quickly than he'd thought they would.

"Brothers, are you not afraid that such a move will provoke the Romans to destroy both our city and our nation?"

"Oh, they'll try; but if we join forces, our nation will, as one, stand up and fight. They cannot kill us all."

Maryam made a small, frightened sound and protectively folded her arms across her chest. Just above a whisper, she urged, "Do not listen to them, Master. The Romans can and *will* kill us all. They have proven it many times."

Dysmas glared at her. To Yeshu, he said, "What do women know of battle? Nothing. Less than nothing."

"And you, Dysmas, have you seen battle? What about you, Gestas?"

Both men straightened, as though offended.

Dysmas replied, "We served as part of the Temple police. While we've never been in war, we've seen our share of fighting. We've also seen the bribery, fraud, and vice that go on in the Temple in the name of religion. Why, High Priest Kaiaphas is the handmaiden of the praefectus! You know it as well as we do. The fool laps the milk of life from a Roman bowl. And it costs us all a pretty sum!"

The "sum" he referred to was the fee that high priests had to pay to remain in office. High priests were Roman nominees, responsible to Roman authority, and removable by the Romans if they did not pay what the praefectus demanded. The sum provided a lucrative source of private income for anyone who served as praefectus. This fact did not make high priests particularly popular with the average person, especially since they charged "temple fees" to help cover the costs.[10]

Yeshu squinted at the rocky hillside. Somewhere in the distance a dog barked, and it stirred every other dog in hearing to yip and howl, serenading the night with a melodious chorus.

In his deep, teaching voice, he said, "Dysmas, I have heard with my own ears the trumpets blare and the noise of rebellion. I have seen with my own eyes the great turmoil that results. I beg you not to do this. Listen to me, and you will be clothed in light and a chariot will bear you aloft. Ignore my words, and this world will pass away before you are prepared."

"We didn't come here to be preached at, Magician! We came to learn your Pesach plans. Will you challenge the Seventy-one, or not?"

Maryam's belly muscles went tight. She looked straight at him, waiting for him to say "no," as he must. Yeshu had subtly been challenging the Council for many months, openly healing on Shabbat, taking food and drink with sinners. But to lead a revolt against them, and by extension Rome, as Yudah of the Galil had done? Horrifying images of gaunt, crucified men with their dead faces twisted in agony filled her thoughts. Maryam rose to her feet, and said, "They need a sacrificial lamb, Master. That's why they're here. They're too cowardly to do it themselves. Let's go."

Rage contorted Dysmas' face. "Best tell your whore to keep her mouth shut, Magician. She's very close to—"

"To me," Yeshu interrupted. "She's very close to me. As I wish you were." He extended one hand to Dysmas and the other to Gestas. "Now, this instant, I challenge you to take my hands and follow me into the light that is to come."

Gestas vented an ugly laugh, and said, "You constantly speak about salvation. How is it possible you do not know that chasing the Romans from our land is the only way to truly save our people?"

Yeshu left his hands out while he mildly said, "I warn you, brothers, resistance can only lead to social and military disaster for our people. Do not take this path. Very soon, God Almighty will renew his covenant with Yisrael and we will all—"

"I told you not to preach at us!" Dysmas shouted and it echoed over the rolling hills. The dogs started barking again.

Yeshu slowly pulled his hands back. Dysmas and Gestas had their jaws clenched.

Maryam moved closer to his side. If they attacked him, she would tear them apart with her bare hands.

Yeshu softly said, "You Zealots remind me of the rich merchant who discovered a beautiful pearl and sold everything he owned to buy it. He clutched that pearl to his chest, forsaking all other things, even food and drink, even his family. Too late did he discover that his treasure brought him only pain and death."

Both men shifted, fists balled in anger. Maryam wondered if they understood that their dream of conquering Rome was the pearl.

"So," Dysmas said, "you will not join forces with us?"

"I am already joined with you in the divine light, brothers. Let that be enough."

"I told you so," Gestas said. "He's a Roman stooge just like the high priest. That's why he told us to pay their taxes. Give unto Caesar! I spit upon Caesar!"

Dysmas fixed Yeshu with a hard eye. "I ask you one last time to tell us plainly if you are with us or against us."

The night breeze tousled the old grass on the hillside and created a soft hissing sound.

"I am against no man, Dysmas. We are all One in the Kingdom. I will pray for you."

"We're wasting our time," Gestas said, raising his hands in frustration. "Let's go and tell the Son of the Father that the Magician refuses to help us."

Dysmas lowered his hand to his belted dagger. "He will be very displeased. Perhaps you should think this over."

Yeshu shook his head. "No, I don't need to."

"Then you are a coward!" Dysmas viciously spat at Yeshu, and both Zealots turned and tramped away down the hill.

He watched them until they disappeared into the dark shadows of the olive trees.

"The fools," Maryam said in a shaking voice. "Why do they persecute you? This world is about to end! They should be tending to their own souls, not rousing the people to fight Rome."

"Don't hate them, Maryam. They are blind in their hearts. For the moment they are intoxicated, but they will leave this earth empty men. If you do not wish to suffer the same fate, you must become a passerby."[11]

"A passerby? Don't joke. After tonight, they'll be working against us, maybe even plotting to kill us. I'm angry. You should be, too."

"Perhaps." He smiled at her. "But only a calm pond reflects the light of the Kingdom."

Her enraged expression slackened. She closed her eyes. He had taught them that sinners only came to them for baptism when the light of the Kingdom shone in their eyes and on their faces.

She said, "Forgive me, Master. I seem to forget your teachings at the moments I need them most. I am ashamed of myself."

"Don't be. You are tired, as I am. Let's . . ."

Down in the olive trees, voices rose. Only then did she realize that a Zealot camp hid there. Maryam's eyes jerked wide and riveted on the spot.

"Blessed God, that's why Dysmas chose this meeting place," she hissed. "How many men do you think he brought with him? All five thousand?"

Yeshu's brows drew together. "I don't know, but let's go." He put a hand on her shoulder. "It's not wise to dally here. Besides, I'm sure the others are awake and longing to hear what happened."

They started down the trail that led back to her family's home in Bet Ani, but she could not help glancing over her shoulder often to make certain they were not being followed.

They walked the entire way in silence. He seemed lost in his thoughts, but Maryam was listening for footsteps behind them. Around every bend, she expected to be ambushed by an angry horde.

When they finally reached her home, her nerves were strung so tight, she said, "You go in, Master. I—I need to remain out here in the cool air for a while."

He touched her hair gently, said, "Don't be long," and walked to the door. When it closed behind him and she heard the voices of the other disciples rise, bombarding him with questions, Maryam could stand it no longer.

She staggered to the side of the road and vomited until there was nothing left to heave, until her belly shredded and caught in her throat, and the only thing coming up was blood.

For a long time, she just listened to her own breathing.

It took a quarter hour, but when she could, she wiped her mouth on the corner of her himation, and straightened her clothing.

He needed her now more than he had ever needed her in his life. She sucked in a deep, fortifying breath, and strode for the house to stand at his shoulder.

Two

The smell of the spiced nightingale tongues mixed sickeningly with the scent of wood smoke, making Pappas Silvester feel slightly ill. He straightened the sleeves of his black robe and let out a shaky breath. His closely shaven head and long nose felt as cold as ice.

The emperor sat in an ornate chair behind a table heaped with colorful platters of meat and fruits. He wore a glittering purple robe, gold-studded jerkin, and sword belt. Constantine was a big man, tall and muscular, with broad shoulders. He didn't even seem to be breathing, just staring unblinkingly at Silvester.

Silvester said, "You summoned me, Excellency?"

The emperor plucked a grape from a platter and crushed it between his teeth. The entire time, his gaze never left Silvester.

Silvester swallowed hard. He was fairly certain why he'd been summoned, but was hoping it was something else. Anything else.

The crackling fire in the hearth threw monstrous shadows over the elaborately painted walls, the great rounded arches, and magnificently vaulted ceiling. There were few pieces of furniture, but each was intricately carved and polished until it gleamed.

Warmth climbed up through his boots, and Silvester glanced down at the mosaic floor. Below, in the subterranean caverns, he could imagine the slaves laboring at the boilers to heat the tiles he stood upon. Ordinarily their warmth would have been a balm, but not tonight. Tonight it was a reminder of the dangerous ground upon which he stood.

"My informants tell me that this afternoon's session was more like a brawl than a sacred council meeting," the emperor said.

"There were many disagreements, Excellency. The heresy of Arius caused much concern. Both sides have strong opinions about whether or not Iesous should be subordinated to God. Our side maintains that our Lord's eternal essence, the Word, is God, while the Arians stress that he was indisputably 'begotten,' though only-begotten, and therefore his creaturely dependence upon the Father's will makes it clear Iesous is less than the Father. This whole 'only-begotten' thing is complicated, of course, by Psalms chapter two, verse seven. Even worse, Pappas Eusebios of Caesarea agrees with Arius! At heart, it's all a discussion of how our Lord could have suffered and saved if he was not human, but wholly God. We will fight it out, I assure you."

A glitter entered the emperor's eyes, and Silvester fought to control his breathing. The emperor obviously considered Silvester's lengthy answer to be a delaying tactic—even subterfuge. He gave the emperor a weak smile.

The emperor smiled back—the effect like a knife at Silvester's throat. "I understand that Pappas Eusebios is, on many issues, our most vociferous opponent. He clearly believes he has some hidden leverage over us."

"Yes, well, the old man is a nuisance," Silvester agreed. His knees had started to quake.

The emperor tilted his head. In a curiously inhuman voice, he asked, "Have you failed me, Silvester?"

A cold wave of fear rolled through him. "No, Excellency, I—I require more time. We've persuaded many of his assistants to tell us what they know of the Pearl, but their knowledge appears very limited."

Silvester shot a nervous glare at Pappas Meridias, who stood just outside the door, waiting for instructions. In the gloom beyond the aura of firelight, the man appeared little more than a tall black silhouette. Fact was, his mere presence sent a cold draft down Silvester's spine.

"Then you didn't use all of the means of persuasion at your disposal. Do better."

"I assure you, Emperor, leniency is not the problem. My people are very thorough."

Meridias sniffed at the affront, but did not enter the chamber. No one who knew him would call Meridias "lenient"—monster, bastard, animal, yes. But never lenient.

"The problem, Excellency, is that Eusebios has spent forty years dispersing his best library assistants to distant parts of the world where we can't find them."

Constantine reached for a pinch of nightingale tongues, tilted his head back, and dropped them into his mouth. As he chewed, he asked, "Are they still part of the True Church?"

"Some of them may be monks. Others have either become hermits or have simply vanished."

"You should be able to locate the monks."

Silvester flapped his arms in frustration. "Men receive new names when they enter monasteries. It makes it difficult to track individuals, especially if they do not wish to be tracked. They can simply move from one monastery to another, taking a new name each time."

The emperor rose from his chair and straightened to his full height. He stepped purposely around the table; the metal of his jerkin, sword belt, and boot tops flashed in the firelight. The man always stood ready to defend himself from hidden murderers, which was prudent, given the number of attempts that had been made on his life.

"As you see it, what is the greatest danger?" Constantine asked as he stopped before Silvester and propped his hands on his hips. He towered over Silvester, his dark eyes like embers. The powerful fragrances of wood smoke and roasted meat rose from his clothing.

Silvester had to tilt his head back to look up at him. "The danger is that they know the location."

"Then it may be gone."

"Perhaps, but I think it more likely that it was covered over around two hundred years ago—as were so many holy sites—by Emperor Hadrian in his zeal to destroy the Jews and everything they cherished. Do not forget that it was Hadrian who changed the name of Jerusalem to Colonia Aelia Capitolina, and as part of the construction of the city turned the *Kraniou Topon,* "Place of the Skull," into a vast landfill upon which he built a

Temple to Aphrodite.[12] "Or"—he waved a hand—"it might have been obliterated in the year 303 when Emperor Diocletian ordered the destruction of all Christian churches and texts."

"Then you believe it's buried?"

"We can't know for certain, but must proceed as though it is." He swallowed hard. "Because if it exists, Excellency, our doctrines will be cast aside like rotted cloth."

The emperor seemed to be considering that. Finally, he took a breath and ordered, "I want the Temple to Aphrodite torn down and the landfill removed. Immediately. If the Pearl is there, I want to know before anyone else does."

"Yes, Excellency. Of course."

Constantine's hard eyes narrowed. "And what of Jairus? Have you located him?"

"We may have, Excellency. At one of the Pachomius' monasteries in Egypt. But again, I need more time to verify the rumors. A few months, that's all."

The jewels Constantine wore flashed and glittered as the emperor turned and walked back toward his chair. Silvester dared to take a breath of relief.

Over his shoulder, Constantine said, "Begin the excavations on the landfill, then find Jairus. After that, find all the men who ever assisted Pappas Eusebios at the library in Caesarea. I want to know where the Pearl is hidden. Our very survival depends upon it. Do you understand?"

"Yes, Excellency." Silvester turned and strode for the door.

Just before he stepped out into the hallway, the emperor called, "And Pappas?"

Silvester turned to face Constantine.

"Do not come back to me until you've accomplished the goals I just set forth."

Terror fired Silvester's veins. The meaning was clear: *You won't live through it.*

Silvester bowed deeply. "Yes, Excellency, I won't fail you."

Silvester stepped out into the brazier-lit hallway. The high-arched corridor was lined on either side with imperial guards. Firelight flickered on immaculately polished armor and gave a deep tone to their red capes. Not one of the ten guards so much as looked at him.

Silvester swallowed hard and locked his knees. The massive gray stone walls seemed to be leaning toward him, as though they were demons bending down to suck away his soul. Try as he might, he could not shake the feeling that a brooding presence stood right at his shoulder.

"Pappas?" Meridias asked, stepping forward and extending a hand, as if for support.

Silvester motioned for Meridias to follow him. Meridias' blond hair and cold eyes shone in the dim light.

As they marched down the hall side-by-side, passing the soldiers, Silvester hissed, "My personal boat is waiting on the dock at Ephesus. Take it to Egypt. Keep me apprised."

THE TEACHING ON THE SWORD

Rain clouds drift through the sky, but there is no rain today, only heat and more heat. You are irritable as you walk down the road toward Yerushalaim. Your brothers and sisters walk ahead of you. You lag, swatting at flies, grumbling to yourself because you want nothing more than to go and sleep in the shade of an olive tree until night comes. But *he* will not allow it. You have finally escaped the crowds, and he says you must rush on. You hear his voice, teaching, as always . . . but can't make out most of the words until he calls:

"Did you hear that, brother?" Yeshu stops and turns around to look straight at you.

You squint against the glare to see him. His black hair haloes his face in tight, sweat-drenched curls. The sun beats down upon your head like a fiery hammer.

"No. I'm too far behind. What did you say?"

"We were talking about the art of the sword. I said that it was, for the most part, the art of being truly present with God."

The disciples gather around him in a milling circle, listening. They can tell by his tone of voice that this is another lesson, and they want to hear it.

Unlike you. You just want to get to a cold drink of water.

As he needs you to, you say, "That sounds ridiculous. Am I not always present with God? How could I be otherwise, for you have told us that God is everywhere, all the time."

He suppresses a smile. It's his way of thanking you for asking the questions no one else will. You are his acknowledged adversary, and he both resents and cherishes it.

Yeshu says, "I think, in fact, that people are almost never present with God. They are thinking about the past or the future, worried about what their enemies are doing, or worse, what their friends are plotting. But rarely do they live truly Now. And that is where God lives."

You flap your arms in exasperation. "Very fascinating, but I don't see what that has to do with the art of the sword."

He cuts the air with his hand, as though swinging an invisible sword. "The sword has a living heart. It beats. It listens. It strikes. But the blow is only lethal when the swordsman acts in an instant of utter awareness of the cause of life and death."

You glance around at the disciples. They look as mystified as you do. Poor Matya, his young face is screwed up in total confusion.

"Truly," you say, "I hate your parables. They are utter nonsense. I wish you would speak straightly."

He tilts his head, and smiles. "I mean that it is only when you are fully present with another that you can know him, or love him."

"Or 'it' in the case of a sword."

"Yes. Very good, brother. I knew you would understand."

He smiles broadly, turns, and heads up the road again.

The disciples fall into line behind him, their sandals kicking up puffs of tan dust. You, alone, remain standing, grimacing at his back.

It takes several moments before you realize he means ". . . or in the case of God."

You shake your head, annoyed that it was meant specifically for you, and run to catch up.

THREE

For the most part the pungent scents of decaying vegetation and damp soil filled the air. But on those occasions when the breeze shifted, the hot dusty breath of the desert could be felt. It was a reminder for the monks of Pachomius that their fertile fields edged a vast, arid waste.

Brother Zarathan wiped his dirt-coated hands on his white robe and gazed out at the fishing boats. They bobbed with the current of the wide Nile River. From his vantage he could see seven of them, filled with men and boys, probably fathers and sons going about their day.

He shifted to look across the fields of the monastery to the great walled city of Phoou where his own family lived. Heat waves rose from the warm stones, making the irregular circular wall seem somehow unreal. Beyond the city, to the north, the high cliff of Gebel et-Tarif was almost invisible, cloaked in a dusty haze.

Zarathan sighed, wondering what his friends in the city would be doing today. Probably helping their families to prepare the fields, just as he was doing. Or, rather, as he was supposed to be doing.

He was sixteen, with bright flaxen hair, clear blue eyes, and, as the girls in the village used to tell him, the face of a freshly circumcised cat. He'd never really understood that, though the insult might have referred to the fact that he frequently felt a little stunned by life. Or maybe it was the thin fuzz of blond beard, the length of a cat's hair, that whiskered his chin. Not that it had mattered much. Though his mother had wanted him to marry, Thaddeus—that had been his name three months ago—had been totally uninterested in matrimony. Even before he'd come here, he'd spent his nights in prayer, yearning with all his heart for one single glimpse of the heavenly kingdom. Sometimes, after he'd prayed until dawn, tiny tendrils of pure aching love had filtered through him, and he'd wept with the knowledge that he had, perhaps, touched the hem of his Lord, Iesous Christos.

"Thank you, brother," Zarathan said as another in a long line of monks delivered an empty seed pot to his washing table beneath the palm tree.

Zarathan sheepishly glanced at the other monks who tilled the soil, planted seeds, and carried water. Then he blinked at the row of clay pots before him. There were so many! When had he gotten so behind?

Brother Jonas had assigned him the simple duty of cleaning the empty seed pots and returning them to their shelves in the monastery. More than twenty unclean pots and a basin of water sat before him—as well as a water jar and ladle to quench the thirst of the laboring monks. Where had the time gone? Had he dreamed it all away?

Another two pots were delivered to his table by silent monks.

His shoulders sagged.

Zarathan absently ran his finger around the rim of the most recent pot. Barley chaff coated his fingertip.

He thought again of those long nights spent in prayer, and the ecstatic memories left Zarathan feeling light-headed. He—

"Zarathan?" The gravelly voice of Brother Jonas surprised him from behind.

He spun around like a dog caught with a roasted lamb shank in its teeth. "Yes, Brother Jonas?"

"Before you realize it, that pile of pots will be as tall as you are, and when they fall and crush you to mush, I will be forced to walk into the city—which you know I hate—and tell your wailing parents that it was not an accident. You, in fact, died from slothfulness."

The other monks in the field turned to look.

Zarathan reddened in shame. "Forgive me, brother. I'll try to concentrate."

"See that you do."

Jonas, over forty, had wild brown hair, a scraggly beard, and a wrinkled nose that reminded Zarathan of a date left too long in the sun. The old monk just shook his head and picked up his water pot again, pouring it out in a thin stream over the freshly planted barley seeds.

Zarathan dunked a pot into the water basin and used his linen cloth to swab out the inside. More pots arrived and thunked on the wooden table.

Zarathan's heart sank. Beneath his breath, he whispered, "This is a waste of my potential. I should be in my cell, on my knees, seeking divine love—"

From his right, a deep voice whispered, "First, wash the pots, then seek divine love."

Zarathan jumped. "Brother Cyrus! I—I didn't hear you approach."

Cyrus suppressed a smile and leaned against the table. He was tall and muscular. Black curly hair hung to his broad shoulders, and he had a thick beard and mustache. His green eyes always seemed half amused. Zarathan guessed his age at around thirty-five.

As Cyrus wiped his sweating brow on his dirty white sleeve, he said, "Would you like some help, brother? Jonas sent me to ask. I think he wants you to finish sometime before the plants mature and are harvested."

Zarathan frowned, dunked another pot, and said, "Yes, thank you, brother."

Cyrus picked up a pot and proceeded to wash it while Zarathan turned his clean pot upside down on the table to drain and dry. The sunlight on this day was painfully bright. When he turned to Cyrus, he squinted against the glare.

"He's such a taskmaster, forever watching," Zarathan whispered. "Has he always been like this?"

Cyrus smiled. "I can't say. I've been here less than a year, but you must understand that Brother Jonas is in charge of seeing that the fields are planted properly so the monastery has food. Abba Pachomius says we must be self-sufficient. It's a heavy burden. Jonas needs each one of us to help him if he's going to succeed."

Zarathan studied Cyrus from the corner of his eye. When he was out of earshot, the other brothers told spectacular stories about Cyrus. They said he'd been a fierce soldier, an archer in the Roman army, and that he'd killed many men.

Cyrus leaned sideways and whispered, "You're dreaming again, brother. Come back to our task."

"What?"

The vision of a thousand archers letting their arrows fly burst, and Zarathan morosely focused on the tall man standing beside him.

"Wash pots," Cyrus repeated, "then seek divine love."

Zarathan grimaced. "I am not meant for the world of pot washing, brother. Mine is a higher calling. I came here because everyone said Abba Pachomius allowed monks to spend their time doing spiritual exercises."

Cyrus' green eyes twinkled. "Planting is a spiritual exercise, brother, though I see you've been brooding too much to realize it." He gestured to the prayer rope that hung from Zarathan's leather belt.

Zarathan looked down. They were ordered to carry their prayer rope, a woolen cord, with them at all times. Each time they said the Iesous Prayer, "Lord Iesous Christos, son of God, have mercy on me, a sinner," they were supposed to tie a knot in the rope. The knots recorded how many times during the day they'd said the prayer. Zarathan's rope had two knots. He glanced at Cyrus' rope. There were too many knots to count.

He said, "Cyrus, I wish to 'pray without ceasing,' as Saint Paulus instructed, but I wish to do it correctly, on my knees in my cell. Standing out here in the hot sun washing pots prevents me from pursuing my holy calling."

Cyrus burst out laughing, and Zarathan gave him an askance look, at a loss to understand what his brother found comical.

From the rear of the monastery, on the south side that faced the Nile River, Kalay, the washerwoman, emerged, along with her young assistant, Sophia. While Sophia was a dark-haired imp from the city who spent afternoons helping Kalay, Kalay was tall and lithe with long wavy red hair and a face that rivaled the legendary beauty of the Magdalen's.

Zarathan looked at her and made a gulping sound. "I don't know why Abba Pachomius lets her live here," he whispered. "She's a harlot. Maybe even a demon."

Cyrus' dark brows plunged down. "She's a washerwoman. Would you rather wash your clothing yourself? I thought you needed every moment to pray without ceasing?"

Zarathan watched Kalay walk down to the river with her tan dress dancing about her long legs. "She truly scares me, Cyrus."

"She scares all of us, brother. But that is not her failing. It is ours."

Fortunately, she was never allowed to interact with the monks. She lived in a hut by herself, ate by herself, and was forbidden to speak to anyone other than Brother Jonas, who delivered and retrieved the wash.

With his eyes still glued to Kalay, Zarathan picked up another pot. When it slipped from his wet fingers, he cried, "Oh!" just before it crashed to the ground and shattered. Shards cartwheeled in every direction.

Jonas must have heard. He straightened in the field, stretched his back muscles, and plodded across the soft earth toward Zarathan.

"I'll be washing pots for the rest of my life now," Zarathan said. "That's the third pot I've broken this week."

"You just need to learn to focus, brother. When you begin using your prayer rope, you'll find it helps."

Jonas walked into the shade beneath the palm tree and dipped himself a ladle of water before he said, "I see a broken pot." He drank the ladle to the last drop and hung it back on the water jar without so much as glancing at Zarathan.

Cyrus said, "I dropped the pot, brother. Forgive me. It was sheer carelessness. I should have dried my hands before I reached for it." He bowed his dark head in apparent shame.

Zarathan stared wide-eyed at Cyrus.

Jonas looked from Cyrus to Zarathan and back again. His mouth quirked. He could not in good conscience ask Zarathan if it were true, because that might force Zarathan to lie, which would mean Jonas was culpable in the sinful act.

Cyrus, his head still bowed, said, "I will accept any penance you give me, brother. I vow to be more careful in the future."

Jonas contemplatively stroked his scraggly brown beard. "It is not my place to punish you. I will refer the matter to Brother Barnabas."

"Barnabas!" Zarathan said in surprise. "The heretic?"

Jonas' bushy brows lowered thunderously. "Brother Barnabas helped Abba Pachomius build this monastery. He has been here for twenty years and is probably the most devoted, certainly the most scholarly, monk we have. Just because he believes in leaving room for compromise on the scriptures does not mean he's a heretic. It would, perhaps, be more accurate to say he is a pragmatist."

"Well," Zarathan said and puffed out his chest, "we will see if the synod of bishops meeting in Nicea agrees—"

"Thank you, brother," Cyrus interrupted, which annoyed Zarathan, who had only just begun his tirade. "We know that Brother Barnabas is a very holy man."

Jonas scowled at Zarathan. "You may *both* go and see Brother Barnabas. Now. And keep in your hearts the fact that Barnabas never assigns a punishment he does not follow himself. If he tells you to scrub floors for a month, he will be there beside you on his hands and knees. Let that knowledge be your burden." He started to turn away, then added, "And maintain silence until he speaks to you."

Cyrus nodded, dried his hands, and started for the monastery. Zarathan hurried behind him. Why had Cyrus taken responsibility for something he had not done? Zarathan knew he shouldn't speak until released from the vow of silence, but he caught up with Cyrus and whispered, "Brother, why did—"

Cyrus gave him a reproachful look and firmly shook his head.

The stunning basilica with its magnificent dome rose in front of them. The walls had been built two cubits thick to support the majestic arches and columns inside and the roof that stretched eighty cubits into the sky.

Zarathan breathed a sigh of relief. This was the place where hearts were weighed. Whoever entered here with faith found the forgiveness of sins and offenses, and the glory of the pure of heart shone over the whole world.

Cool air rushed from the door when Cyrus opened it, and they stepped into the shadowed interior. High above, in the vaulted ceiling, dust danced and spun in the light streaming through the windows. Paintings covered the walls depicting sacred moments in the life of their Lord: his birth, the breaking of the bread at the Last Supper, his trial, the crucifixion.

They walked side-by-side toward the library where Brother Barnabas spent the day, every day, translating tiny fragments of ancient documents brought to him by nearby villagers. Sometimes even traders passing through, who knew of his peculiar interests, brought him scraps of papyri.

Zarathan hissed, "Cyrus? What do you think of Brother Barnabas? Do you agree that he is a heretic? I've heard him say, for example, that our Lord did not rise in the flesh, but that it might have been a spiritual resurrection of the soul! The emperor has ruled such utterances heresy. What do you think?"

He gave Cyrus a sidelong glance and saw his brother lift his eyes briefly to heaven, as though begging God to give him patience.

"Cyrus," he continued, "you know the synod of bishops recently met in Nicea to decide such issues once and for all. Has there been any word as to their decisions?"

When Cyrus kept his green eyes on the massive wooden library door ahead, Zarathan added, "I have truly been eager to learn what day they have decided is Easter. Will it be on the date of the Jewish Passover, as the Gospel of Ioannes says, or the day after as told to us in the Gospels of Markos, Loukas, and Maththaios. Personally, I think the correct date—"[13]

Cyrus stopped and gently put his fingers over Zarathan's mouth. He said nothing, but just stared down into Zarathan's eyes.

Grudgingly, Zarathan nodded.

Cyrus continued toward the library door. The iron hinges groaned when Cyrus swung it back, and they stepped into the musty air. The room smelled like moldering books and dust. Candlelight fluttered over the stone walls like amber wings flying toward the high vaulted ceiling above.

Zarathan stood quietly, as he'd been instructed, waiting for Brother Barnabas to speak to him. The old man, at least fifty, sat on a long bench, hunched over a table covered with scraps of papyrus. They resembled dried golden leaves inscribed with black ink and looked very old. He seemed to be arranging them in some kind of order.

Barnabas squinted and exhaled hard. As though having difficulty deciphering the ancient text, he muttered to himself. His gray hair and beard shimmered slightly when he cocked his head. He had a curious face; all of the proportions seemed to be oversized. Though his skull was long and narrow, he had a grotesquely wide mouth, long hooked nose, and brown eyes that were too deeply sunken into his head. Truly, he looked more like a recent corpse than a living man. Like every other monk, he wore a long white robe with a leather belt and prayer rope.

Zarathan heaved a sigh and studied the shelves filled with ancient parchment books and papyrus scrolls of scripture, most of which he knew to be heretical. He'd once seen Brother Barnabas studying the forbidden Gospel of Maryam.

The faint scent of ink pervaded the air, as though Barnabas had been writing just before they'd entered the library. A calamus—a pointed reed split to form a nib—rested in an inkstand to Barnabas' right. The red ink, made of iron oxide and gum, resembled old blood. An assortment of other writing supplies rested close at hand: a knife for sharpening the pen, a whetstone for sharpening the knife, a chunk of pumice for smoothing the papyrus, a sponge for making erasures, a pair of compasses for making the lines equidistant from each other, and a ruler and a thin lead disk for drawing the lines.

Zarathan scratched beneath his armpit. The linen robes itched. There were times at night when he pulled his robe over his head and found his arms and belly covered with red welts. But he understood; it was part of the price he had to pay for seeking the divine love of his risen Lord.

Brother Barnabas pulled a fragment of papyrus from a distant spot on the table, said, "Ah!" as though he'd made a great discovery, and rearranged the fragments to put it in the proper place. After several moments, his breath seemed to catch, and in a dire voice, he whispered, ". . . *buried shamefully.*" He didn't seem to be breathing. Finally, he whispered, "I need more . . . details. . . ."

Zarathan cast a look of incomprehension at Cyrus, who softly cleared his throat.

Barnabas whirled and stared at them in surprise, as though they'd sneaked up on him with battle-axes in their fists. A little breathlessly, he said, "Forgive me, brothers, I did not realize you were there. Zarathan, you're not in trouble again, are you?"

Zarathan blushed and shifted his weight to his other foot. Cyrus turned to Zarathan, giving him the opportunity to confess.

In a morose voice, Zarathan said, "I broke another pot, brother."

"I see." Barnabas looked at Cyrus. "And your offense, Cyrus?"

"I lied to protect Zarathan from Brother Jonas' wrath. I said that I dropped the pot."

"Then your offense is worse; you realize that? Even though you meant good by it?"

Cyrus nodded obediently. "Yes, brother."

Barnabas rose to his feet and the mere motion fluttered the fragments spread over the table. His eyes flew wide, and he eased back to the long bench.

"I'm supposed to prescribe some punishment, I suppose." He folded his hands in his lap and appeared to be thinking. After a time, he said, "In penance, I want both of you to fast for three days and—and to help me translate a recent library acquisition. Cyrus, I believe you are skilled in the Aramaic language?"

Cyrus nodded. "Yes, brother."

"Good. I want both of you to go to the library crypt beneath the oratory. There are leaves laid out on the table there. Please translate them into Greek."

The library crypt was where they kept their most valuable documents. Zarathan had never even seen it. Few of the monks had.

"Greek, brother?" Cyrus asked. "Not Coptic?"

Though they often spoke in Greek—the language of the Gospels—Coptic was the common language of Egyptian Christians. Why would Brother Barnabas want them translated into Greek?

"Yes, Greek. I want the book to have a wider audience. I believe the Gospel of Petros is important—"

"The Gospel of Petros!" Zarathan blurted. "Hasn't that book been banned?"

Barnabas seemed to barely register Zarathan's objection. He said softly, "To the earliest Christians, books like the Gospels of Petros, Philippon, and Maryam *were* the holy books, Zarathan. You need to read them to understand why."

"But they've been—"

Barnabas lifted a hand to still him. "Do not make the Kingdom of God a desert within you, Zarathan. Read our Lord's words wherever you find them . . . and be grateful."[14]

Zarathan let out a pained sound.

Cyrus answered, "Yes, brother."

Barnabas waved his hand, dismissing them, and turned back to his little bits of papyrus. "The key to the crypt rests above the altar to the Magdalen. Please remember to put it back."

"We will, brother." Cyrus turned and pushed open the heavy door.

As they walked into the corridor, Zarathan complained, "I am being forced to read *heresy*! The emperor has made it a death sentence!"

Cyrus drily replied, "Emperor Constantine is, fortunately, far away. I suggest you heed Brother Barnabas' advice and read everything before such opportunities vanish."

"If I'm not executed first. I don't see how you can be so calm about this, when—"

"Brother," Cyrus interrupted and stopped in the middle of the long quiet hall to peer down at Zarathan. "Earlier you asked why I had taken responsibility for the broken pot."

"Yes. Why did you?"

Cyrus gave him a serious look. "When I lived in Rome, I was taught never to let a day pass without performing at least one act of mercy. Today, you helped me remember. Now it's your turn. Be merciful—and quiet."

Cyrus started down the corridor again, taking long, measured steps, much longer than Zarathan's stride, which forced him to run to catch up.

"You lived in Rome?" Zarathan asked in awe. "What did you do there? Were you a soldier as everyone says, or—"

"Mercy, Zarathan. I beg you."

Two men turned the corner ahead and strode toward them. One, Abba Pachomius, they knew. The white-haired Abba, which meant "father" in Hebrew, was fondly regarded as the founder of Christian monasticism. So far, he'd established four monasteries in Egypt and had several more planned. Usually, Pachomius looked serene, but today, he wore a slightly frightened expression. The other man, dressed in a black robe, had short blond hair and seething eyes. Zarathan had never seen him before.

As they passed, Cyrus bowed his head and said, "The Lord be with you, Abba, brother."

"And with you, Cyrus and Zarathan," Abba Pachomius said.

The blond man did not even deign to speak to them. He just marched toward the library like a man on a holy mission.

When they heard the heavy iron hinges squeal, Cyrus frowned and turned to watch. Abba Pachomius entered first. The other man remained standing outside, staring back at Cyrus. Zarathan would have sworn their locked gazes were those of wary lions appraising each other from afar.

Cyrus swiftly turned to walk away, but a harsh voice called: *"Wait."*

Cyrus tensed and turned back. "Yes, brother?"

The blond man's eyes narrowed. He said, "Are you Jairus Claudius Atinius?"

Zarathan saw the muscles in Cyrus' shoulders begin to bulge through his white robe. In a firm voice, he answered, "No, brother, I am not."

Tendons stood out on the backs of Cyrus' clenched hands, and Zarathan instantly suspected Cyrus had committed yet another sin he would have to confess.

The black-robed man stared hard at Cyrus' face. Romans shaved their faces and kept their hair cut short. Was the black-robed priest trying to see through Cyrus' thick beard and curly shoulder-length hair?

The Roman grunted, said, "Do you know where he is? I heard he was here, though I did not believe it."

Cyrus answered, "We are given new names when we come to our Lord. I do not know the name of the man you are seeking."

"No, of course not," the Roman replied skeptically. For three or four heartbeats, he hesitated, then he stepped into the library, leaving the heavy door ajar.

Zarathan whispered, "Do you know that man?"

"No." Cyrus shook his head. "But he's a messenger from Rome. You wanted to know about the synod's conclusions in Nicea? I think you are about to have your answers. We had better—"

Voices rose from the library.

Brother Barnabas cried in shock, "It cannot be true. They wouldn't order us to consign them to the fire! They are the words of our Lord."[15]

In a strident voice, the Roman said, "The bishops have ordained twenty-seven books as the New Testament. Another fifty-two books have been declared heretical, a hotbed of manifold perversity. The Council of Nicea orders that they are not only to be forbidden, but *entirely* destroyed. Anyone found reading or copying these books is to be declared a Christian heretic and executed."

Steps moved across the floor, pounding out authority. "Also, I am to inform you that the doctrine of the resurrection has been ordained. It was a *fleshly* resurrection. Our Lord rose in the body. Is that clear?" After a moment, the blond continued: "In addition, the Council has established that

Miriam was a virgin. They are even considering ordaining that she was a perpetual virgin, that she was a virgin when she gave birth to our Lord, and she remained a virgin for the rest of her life."

"But . . . ," Barnabas said in disbelief. "Our Lord had four brothers: Iakobos, Ioses, Iuda, and Simon. And he had two sisters, Mariam and Salome. What about them?"[16]

"The Council has declared that they were not true brothers and sisters. They were stepbrothers and sisters, perhaps even cousins, but *not* real brothers or sisters."

There was a short pause, and Zarathan heard the Roman ask, "What's that you're reading?"

In a soft, fearful voice, Brother Barnabas said, "I'm not certain, yet. I believe it is a book written by the brother, uh, cousin, of our Lord: Iakobos. It is in Hebrew, so naturally, it's called the Secret Book of Yakob. I've only just begun to translate—"

The Roman ordered, "Burn it! Burn every book in this room that has been judged heretical. I'll provide you with a list, and I want you to give me a list of the monks who have read these books."

"But," Abba Pachomius objected, "the entire monastery has read at least parts of these books."

"Then bring every man before me, tonight at supper. That's two hours away, isn't it? I must make certain the monks understand the Council's declarations."

The Roman stalked from the library with a pale and devastated Abba Pachomius trailing a few steps behind. "Pappas Meridias, please wait."

"You have another monastery just upriver, Abba. When I have finished here, I'll meet you there. Then we'll discuss the situation in greater detail." Meridias had his chin up and wore an arrogant expression.

"Yes, Pappas Meridias," Pachomius obediently agreed. "I'll be waiting. There is much we need to clarify before we ask our monks to . . ."

They rounded a corner and their voices dropped too low to hear.

"So, he's a bishop," Cyrus said.

Pappas, Greek for "father," referred to bishops.

Cyrus quietly said, "Come on. We're supposed to be in the crypt translating a book."

Cyrus turned right and headed down the corridor. Light streamed through the high windows and illuminated the magnificent vault above them.

Zarathan whispered, "Translating a book we've been ordered to burn. If anyone finds out, we'll be executed."

He studied Cyrus from the corner of his eye. Jairus Claudius Atinius? Why would a bishop from Rome call him by name? If the man had not known Cyrus personally, then someone must have described Cyrus in great detail for the Roman to have recognized him . . . if indeed he really had recognized him.

Just before they exited into the sunlit garden where palms swayed in the late afternoon breeze, Cyrus stopped and turned. "Zarathan, I suppose it is impossible for you to forget the Roman name you just heard."

With hurt pride, he straightened and answered, "I can keep a secret."

The lines at the corners of Cyrus' eyes deepened. He gave Zarathan a short, relieved nod. "I would take that as a great favor, brother."

FOUR

Mahanayim

NISAN THE 15TH, THE YEAR 3771

Thunder rumbled in the distance, and the earthy scent of the coming storm was heavy on the breeze that swept the dark mountain. Already rain had begun to spot the wool of Yosef's cloak, and catch like jewels in the golden threads that stitched the fabric.

As they guided their horses up the steep trail toward the pass, starlight glimmered from the leaves of the olive trees and cast uncertain shadows across the rocky slopes.

Yosef studied the darkness, and found himself listening intently for the sound of soldiers, for reins clinking, or a sword being drawn from a scabbard, perhaps spears cutting the air. It would not be long before their crime was discovered, and centurions were sent to hunt them down. He did not know how much time they had. To his servant, riding ahead of him, he called, "You are a Samaritan, Titus. When will we reach the mountaintop?"

Titus, twenty-five years old, with gray eyes and curly brown hair, had the stony expression of a brave man awaiting his own execution. He replied, "We should reach the tor by the fifth or sixth hour of night, Master."[17]

"Good. I will be glad when our task is finished. You know the place we are seeking?"

"Yes, Master. I grew up here. I know it well."

Yosef hesitated a moment, then more softly asked, "And, as well, you remember what we must do if we fail here?"

"I do, Master, though I pray that is not required of us."

"As I do, Titus."

The third man among them had a face like a scavenger bird's, narrow and beaked, with alert brown eyes. He wore a long white robe. His name was Mattias, though he'd asked Yosef never to say it aloud in public—a precaution in case they were caught. He walked two paces behind, leading the packhorse. The poor animal struggled up the trail with its head down, as though the linen-wrapped burden strapped over its back was almost too heavy to bear.

"Do you think they are already after us?" Titus asked.

Yosef reined his horse around a rock before responding, "Probably not. The Law forbids our people from leaving their houses for another two days. That's when they'll know and notify the praefectus. I pray Petronius makes a good excuse."

Petronius, a centurion of some reputation, would still have a hard time explaining his failure.

In the rear, young Mattias said, "He will tell them he fell asleep."

A tremor shook Yosef. The past few days had been terrifying. The whispers and secrecy had drained his strength. He drew in a breath and let it out slowly. "I hope not. No one will believe him. They'll kill him for it."

"No, they won't," Mattias responded. "The two who stood guard with him will support his story. Our bribes were enough to buy them each a kingdom of their own."

Titus cast an unkind glance at the youth, and said, "I thought the Dawn Bathers had forsaken worldly wealth. Where would you get such a ransom?"

The Dawn Bathers, so called because of their custom of taking a ritual bath each morning, were also known as the Essenes. The name of the sect came from a lost sacred artifact, the oracle, or *essen,* a breastplate worn by ancient high priests. Twelve stones, each inscribed with the name of a tribe, in four rows, gleamed on the *essen,* and the Lord God had always signaled victory in battle by sending his power flowing into the stones and causing them to shine brilliantly enough to light the soldiers' way. According to lore, the *essen* had ceased to shine two centuries ago. After God had abandoned the sacred artifact, it had disappeared, or perhaps been cast aside in the desert by frustrated men.[18] Yosef had heard rumors that the Dawn Bathers kept it hidden deep in a cave near Qumran, where it was guarded by giant fanged beasts with wings.

Mattias said, "We have ways of acquiring necessary funds."

Titus waved a disparaging hand. "Forgive my impudence, Master, but I don't know why you listen to these people. They are sinners of the worst sort. I wouldn't let them tie my sandals, let alone—"

"Silence!" The surly tone of Titus' voice had obviously rankled Mattias. "Do not forget that I was there when Yeshua first began studying with Yohanan Baptistes at Qumran. I was there at his arrest! I was his last chosen apostle! My brothers will meet Maryam at the tomb in the morning, give her the sacred artifact, and tell her we have executed her plan. My community has taken great risks, and thereby earned certain rights—the least of which is your courtesy."

Titus' stiff neck eased and he looked away.

Taking it for contrition, Mattias continued in a milder voice. "There are many people who share our beliefs, but who are not members of our community. A few are wealthy—though I fear we may have asked too much this time. I think some of them emptied their homes to fill this last request. If any of their servants speak of it, word may get around . . . and then we will all be lost."

Titus glanced at Yosef as though waiting for a response.

Yosef finally said, "You, too, have earned certain rights, Titus. Especially the right to be impudent. Go ahead and say what you wished to."

Titus had been Yosef's faithful servant for more than ten years. It had been Titus and Maryam who had performed the most difficult tasks. They had accepted the ceremonial uncleanness associated with touching the dead, and done it without complaint, so that Yosef might cleanse himself of the impurity before the holy days and thereby salvage his political and religious careers. Little did they know that Yosef had already surrendered both. This night he would flee Palestine forever, before the Romans could accuse him of the role he'd played.

Everything that he had ever wanted or loved was here. For days and nights his head had been drumming with the agony of loss, ready to split. Now all he felt was a gut-wrenching loneliness.

Titus shoved brown curls away from his eyes and said, "The man was a criminal, Master. You should not have allowed the Dawn Bathers to talk you into this insanity. The body should have been released to his relatives, as is customary."

"His relatives." Mattias spat in disgust.

Titus shifted on his horse to glare back at the man.

Yosef patiently explained, "His relatives did not want the body, Titus. They thought him mad. They cast him aside many years ago. There was no one else. If I had not pleaded for the right to give him an honorable burial, his body would have been left out for days to be devoured by jackals and vultures. I could not have borne it."[19]

"Nevertheless, I do not understand why you place yourself in such peril. If they discover—"

"These are the Last Times, the last hours," the young man in white interrupted. "The Kingdom of God is almost upon us. We must all accept the utmost peril."

Titus acted as though he had not heard. He continued. "Master, this is exactly what the Romans feared. If they discover what you've done—"

"They will discover it, Titus. You may be sure of that," Yosef said in a tired voice. "And as to why . . . I believed him."

For several moments, Titus remained silent, riding along with his brow furrowed. Then he murmured, "I did not suspect that."

Yosef smiled sadly. He had surprised even himself in that regard. Over the past year, his longing for the Kingdom had become a physical ache, a torment that no worldly comfort could ease. "You mean because I am a member of the supreme Council of Seventy-one?[20] I think even the great teacher, Naqdimon, believed, though he never said so."

With each breath of wind, the fragrances of myrrh and aloe rose from the Pearl, wrapped in a linen shroud and bound to the packhorse. The perfumes were so powerful, they seemed to surround and penetrate him like the Holy Spirit herself. Naqdimon had provided the lavish spices—surely the act of a believer, if not a disciple—and then Maryam alone had carefully, secretly, bound the Pearl in its linen disguise.

As they climbed higher, Mount Ebal, to the north, seemed to rise with them. Yosef looked down into the valley that lay between mounts Ebal and Gerizim. Oil lamps glittered in many homes, making the valley resemble a gigantic overturned jewel box. A few lamps even glowed amid the tumbled stones of the ancient ruined city of Shekem.

They rounded a bend in the trail and the olive trees vanished, giving way to a forest of tall pines, where the air grew cool and crisp.

Yosef drew his fringed cloak more tightly about his shoulders. In the star gleam, the golden threads woven into the fine linen fabric, dyed with costly indigo, shimmered. The cloak was a symbol of wealth and status, a sign of the high position he'd held in the council. Tonight, when all was said and done, he would give it to one more deserving, along with anything else that might identify him. He looked down at his empty first finger, where that morning there had been a large golden ring bearing the pomegranate design of his family. It had belonged to his great-grandfather. All his life, Yosef had used that ring to make an imprint on wax that acted as a legal seal for letters and documents. He had cherished it. Now, it encircled the finger of a dead man. A small gift, no bigger than a mustard seed in the grand scheme of things, but it had been the best he could offer.

He rubbed his aching eyes and lifted his gaze to the craggy tor of Mount Gerizim. As the night deepened, it appeared to be a huge black tooth embedded in the deep blue belly of the sky. Clouds clung to the western slope, trailing streamers of rain. Before the third hour of night they'd be in the middle of the downpour.

"Do you believe it, Titus?" he asked softly. "Do you believe what Maryam said about this mountain?"

Titus' gaze drifted over the rain clouds, assessing the storm, and finally came to rest on the crag. "This mountain has always been known among my people as the *tabbur ha'ares,* 'center of the land,' the one place where heaven meets earth. Moshe is said to have buried the Ark of the Covenant there on the highest peak." He pointed.

"I caution silence," Mattias, who led the packhorse, hissed. "It is dangerous to even speak of these things. What if Praefectus Pontios Pilatos[21] were to hear of this? He would send his troops to ravage the mountain to find and destroy the tabernacle, then he would kill anyone caught worshipping there!"[22]

Titus clenched his jaw, clearly on the verge of an unpleasant tirade. He had, after all, merely been answering Yosef's question.

"Dangerous or not," Yosef said, "Maryam believes the Samaritan tradition. So I, too, believe it."

The image of her tear-filled eyes and beautiful face surrounded by its halo of black hair reared in his mind. *"Yosef, please, I beg you. The savior himself must be saved . . ."*

Not an easy task for Yosef or anyone else. Nothing in the holy books had ever prepared them for a messiah who could suffer such a fate. The way he'd died had been scandalous, a sign of extreme shame, proving to the world that he was not the Annointed One, that, in fact, he had been cursed by God.[23]

A curious pain began around Yosef's heart, like a stab wound that would not stop bleeding. He bent forward and stroked his horse's mane. The horse, Lightning, tossed his head as though upset by Yosef's trembling hand.

Yosef patted the horse and whispered, "It's all right, Lightning. We are well. Do not be afraid," and he wondered if perhaps he was not speaking as much to himself.

Titus gestured to the boulders that lined the trail ahead. "When we round that outcrop, we must leave the trail and head into the trees. There is a hidden game trail through the pines; it is more difficult, but ultimately faster."

"Very well," Yosef agreed.

Passing the rocks, they turned into the trees, and rode along the dark, twisting trail for another two hours, until the falling rain turned the world into black sackcloth. The horses began to slip in the mud, which forced them to slow their pace. Though Yosef had long ago drawn his cloak over his head, it did little to protect him from the deluge. Water sheeted from his face, making it difficult to see, except when flashes of lightning penetrated the gloom.

Around the sixth hour, as they were nearing the mountaintop, a strange sound penetrated the storm, like distant thunder, only different in a way he could not define. Yosef sat up straighter on his horse and strained to hear over the roar of the downpour that battered the pine boughs.

"What is it?" Titus asked in a low voice. "Why did you stop, Master?"

"Do you hear it?"

No one spoke for several heartbeats.

Finally, Mattias said, "All I hear is the storm."

Titus still had not responded. Yosef blinked the rain from his eyes and searched the darkness to his left, where he knew Titus sat his horse. He saw a vague outline of a man, a darker spot against the charcoal background. "Titus?" he softly called.

A lightning bolt slashed the inky sky, and he saw his servant surrounded by swirling veils of rain. "It's more than the storm," Titus whispered. "It's . . ." He cocked his head, listening.

The sound grew sharper.

In a shaking voice, Yosef finished the sentence. ". . . horses, pounding toward us."

"Dear God," the Dawn Bather cried. "Someone betrayed us! They've come for us!"

Yosef ordered, "Give me those reins!"

He rode over, jerked the packhorse's reins from the Dawn Bather's hand, and yelled, "Quickly! Both of you hide! I'll make a run for—"

Before he could finish his sentence the first horses burst through the forest and rode down upon them like a frothing midnight wave. Yosef saw the glint of burnished shields and armor, and the silver flashes of raised swords.

One of the centurions yelled in Greek, "Take the packhorse! Kill the riders!"

A silver-silk flash of light cut the rain and Yosef was knocked backward off his horse. He hit the ground hard. The arrow had pinned his cloak to his shoulder. In an enraged voice, he shouted, "Titus! Take the horse and ride!" He lifted the reins.

Titus kicked his horse and it leaped forward, its hooves slashing across the mud to Yosef, where Titus grabbed the reins of the packhorse and charged away into the night.

Yosef lunged to his feet and careened down the slope through the forest, with the Dawn Bather close behind him. There was a moment of confusion among the Romans. They shouted at each other, asking which direction the packhorse had gone, and had anyone seen the "priests." Then most of the horses thundered after Titus.

Yosef slid and staggered through the mud on the steep mountainside, trying to pick a path the remaining horses could not follow. Behind him, he could hear the Dawn Bather weeping, his voice like a man suffocating.

Roman calls echoed up the hill, but in the storm he could not make out any of the words.

Finally, bleeding badly, unable to go farther, he worked his way into a head-high pile of deadfall along a near vertical cliff and collapsed.

Mattias followed him, scrambling into the deadfall on his belly.

An eerie web of lightning crackled across the sky and thunder roared. High up the slope, Yosef caught glimpses of soldiers fighting to control their frightened horses.

Mattias choked out the words, "This is madness! Can't we do something? Are we to be nothing but witnesses?"

Yosef watched the Romans' horses struggling to stay upright in the soggy mountain mud as they trotted along at the edge of the trees. The centurions shouted at each other, trying to find Yosef's trail—almost impossible in the darkness and rain.

Yosef sank back against a fallen log. His shoulder had begun to ache as though on fire. In a tormented voice, he answered, "We are not witnesses. Yeshua said there would only be three who would bear witness: the spirit and the water and the blood."[24]

Mattias began to weep again.

A mournful gust of wind ravaged the slope, battering them with old leaves.

Through gritted teeth, Yosef whispered, "Stop that and help me pull this arrow out. We must be gone long before the storm passes."

FIVE

Cyrus had lit one single oil lamp when they'd entered the library crypt. It cast a weak, flickering glow over the coffins stacked five high along the walls and the piles of codices, scrolls, and papyri that littered the tables. Many more scrolls peeked from hundreds of holes in the walls. The crypt, which stretched ten fathoms across, resembled a giant honeycomb.

Zarathan looked up. The rounded ceiling soared four times his height to the trapdoor that led into the oratory, the prayer chamber. Massive stone stairs, hewn from the native rock walls, led to the trapdoor.

"This must have been a cave first, then it was enlarged to serve as a crypt," Zarathan whispered, and his voice echoed in the gloom. "I wonder if Abba Pachomius chose to build his basilica on this spot because of this cavern?"

"Possibly," Cyrus said as he dipped his calamus and wrote a line on the parchment before him. "Many of these coffins look centuries old."

Zarathan's nose wrinkled. The musty smell of dry decaying corpses and ancient manuscripts pervaded everything. He draped his white sleeve over his nose to filter the odor.

"Why has no one ever mentioned that this really is a crypt?" Zarathan complained.

Cyrus, who bent over the forbidden manuscript, replied, "Very few men have seen this crypt, and those who have, never speak of it. You should count yourself fortunate. As a result of a dropped pot, you have become one of the chosen."

Cyrus dipped his calamus in the inkwell again and carefully wrote another line, repeating it softly in Greek. "Do you wish to know what this says, Zarathan?"

"Certainly not! If anyone asks, I can truly say I have never read a forbidden book."

A faint smile turned Cyrus' lips. "You wouldn't be reading it. I would. It's about our Lord's death. Are you sure you don't want to hear it?"

Zarathan hesitated. "Is it different from the approved gospels?"

"Some of it. Don't you at least want to know the name of the centurion who stood guard at our Lord's tomb after the crucifixion?"

Zarathan's eyes widened. "The *real* centurion's name?"

Cyrus whispered, "Petronius."

Petronius, Zarathan mouthed the forbidden name, then said, "Cyrus, are you sure they won't put me to death for knowing this?"

"I suppose they'd want to, but I'm not sure they could. The order only relates to the reading and copying of heretical books. They appear not to have condemned the 'hearing' of such forbidden teachings. Probably because they know it's difficult to prove."

Zarathan swallowed hard. "What else does it say?"

Cyrus replied, "The elders went to Pilatos and asked him for soldiers to guard the crypt for three days to make sure the disciples didn't steal the body. They were afraid that if it vanished people would assume our Lord had been raised from the dead, which would prove he was the messiah."

"But we know most of that already. What else?"

Cyrus read the document with his brow furrowed. "Two bright shining men came down from heaven and the stone rolled away by itself. They entered the tomb, and three men came out, followed by the cross."

"The cross?" Zarathan said suspiciously. "What was it doing in the tomb?"

"The cross was not dead, but alive. God's voice came down from heaven and asked, 'Have you preached to those who are asleep?' The cross told Him yes."

Zarathan blinked. "I don't understand. What does it mean?"

Cyrus shrugged. He had his eyes glued to the leaf, reading. "I don't know, but Pilatos ordered Petronius not to say anything about what he'd seen."

"No wonder. If Petronius had revealed the truth, our Lord's followers would have torn the Romans and the high priests to pieces. But . . ." He tilted his head, thinking while his gaze drifted over the coffins stacked around the cave. "I still don't understand how the cross got into the tomb."

"Think of it as poetry, brother."

"Poetry?"

Outside, the dinner bell clanged, calling the monks in from the fields. Zarathan started to rise. His belly had been growling for over an hour.

"Where are you going?" Cyrus asked.

"Didn't you hear the bell? We should be assembling with the others for supper."

Cyrus leaned back on the bench and smiled. "You and I, brother, are to fast for three days. We can't join them."

Zarathan had forgotten. He sighed and slumped to the bench again. "Three days," he whispered in agony. "I'm going to starve to death."

Cyrus bent over his work. "Look about you, brother. This is a place for reflection and patience. Think of the dead over there. They probably fasted for half their lives in the hopes of gaining one tiny glimpse of the Kingdom of God. If you meditate on that, the dead can teach you many things."

Two beautifully tooled gazelle leather bags rested on top of one of the coffins, and on top of the bags were four magnificently bound parchment books. It looked as though someone had just taken the books from the leather bags and forgotten to put them back.

Zarathan pointed. "It must have taken forty goats to produce those books alone, never mind all the other books in this crypt."

Parchment was made by removing the hair from sheep- or goatskin, then processing the hides with lime to produce smooth and extremely fine leather.

"Yes, they're very beautiful, aren't they?"

Cyrus rose from the bench and walked across the crypt. He carefully lifted the book on top and opened it.

Zarathan watched him read for a time, before asking, "What is that?"

"*The Exposition of the Lord's Logia:* sayings by Papias. There are supposed to be five divisions, or five books, in this volume." Cyrus tilted the book sideways to read something. "There's a handwritten note in the margin, in Greek, which says that Papias was the bishop of the community of Hieropolis in Asia Minor, and lived about thirty years after our Lord's death."[25]

Cyrus flipped through the leaves for a time, reading, until he found something that obviously caught his attention. In awe, he whispered, "I didn't know that."

"Know what?"

"Papias says that Markos served as Petros' interpreter, *hermeneutes,* and that he wrote down everything he heard Petros say about the words of our Lord."

"Is he referring to the Gospel of Markos?"

"According to Papias, he didn't like written sources. He only recorded the words of living people. He claims to have spoken directly to the presbyter Ioannes, and someone named Aristion, as well as 'those who actually attended the presbyters.' Which means he got his information from the disciples second- or thirdhand." Cyrus scrutinized something and murmured, "Really?" as though surprised.

"What did you find now?"

"Have you ever heard the names of the two thieves who were crucified on either side of our Lord?"

"No," Zarathan whispered in awe. "Who were they?"

"Dysmas and Gestas.[26] Except this says they were Zealots, not thieves. Hmm." He squinted. "There's another editorial note that refers the reader to a passage in division four."

"Look it up."

Cyrus glanced at him, smiled, and flipped through the parchment leaves. As he read, he whispered, "Are you sure you want to hear it? It's *definitely* heretical."

Zarathan wet his dry lips. "You won't tell anyone, will you?"

"Of course not. I'm your brother in Christos."

"Then I'm not afraid. Read it to me."

Cyrus read for a few heartbeats, and his eyes narrowed. He whispered, "I wonder what this is?"

"What?"

"It looks like some sort of substitution cipher, using Aramaic, Greek, and Hebrew letters."

Excited, Zarathan said, "You mean it's a secret saying?"

As Cyrus continued reading, his green eyes grew shiny, then he gently closed the book, placed it back on top of the gazelle leather bags, and sank down on the bench.

Zarathan's heart began to pound. "What's wrong? What did it say? Why aren't you telling me?"

Cyrus stared at the far side of the crypt. "Have you ever heard a story about Ioses of Arimathaia—"

"And the cup of Christos? Of course. It's said that he—"

"No, not the grail legends. This is a story about Ioses fleeing Jerusalem the night after he placed our Lord's body in his garden tomb."[27]

Riveted by the expression on Cyrus' face, Zarathan's voice grew hushed. "No, I've never heard that story."

Cyrus seemed to be gazing into eternity. "I'm not sure I understood correctly. Most of the passage is in cipher, and a good deal is so faded I can't make it out. But . . ." He turned to Zarathan. Their gazes locked. "Papias said he heard this story from the grandson of a centurion who had been ordered to ride hard to catch Ioses of Arimathaia and his band of thieves."

"Thieves? What had they stolen?"

Cyrus shook his head. "I don't know. The only words I can definitely translate are about the Pearl. Then there's something cryptic about 'a headless demon whom the winds obey,' and 'the son of Pantera.'"

"A headless demon?" Zarathan rubbed his arms, feeling cold to the bone. It must have been getting dark outside, and the temperature of the desert falling.

The cavern had turned cold and haunted, as though the spirits locked in the coffins had risen and begun their nightly walks, circumambulating the narrow confines of the crypt.

Zarathan lurched to his feet. "Even if we can't eat, I'm thirsty. Let's go to the kitchen and get a cup of water."

Cyrus rose. For several moments, he just stared at Papias' book.

"What's the matter?"

"I don't know, I . . ." Cyrus shook his head. "I have the feeling that book may be gone by the time we get back."

"We're just going for a cup of water, Cyrus. It'll take no more than a quarter hour."

Zarathan walked up the gray stone steps to the trapdoor in the ceiling and heaved it open. A flood of river-scented air blew around him.

Cyrus, carrying the small oil lamp, climbed out behind him and closed the trapdoor. As he inserted the key into the lock and turned it, the lamp's flame spluttered and went out.

Zarathan frowned. The door that led from the oratory out into the garden was wide open. Even stranger, the oratory was empty. Ordinarily after dinner, monks came here to pray before the evening rituals.

"Perhaps dinner is not yet over," Zarathan said and started to stride for the kitchen.

Cyrus' hard hand caught his shoulder, forcing him to stop.

"Wait, brother," he whispered.

Cyrus' gaze swept the oratory, missing nothing—the open door, the wind fluttering the cloths on the altar. Then he cocked his head to listen.

And Zarathan noticed it, too.

Absolute quiet.

Though they were instructed not to speak during dinner, there were always sounds: plates being shifted, footsteps across the floor, cups thudding on the long wooden tables.

Tonight, there was nothing.

Just above a whisper, Cyrus said, "Brother Zarathan, I want you to walk behind me. Do not speak. Do you understand?"

Cyrus' tone made the hair at the nape of Zarathan's neck stand out. He jerked a nod and kept pace behind Cyrus as he quietly moved across the oratory toward the heavy door that led to the kitchen.

Cyrus pushed the door open a handbreadth, minimizing the squeaking of the hinges, and peered inside.

Zarathan sniffed the air. From the kitchen, he caught the scents of freshly baked bread and roasted goat, but there was something else. The acrid odor of urine. He whispered, "What—"

Cyrus slapped a hand over his mouth so hard the blow nearly knocked Zarathan off his feet. He gaped at his brother in horror.

Cyrus leaned down until his nose almost pressed against Zarathan's and mouthed the words, *Do not make a sound.*

With tears in his eyes, Zarathan nodded.

Cyrus pushed the door open wide enough to slide through. Zarathan followed close behind.

Had Cyrus not just warned him, the sight would have made him scream.

Monks slumped over the dinner table with chunks of food in their hands, or lay sprawled on the floor in impossible positions. Pools of urine spread around their bodies.

Zarathan's heart thundered. His entire body might have been on fire. He reached out and tugged Cyrus' sleeve. Cyrus looked at him, seemed to understand that Zarathan wanted to run, and shook his head.

Cyrus moved around the overturned benches, avoiding the shattered plates and cups that covered the stone floor. Zarathan followed on trembling legs.

A man sprawled facedown at the head of the table, his hand outstretched as though he'd been trying to reach for the leaf of parchment that rested just beyond his fingers.

Cyrus gently turned him over.

Brother Jonas! A wrenching pain twisted Zarathan's heart. He desperately longed to ask Cyrus what had happened, but the cold, fierce look on his brother's face kept Zarathan mute. Not only that, his throat had constricted so tightly he was having trouble breathing.

Cyrus picked up the leaf of parchment and read it. It seemed to take forever before he handed it to Zarathan and whispered, "The list of forbidden books."

Zarathan didn't even look at it. He just crumpled it in his fist and followed Cyrus as he stealthily moved out of the kitchen and into the hallway that led to the rectory. No lamps burned in the monastery, and as night deepened, it became more and more difficult to see. Cyrus moved methodically down the hall, opening doors, closing them, and resolutely moving on, like Sisyphus with his stone, condemned to forever repeat the same hideous act.

Bodies were usually sprawled on floors, other times slumped over tables. In two cases, they found men hanging out their cell windows, as though at the last instant they'd tried to jump.

What madness is this?

A plate of food rested near every corpse, usually knocked over, with the bread and meat thrown across the floor.

And each man had a bluish face.

When they'd made it to the far end of the monastery, and stood in a square of moonlight streaming through the window, Zarathan could stand it no longer. He whispered, "Cyrus, please tell me—"

"Cyanide, probably in the meat, but it's possible the murderers added it to the water and bread, too. Don't touch anything."

"But . . . why would someone do this? We are just monks!"

Cyrus stared at him unblinkingly. Despite the silver gleam, it was hard to see him. His black hair and beard obscured his face. Only his green eyes were clearly visible, because they reflected the moonlight like polished mirrors.

"At first, after Pappas Meridias' questions, I thought they'd come for me," Cyrus explained. "But that doesn't make any sense. If they'd wanted me, centurions could have marched in and simply taken me."

"Why would they want you?"

Cyrus looked away, his gaze scanning the darkness for the hundredth time. Rather than answering, he said, "They obviously did not come for me. They came to destroy some evidence that's here, in the monastery."

Zarathan wrung his hands like an anxious child. "What evidence? Why couldn't they just order us to turn it over? They could have taken whatever they wanted."

"Because, my brother, you can't take what is in men's hearts. You have to kill them."

Cyrus touched a leaf of parchment that rested on the dead monk's table. When he tipped it up to the moonlight, Zarathan saw the large letters that proclaimed it the Gospel of Thomas, a text written by the Lord's twin brother, and revered since the earliest years of Christianity. Probably the monk had been pondering a particular passage.

Cyrus whispered, "The Gospel of Thomas is on that list we found in the kitchen."

Shocked, Zarathan said, "They have forbidden us to read *Thomas!* But that's absurd. Christians have been reading that book since the beginning! It is my own mother's favorite gospel."

"No longer, I'm afraid. Not if she wishes to continue breathing."

Cyrus eased over to the side of the window and studied the monastery grounds and the desert beyond. In the moon glow, the palm trees gleamed as though sheathed in silver dust.

"They're out there," Cyrus said.

Fear prickled Zarathan's belly. "Who? What are you talking about?"

"The men who are supposed to make certain we are all dead. They'll be coming. Soon. If they were willing to do this to protect themselves, they can't leave anything to chance."

"You mean like two monks who were not at dinner?" Zarathan felt like he was going to throw up.

Cyrus abruptly turned to look at him. "Do you recall Brother Jonas saying that Barnabas never assigned a punishment that he himself did not follow?"

"Yes, why?"

Cyrus' white robe flapped around his long legs as he swiftly strode out of the room and down the hall.

Zarathan whispered, "Where are you going? If they are coming, shouldn't we get out? While we still can?"

Cyrus didn't even slow down. He went directly to Brother Barnabas' cell and called, "Brother? Brother, are you awake?"

When no answer came, he opened the door and looked inside. After a few moments, he closed the door. "He's not there. Where else might he be?"

"Still in the library, perhaps?"

Cyrus nodded and headed for the basilica, following the path they had taken only that afternoon to see Brother Barnabas.

The echoing passage of their footfalls had an eerie, surreal quality, as though somehow not human.

As they hurried through the dark corridors, Zarathan pleaded, "Cyrus, how long do we have before they come looking? Shouldn't we run?"

"That, brother, is the last thing we should do. The first person who flees the monastery will be cut down in a heartbeat. We need to wait until it's too dark for them to see us leave."

"How long will that be?"

"Perhaps another half hour before the moon sets."

"We could be dead by then!"

They walked back through the grisly kitchen and out into the oratory, where Cyrus stopped dead in his tracks.

The trapdoor to the library crypt was open. The amber glow of an oil lamp created a halo over the entry and illuminated the oratory.

Cyrus said, "Who else has a key to the crypt?"

"How would I know?" Zarathan hissed. His heart was beating so hard it felt like it might jump out of his chest. "Please, Cyrus, let's run!"

Cyrus said, "Wait for me here. Do not move unless I tell you to. Do you understand?"

"Y-yes."

Cyrus moved across the floor like a lion on a hunt, one cautious step at a time. When he neared the crypt, he got down on his belly and slid forward until he could see over the edge.

"Brother," Cyrus called softly, "what are you doing?"

"Hmm?" Brother Barnabas' frail, confused voice responded. "Oh, I—I wanted to see these books. One last time. I thought I might spend the night reading them, trying to memorize their words. I have memorized many, but not all of them."

Cyrus rose and hurried down the steps into the crypt, disappearing from Zarathan's view, leaving him absolutely terrified. He scurried across the room, breathing hard, and called into the crypt, "Let's go! Hurry!"

Cyrus didn't even look up at him. He had taken the two gazelle leather bags and was stuffing them full of every book that would fit, while Brother Barnabas watched in utter bewilderment.

"Cyrus, what are you doing?" Barnabas asked.

"Saving as many as I can. Brother Barnabas, do you realize what's happened here tonight?"

As Barnabas tilted his gray head, his long hooked nose cast a shadow across his cheek. "What do you mean?"

"Everyone else is dead. They were poisoned tonight at dinner."

Barnabas' elderly brow furrowed, as though in anger. "Cyrus, that is not amusing. I don't know what would possess you to say—"

"Brother?" Cyrus glanced up at Zarathan and said, "Please show Barnabas the kitchen."

"Me?" Zarathan asked in horror. "But I—"

"Do it!" Cyrus ordered in a voice that sent a shiver down Zarathan's spine.

Zarathan began shaking violently. He had never been brave. Since childhood, he'd hated lightning storms and banging cartwheels. Fisticuffs appalled him. Even loud, angry voices made him shriek and hide. "Brother," he whined, "please, don't make me go back in there!"

"If I have to climb out of this crypt and drag you, brother, you'll regret—"

"Wait." Barnabas gave Cyrus a frightened glance, and climbed the stairs. When he stepped into the oratory, he said, "Show me, Zarathan."

Zarathan scurried for the door to the kitchen, pushed it aside, and held it open for Brother Barnabas to peer through. The odor of urine now overpowered that of the bread.

Barnabas froze in the doorway, his throat working. He kept swallowing convulsively, and his long, narrow face had gone as white as the moonlight. His gaze fixed on each dead face, studying it in disbelief. "Who . . ."

Zarathan answered, "We don't know. But Cyrus said they're desperate and can't leave anything to chance. Which means that soon someone will be coming into the monastery to make certain we are all dead. We have to go, brother."

Tears traced silver lines down Barnabas' wrinkled cheeks. He wiped them on his white sleeve and whispered, "Is it the books?"

"I don't know, brother."

When he didn't move, Zarathan took him by the sleeve and gently tugged him away from the kitchen and back toward the trapdoor over the library crypt.

Cyrus trotted up the stairs with two hugely overstuffed bags and gave one to Barnabas. "Can you take care of this, brother?"

Barnabas took the bag and ran his hand over the beautiful leather as though it contained something more precious to him than life itself. "Yes."

Cyrus fairly threw the other bag at Zarathan, saying, "If my suspicions are right, what's in that bag is worth the lives of one hundred monks. Keep it safe."

"But why do I have to carry it?" Zarathan complained. "I don't even want to touch heretical books!"

Cyrus ignored him, trotted across the oratory, then silently eased up alongside the open door that led to the garden. With great care, he looked outside. It seemed to take forever before he waved for Zarathan and Barnabas to join him.

Their heavy bags clutched to their breasts, they sprinted across the floor.

Cyrus whispered, "We have to wait for the right moment."

"When will that be?" Zarathan demanded. "We should go now! If we don't escape, they'll find us and capture us, and—"

"Zarathan," Brother Barnabas said in his deepest, calmest voice. "Fear not, stand still, and see."

He extended a finger to the darkness beyond the garden, and Zarathan saw black shapes moving against the sand. Four of them. They were creeping toward the monastery, bent over, as silent as ghosts. Something, probably weapons, glinted in their hands. They must have had their faces blacked with charcoal because the moonlight did not reflect from them.

As it will ours . . .

Cyrus hissed, "They're splitting up. One man is going to come through this door. Both of you hide in the kitchen until I call you."

Zarathan was already on his way at a run when he heard Brother Barnabas say, "Cyrus, please. Don't do this. I would rather die than see you return to your former life of sin. Your soul—"

"There's no time to discuss this, brother. Someone must save the words of our Lord." Cyrus gestured to the books, probably realizing it was the only argument that would persuade the old monk.

Barnabas clutched the gazelle leather bag to his chest, murmured, "Yes, I—I . . . will," and reluctantly turned away to follow Zarathan to the kitchen.

Zarathan rushed ahead, swung the door open, and almost fainted when someone moved in the rear. "Oh, dear God, what are *you* doing here?"

Kalay straightened from where she'd been sniffing Brother Jonas' cup of water. She carefully placed it back on the table. Wearing a black cape with the hood pulled up, she would have blended with the darkness were it not for the wisps of red hair that glinted in the faint light. "I knew something was wrong. It was too quiet. I came to look."

"Well, run! We're in danger!" Zarathan urged.

The hem of her cape brushed the floor as Kalay came around the table to stare at them. "What's happening?"

"There are men, killers, coming into the monastery!"

"To make sure the job was properly done?"

He nodded, trying to say as few words to her as possible.

She swept around the table and peered out the ajar kitchen door. "Is Brother Cyrus going to try to protect you?"

Zarathan gestured with the heavy bag in his hands. In an insistent whisper, he said, "I don't know what he's doing. Now please run away!"

Barnabas put cool fingers on Zarathan's shoulder. The mop of gray hair that surrounded his cadaverous face made it look even more skeletal. His cheekbones protruded as though ready to burst through the thin veneer of skin. "God has cast her lot with ours, Zarathan. She must remain until our fates have been decided. One way or the other."

The iron hinges on the oratory door groaned as someone pushed the door back, opening it wider. Kalay's mouth tightened.

Zarathan felt as though his chest was about to burst. He flattened himself against the wall, and fought to see, but Kalay's head blocked his view. She was too tall for a decent woman!

"What's happening?" He breathed the words. "Can you see—"

He heard a gasp and a groan, a body toppling to the stone floor, then the sounds of two men struggling.

Like lightning, Kalay shot through the open door and dashed across the oratory with her cape flying.

Zarathan remained frozen, watching with his mouth open. Cyrus had grabbed the killer around the throat. They were both rolling across the floor. Though Cyrus' muscular arm was clamped over the man's throat to mute his cries, ragged squeals still escaped; the man kept ripping at Cyrus' robe, trying to pull Cyrus off him.

"Brother!" Kalay called as she ran headlong for Cyrus. "Move your arm!"

He looked up in time to see her pull one of the kitchen knives from her belt. Cyrus jerked his arm aside, and Kalay lashed out with the blade, neatly slitting the man's throat. A brief shriek erupted, followed by an awful gurgling sound.

Cyrus let the man drop to the floor, took the knife from Kalay's hand, and plunged it into the killer's chest.

"Brothers, hurry!" Cyrus called.

Zarathan sprinted for Cyrus and heard Barnabas padding behind him.

Kalay said to Cyrus, "Have you a plan for escaping?"

"No, but I thought—"

"Quiet your tongue and follow me. I have a boat stashed on the river below my washing hut."

Kalay slipped out the door and ran headlong across the garden. Her black hood fell back and her hair streamed around her like flames straight out of Hades.

Cyrus followed her, though Zarathan had no idea why. With no other viable choice, he ran after Cyrus, and Barnabas followed. They passed through the garden gate, four dark figures taking the path that led past the washhouse. Within moments, Zarathan was panting, his feet hammering the hard-packed trail. The heavy bag of books was like a block of stone in his arms. His first thought was to drop the load, but Brother Barnabas was clinging to his as through his life depended upon it. To save face, he had to keep hold of his own bag.

Zarathan kept shooting frightened glances over his shoulder, sure that they were being pursued. His imagination filled the dark with sinister figures, each about to sink a dagger into Zarathan's back.

When they lunged down the bank toward the dark, glistening waters of the Nile, Zarathan saw only the thick reeds that lined the shallows. Kalay darted into the reeds, the stalks whispering against her clothing.

Zarathan followed the others, the smell of mud, vegetation, and the river thick in his nose. Insects hummed about his head. He batted at the ones that landed on his face.

The boat wasn't the sort of thing Zarathan would have expected of a washerwoman. It was of plank construction, perhaps fifteen cubits in length. The high bow was tethered to the bank with a rope. Three bench seats could be seen inside, and several oars were propped on the seat.

"Where is Sophia?" Cyrus asked, knowing that she and Kalay often worked late into the night.

"Back in the city. She's safe." Kalay was already picking at the knot on the bow rope.

Even as she spoke, Zarathan could hear shouts in the darkness behind them. He swallowed hard, expecting assailants to leap out of the reeds at any moment.

Cyrus shoved the boat into the water and held it while the others got in. Zarathan, panting for breath, felt the thing rock under his weight, and quickly sat, the book bag pressed to his heaving chest.

Cyrus pushed off, wading out from the bank, then clambered into the rear and reached for a paddle. Kalay already sat in the bow with her own paddle and was propelling them out into the current. Barnabas and Zarathan, with their overstuffed leather bags, sat in the middle.

By the time Cyrus and Kalay had paddled to the middle of the river, a gaudy glare lit the sky. Through the trees that lined the shore, Zarathan glimpsed flames shooting from the basilica's windows. The crashing of wood and stone thundered over the river.

Zarathan whispered, "Dear God, what did we do to deserve this? Are we being punished? Where is our Lord?"

From the darkness beside him, Barnabas softly answered. "Split a piece of wood and he is there. Lift up a stone and you will find him."[28]

Scared and on the verge of tears, Zarathan said, "It's dangerous to quote from the Gospel of Thomas, brother. It's not one of the twenty-seven approved books. What if someone were to hear you? You could be charged with heresy and executed! We all could!"

"I will continue quoting Thomas, brother, and the gospels of Petros, Philippon, and Maryam. Their words are the light. I refuse to live in darkness, even when ordered to do so by my own church." Barnabas heaved a sigh and, as though coming to a difficult decision, called, "Cyrus? Please stay close to the shore. I wish to stop at a place near the cliff of Gebel et-Tarif."

"Yes, brother, but we mustn't remain long. We will be in danger until we are far from here."

"I understand."

Zarathan propped his arms on his bundle and let the rocking of the boat soothe him.

Barnabas said, "Zarathan, please give me your bag."

Zarathan handed it to Barnabas, and the elderly monk began sorting through it, pulling out some books and setting them aside, leaving others inside. He did the same with his own bag until he had two distinct piles, then he refilled the bags.

"Why is Brother Barnabas so worried about those books?" Kalay turned to ask Zarathan.

"A synod of bishops recently met in Nicea, a city in Asia Minor. They declared that many of the holy books we cherish are heretical, and that anyone caught reading or copying them will be charged with treason and put to death."

Kalay turned back and dipped her paddle again. "Well, if they had orders to kill only those that could read and write, I guess I was safe, since I can't do neither."

"You were safe," Cyrus said from the rear, "until you helped us. Now you're in as much danger as we are."

"You think they'll be looking for you? Coming after you?"

"Oh, yes," Cyrus said.

For a long time, no one spoke. They just stared at the silver waves that rolled away from the boat.

In a faint voice, Brother Barnabas said, "Yes, they must come after us. They have no choice. They're afraid we know where it is."

A camel brayed somewhere to the south.

Cyrus asked, "Where *what* is?"

Barnabas did not answer. He clasped his hands over the bag of books, and closed his eyes in prayer.

THE TEACHING ON FORGIVENESS

The summer day is bright and warm. To your right, Lake Kennaret shimmers as though strewn with fine fragments of jade. The scent of roasting lamb fills the air, and down the shore you see children playing around the cook fire, where the lamb drips fat onto the flames.

"But it makes no sense, Yeshu," you object. "Why should we forgive evil people like the Romans? If God were truly just, he would pluck them up and cast them straight into the pit to rid us of their scourge."

Yeshu's tanned face is damp with sweat, his dark eyes tired. He adjusts the white himation over his head to shield his brow from the scorching sun. "I, too, have struggled to understand why evil people deserve forgiveness . . . or perhaps why anyone does. We are all thoughtless and cruel, concerned only with ourselves and our own needs. That is, I suspect, the point."

You shake a fist in the hot air. "The point? What is the point? That forgiveness has no reason? That it is simply a moment of God's grace?"

The lines around his mouth tighten. "No. Ultimately, I think forgiveness is a hard-fought, relentless battle to give of one's self until there is nothing left, and to do it only for another's sake."

Anger tingles your breast. "Tell me you are not suggesting that we forgive the Romans for what they have done to us? They have murdered our people by the thousands. Are you saying that I should give all of myself, everything that I am, so that God might release them from the punishment they deserve?"

He stares at me with longing in his eyes. When he answers, his voice is soft, but rich and melodic. "Yes. Of course. I am. Because to truly forgive is to feel the presence of Sinai in your heartbeat. Can you feel it, brother?"

You just stare at him with your lips pressed into a white, bloodless line.

Yeshu continues. "Can you hear the echo of God's voice in your own breathing? It's there. It's been there all along, but until you can hear and feel the presence of the divine you will not be able to forgive either the Romans or yourself."

You fold your arms arrogantly. "I think perhaps, Yeshu, you have gotten lost amid the leaves of the lesson-tree while digging for its roots."

He smiles and bows his head. "Yes, perhaps. If so, I must work harder and hope that God finds me."

SIX

They'd been paddling for an hour when Barnabas suddenly said, "There, Cyrus. Put ashore near that gap in the reeds."

As the reeds slid along the side of the boat, Zarathan, who'd been vomiting over the side, lifted his head, and watched Cyrus and Kalay guide the boat to the shore. The starlight reflected from the sand with such brilliance, it appeared to be a shimmering blanket of diamonds.

"Why are we stopping?" Zarathan asked as he wiped his mouth on his sleeve. The awful taste of bile made him long to retch again.

"We won't be long," Barnabas said.

"We shouldn't stop!" Zarathan said, but no one seemed to be listening. They all continued exactly as they had before he'd opened his mouth. What was the matter with them? The images of his dead brothers' faces seemed to be carved into the back of his eyelids. He couldn't even blink without seeing them, and Barnabas wanted to stop! "We have to keep going," he cried. "We can't stop! If we stop, they'll find us and kill us!"

"Zarathan, please calm down. Everything is well," Barnabas said and patted his shoulder gently.

As though the pat had triggered it, the acrid scents of urine and blood filled his nostrils. He lurched to the side of the boat and vomited again. When his stomach stopped heaving, he propped his chin on the edge of the boat and stared blindly at the stars that reflected in the smooth surface of the river. He felt like he was burning up with fever.

The massive cliff, Gebel et-Tarif, fifty times the height of a man, almost seemed to lean over the water here. Zarathan sucked a breath of cool air into his hot lungs and studied it. The stone wall was filled with holes and cut by starlit ledges, upon which owls perched. He could see their eyes shining.

Cyrus jumped into the water and dragged the boat up onto the beach.

Wet to his knees, he went to the bow to help the others out.

Zarathan stumbled out first. When he turned, he saw Barnabas pick up Zarathan's book bag and waddle forward, his feet slapping a clumsy rhythm on the sand. He looked like a drunken, overweight ibis. What could he want with that bag out here in the darkness? Surely he wasn't thinking of lighting a fire to read by? The old fool. That would end their flight quickly and lethally.

"Let me help with that bag, brother." Cyrus took it from Barnabas' protective arms.

"Thank you, brother."

Barnabas stepped onto the sand, immediately took the bag back, and walked straight for the cliff. His head trembled on the slender stem of his neck, as though he could barely put one foot in front of the other.

Zarathan glanced at Cyrus. "Where's Barnabas going? We shouldn't get too far from the boat."

Before Cyrus could answer, Kalay leaped to the sand in front of Cyrus and said, "You've had some practice at killing, haven't you?"

Cyrus' eyes tightened. "Some, yes."

She propped her hands on her shapely hips. "I think a lot more than 'some.' You're just being modest."

Cyrus gave her an evaluative look. "You saved my life back there. Saved our lives. I haven't properly thanked you. I'm grateful."

She tossed her head, and her hair shook out into glorious waves. "There's no need. Even though I think you're all mad, I wouldn't see you harmed, especially not by brutes from Rome."

Cyrus paused. "How do you know they were from Rome?"

"I was in Phoou this morning, buying soap, and saw that blond bishop when he got off the boat. He had four men with him. One of them was the man we killed. Why'd they come after you?"

Cyrus' eyes remained on Kalay, apparently deciding whether or not to answer her, and she seemed to feel his gaze like a hand upon her body. She drew her black cloak up over her shoulders and tucked a stray tendril of her tumbled hair behind her ear. The action was perfectly natural, almost instinctive, feminine, alluring.

Zarathan felt as though he'd been bludgeoned. A choking sound seeped from his lips before he caught himself.

Kalay turned to him. "Aren't you the one they call Zarathan?"

"I'm not telling you my name! It's common knowledge that if a demon knows your name, it can control you." He glared at her.

Kalay pulled up her skirt, revealing a bare leg, and scratched her ankle. "You must be Zarathan. I see the resemblance to a circumcised cat."

Zarathan's mouth fell open and he shot a mortified glance at Cyrus.

But Cyrus had already turned and begun walking across the sand after Brother Barnabas.

"Don't worry," Kalay whispered almost in his face, "you're safe with me. Your puny soul isn't worth the effort."

She had the audacity to wink at Zarathan just before she lifted her skirts even higher and tramped after Cyrus.

Zarathan stood as if planted. He didn't want to be anywhere near those bare legs. He cupped a hand to his mouth and called, "I'll stay and guard the boat!"

Brother Barnabas had set the bag down, and now walked along the base of the cliff with one hand on the cool stone. In the starlight, his gray hair and beard shimmered as though coated with frost. Cyrus and Kalay silently plodded along behind him.

Finally, Barnabas stopped, and said, "I think this is it."

Barnabas knelt and began scooping away sand. Both Cyrus and Kalay fell to their knees to help him.

In no time they'd heaped up a mighty mound and still found nothing.

Zarathan wandered toward them, casting glances over his shoulder, expecting to see a boat filled with black-robed killers paddling around the wide river's bend. "We should be going. This is taking too long."

No one answered him, and despair wrung his soul. By now his parents would know about the monastery fire. People in the city would have seen the flames almost immediately and begun running out to see what had happened. His poor mother. He could imagine her searching the charred remains for his corpse while his father carried the torch to light the way. She would be weeping. He suddenly longed to go home so badly he could barely stand it. If only he had the courage, he would. . . .

"Brother," Cyrus said, "I think I've uncovered the lid of a jar."

"Let me see!" Barnabas crawled over, out of breath from his labors, and felt the object. "Yes, let's continue until we have enough space to twist off the lid."

Zarathan watched them uncover the shoulder of the pot. It looked big.

Curious, Zarathan moved as close as he dared. The demon woman was still giving him occasional glances.

Cyrus said, "What's in the jar, brother?"

Barnabas wiped his hands on his dirty white robe. "I believe it may be . . ." He paused. "It may be what they're looking for. Can you open it? The lid is sealed with wax."

Cyrus twisted and the aged wax cracked loose. As he lifted the lid, Kalay bent forward to look inside, then frowned at Barnabas.

"More old books?" She sighed. "Aren't you in enough trouble?"

Zarathan shook his head. If the jar had been standing on the sand, he suspected it would have been nearly as tall as Cyrus.

As though reaching for a precious child, Barnabas slipped his hand deep inside, and drew out a brittle leather pouch. "Cyrus, could you retrieve the bag of books I carried from the boat?"

"Yes, brother." Cyrus trotted across the sand and brought it back.

Barnabas pointed a gnarled finger to the jar. "Put it in there, with the other books."[29]

Cautiously, Cyrus slid the gazelle leather bag into the jar.

"Now," Barnabas said. "We must make a fire to heat the wax so that we can reseal the jar, and bury it again."

Cyrus ran a hand through his curly black hair. "Brother, I don't think that's wise. What if they're pursuing us? They will see the blaze."

"Yes, yes, I . . . I'm sure you're right, but—" His voice faded. As though too exhausted to argue, Barnabas clutched his precious leather pouch to his heart and unsteadily walked away. He slumped to the sand like an old rag doll.

Kalay glanced at Zarathan, saw him flinch, and walked straight toward him. He considered running, but didn't want to appear to be afraid of a mere woman.

"What do you want?" he asked sharply.

She stopped in front of him. "You really hate it when women get close enough to see the whites of your eyes, don't you?"

"It's not women. It's *you*," he said.

Her brows arched. She tipped her head toward Barnabas. "What's in the pouch?"

"I don't know! I've spent my whole life avoiding heretical books."

"You mean until recently."

"Well, it's not my fault the bishops declared one of my favorite books to be heresy. I had nothing to do with it."

Kalay grunted, and then said, "How did the old man know where that pot was?"

"Go ask him. I'm just running for my life."

Cyrus went to kneel before Brother Barnabas, who had removed a palm-sized fragment of papyrus from the pouch and gazed at it with tears in his eyes.

Cyrus' white sleeves blew in the faint wind that swept the Nile. Gently, he asked, "Are you well, brother? Do you need a drink of water? I'll have Zarathan fetch you some from the river."

Barnabas' eyes glistened. "I—I have not always been so faithful, Cyrus," the old man confessed. "All my life people have brought me books, or tiny fragments of books. I knew some of them contained information that the church would find frightening. Especially . . . this one."

Cyrus patiently waited for more. When it didn't come, he said, "So you buried them to protect them?"

Shamefully, Barnabas nodded. "I didn't trust our church."

From the corner of her mouth, Kalay said, "Well, that proved your salvation."

"That's blasphemy!" Zarathan scolded. "Salvation only comes through our Lord, Iesous Christos."

"Really?" she said with a canny tilt of her head. "Tonight, it looked to me as though it came through Brother Cyrus' skill with a carving knife. Not to mention *mine*."

"Why are you talking to me?" Zarathan demanded to know. "Are you trying to tempt me?"

Kalay looked him over the way she would an annoying insect. "Are you truly so stupid? Or are you just pretending?"

Zarathan couldn't think of an answer.

Cyrus gently said, "Brother Barnabas, please sit here and rest. I'll make a small fire to heat the wax so that we can reseal the pot."

Barnabas nodded. "Thank you, brother."

Cyrus walked back across the sand to where Zarathan and Kalay stood. "Brother, please watch Barnabas. He's frail and heartbroken. I'll return soon."

Zarathan said, "Of course, brother."

Cyrus turned to Kalay. "Sister, would you like to help me gather drift-wood?"

"I will if you'll stop calling me "sister." I don't believe in that crucified criminal you call a savior. I'm a pagan. I worship the Goddess, and my name is Kalay." She pronounced it *Kuh-lay*.

Cyrus inclined his head agreeably. "I would appreciate some help gathering wood, Kalay, if you would not mind."

"I wouldn't, Cyrus."

They walked down to the water and drifted through the starlit reeds like pale ghosts, bending, picking up sticks, talking softly.

Zarathan walked over to Barnabas and found the old man shivering. "Brother? Are you all right?"

"Just cold."

Zarathan sank to the sand beside him and wrapped his arm around Barnabas' shoulders, trying to warm him. He might be a heretic, but he was his brother. "Barnabas, you mustn't worry so much. You'll wear your-self out."

Barnabas shook his gray head. "I keep seeing the faces of our dead brothers. I can't believe someone would kill them for this." He tucked the papyrus fragment back into the leather pouch and tied it to his belt.

"What is that? And why do you think they were killed because of it?"

Zarathan's eyes moved to where Kalay and Cyrus walked down the shore.

Barnabas followed his gaze. Instead of answering his question, Barnabas said, "Are you concerned about the woman, Zarathan?"

"No! Well, not exactly. At least I wouldn't be if I were sure she was human. I fear she may be a demon."

"Be of good courage, Zarathan, for the Son of Man is within you. Follow after him, and all will be well."

"That's from the Gospel of Maryam!" he said in terror. "Stop that!"

"I thought you didn't read 'heretical' books?"

"Well . . ." Zarathan sheepishly lifted his shoulders. "There were so many copies lying around the monastery. It was hard not to see a *few* passages."

Barnabas smiled and bowed his head. "What I meant is that the only one who can violate your vow of chastity is you, Zarathan. That bit of knowledge should comfort you."

"It should?" He couldn't imagine why.

Cyrus and Kalay walked up the sand together, talking. She smiled at something Cyrus said. A short time later, a tiny blaze flickered to life near the pot.

Barnabas got on his knees and clasped his hands in prayer. His lips moved with soundless words. When he opened his eyes again, they fixed on Cyrus with such intensity that Zarathan said, "What's wrong? You look like you just saw Beelzebub himself."

"I'm afraid for Brother Cyrus."

Astonished, Zarathan said, "He's the last person you should worry about. He can take care of himself."

Barnabas' eyes tightened. "Can he? Perhaps you see a less tormented soul than I do."

The old man rose and walked unsteadily across the sand toward the fire.

SEVEN

When Cyrus saw Barnabas coming, he immediately rose and took Barnabas' arm, helping him to the fire. "Are you cold, brother? Why don't you warm yourself while I melt the wax."

Barnabas sank down and extended his icy fingers to the tiny flame. "Kalay? Would you allow me a few moments alone to speak with Brother Cyrus?"

Her eyes narrowed. "Plotting again, are you?"

Barnabas smiled. "Yes."

She got to her feet and headed for Zarathan, who threw up his hands in exasperation and backpedaled across the sand.

Kalay called, "Stand still. You're vexing me."

When Barnabas and Cyrus were alone, Cyrus stopped adding twigs to the flames, and lifted his gaze to stare into Barnabas' eyes. Barnabas saw the fear that lived there. Before he could speak, Cyrus bowed his head.

"I also am worried about my immortal soul, Brother Barnabas. I just . . ." Cyrus toyed with a twig and then tossed it into the fire. "I could not see any other way at the time."

Barnabas reached out and put a hand on Cyrus' bowed head. "I fear that I am the one responsible for your sins tonight, Cyrus. Were it not for my literary obsession, I doubt you and Kalay would have needed to—to do what you did."

Cyrus looked up. Sternly, he said, "That was not your fault, brother. No more than—"

Barnabas softly interrupted. "We can both worry about forgiveness at another time, and probably for the rest of our lives. Actually, I wanted to speak with you about something else."

Cyrus' thick black brows drew together. "Yes?"

Barnabas cast a glance over his shoulder, making certain that Zarathan and Kalay could not overhear. Then he whispered, "Please try to answer me honestly."

"Of course, brother."

"How did Pappas Meridias know you?"

For several moments Cyrus didn't seem to be breathing. Barnabas studied him. He must have been considered a handsome man when he was in the world. The curly black hair that hung to his shoulders framed his oval face, accenting his straight nose and green eyes.

Cyrus replied, "I don't think he knew me, that is, recognized me, but he probably knew my reputation—"

"How did he know you were in our monastery?"

Cyrus lifted his shoulders in a confused shrug. "Truly, I don't know."

After more than thirty years of working with monks, Barnabas could assess truth and falsehood with fair ease. He saw no guile in Cyrus' face.

"I am concerned," Barnabas explained, "because when a man enters our monastery, we do not ask about his former life, or name. It is enough that he wishes to seek God, and help us usher in the Kingdom. To discover a monk's former name requires a great deal of effort." He held Cyrus' gaze. "Pappas Meridias was hoping to find Jairus Claudius Atinius in our monastery. Why?"

Cyrus stared at the river as though seeking hidden enemies, expecting them to arrive soon. Perhaps the fire had been burning for too long.

Cyrus pulled the lid from the big pot and held it near the flames, turning it to melt the wax all around. "If I knew the answer to that, brother, I might be able to solve part of the puzzle about the attack on our monastery. But I don't."

"Are you certain you have no idea—"

"I swear to you on my baptism, brother. I do not know why a bishop would wish to find me."

Barnabas shivered and stared into the flames. It was a small fire, no more than a clutter of burning twigs, but it felt good. "Cyrus, how old are you?"

Cyrus wet his lips, as though worried Barnabas might put something together. "I am thirty-four, brother."

Barnabas did not take his eyes from the flames, but his mind was running calculations. "You have been a monk with us for almost a year. Were you a monk anywhere else first?"

"In Rome, for one year. Another year in Milan. I spent eight years moving through monasteries in Asia Minor, then I spent a little over a year in Palestine."

"Is it possible that men from the highest levels of our Church have been searching monasteries for years trying to locate you?" When Cyrus hesitated for an unusually long time, Barnabas said, "If you don't wish to tell me, Cyrus, it's all right."

"Truly, brother, I can't imagine why they would."

There was something in his voice that told Barnabas he wasn't telling the whole truth, but he said, "Well, keep thinking about it. Perhaps you will come up with a reason. In the meantime, hand me that lid. I'll reseal the pot, then we'll quickly bury it, and be on our way. I know you're frightened for us, as I am."

Cyrus handed him the warm jar lid and Barnabas pressed it down hard on the pot rim, sealing it. As Cyrus kicked sand over the fire, Barnabas began shoving sand over the top of the pot.

It didn't take long. By the time the night wind had done its job, the pot and its hiding place would again be invisible.

Barnabas struggled to his feet and found Cyrus standing awkwardly, his fists clenched at his sides. "What is it, Cyrus?"

"Brother, I would like to ask you a question now."

Barnabas' heart skipped. There was only one question that could be plaguing Cyrus.

The river-scented breeze blew Cyrus' black hair around his face, tangling it with his beard.

Barnabas sighed. "I cannot tell you, Cyrus. If I did, it would be dangerous for you. For all of us. That said, I must ask for your help. I cannot do this alone."

"What is it you wish to do?"

"I must undertake a mission that I should have undertaken twenty-five years ago, when I first discovered the papyrus. Please, don't ask me anything else."

Cyrus propped his hands on his hips and his broad shoulders strained against the linen fabric of his white robe. "Brother, I will do anything you ask of me, because I trust you, but will you at least tell me what the Church is afraid of? It would help me to know that."

The night air had grown cool. Barnabas stared up at the wealth of stars in the heavens, wondering what he could say that would be true, but not the Truth.

"Cyrus," he began in a low, confidential voice, "they err who say, 'The Lord first died and then he arose.' For first he arose, and then he died. *That* is what they fear."[30]

Just before he turned for the boat, Barnabas caught the sudden glint of fear in Cyrus' eyes . . . and it cut him to the heart.

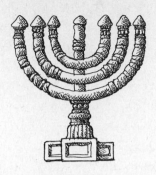

EIGHT

Mehebel

Wind rustled the boughs of the fig trees and fluttered Yosef's cape where he'd drawn it tightly about his legs. The intense darkness on the mountainside made it difficult to see anything clearly, but at least he did not hear horses, or men moving through the trees. In the distance, the lamplit homes of the farmers who cultivated the land gleamed. Both the broad fertile valley bottom, and the terraced hillsides between mounts Ebal and Gerizim were farmed. Vineyards and orchards flourished on the slopes.

Titus, I pray to God you are safe.

He rolled over and had to grit his teeth to keep from crying out. The pain in his wounded shoulder was staggering. After they'd taken refuge in this orchard, he'd barely slept. All night long, he'd worried about Titus, and gone over every possible person who might have betrayed them, remembered every argument.

The traitor must have been one of the inner circle. No one else knew of their plan. But who could have so hated them he would betray even their final act of devotion?

The scents of damp earth and blossoms blew through the orchard. He inhaled deeply, and closed his eyes, trying to force himself to sleep. Bone-numbing pain throbbed in his shoulder with each beat of his heart.

As his breathing dropped to the deep rhythms of sleep, voices whispered to him, and faces drifted before his eyes. . . .

I lean against the doorway of my house just outside the walled city of Yerushalaim and casually watch the passersby.

The purple gleam of dawn streams through the grapevines that cover the white limestone cliff behind my house, and casts dappled shadows across the road twenty paces away. Titus kneels near the road, apparently mending a leather harness. His job today is to watch for Roman soldiers. As a member of the Council of Seventy-one, I know my house is occasionally under surveillance. The occupiers rightly fear that I have sympathy for radicals.

In the room behind me, three such men talk in low voices: Yakob and Yohanan, the sons of Zebedaios, and Kepha, the Rock, who is also known as the skandaion, *the stumbling block,*[31] *because of the constant gloom he seems to inflict upon everyone.*

A wagon filled with large clay jars bangs down the road, the wares jostling in the back. I watch it pass. Many people walk the road today, carrying goods for sale in the city. Others are just travelers coming for the Pesach celebration. By the end of the week more than two million people will have arrived from all over the world.[32]

My gaze moves over the nearby houses. Most are carved into the limestone cliff, or built against it so that the cliff makes up one wall. My house is larger than most, but not ostentatiously large. I have six rooms. The recently hewn tomb in my garden resembles a dark hole. I built it out of fear that my ailing father will soon require it. He's been dying for a month, but soon, I pray, his misery will be over.

Titus stands and whispers, "The Two are coming, Master."

I turn and softly call to the men inside my house, "They're coming."

Behind me, I hear robes rustling, sandals scuffing the stone floor.

I straighten and smooth the wrinkles from the front of my yellow himation. Beneath it, I wear a simple blue linen tunic and sandals.

Titus dips his head politely as Yeshua and Maryam walk onto the path. Both wear white tunics tied over their left shoulders, with the other shoulder bare, and white himatia draped over their heads to hide their identities, lest the crowds should follow them here. Maryam has her wealth of black hair pulled back and tied with a leather cord. The style highlights her perfect face, but also accentuates her worried expression. She keeps glancing fearfully at Yeshua, though he doesn't seem to notice. He has his gaze fixed on me. He is a slender man, of medium height,[33] but his eyes capture the hearts and souls of men and women alike. There is a serenity there, centuries deep, that makes me long to stare into those dark eyes forever.

I step forward. "Rab, welcome. Please go inside quickly."

Maryam gently touches my shoulder as she passes and enters my house.

Yeshua stands for a moment longer, just staring at me. His long curly black hair and beard blow in the wind that gusts down over the cliff. "Thank you, Yosef. For everything. I know we place you in great danger. You are a true friend."

"Yes, well, that won't matter if we're caught. Please hide yourself."

Yeshua nods.

As he passes, my gaze lingers on the strange tattoos that cover his arms. His flesh bears the marks of many powerful magical spells. There are those who claim to have been healed just by touching those marks.[34]

I take one last look around—see Titus shake his head, telling me there is no sign of pursuit—then duck inside and close my door.

After the rich colors of dawn, it requires time for my eyes to adjust to the darkness.

The five exchange holy kisses, then Yeshua extends a hand to the floor mats. "Please, sit. We haven't much time."

Maryam kneels between Yakob and Yohanan, but Kepha remains standing, facing Yeshua. Tall with sandy hair and a thick beard, he always looks angry. He is known for being hot-tempered.[35]

Yeshua smiles at Kepha. "Brother, please sit down. We have much to discuss."

Kepha's eyes narrow at Maryam. The rivalry between the two has been growing for some time. They clearly dislike each other.[36] Kepha thrusts out a hand to Maryam. "Master, please, let Maryam leave us, for women are not worthy of life."[37]

In the Jewish tradition, women are not allowed to become disciples of prominent religious teachers, much less be a part of a wandering ministry. Such behavior is scandalous. Kepha is voicing what many men in their religion believe, but it is not what Yeshua believes. Yeshua has always accepted men as well as women as his disciples and traveling companions. Radical ideas like these are what get him in trouble. Temple authorities see his teachings as threats to the very fabric of Jewish social life.[38]

Maryam's jaw clenches. She starts to stand, and Yeshua softly says, "No, Maryam, stay." To Kepha, he gently adds, "Brother, the heavens and earth will be rolled up in your presence,[39] *why are you troubled by Maryam?"*

"Because," Kepha gestures his frustration, "she always dominates the conversation, displacing the rightful words of your true apostles."[40]

"Master," Maryam says, starting to rise again. "I will go so that my voice does not hinder Kepha."

Yeshua lifts a hand to stop her. In a tender voice he says, "I tell you truly that for the rest of time you will be known as my most beloved apostle and praised as the woman who knew the All. Please, sit down."[41]

He kisses her again on the mouth, and she sinks back to the mat.

Kepha clenches his fists. "Lord, do you love her more than us? You kiss her often."[42]

Yeshua sighs. "I love equally all those who walk in the spirit of the life. Here, Kepha, sit by my side and let us speak of more important things."

Kepha grumbles, but he sits on a mat opposite Maryam, as far from her as he can get.

"Now," Yeshua says, "let us get to the business at hand. Yosef? The Council recently met?"

I walk forward. "Yes. They're very worried about you. Your movement is attracting increasing numbers, and the Council fears that during the Pesach feast there may be a riot. Many of the uneducated are already shouting that you are the messiah, the 'annointed king' who will overthrow the Romans and restore the Jewish State."

"I have never said that, Yosef."

"I know, but it's difficult to control such feelings of Jewish nationalism. The people are looking for a savior, and their hatred for Rome is like a smoldering torch, ready to ignite. The Council fears that over the holy days people might rally around you."

"All of the Council, or just certain members?"

I shrug. "Not all, but the most powerful members. High Priest Kaiaphas says that if we let you go on like this, the people will revolt and the Romans will come and destroy both our Temple and our nation."[43]

"And Councilor Hanan?[44] What is he saying?"

Hanan is the former high priest of the Council, and a wealthy business-man. His family sells the lambs and doves necessary for ritual sacrifices. I don't know all the details, only that there is a blood feud, generations old, between Hanan's family and Yeshua's.

"Hanan says you are a Zealot, maybe even one of the secret leaders of the movement. He says that's why you call yourself the Son of Man, just as the other secret leader calls himself the Son of the Father. He says the Zealots are trying to fulfill the prophecies of the Essenes regarding the coming of two mashiahims, the Mashiah of Yisrael, and the Mashiah of Aaron."[45]

Yeshua bows his head. For a time he merely seems to be staring at the floor.

Yohanan looks around and says, "But, Master, all of this is about to pass away. Why are they worried? They should forget about politics and gird them-selves for the coming Kingdom." He has bright brown eyes and a mass of brown curls. He smiles at Yeshua as though the light of the world emanates from him.

Without lifting his head, Yeshua replies, "The Kingdom is right before their eyes, spread out all over the earth, but men are blind, so they do not realize it."[46]

The words seem to pierce straight to my heart. I am not one of the chosen, not an apostle, merely a helpful bystander; but I feel grateful to be in the pres-ence of this man. So many of his words seem to open my eyes to a bright para-dise I never thought possible.

Yeshua turns to look up at me. "What else, Yosef? Is there more?"

"Not much more. During the feast, the Council is responsible for main-taining peace between the Jews and the Romans. I'm afraid they will do what-ever is necessary to see it accomplished."

"Including arresting Yeshu?" Maryam asks.[47]

"I'm afraid they might, though no one has suggested it yet. The councilors are more afraid that Rome might arrest him, and they will have to protect him. He is greatly beloved by the people, who will expect the Council to do something to save him."

Maryam reaches out to touch the hem of Yeshua's himation. "Please don't do this. It's too dangerous."

Kepha says, "Do not listen to Maryam. She is a coward, as are all women. We must enter the city as planned. It is the heart of the matter!"

Yeshua's gaze has not left me. "On what charges would the Council arrest me?"

"Probably sedition. I hope they would not charge you with being a magician. If found guilty, you would be stoned to death."

Kepha says, "Well, that's better than being charged as a magician by the Romans, where the sentence is death by crucifixion."

Yeshua's dark brows lower. In a very soft voice, he says, "I pray God does not require that."

His words bring tears to Maryam's eyes, but whether they are tears of anger or mourning, I cannot tell.

"Yeshu," she says, "Only Praefectus Pontios Pilatos can condemn a man to be crucified. Surely the Council would not refer such a case to the praefectus."[48]

All eyes turn to me.

"Truly, I do not know. I think it doubtful that the Council would bother the praefectus over such a matter, but I can't be certain. Kaiaphas is genuinely terrified about the possibility of a revolt."

Kepha says, "Then we should enter Yerushalaim as planned and take our chances. Lord, I am ready to go with you to prison and to death, if necessary."

A small, sad smile touches Yeshua's face, as though he knows something Kepha does not, and it's breaking his heart.

Yeshua draws his himation up over his shoulders and through a long exhalation says, "We will enter Yerushalaim as planned. The End is coming. The Kingdom must be revealed."

He rises and his followers rise with him. One by one they file out of my house into the lavender hues of dawn.

When there are only three of us left, Yeshua looks at Maryam. "You were too quiet. I had hoped you would say more."

"Kepha makes me hesitate. I'm afraid of him, because he hates all women."[49]

"Kepha does not determine who has the right to speak and who hasn't, Maryam. Whoever the Spirit inspires is divinely ordained to speak, it doesn't matter whether he is male or female. You must not let him silence your words. I need to hear them."

Maryam glances at me, then whispers, "Yeshu, I know you have confidence in Kepha, but I tell you he is not trustworthy. He is faithless and fickle. I fear you will find out his true nature—"

"Enough," he gently chastises her, and kisses her lips again. They stare into each other's eyes. It is a quiet, beautiful moment. Rumor has it that she is his

consort, his lover,[50] *though neither of them has ever said this aloud. Still, I have only heard Yeshua mention loving two women: Maryam and her sister, Marta.*

She looks up at him. "Master, promise me you will not risk yourself this week. I couldn't bear it if. . . ." She can't finish the sentence.

"If I were to die?" He smiles tenderly when tears fill her eyes. "Have I not told you that a man or woman becomes what he sees, Maryam? If you see death, you become death. If you see light, you become light. If you—"

She continues the teaching for him. "If you see the mashiah, *you become the* mashiah. *If you see the Father, you become the Father. See yourself, and what you see, you shall become."*[51]

"Yes," Yeshua praises. He strokes her hair. "Our time here is over. Let's go before we further endanger Yosef."

"Yes, Master."

Maryam ducks through the doorway.

Yeshua remains a time longer, looking at me. A man could get lost in those eyes. I cannot tear my gaze away. "Yosef, if the worst happens, will you ask the Council not to refer my case to the praefectus? I would rather have my own people judge me."

The words are like daggers in my heart. "If it comes to that, I will. But let us work very hard to make sure that neither the Council nor the praefectus charge you with a crime."

Yeshua places a hand on my shoulder, and closes his eyes, as though savoring these last moments with me. He smiles, but it is a frail, frightened gesture.

"I came to crucify the world, Yosef. I'm not sure it can be stopped now."[52]

He walks by me, through the door, into the day.

It is the morning of Nisan the 10th. I will never forget . . .

Yosef woke with a start, his heart pounding, and tore open his shoulder wound. He bit back the cry that climbed his throat as warm blood drenched his clothing. The first glimmers of dawn had touched the sky, and begun to chase away the stars.

He reached out to shake his companion. "Mattias, wake up. It's almost dawn."

The young man rolled to his back and rubbed his eyes.

They'd spent most of the night running across the muddy mountain, evading soldiers. He'd lost count of how many times they'd stumbled and fallen. Mattias' white robe was a good reminder of how difficult their escape had been. It was filthy and torn to shreds. Bloody scratches and bruises shone in the gaps.

Yosef looked down at his own robe. It bore many of the same signs of their flight, rips and caked mud. Clotted blood glued his robe to his shoulder. Mattias had, as well, cut off the hem of the linen garment and used it to bandage Yosef's shoulder. But his fine indigo-colored cloak looked worse. Golden threads frizzed the edges of every tear like a perverse fringe. Impossible to mend, he would have to discard it.

Yosef made a vain attempt to comb his filthy black hair away from his round face.

Mattias sat up. "Do you think they're still looking for us?"

"Of course they are. And if we do not reach the house of your friends before full light, we are certainly dead men."

NINE

Morning arrived cool and bright, without a cloud in the sky, though streamers of smoke continued to stretch over the desert and fill the air with an acrid scent.

Pappas Lucius Meridias pinned his black cloak over his left shoulder and continued toward the charred husk that had been the monastery. The sound of weeping floated on the wind, and he could see dozens of people moving through the ruins like smoke-blackened scavengers. Had they been here all night? It was a wonder they hadn't been killed by collapsing walls or roofs.

The dome of the basilica remained, as did several of the great arching hallways, but the monks' cells were little more than smoldering debris.

Three men stood in the oratory doorway, waiting for him.

Meridias strode forward. When he reached the door, the men in black bowed. He stepped inside. The shrine to the Magdalen still stood on its pedestal. The white marble was coated with soot, but otherwise it looked untouched. Surely it was a miracle. Everywhere collapsed roof beams lay jumbled, many still burning. Red flickering embers glittered across the floor.

He said to the leader, "Loukas, did you find the body of Brother Barnabas?"

Loukas wet his lips nervously. At the age of twenty-nine, he was an accomplished killer. He had the face of a big cat, with a broad nose, slanted green eyes, and short red-gold hair. A failure would damage his reputation—as it had on one very notable occasion in the past. Not only that, the emperor might have him executed for it.

"No, Pappas, we didn't."

"You searched his cell and the library?"

"We searched every room and every body. He is not among the dead."

Meridias' gaze drifted over the other killers. "The emperor will not be pleased."

A charred dead body lay to his right, just inside the door. "One of yours, Loukas?"

"Yes. Mattithiah. He was—"

"Don't tell me his name. Don't tell me anything about him. He failed his emperor and his God. His name will be forgotten in heaven."

Loukas stiffened, but wisely kept silent. His accomplices, however, whispered among themselves. The Militia Templi fervently believed that their reward for doing the work of God was eternal life and happiness.

Meridias saw the open trapdoor in the floor of the oratory, frowned, and said, "What is that?"

"It's a crypt. We found it when we were searching the ruins. There are several coffins inside, plus many books and scrolls."

Meridias picked his way through the burning embers, and looked down into the crypt. Large stone steps had been hewn into the wall. Coffins were stacked four and five high on one side. The other side was filled with shelves of books, scrolls, and loose leaves of papyri.

"Abba Pachomius said there were one hundred monks here. Were any others missing?"

Loukas' cold green eyes glittered. "We counted ninety-seven bodies, therefore three men are missing."

"And Jairus Claudius Atinius?"

Loukas shook his head. "He was not among the dead."

"You're sure? His name now is Cyrus. Brother Cyrus."

"I served with him at the battle of Milvian Bridge on the Tiber. He was a large, impressive-looking man with fierce eyes. It's been thirteen years, but I would know him in an instant—no matter what name he has taken." He squared his shoulders. "As would any soldier who served with him."

Meridias noted the hatred in Loukas' voice, and said, "We hired you to give you a chance to redeem your previous failures. Though none of us could have imagined it would take you years to search monasteries across Asia Minor, Palestine, and Africa to find him."

Loukas looked very much as though he'd enjoy getting his hands around Meridias' throat. He said, "He did not wish to be found, Pappas. He made it particularly difficult. His appearance is much changed—though his eyes are the same. That's how I recognized him."

Meridias peered down into the crypt again. The scent of ancient parchment and lamp oil rose.

Barnabas, widely known as "the Heretic," had once studied in Caesarea—the administrative capital of Roman Palestine—with the famed scholar, Pappas Eusebios. The library at Caesarea, consisting of more than thirty thousand volumes, had been a breeding ground of heresy.[53] Meridias assumed that there were simply so many books they confused the mind.

Through a series of recent interrogations, Meridias had learned that, while serving as research assistant to Pappas Eusebios, Barnabas had made a discovery that threatened the very foundation of the True Church. He could still hear the grave voice of Pappas Silvester: *A monstrous thing. No one must be left alive who can spread the lie.*

Or worse, Meridias thought, prove it.

A breeze whimpered through the oratory and black veils of ash whirled across the floor. As Meridias covered his nose with his sleeve and waited for them to pass, he wondered why his superiors had not ordered him to eliminate Pappas Eusebios, as well.

Eusebios was definitely a heretic. At the recent ecumenical council in Nicea, Eusebios' doctrinal arguments with Eustathios, the pappas of Antioch, and Athanasios, the pappas of Alexandria, had been heated, and though the old man had finally agreed with the conciliar decisions regarding the fleshly resurrection of Iesous Christos, the virgin birth, and the list of approved books, he had complained mightily that such decisions would fragment the Church rather than unify it.[54]

These were desperate times for Christians. The Great Persecution had ended only fourteen years ago. Anyone with a shred of wisdom knew they had to do whatever was necessary to assure their own safety, which meant they had to codify the tradition, hone the teachings, no matter the cost. Establishing the Truth and eliminating heretics was a necessary beginning.

His gaze moved over the hundreds of books in the crypt. He did not know exactly what books the emperor's religious advisers feared most, so it was better to be thorough.

He turned to Loukas. "Burn this crypt. Make certain none of the books survive. Then find Barnabas and the others and carry out your orders. If they have any documents with them, any at all, you are *not* to read them, but destroy them immediately."

"Of course, your excellence. I will, however, be required to call in more resources to pursue them."

"Why?" Meridias snapped. The need for secrecy was paramount. More men on the trail meant more loose ends.

Loukas said, "I suspect Atinius fled down the river. It is the fastest escape, and he may even make it to the sea before we can stop him. But he has fooled many men before. He may be leading them overland. Three people cannot possibly cover all the possibilities. Therefore I request permission to hire two *sicarii*."[55]

"I presume you know these 'dagger men' well?"

"Yes, Pappas."

Meridias hesitated. "Do it, but do not tell me who they are. I don't want their souls on my conscience."

"I understand."

The young man standing beside Loukas cleared his throat. He was perhaps twenty, a student killer at best, of medium height, with brown hair, and a totally forgettable face that vaguely resembled a fox's. "Pappas, there is one other thing you should know."

"And that is?"

"The washerwoman who lived in the hut beside the river is also gone. We did not find her body. She may be with the monks."

Meridias waved a hand. "She is a woman. Probably illiterate. She is of no consequence."

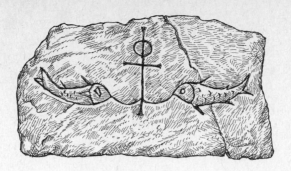

TEN

"Lord Iesous Christos, son of God, have mercy on me, a sinner." Cyrus tied a knot into his woolen prayer rope, and scanned the water. Dark reeds and rushes whiskered the bank where he crouched. A dozen men could be hiding in there, waiting their chances.

"Lord Iesous Christos, son of God, have mercy on me, a sinner."

The night air was cool and sweet with the scent of the Nile, underlain by the faint metallic tang of the blood that clung to his robe.

"Lord Iesous Christos, son of God, have mercy on me, a sinner."

He shifted the rope from his right hand, which had begun to ache from the tight holding of it, to his left. The river flowed lazily by, and was so still that the stars reflected from the surface with almost perfect clarity.

"You're out there," he whispered to their unseen pursuers. "I know you are."

The dedication of the killers who'd attacked the monastery spoke of a professionalism he understood. They had carefully planned and executed the assault, then cleaned up afterward. They had been soldiers, not hired murderers. And if they were being pursued by Roman soldiers, Emperor Constantine was behind it. Despite what he'd told Barnabas, Cyrus feared he *did* know why their friends had been killed. And it was more than the papyrus.

"Lord Iesous Christos, son of God, have mercy on me, a sinner."

As he knotted the rope, a strange series of images flashed before his eyes, the dead, stricken faces of men he'd loved—innocent men whose only crime had been heir devotion to seeking God—interspersed with brief, garishly intense images of the death of his wife.

As though it had seeped from a locked door buried deep inside him, he heard her cry, *"Cyrus!"*

It was so vivid that, for a moment, he actually thought he'd heard it. His muscles bunched in preparation for leaping to his feet, for doing battle.

"No," he soothed himself. "She's been gone for twelve years. She's gone."

He glanced to where Barnabas and Zarathan slept on the sand, then to Kalay, and tried not to let his eyes rest too long on her starlit face. They were all in mortal danger. He could not afford the luxury of dreams.

"Lord Iesous Christos, son of God, have mercy on me, a sinner."

He tied a knot, expelled a breath, and hung his head.

Even after they'd slit his wife's throat and hurled her to the floor, she'd twisted around to look at him, as though she knew if she could just see him, she would be safe, she wouldn't die.

A sensation, like insects crawling over his skin, tormented him. "My fault . . . all my fault."

Guilt was eating him alive. Terrible, wrenching guilt.

The man he'd killed at the monastery formed in his mind and looked at him with dark, glistening eyes. . . . *I was already dead. Why did you have to take the knife from Kalay and plunge it into my heart?*

Cyrus clutched his prayer rope as though it were a raft in a hurricane-swept ocean.

Because a good soldier never takes chances. You would have done the same.

"Lord Iesous Christos, son of God, have mercy on me, a sinner."

Try as he might, he could not suppress the memories of his wife's dead eyes. . . .

ELEVEN

The morning breeze still wore the thin chill of night.

Kalay rubbed her arms, and gazed across the wide, muddy Nile River to the distant eastern horizon. The sun had not yet risen, but a halo of sun fire gleamed on the hills, and cast long shadows across the sand. In the distance, clusters of palm trees swayed. Each marked an oasis. Here and there, she could see the dim walls of villages.

She finished washing her face and sat back on the sand. They'd pulled the boat ashore just a quarter hour ago. All of them were exhausted, but especially Brother Cyrus. Since the slaughter at the monastery last night, he hadn't closed his eyes for a heartbeat.

As she tied her wavy red hair back with the leather cord, she looked at the three brothers ten paces to her left. The young blond one with the perpetually stunned expression was asleep. He lay curled up on the bank next to Brother Barnabas, who had his nose pressed against that scrap of papyrus they'd retrieved from the pot last night. Only Brother Cyrus was doing anything truly practical. He'd found a dessicated goat carcass on the shore and pulled out several of the bones. He was rubbing each on a stone, grinding it to a sharp point to fashion it into a stiletto.

Now there's a man worth a woman's respect.

When he noticed her attention, Cyrus tucked the four stilettos into his belt, rose, and walked down the shore toward her.

She let her gaze roam across his broad shoulders to his trim waist and finally down the length of his long legs. If she'd had any longing for a handsome man, he would have stirred the dead embers of her passions.

He knelt in front of her, and looked straight into her eyes. A deed few men had the courage to do. "Kalay, I have a question for you."

"First, ask me if I'm well. If I'm hungry. Or maybe what I think of the sunlight on the river."

Cyrus frowned in confusion, then a smile slowly came to his lips. Perhaps he realized that monks never treated women as human beings, but merely as objects to be dealt with as little as possible. That had been the most difficult part of working at the monastery. The loneliness. Except for the mute Sophia, she'd had no real human contact. Just orders from monks who refused to look her in the eyes. Men were such frail creatures, so susceptible to the attentions of beautiful women—though, if Cyrus was, he was doing a valiant job of not showing it.

"I'm sorry," Cyrus said. "Are you well, Kalay?"

"Yes, for the most part, thank you. I appreciate you letting me sleep some in the boat last night. I think everyone got to rest a bit, except you."

His dark brows drew together and he looked out at the river.

She asked, "Are you calculating how far they are behind us?"

"Actually, I'm worried they may not be on the river."

She stared at him a moment. "Ah. I understand. If they travel overland, they can avoid the water's twists and turns. So you're afraid there will be an ambush waiting for us somewhere ahead." She arched an eyebrow. "Alexandria? Or Leontopolis?"

"I'm betting they'll race us to Alexandria. It's the smartest bet. The city is huge, with lots of places to hide. They'll assume that Barnabas has connections there, men who will aid him."

"And that's the best place to hire passage on a ship," she added.

"All the more reason why we shouldn't go there." His black curly hair blew around his handsome face. "But that means purchasing passage, either by camel or wagon, to continue our journey." He let the implication sink in.

She laughed softly. "Cyrus, I didn't have time to gather my meager shekels, if that's what you're asking. I can't pay for my own passage, let alone yours."

"Would you consider selling your boat?"

She tilted her head. "Well, there's a thought. It's not going to be of much use to me if I'm on camelback. Besides, I stole it, so it never cost me a coin. Of course I'll sell it"—she tucked a lock of windblown hair behind her ear—"if you'll tell me where we're going."

Cyrus turned to look over his shoulder at Brother Barnabas. When he turned back, he said, "My brother tells me that we must head north, but that's all I know."

" 'North' is not much of a destination."

"I know. I'm sorry."

"Do you trust him that much? That you'll just go where he says to?"

"I trust him with my life."

Kalay shifted to peer at Barnabas. The gray-haired old man had not moved since it had grown light enough to read. "He's had his nose pressed on that scrap of papyrus all morning. What's it say?"

Cyrus gave her a faint smile. "He won't let me read it, so I don't know."

"What language is it? I couldn't tell."

"It's Latin, I think."

"Is it truly dangerous?"

An agonized expression tightened his face. He frowned at the river again, his gaze searching the water and shorelines, lingering on the shadows cast by the trees. "Ninety-seven of my brothers died last night and Barnabas is certain they were killed over that 'scrap,' as you call it. I'd say it's very dangerous."

She grunted and watched a camel loping across a hilltop in the distance, while she considered her curious position. She couldn't return to Phoou. They might be looking for here there. She had no relatives. But what future did she have with three monks of questionable sanity?

"Cyrus, what did you do in the army?"

He gave her an evaluative sidelong glance. "What makes you think I was in the army?"

"No man kills as cleanly as you did without being trained to do it. Were you some general's personal cutthroat?"

"It would be more accurate to say I was some general's personal guard."

"But you've seen fighting. I can tell it in the way you carry yourself."

She'd always found it interesting the way people revealed their pasts in the motions of their bodies. A tilt of the head, a wave of the hand, told her immediately whether a woman was noble born, or a courtesan. Men were the same. A clumsy tread and he was a merchant. A lion's stealthy gait, he was a soldier.

Through a long exhalation, Cyrus said, "Yes. Too much fighting. Most of it senseless. Emperors are passionate about vainglorying."

Emperors? He was the personal guard to an emperor?

They were quiet for a time.

Finally, he asked, "And what about you? How does a simple washerwoman develop the instinct and skill to slit a man's throat to the bone like that?"

"I worked in a"—she smiled—"a butcher shop. And one pig's throat is pretty much like another's."

He stared at her. "And how did a butcher's assistant, not to mention a pagan goddess worshipper from Palestine, come to be a washerwoman for a Christian monastery in Egypt?"

"Let's just say I believed no one would come looking for me there. Nor did I have to worry about the good brothers coming to visit after dark." She paused. "And . . . I was a Christian once, a long time ago."

"Really?" He clearly wanted to ask her why she'd left the faith, but instead asked, "Were your parents Christians?"

She drew up her knees and propped her elbows on them. The morning air was luminous with sunlit dust. She could smell the musk of the silt-laden Nile in the air. Cyrus had an interesting face, she decided. His eyes most of all. Heavily lidded, they were the color of dark emeralds, and had the same mysterious sparkle. No matter how hard she looked, she couldn't quite see him in there. He'd had practice at putting up shields, too.

"Yes, my family was Christian," she answered. "I was six when the Great Persecution came roaring down upon us. After eight years of running and hiding, my family was cornered by Roman soldiers on the outskirts of the city of Emmaus. I watched both of my parents tortured to death. My little brother was carried off as a slave." She hesitated, before adding, "The only thing I ever wanted was family, Cyrus. The Church took even my hope of a family away from me."

Cyrus betrayed no emotion. "When did you become a pagan?"

"As soon as I could."

Surely he knew why. Even if he did not know the history of the persecution in Palestine, he would have seen it in Rome. It had been a horrific
time. Christian churches and houses where Christian scriptures were found
were ordered to be destroyed and the scriptures burned. Christian worship
was forbidden. Christian clergy were arrested. Those who persisted in proclaiming themselves Christians lost all rights as members of the Roman
Empire, even the right to bring actions in court—which meant they were
totally vulnerable to *anyone* who wanted to do *anything* to them. Many,
many people were simply murdered for their faith.[56]

The corners of her mouth turned up. "It's curious, don't you think?
Twenty-two years ago, it was the Romans who were burning Christian books.
Now it's Christians burning Christian books. Where does it end, Cyrus?
What can be so dangerous about a few black squiggles on parchment?"

"Sometimes," Cyrus said, "black squiggles are the most fearsome
weapons in the world."

She found it interesting that he hadn't asked for more details about her
life before she came to the monastery. Perhaps he didn't want to know.
Men rarely did. Such ugliness seemed to wound the good ones deep down.

"I don't know why you monks don't just take to worshipping Satan,"
she said.

"What?"

"He constantly proves he's more powerful than God. If I were going to
be a Christian, that's who I'd be begging for help."

Cyrus smiled, apparently thinking she was joking, and pointed out,
"You didn't answer my question. How did you get to Egypt?"

"Well, it's a long story, Cyrus." She made an airy gesture with her
hand. "It began with a wealthy spice merchant who had an unhealthy pas-
sion for ropes. One night his vital signs mysteriously stopped in my presence. He had friends who either took it personally, or wanted to try the
same rope tricks. After that, one thing led to another."

For a few moments she feared he might adopt the "crucifixion look,"
that morally tormented expression that so many of his brothers plastered
on when faced with the unsavory details of life, but he caught himself. His
expression relaxed and he calmly held her gaze. "And now?"

"I think you need my help."

"We do." He nodded, rose to his feet, and asked, "Are you hungry?

Why don't you help me catch some fish? We'll roast them quickly, and be on our way."

She got up and walked at his side down the shore. "You're not going to preach at me, are you?"

"No." He shook his head. "I am no longer worthy to speak my Lord's words . . . if I ever was."

TWELVE

A dusty radiance filled the morning air, turning the sky into a shimmering blanket of pure amber.

Zarathan knelt beside the small fire, watching the fish skins turn brown and peel. Watching fish was much easier than watching Kalay cook. The woman had skewered the fish on sticks of driftwood, then stuck them in the sand and leaned them over the small blaze. At his age, the strangest things caused overpowering lust. As she moved about adding twigs to the fire, wisps of her long red hair danced around her tanned face. He occasionally caught glimpses of her breasts as she leaned down to turn the fish so they wouldn't burn. It was agonizing.

Cyrus and Barnabas sat ten paces away, talking quietly. He only caught pieces of what they were saying, but the expression on Cyrus' face was dire.

"What are they talking about?" Kalay asked, jerking her head in Cyrus and Barnabas' direction.

To say her eyes were blue would have been like describing the most magnificent amber as yellow—words could not convey the sparkling un-earthly depth and richness.

"Something about the city of Leontopolis."

"So that's our final destination?"

"I don't know, but Barnabas says he knows a man, an old hermit, who lives in a cave a few days' hard ride north of the city, on the coast."

"Are we going to the hermit's cave?"

Annoyed, Zarathan replied, "Does it look like I've been included in the planning? I'm guessing, just like you are."

Kalay propped her hands on her hips and her full lips quirked. "Zarathan, did it ever occur to you the cat comment might have been inspired by that yowling tone of voice you so often affect?"

His cheeks reddened. "You are so infuriating! You prove beyond question that Saint Petros was right. Women are not worthy of life."

"Did he say that?"

"Yes. In the now forbidden Gospel of Thomas. It's one of my favorite books."

"I see why."

She bent down to turn the fish again, and he squeezed his eyes closed until he heard her straighten up. When he opened one eye to peek at her, she glared at him.

His stomach growled, loudly, and knotted up.

Kalay said, "You're not eating this morning, are you?"

"Of course, I'm eating. Why?"

"Well, it's none of my concern, of course, but yesterday afternoon I heard some of the monks say that you and Cyrus had been ordered to fast for three days, because of a broken pot, or some such."

Zarathan could feel the blood drain from his face. He felt faint. "Surely, Brother Barnabas isn't going to—"

"You can ask him. Here he comes." She extended a hand.

He swiveled around and saw his brothers walking toward the fire. Cyrus' white robe was filthy and blood-spattered from rolling around the oratory floor. Then their time on the river had added to the patina. It contrasted sharply with the pure white of Barnabas' robe.

Zarathan tried to interpret his brothers' expressions: Both men had a tightness about their eyes, and mouths.

Kalay pulled the four sticks with the roasted fish from the sand and began handing them out. Zarathan eagerly took his and bit into it before anyone could tell him otherwise. Then he winced in horror when Barnabas and Cyrus got on their knees and bowed their heads.

Barnabas softly murmured the Creed established by Hippolytus in the year 215: "Do you believe in God the Father all-governing? Do you believe in Iesous Christos, the Son of God, who was begotten by the Holy Spirit from the Virgin Miriam? Who was crucified under Pontios Pilatos, and died, and was buried, and rose on the third day living from the dead, and ascended into the heavens, and sat down on the right hand of the Father, and will come to judge the living and the dead? Do you believe in the Holy Spirit, in the holy church, and in the resurrection of the body?"

Cyrus reverently whispered, "I do."

Around a mouthful of fish, Zarathan slurred, "I do."

Kalay said, "What a lot of twaddle that was," and bit into her fish.

While she chewed, the brothers stared at her.

Cyrus rose, walked around the fire, and handed his fish to Zarathan. "You need this more than I do, brother. Please, take it."

Zarathan took the stick and propped it across his lap. "Thank you, brother."

Zarathan wondered if Cyrus was still keeping his fast, or if giving away the fish was his "one single act of mercy" for the day. Both, perhaps. In either case, Zarathan's squealing belly was grateful.

Barnabas ate his fish distractedly, his faraway gaze fixed on the flickering fire.

"You don't really believe all that drivel, do you?" Kalay asked between bites.

"Of course, we believe it," Zarathan snapped. "What a silly question. Do you think we'd say the words if we didn't—"

Almost inaudibly, Barnabas said, "Mostly, yes, except for the part about the resurrection and, of course, he was a *mamzer*."

Kalay's eyes flew wide and Cyrus froze as though he'd just been slapped.

The word seemed to tremble in the desert-scented air, inviting swift and terrible divine retribution.

Zarathan swallowed and asked, "What's a *mamzer*?"

Kalay answered, "It's Hebrew for bas—"

Cyrus interrupted, "The Aramaic term, which is similar, refers to an illegitimate child."

Zarathan's gaze went from one person to the next, trying to fathom what they were talking about. No one seemed to want to tell him. "Who's an illegitimate child?"

Barnabas, who seemed totally oblivious to the shocked faces, took another bite of his fish, and replied, "Our Lord, Iesous."

Zarathan blurted, "That's blasphemy!"

Cyrus and Kalay sat in stunned silence, their eyes riveted on the old man.

Barnabas chewed his fish and swallowed. Distractedly, he said, "Didn't you ever notice that in the earliest Christian documents, he's never referred to as the 'son of a virgin'?"

"He isn't?" Zarathan tried to recall.

"No." Barnabas shook his head. "Outside of the gospels, we have records that tell us Iesous' father was a man named Pantera. Our Lord is often referred to as *Yeshua ben Pantera,* that is, 'Iesous, son of Pantera,' though there are variations on the man's name. Sometimes it's 'Panthera,' or 'Pantiri,' 'Pandora,' or even 'Pandera.' "[57]

In an awestruck voice, Cyrus said, "Pantera."

And Zarathan remembered the passage Cyrus had read to him from Papias' book. It had mentioned the "son of Pantera," and something about 'a headless demon.' His gaze was involuntarily drawn to the gazelle leather bag that Barnabas kept beside him at all times. He had the uncomfortable feeling that voices whispered inside that bag, just beyond his range of hearing.

Cyrus asked, "Where is this information about Pantera recorded, brother?"

"Oh, in many documents, both Roman and Hebrew. The scandal was well known at the time our Lord walked Palestine. One of the earliest rabbinic references dates to around the year seventy, or forty years after our Lord's death, which is also when the earliest gospel, the Gospel of Markos, was being written—and you will notice that Markos does not mention the name of Iesous' father at all."

Zarathan narrowed an eye. Surely it had just been a simple omission on Markos' part.

Cyrus leaned closer, his gaze fixed on Barnabas. "What does the rabbinic document say?"

"It's a story about a rabbi, Eliezer, who was arrested and charged as being a Christian because he had listened to an heretical teaching 'in the name of Yeshua ben Pantera,' which violated the rabbinic ordinance prohibiting any intercourse with heretics. We have the record because his case was submitted to the Roman governor."

"What happened to Eliezer? And what was the teaching of our Lord that he had listened to?"

Barnabas peeled off some of the fish skin and ate it. Zarathan couldn't take his gaze from the old monk's wrinkled face. He appeared totally unconcerned, as though he'd known and thought about these facts for most of his life, and therefore found nothing heretical about them. They were just facts.

He's lost his mind! It's the stress . . . or the lack of food! Zarathan had to make a conscious effort to close his gaping mouth.

Barnabas continued. "Eliezer was pardoned and released, but the issue for which he was arrested apparently regarded a question about whether one who cuts tattoos on his body during the Sabbath is guilty of violating the law prohibiting work on the holy day. Rabbi Eliezer declared him guilty."

Zarathan wrinkled his nose. "Our Lord cut tattoos on his body on the holy day?"

"Well, we don't know for certain, but the story of Rabbi Eliezer goes on to say that our Lord 'brought magic marks from Egypt in the scratches on his body,' so he apparently carried such marks on his flesh." He lifted a finger to emphasize his point. "And let us not forget that the book of Galatians says Saint Paul bore 'the marks of Iesous,' probably the same spells our Lord carried."

Angrily, Zarathan said, "That's the only reference? A Jewish source about cutting marks on the body? This is absurd!"

"No, no, there are others. One dates to around the year 100. It's about Rabbi Elazar ben Dama, who was bitten by a snake. A man named Yakob, from Galilaian, came to cure him in the name of *Yeshua ben Pantera*. Then, a century later, a similar incident occurred in Galilaian where the son of a well-known rabbi was healed by a magician who cured him in the name of *Yeshua ben Pandera*. Those are the only three references I know from rabbinic literature, but there are other sources—"

Cyrus said, "I would appreciate it if we could return to the subject of our Lord's father. Who was he?"

"His father was God!" Zarathan's heart had risen into his throat where it was beating hard enough to half-choke him. He fought to swallow the lump.

Barnabas blinked, took another bite of his fish, and seemed to be shifting his thoughts back to the original topic. As the dawn light changed, his gray hair picked up a tinge of pink. "My best guess is that he was a Sidonian archer named Tiberius Julius Abdes Pantera."

"He was a *Roman* archer?" Cyrus asked, as though that small detail had bridged the centuries, allowing him to connect with the long-dead Tiberius Pantera, and Zarathan remembered the stories told around the monastery that Cyrus, too, had been a Roman archer.[58]

Zarathan tugged at his collar, trying to get more air.

"Yes," Barnabas replied. "We know from Roman records that he was serving in Palestine at the time of our Lord's birth. He was transferred out of Palestine in the year six, when our Lord would have been twelve."

"Twelve?" Cyrus whispered. "You mean . . . the Missing Years? Did our Lord travel with his father to his new post?"

Barnabas tilted his head and his gray beard flashed in the gleam. "To my knowledge, there are no records to either support or reject that notion. But, I suppose it's possible." In a soft, sympathetic voice, he continued. "It would have been a blessing for Yeshua, given the torment he must have suffered as a child because he was a *mamzer*."

This isn't happening. Cold sweat had broken out on Zarathan's skin. He shifted uncomfortably and noticed that Kalay was watching him with an amused look on her face.

She moved to curl her legs around her hips and propped a hand on the sand. Her thin tan dress conformed to the curves of her body like a second skin. The sensual position barely seeped through Zarathan's general horror.

Kalay asked, "Why? What happened to bastard children?"

Zarathan flinched at the term.

But Barnabas seemed unaffected. "Terrible things. Being called a *mamzer* was the worst insult. Such children were considered the 'excrement of the community.' Both the mother and the child would have been social outcasts. In fact, the Wisdom of Solomon, in chapter three, verses sixteen through nineteen, and chapter four, verses three through six, says that such children should be held 'of no account,' and even in their old age should be without honor. They were denied entry to the Kingdom of

God after their deaths. Deuteronomy, in chapter twenty-three, verse three makes it clear that 'No *mamzer* will enter the assembly of God even to the tenth generation.'"

"I don't care about after death." Red wisps of hair blew around Kalay's face. "What about during his life? Would he have been punished?"

Zarathan wiped his sweating palms on his robe and licked his lips. His throat had gone dust dry.

"Iesous would have been punished in every way possible. *Mamzerim* couldn't hold public office, and if they took part in court cases, the decision was invalidated. They could not legally marry any other legitimate Israelites. If they did have children, there was a good chance those children would be killed. The Wisdom of Solomon says that 'The offspring of such an unlawful union will perish . . . by the violence of the winds they will be uprooted.'"

"Is that why our Lord never married?" Cyrus asked. "He couldn't?"

"Possibly, though it is also possible he chose to be celibate, which is what I believe. There were many religious groups who taught that the Kingdom was coming very soon, and so there was no point to marriage. That is, for example, what the Essenes taught in Palestine, and the Theraputae in Egypt. If our Lord was a member of either of those ascetic groups, his inability to marry and have children would have been irrelevant."

"Do you think he was a member of one of those groups?" Cyrus asked.

My Lord a bastard child? I don't believe it. This is heresy!

The sublime, mystical stories of the virgin birth were some of Zarathan's favorites. The most powerful moments in his nighttime prayer vigils came when he was contemplating the virgin birth.

Barnabas said, "I think it likely that our Lord studied healing and magic with the Theraputae in Egypt and then returned to pursue his education with the Essenes in Palestine. And the Platonist philosopher Celsus wrote in his book *True Doctrine* that Iesous went to Egypt to study magic. Both groups were reputed to have great medical knowledge, the best of their day."

Nonchalantly, Kalay the pagan said, "That's probably how he did his 'miracles.' He could heal because he was a master of the medical arts."

Zarathan gaped. "His miracles came through the power of *God*! How do you explain that he could raise the dead?"

Kalay opened her mouth to say something unpleasant, but Brother Barnabas softly interrupted, "I've always believed it was the Iesous ointment."

Kalay frowned at him. "He invented an ointment that raised the dead?"

Zarathan cried, "That's ridiculous!"

Barnabas propped the stick on which his fish was skewered across his lap and pulled off a flaky piece of meat. As he chewed, he said, "The *Marham-i-Isa,* the ointment of Iesous, is referred to in many ancient medical treatises. Apparently it could heal wounds with stunning rapidity, and even raise the dead, or at least those who appeared to be dead."[59]

While Zarathan was staring at Barnabas in shock, Cyrus said, "Brother, who is 'the headless demon whom the winds obey'?"

Zarathan's gaze jerked back to Cyrus. In the holy name of God, why didn't Cyrus reach over and slap some sense into the old man?

Barnabas replied, "Anyone who has read Psalms knows whom the winds and seas obey. God. But the Egyptian Magical Papyri specifically state that the headless demon is 'the Lord of the world, this is he whom the winds fear.'[60] He's a powerful figure in ancient magic. Why do you ask?"

As though terrified someone might be listening, Cyrus cast a glance over his shoulder, then scanned the river and desert, before saying, "When Brother Zarathan and I were in the library crypt we found Papias' book *The Exposition of the Lord's Logia.* There was a reference—"

"Ah, yes, in division four." Barnabas' thick gray brows lowered. He gave Cyrus a serious appraisal. "Could you read it, brother?"

Embarrassed, Cyrus said, "Well, no, not all of it. The passage was clearly written in cipher, but I understood the part about Pantera, and the headless demon, and the reference to the Pearl."

Barnabas nodded approvingly. "That is a great deal more than most monks would have gleaned from that passage—even after years of study. Have you had experience with ciphers?"

Cyrus hesitated a long time before saying, "When I was in the army, I was required to decipher coded messages for the generals. I'm not very good at it, but that particular passage was clearly a substitution cipher using Hebrew, Aramaic, and Greek letters."

"Only a man who knew all three languages would realize that, Cyrus. I didn't know you read Hebrew?"

"I read it poorly, brother. Hebrew is close enough to Aramaic that I can get a general idea of what is being written, but I'm not skilled at translating Hebrew."

Kalay drew up her knees and propped her forearms on them, revealing her bare legs. "I can translate it. My grandmother was Jewish. She started reading me the Hebrew Scriptures when I was four. I don't read Hebrew, but I understand it, which means I can also get along understanding Aramaic—though I wouldn't have Cyrus' talent."

Zarathan madly bit into his second fish. He was feeling a little dizzy. Chewing and swallowing seemed to help his constricted breathing.

Barnabas still had his gaze fixed on Cyrus, and the expression on his face suggested he was seeing Cyrus in a different light. "Cyrus, perhaps Zarathan and Kalay could row us to the next village while you sit beside me in the boat. There are some things I would like to show you. You may understand them better than me."

"Of course, brother."

Zarathan tossed the fish bones into the fire and loudly challenged, "You said there were many records that document that our Lord was a *mamzer*. The ones you've named are Jewish. They're all lies meant to hurt our Lord. You can't believe—"

Barnabas gently interrupted, "There are other records, Zarathan. Some of them you know very well."

Zarathan blinked, trying to clear his reeling head. "I do?"

"Do you recall these words: 'He who knows the father and the mother will be called the son of a whore'?"

"Of course. Our Lord says that in verse one-oh-five of the Gospel of Thomas, but he meant—"

"I think he meant what he said, brother. We even have clues in the approved gospels, though not the versions written after the year 200. By that time, the gospels had been edited by so many writers with points to prove that you can't believe them. They—"

"You're possessed by demons! No wonder the Church sent people to burn our monastery! Maybe I should have helped them!"

Cyrus, who had closed his eyes at the term "whore," ignored Zarathan, asking, "Barnabas, where in the approved gospels does it speak of these things?"

"Oh, Cyrus," the old man said gently, "think about Markos' story. In the temple in Nazaret the people call our Lord the 'son of Miriam.' The Jewish people didn't trace descent through the female until after the destruction of the Temple in the year 70. At the time our Lord was in Nazaret, descent was traced through the male. To refer to a man as being the son of his mother was gravely offensive. It meant that his paternity was uncertain. Gospels written twenty or thirty years after Markos' gospel, like the gospels of Maththaios, Loukas, and Ioannes, go to great efforts to eliminate this reference. So, for example, Maththaios, chapter twelve, verse fifty-five, replaces Miriam with Ioses, as does Ioannes in chapter six, verse forty-two. Later editors changed Markos' words to read things like 'the son of the carpenter.' The Gospel of Markos was often 'corrected' by later writers to echo the glosses of Maththaios and Ioannes. Such things are a disgrace. The original documents should be allowed to speak for themselves." He shook his head. "Then there is the fact that the Gospel of Ioannes never mentions the name of Yeshua's mother. Nor do the epistles of Paul. She was an outcast whose name was to be forgotten."

Zarathan simply could not speak.

Barnabas looked out at the dawn. As the sun rose in a huge orange orb, a golden flood of light swept across the desert. The horizon became a vast, shimmering plain, as though earth was melting into sky.

Barnabas added, "And there are many other documents from the second century that relate the story, like the works of Celsus, who was writing sometime between the years of 150 and 178. He also knew and reported the story of Yeshua ben Pantera."

Zarathan glanced at Cyrus. He looked as though he'd been hit in the head with a rock. Stunned, his mouth was hanging open.

Cyrus said, "But, brother, where does the story about Iesous' father, Ioses, come from?"

"By the year 85, the Temple had been destroyed, Judaism and Christianity had split, and Iesous' followers were desperate to make sure he fulfilled every Hebrew prophecy about the coming messiah. For example, think of Micah, chapter five, verse two, and Isaiah, chapter seven, verse fourteen. As well, the crucifixion story is strikingly similar to Psalms, twenty-two. With regard to his father, the passages were Zechariah, chapter six, verses eleven through thirteen."

Cyrus seemed to be running verses through his head. "You mean the Hebrew verse that says, 'Take the silver and gold and make crowns and set them upon the head of Yehoshua, the son of Yosadaq.'"

Zarathan shouted, "That's about the prophet Ioshua, not our Lord, Iesous Christos!"

Cyrus clasped his hands around one knee and softly replied, "*Yehoshua is* our Lord's name, Zarathan. Iesous is the Greek form of the Hebrew name, Yeshua, and Yeshua in formal Hebrew is Yehoshua. So, Yosadaq?"

Barnabas nodded. "The shortened form in Greek is Iose or Ioses, and in Hebrew—"

Kalay finished for him, "Yosef."[61]

Cyrus placed hands on either side of his head and squeezed. "Forgive me, but this is too much to hear all at once."

"That's because it's blasphemy!" Zarathan insisted. "Ioses was our Lord's adopted father. That's a fact! You're all going to be struck by lightning and then cast into flames that burn forever!"

Kalay said drily, "Well, that will certainly make me think twice."

Barnabas ignored them, reached out, and placed a hand on Cyrus' curly black hair. "You are not the first to be troubled by these things, Cyrus. My own teacher, Pappas Eusebios, at the library in Caesarea, had difficulty with these ideas. That's why he believed in religious tolerance and pluralism, and opposed all persecution of pagans or heretics in the Roman Empire. He maintained that through discussion ultimately the purity of the gospel truth would be revealed."

Kalay smoothed windblown hair away from her blue eyes. "I heard he's had some problems with his library assistants," she said offhandedly, and gazed out at the palm trees swaying over the distant oasis.

Barnabas took a big bite out of his fish and chewed. Around the lump, he asked, "What problems?"

"They keep disappearing."

Barnabas swallowed his mouthful of fish. "What do you mean, 'disappearing'?"

"You monks never get into the city. It was big news a year ago. Then just six months ago another of his assistants up and disappeared. They found his body shortly thereafter. He had his heart in his hand and his balls and cock in his mouth."

Zarathan gasped. "He'd been tortured?"

Barnabas' elderly face slackened as though with terrible knowledge. His fish fell from his numb fingers and rolled across the sand.

Cyrus leaped to his side. "Brother? Are you well?"

Barnabas was staring wide-eyed at nothing. In a deathly quiet voice, he said, "Dear God. They're hunting us down."

"Us?" Zarathan cried. Terror fired his veins. He stumbled to his feet, careened off into the reeds, and while bitter tears leaked from his eyes, his stomach pumped.

THIRTEEN

Mahray

Yosef dozed on the back of the horse as the animal plodded down the trail that led toward the city of Gophna. Last night they'd made it to an Essene community where his wound had been properly cleaned and bandaged; his pain had diminished somewhat, though he could still smell the odors of pus and torn flesh.

Three youths rode horses in front of him, all Dawn Bathers who had eschewed their traditional white robes for something less distinctive: brown sackcloth. Yosef himself had traded for a modest red Roman toga. If necessary, since he spoke both Greek and Latin, he could pass as a Roman citizen traveling with his three slaves.

Truly exhausted, he was trying to sleep, but the horse kept breaking into a trot, which ripped open his wound and the pain woke him long enough to see the passing vineyards and farmers who waved at them. Cedar, acacia, and box trees fringed the fields. Often blackberry brambles filled the spaces between the trees, creating a very effective, thorny fence. The bleating of goats and braying of camels carried on the fragrant wind.

Yosef let his head fall forward, and closed his eyes. Behind his lids images flitted, faces of people now dead interspersed with strange flashes of *ephod* cloth. Made from a mixture of fine linen and gold leaf, with blue, purple, and scarlet threads, *ephod* cloth was the apparel of the high priest.

As he drifted deeper into sleep, he wondered why the flashes of *ephod* cloth kept appearing? Was his soul trying to reveal some secret?

A voice, deep and melodic, twined through the flashes, growing louder, more distinct. . . .

"I knew you'd come, Yosef."

I walk up behind him and prop my hands on my hips. Twilight has settled over the Kidron valley in a smoky veil. All around me, limestone cliffs, filled with tombs, thrust up, and the massive stone wall constructed by Herod to encircle the City of David has turned the color of charcoal. Oil lamps from nearby homes cast a fluttering halo over the hills, and their sweet fragrance rides the breeze.

Yeshua kneels on the ground five paces away, carving a stone. He has not looked at me, but is patiently, expertly chipping the limestone away with a hammer and chisel, forming a symbol that is not yet clear. He wears a white robe and sandals. His black hair and beard shine, as though freshly washed.

"Maryam told me you would be here, Rab. She's worried about you."

He bows his head for a moment and stares at the base of the limestone outcrop where a large stone blocks the entry to the underground tomb. "I needed some time alone. Today was . . . difficult."

I expel a breath. "Your actions have enraged the Council. You should have lodged a formal complaint and asked for the proper actions to be taken."

"The Council doesn't care that the Temple has become a den of thieves where the vendors rob the poor, or they would put a stop to it."

"Of course the Council cares. The vendors carried their merchandise and sacrificial animals beneath one of the Temple porches. They entered the Temple in a state of impurity. Entry is forbidden even with dusty feet. The Council understands that what you did was natural and lawful, but it was not done properly. You started a riot." I take a deep breath, and say through a long exhalation, "Rome noticed. After you left, they had to send in soldiers to quell the uproar. Three Roman soldiers were killed and several Zealots were arrested."

Yeshua hesitates an instant. Then he heaves a breath and expertly uses his tools to remove a stubborn bit of stone. Finally, he wipes away the dust and examines his work.

"Rab, try to understand the situation from the Council's perspective. Rumors are flying. The crowds are ready for anyone who will stir things up against the Romans and their supporters. People are crying 'Hosanna to the son of David' and 'Blessed is the Kingdom of our father David that is coming.' The crowds believe you are of David's lineage and—"

"I have never claimed that, Yosef."

"I know, Master, but you did say: 'Seek and you shall find; knock and it shall be opened to you.' These people are seeking the mashiah with all their hearts. They are knocking as loudly as—"

Almost angrily, he cries, "Away with the person who is seeking where he never finds, for he seeks where nothing can be found! Away with him who is always knocking, because it will never be opened to him, for he knocks where there is no one to open."

"Rab, they are just asking—"

"And especially away with those who are always asking, because they will never be heard, for they ask of one who does not hear!"

His words silence me.

The scene in the Temple was disgraceful. He knows this. As Pesach nears, people devoted to fulfilling God's commandments arrive from all over the world. The vendors help them to fulfill their ritual obligations. Men over twenty must donate a half-shekel of silver, as Moses commanded in the Book of Exodus. This offering, due once a year by Pesach, necessitates that special "money-changing" tables be set up three weeks before to handle the huge crowds that come to Yerushalaim for the festival. It is also required that people make a sacrifice to God. The wealthy will sacrifice over two hundred thousand lambs on the day of Pesach alone. The poor will substitute doves. This means that animals acceptable for sacrifice must be sold. As well, because the Council charges fees of the vendors, such sales are stunningly profitable for the Temple. No one wants to see the Temple desecrated, but sometimes it happens purely by accident. There are proper steps to punish the guilty. He chose not to follow them.

I spread my hands in a gesture of futility. "Master, I don't know what to say to you."

His gaze softens. He turns away and uses his tools to fashion what is becoming clear as the symbol of the tekton,[62] the stoneworker. For many generations his family has made its way as stoneworkers. Is that what this is? The tomb of a lost friend, another tekton?

Yeshua uses his finger to trace a small crack, then pets the stone as though it is alive and can feel his touch. "This stone would never have been set by a builder. But it's beautiful, isn't it? Flawed, but beautiful. All things have a purpose."

He seems to be absorbed by the stone. His gaze focuses on it to the exclusion of everything else. I say, "I think, Master, that perhaps your mind is on other things."

"My mind," he says stiffly, "was on three things today, and three only: Zechariah, Isaiah, and Jeremiah."

I shift uneasily.

Zechariah had prophesied a time when "there will no longer be traders in the house of Yahweh," and Jeremiah had gone into the Yahweh's Temple and declared, "Has this house, called by my name, become a den of robbers in your sight?" Finally, Isaiah had foreseen a time when the Temple would be a "house of prayer for all nations."

I understand that his actions were a prophetic protest meant to herald the overthrow of the corrupt Temple system by the arrival of the Kingdom of God. But understanding this does not help me.

I say simply, "Master, the crowds cheered you today. People died. You gave the Romans the reason they need to arrest you."

His hammer hesitates over the stone before it comes down hard. "We will spend the night in Bet Ani, Yosef. Tell the Seventy-one that I am not with the crowds stirring them up. Tomorrow I will go to the Temple and speak with the priests, or anyone else who wishes to speak with me, including the praefectus himself."

In panic, I say, "Please, please, do not go to the Temple! I beg you. People will flock to hear you, as they did today. Your enemies will be frightened of another riot and the intervention of Roman forces that will be necessary to quell it. You must stay out of the city until after the holy days are over."

This year, since Pesach falls on Friday, Nisan the 15th, and the usual Sabbath day is Saturday, two Sabbaths will occur back-to-back.[63]

He turns to me. "I will be in the Temple tomorrow morning. Whoever wishes to question me should come and do so. If the crowds are truly as great as you imagine, the Romans will be afraid to arrest me, because that surely will cause a riot."

"Oh, Rab," I say in exasperation, "they will just wait until a more oppor- tune time, at night, when you are alone and vulnerable."

"And after my death? What are their plans?"

I lower my arms and stare at him. He speaks of his death as if it has al- ready occurred. My heart is breaking, and he looks perfectly calm.

I answer, "The Council is terrified that if they kill you, your disciples will steal your body and proclaim that you were resurrected in accord with prophecy. They've already planned for that possibility. They—"

"Yosef," he interrupts in a voice that makes my soul quake, "flesh and blood shall not inherit the Kingdom of God. I have told you this. Those who say they will die first and then rise in the flesh are in error. Have I not pounded it into you over and over that it is necessary to find the resurrection while you live?"[64]

"You have told me, Master, but I do not understand." I flap my arms help- lessly. "I know you teach that we must be reborn into the divine light while yet we live, but I have never grasped what that means."

His bright, hopeful eyes go dark, as though I've disappointed him. "If you do not understand," he whispers, "does anyone? Or are all my words just the fearful wind?"

He exhales a long, difficult breath and returns to the image he's carving, giving it a few final taps, then he fills his lungs, blows the symbol clean, and brushes at it with his hand. The symbol of the tekton has two elements: a builder's square for truing a foundation, and a circle, showing the point at which the master stoneworker strikes to shape the stone.

With tears in my voice, I proclaim, "They'll kill you, Rab."

He rises to his feet and looks at me with those centuries-deep eyes. Softly, he responds, "God is a man-eater, Yosef.[65] Our sacrifices give him life."

He pulls up his himation to hide his face and walks away, carrying his hammer and chisel.

"You should not move through the streets alone tonight, Master! Let me es- cort you to Bet Ani." I run to catch up, and he—

The horse leaped forward, broke into a trot, and the pain in Yosef's shoul- der jolted him from his dreams. He grabbed for the reins with a gasp. The other riders didn't even turn. He'd fallen far behind. He kicked his mount and rode to catch up with them. Dust puffed from his horse's hooves and lifted into the sky like ghosts ascending toward heaven.

As he thundered past the other conspirators, their horses shied and whinnied. Yosef was suddenly desperate to find Titus, to see if he was still alive and had accomplished their sacred task, or if everything they'd risked had been for nothing.

FOURTEEN

Barnabas sat beside Cyrus in the rocking boat, watching the shore pass. As they neared the sea, the vegetation began to change, becoming taller and ever more lush. In many places, trees overhung the water. The green scents of wet leaves and bark suffused the air.

Birdsong filled the air, and Barnabas tried to enjoy the melody. What had once filled him with peace now barely registered. At the edge of his vision, he noticed the thousands of insects, their wings shimmering in the slanting morning sunlight.

Barnabas forced himself to take a breath. Fear rode his shoulders like the angel of death, leaving every tendon in his body humming, strung so tightly he had to work not to tremble.

One by one the faces of his brothers stared out from his memory. From Brother Jonas on down, he forced himself to recall them. He engraved each face in his memory, that at least during his life none of them be forgotten. He recalled the cool, shadowed arches of the monastery, heard his brothers' soft whispers as they assembled for prayer.

Gone. All gone, lost in an orgy of poison and banished by a sordid wall of flame. How could life with its hopes and dreams be so transitory? Were ninety-seven men no more than a soft exhalation in the vastness of time?

A cold shiver traced down Barnabas' back as he glanced over at the delicate fragment of papyrus in Cyrus' hands.

Have they already found it? The most sacred place on earth? Did they destroy it with the same ease that they murdered my brothers?

He bowed his head and silently prayed for the library assistants, many of whom had probably known nothing more than Barnabas' name and the general nature of the discovery—tiny details they would have gleaned from the notes he'd left in the margins of the original documents. How long had they been forced to suffer?

Guilt ravaged his soul.

Dear Lord, grant them swift entry into heaven. For as you promised, all those who walk in the spirit of the life will wear the garment of honor in the everlasting light. Amen.

As Zarathan and Kalay guided the boat into the shallows, the tree-filtered morning light dappled the ancient papyrus in Cyrus' hands, flashing upon the letters, as though God himself was trying to point something out. The thin parchment appeared incredibly delicate, almost light enough to float out of his fingers.

Cyrus murmured, sounding out the words; then he frowned and studied the papyrus again. The once black ink, made from a mixture of soot, gum, and water, had faded to a handsome rusty-brown, but the letters remained perfectly clear:

MAHANAYIMMEHEBELMAHRAY
MANAHATMAGDIELELSELAH
MASSAMASSAMELEKIELEL
MAGABAEL

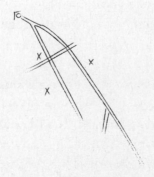

Cyrus shook his head in frustration. He seemed to feel it, that enormous pattern just beyond the reach of his understanding.

Barnabas knew the feeling well. For most of his life, the fleeting moments of illumination had alternately tantalized and terrified him. So much so, that while he had hidden several copies of the papyrus in different locations, he had never once carried it with him—except in his memory.

"What do you see, Cyrus?"

Cyrus lifted his gaze from the papyrus and looked at Barnabas with clear green eyes. "I see ten proper names, maybe twelve, or I think I do."

Barnabas nodded in approval. "What are they?"

At the mention of the names, Kalay turned slightly in the bow to hear better.

"Mahanayim, Mehebel, Mahray, Manahat, Magdiel, El, Selah, Massa, Massa, Melekiel, El, Magabael."

Barnabas studied Cyrus with curious eyes. While a substantial variety of texts about their Lord had, until recently, been available in the monastery, few of the Hebrew Scriptures were available in any Christian monastery. Most monks saw little point in reading them, since their Lord had fulfilled and superceded the Hebrew Scriptures. No one would realize these were names unless he had a knowledge of the Hebrew Scriptures that was both thorough and exacting. Where had Cyrus gained such knowledge? Rome? More likely, Palestine.

"Yes, I, too, think they are names. Do you know the history of those names?" Barnabas watched him closely.

Cyrus shoved damp black curls away from his bearded face. "The first name, Mahanayim, is the place along the Iabbok River where Iakobos and his family encountered the troop of angels."

Barnabas nodded. "Yes, good. What about the others?"

"Mehebel may be one of the towns conquered by King David."

"Yes, go on."

Cyrus' thick black brows lowered as he studied the papyrus again. "Mahray . . . I'm not certain. It may be the city—"

Kalay interrupted with, "Mahray was one of King David's special warriors. His champion. Mahray came from just southwest of the village of Bet Lehem. He was one of the twins born to Yehudah and Tamar."

The boat went silent. Kalay kept paddling as though such obscure historical facts were common knowledge. As the day warmed, locks of her red hair stuck to her long, slender neck.

Barnabas sat back in the boat. "Forgive me, Kalay, did I hear you say this morning that your grandmother had started reading you the Hebrew Scriptures when you were four?"

"That's right. She thought all the Christian teachings were drivel. She was trying to set me straight."

Barnabas chuckled. She might be misguided, but she always spoke plainly. He liked that.

Zarathan, who still looked soul-sick, said weakly, "Is it a veiled reference to our Lord's birth in Bathleem?"

Without thinking, Barnabas replied, "He wasn't born in Bathleem. The infancy narratives are a poor attempt to make our Lord appear to be the son of David, which he was not."

"But Maththaios and Loukas say he was!"

"Yes, well, they're trying to make him fulfill prophecy. In this case Psalms, chapter one hundred thirty-two, verses five and six, and Micah, chapter five, verse two. Didn't it ever strike you as odd that in the seventh chapter of Ioannes many of those listening to our Lord knew that Bathleem was the birthplace of the son of David, but these same people show no knowledge that it is the birthplace of Iesous of Nazaret? More importantly, in the earliest versions of the Gospel of Maththaios, used by the Nazoreans, there is no genealogy of our Lord.[66] He was most likely born in Nazaret."

Stubbornly, Zarathan insisted, "His parents went there for the census! That's why he was born there! They—"

"There was no census, brother. Loukas was wrong about that," Barnabas quietly corrected. "The only census recorded during our Lord's lifetime was ordered by Quirinius in the year six. Our Lord would have been twelve at the time."[67]

Zarathan, apparently shocked senseless, just stared at Barnabas. His oar was dragging uselessly in the murky water.

Cyrus softly said, "Brother, perhaps Kalay is the one who should be looking at the papyrus."

Zarathan found enough voice to angrily blurt, "She can't read. What would she do with it?"

Zarathan's shoulder-length blond hair and the thin fuzz of blond beard that covered his chin glistened with sweat. His startled blue eyes kept darting about as though he couldn't keep them still. In the name of God, the youth was frightened clear down to the marrow of his bones.

"Thank you, brother, for reminding me," Barnabas replied in a gentle voice. "I'd forgotten. It's terribly unfortunate, though, since we could use—"

"She doesn't have to read it," Cyrus said. "If we read it to her, she can still help us to understand it."

Kalay cast an unpleasant glance over her shoulder. "Instead of discussing it amongst yourselves, try asking me."

Barnabas blinked. "My apologies, Kalay. Would you be willing to advise us on the proper meaning of these Hebrew names? We would value your help very much."

She dipped her head. "I would be happy to help, Brother Barnabas. What's the next word?"

Cyrus read, "Manahat. Wasn't that the place where the clan of Benjamin was exiled to?"

"Yes," Barnabas said, nodding. "I've often wondered—"

"Not necessarily," Kalay interrupted.

Barnabas closed his mouth and stared at the back of her red head. "No?"

"No. Manahat was the grandson of Seir, the Horite. He was an Edomite."

A gust of wind thrashed the trees on the banks and a shower of leaves fell into the water around them.

Barnabas cocked his head. To Cyrus, he said, "She may be right, though the form of the name is difficult to explain. Which is why I think it's a place, but let's move on. Kalay, what about Magdiel?"

"Another Edomite chief."

"Yes, perhaps, though my own teacher, Pappas Eusebios, believed it to be the name of a place in the Gebalene. Just as—"

Kalay said, "Actually that would make more sense."

Barnabas squinted at her. "Why?"

"Because Selah, the next word, is also a place, an Edomite rock city conquered by Amaziah, king of Judah."

"Why did you say it made more sense?"

She turned to give him a look that made him feel distinctly inferior. "Place, place—person, person—place, place."

Barnabas considered it. The first two names had, probably, been places, the second two, names, the third two, places. Would the next two prove to be names? "That's an interesting observation, Kalay, let's see—"

Cyrus said, "Forgive me, brother, while I grant that it is possible, let me also suggest that the reference could be to Selah, the place in Moab cited in Isaiah's prophecy, chapter sixteen, verse one."

Kalay turned halfway around to give Cyrus an admiring look. Her sculpted face was flushed with the effort of rowing and shiny with sweat. "Well done, Cyrus."

In a complaining voice, Zarathan said, "Why doesn't someone ask me something? I'm not completely ignorant. For example, I noticed that you forgot to translate the word *El* after Magdiel. And it means 'God.'"

The irritated pride in his voice made Barnabas reach back and pat his knee affectionately. "Forgive me, brother. Thank you for pointing out our error. You are right, it means God. Would you like to comment on the next two words? They are the same: Massa, Massa."

Zarathan's young face pinched with effort. He shifted his paddle to the other side of the boat and stroked the water. "Is that from Psalms?"

Psalms was one of the few Hebrew texts—translated into Greek—that was available at their monastery, and it pleased Barnabas that Zarathan had read it.

"Possibly." Barnabas turned back. "Cyrus? What do you think?"

He shook his head. "The son of Ishmael? Or maybe the tribe of Ishmaelites?"

Barnabas looked to the bow. "Kalay? What is your opinion?"

She tilted her head to the side and damp wisps of red hair draped her narrow shoulder. "I'm inclined to agree with the boy that it's from Psalms—"

"Don't call me a boy!" Zarathan objected.

With hardly more than a breath taken, Kalay continued. "—and deals with *Massa umeriba*. Massa being 'the day of testing.'" She took two more strokes with her paddle. "What do you think, Brother Barnabas?"

He thoughtfully smoothed his gray beard. He had, of course, thought of all these things before, but it was comforting to hear others discuss them. He had never had the luxury of openly discussing the papyrus—

except with his friend Libni, in Caesarea. But that was more than twenty years ago.

"I agree with you that it's about Massa and Meriba, but I've often wondered if it doesn't refer to a passage in Exodus."

Kalay paused for a few moments, then said, "Where Moshe strikes the rock and water comes out?"

"Yes. He called the place *massa,* which meant 'proof,' because they had proved the power of the Lord."

"I like my 'day of testing' better."

Cyrus lifted the fragment of papyrus and studied the next letters. "What about Melekiel? Melek was the great-great-grandson of King Saul, but I don't understand the ending here."

"*Melek* means 'king,' " Kalay said. "*El* is 'God.'"

Barnabas turned around to Zarathan, whose eyes narrowed at the attention. "Can you guess, brother?"

Zarathan said, "Melek. El. The king of God?"

"Excellent work," Barnabas praised. "Don't you agree, Kalay?"

"Well, that's fairly close, I guess. I'd translate it, 'My king is God.' And the last one, Magabael, is neither a place nor a name. It means 'how good is God.'"

"Or maybe just 'God is good'?" Cyrus suggested.

Kalay braced her paddle over her knees and let Zarathan guide them along the bank while she turned to face them. Her damp, tan dress clung to her body. Barnabas, and, he assumed, his brothers, tried not to notice the way it perfectly sculpted her feminine form.

"If you don't mind my saying," she said, "all of that comes down to nothing. The final translation is:

The place where Yakob encountered the angels.
The town conquered by King David.
David's champion warrior.
The place where the Benjaminite clan was exiled to, or the Edomite, Manahat.
A place in the Gebalene, or another Edomite.
God.

The Edomite rock city, or a place in Moab.
God.
The son of Yismael, or maybe 'the day of testing,' or maybe again it means 'proof.'
Lastly . . . my king is God—God—and how good is God.

Kalay made a deep-throated sound of irritation. "It's a whole lot of gibberish."

Under his breath, Zarathan muttered, "Just like our Lord being a *mamzer.*"

In a soft, contemplative voice, Cyrus asked, "Do you think it's a map?"

Kalay's head jerked up, and Barnabas smiled. "Do you?"

"Well, I—I don't know, but if we assume that few of these names refer to people, then we're left with a series of place names. Except for Melekiel-El-Magabael, which seems to be some sort of affirmation of faith. Have you ever tried to plot the places on a map?"

An ache squeezed Barnabas' heart. "Many times. Some of the places are impossible to locate now, which means the map makes no sense. But you are welcome to try, Cyrus. In fact, I hope you will."

As they rounded the bend in the river, the city of Leontopolis came into view. People crowded the landing just up from a dock that jutted out into the water. They had apparently arrived on market day. Men and women were milling around the hundreds of booths where merchants and artists sold their wares. Flute music and the sound of singing rose, along with the delicious scents of roasted meat and freshly baked bread.

Zarathan took a deep breath, and his stomach growled. "Dear Lord, please let someone give us food."

Barnabas glanced at Cyrus, who'd had nothing to eat in two days. He didn't even seem to notice the enticing smells. He continued to stare hard at the papyrus.

"What's wrong, Cyrus?"

Cyrus looked at him from the corner of his eye. "I assume you have noticed the number of letters."

Barnabas nodded. "Yes, but what does it tell you?"

"There are seventy-one letters. There were seventy-one members of the

Jerusalem Council, the Great Sanhedrin Court that met on the Temple Mount."

Cyrus was getting close, his mind moving silently into the ancient Chamber of Hewn Stone, a place where frightened voices whispered dark truths, and the shadows carried daggers. Every letter, every word, was an echo of the deepest secret of their faith.

"Yes," Barnabas answered quietly. "So?"

Cyrus swallowed hard. "Is it possible this is a clue?"

"A clue to what?"

In a hushed voice, Cyrus said, "The person who wrote this."

A tiny flame grew in Barnabas' chest. "I think so, yes."

In a bare whisper, Cyrus asked, "Which Council member?"

Barnabas looked ahead to the shore where brightly colored lengths of fabric danced in the wind. As their boat drew near the long wooden dock, several merchants ran down with baskets of food, blankets, and clothing over their arms. They were already shouting prices and smiling.

"I believe," Barnabas whispered, "that he was the first member of the Occultum Lapidem, the Order of the Hidden Stone."

Cyrus leaned forward with his eyes glittering. "And are you another?"

Barnabas swallowed hard. "Let's sell the boat and arrange for trans-portation to Palestine, then we'll discuss it more."

Kalay said, "You monks are all fools. You're discussing secret societies when the answer is clear as the day."

Barnabas had forgotten her. He shifted to face Kalay. "What's clear?"

"The person who wrote the message," she said as she pulled her black cape from the boat and swung it around her shoulders.

Barnabas' heart started to pound with anticipation. He glanced at Cyrus, who seemed to have stopped breathing. "Who?"

Kalay dipped her dirty hands into the water and washed her sweaty face before she said, "David's champion, who believes that his king is God, and has the proof of it."

Cyrus sucked in a sharp breath, and his gaze again fixed on the papyrus, putting the words together as Kalay had suggested. "She may be right."

Barnabas stared at Kalay, then nodded, and whispered, "She is right."

THE TEACHING ON THE CROSSROAD

You perch on a sandstone ledge, dangling your feet, studying the men and women sitting in a circle around Yeshu ten paces away. They have their white himations pulled over their heads, praying.

You all stand on the verge of disaster . . . and they waste their time praying when they should be gathering weapons and allies to fight the coming war against the Romans. In the beginning, you were naive enough to believe that's what Yeshu wanted, too. You heard him speaking one day, about Rome and the Romans. He said, "I will destroy this house and no one will be able to rebuild it. He who is near me is near the fire."

You longed to be aflame in the fight against Rome. You fell into the line of those following him. But your faith has faded, because you've never really understood him.

As though he has heard your thoughts, Yeshu raises his voice, obviously for your benefit, and says, "Do not give what is holy to dogs, lest they carry it to the dung pile and endlessly gnaw upon it."

Your mouth quirks. You are not amused.

You call, "Through our cowardice, we have given our holy Temple to the Romans to defile. They are gnawing upon its bones as we speak. Let us make allies of the Zealots and go down and destroy our enemies!"

The disciples turn as one to stare at you, and the breeze flaps their white himations around their stunned faces. Yeshu has been teaching about peace all morning. They must wonder where you have been. You can almost hear them whispering, "Hasn't he heard a word the master has said?"

Yeshu calls, "I had a dream, brother. In it, I saw a long caravan coming across the desert and heading into a great darkness. Each wagon was filled with weapons, so full that with each bump or sway of the wagons, swords and knives tumbled down onto the sand. Hordes of people ran behind the wagons, picking them up and clutching them to their chests."

"Yes?" you call. "Please tell me where this wagon is that I may go and arm myself as well."

A few of the disciples laugh.

Yeshu does not. An eerie calm comes over him as he replies, "If you wish, brother, but you would do better to arm yourself in the light. The battle that is coming is not of this earth."

"Light is useless, Yeshu, if it does not have the strength to burn our enemies to ashes. We are at the crossroads! We must act, not spend all day in useless prayers."

"The crossroads," he murmurs, almost to himself and his eyes take on a faraway look, as though he's gazing into that same great darkness the caravan moves toward in his dream.

Several of the disciples are scowling at you now. Not that you care. You are readying yourself to leave this movement, to go and join the Zealots where the real war will be waged.

Yeshu finally looks up and nods to you. "Forgive me, my adversary. You are right. We are at the crossroads. The center of all paths, the place where we must make choices. Make your choice, brother . . . and I will be there . . . and you will defeat Rome."

You just gaze at him, unblinking.

He says, "Do you understand?"

"No."

In a kind voice he murmurs, "I cannot cease asking your heart to generate something from nothing, brother. Creation is the single greatest moment of forgiveness in any man's life. As it was in God's."

FIFTEEN

Loukas stood in the shade of a merchant's booth, examining a fine indigo fabric made from pure linen. It was gorgeous, as the merchant well knew. The price was exorbitant. The merchant—a tall man with two missing teeth and a sun-swarthy face—smiled broadly. He was a well-to-do Roman; that much was clear from his accent and attire. The yellow toga he wore, banded along the collar and hem with black diamonds, was surely of imperial manufacture.

Loukas idly pondered what curious twist of fate had brought the man to Leontopolis to sell wares from a street stall.

The merchant lifted a corner of the deep bluish-purple fabric and rubbed it between his fingers. "You will never again find such a fabric in all of Egypt. I purchased this on a caravan trip to Aelia Capitolina. It had been reserved for the wife of a Roman centurion, but he was transferred before she could purchase it. I was lucky enough to be in the right place, at the right time. Her loss will be your gain."

"Yes, the color is extraordinary," Loukas said, "but I can't afford it."

Loukas turned to examine the river, and the merchant hastily said, "As one Roman to another, I'll drop the price. Two hundred drachmas! Hmm? What do you say? It would make a magnificent garment for your wife."

"I don't have a wife."

"Ah, well, your mother then, or perhaps a sister?"

"I have no family."

The merchant spread his arms wide in a flamboyant gesture. "Give this to a woman . . . and you will!"

Loukas smiled. As he walked away down the line of booths that packed the shoreline, the merchant kept calling to him, further lowering his price.

On the dock below, fishermen sold catches from their boats, which bobbed on the muddy water. People who could not afford to put up a merchant's booth carried goods over their arms, trying to sell them to each person who passed.

Loukas shouldered through the bustling crowd until he could see Janneus and Flavius standing down on the dock, smiling and talking as though waiting for a boat to come in.

That they remained alert was a tribute to their stamina. It had been a hard ride, broken only by stops to scan the river for the fugitives. The Nile, however, was immensely wide, and thousands of boats plied its waters.

The best chance was to intercept the fleeing monks at the ports. Loukas and his men had changed clothes, selecting common coarsely woven tan robes so they would blend in with the local population. It was a gamble, a hunch on Loukas' part that had brought him here.

Pappas Meridias had dispatched the remainder of his men to guard the ports where the Nile emptied into the sea, and the main caravan route into Palestine. Loukas had decided on Leontopolis.

He had served under Centurion Atinius, and this was the route he thought the man would choose. It was the route Loukas himself would have selected. Coming here required traveling down a muddy offshoot of the main Nile—a place tormented by bandits and cutthroats—and it led to Leontopolis. Though small, it was a hive of inequity, and generally very crowded. A man could easily obtain anything he needed from this press of people, or lose himself in the maze of merchants hawking their wares.

Loukas casually headed toward the dock, stopping frequently to examine a pot or scabbard. One booth, run by a plump elderly woman, sold exclusively roasted tripe, lamb's lips, and sow's genitals. A long line of people waited for their chance to buy one of the delicacies. For a moment he considered it, but temptation wasn't worth enduring the line.

Everywhere men and women of questionable integrity lounged about. The variety was astonishing: robbers, runaway sailors, bond or debtor slaves, murderers, coffin makers, drunken eunuch priests, and, of course, prostitutes by the bushel. Leontopolis, it appeared, was as bad as the cook-shops, the *popinae,* in Rome.

While Loukas was fingering a beautiful ivory-handled sword in a tooled leather scabbard, he saw Flavius lift both hands over his head, as though stretching. *The signal!*

Without thinking, Loukas gripped the sword and turned to leave.

The merchant shouted, "Thief! Bring it back!"

Loukas quickly tossed the man four tetradrachmas, more than enough to pay for the sword. The man grinned, and called, "Return later, and I'll bring out my good stock!"

Loukas drilled through the crowd at a run, dodged a big, smiling mer-chant who tried to grab his arm to drag him into his booth, and bounded around a table filled with fish. Reaching the landing, he belted on the sword and slowed again, blending in with the onlookers who were clustered at the foot of the dock.

Ahead of him, he saw Flavius and Janneus staring out at several waiting boats. Most of the spaces to tie up had already been taken. Since neither Flavius nor Janneus had ever seen Jairus Atinius, their signal had meant only that they'd spotted a boat with three men and one woman, which met the minimum description of their prey.

Loukas slipped through the crowd, and studied the boat in question. It had drifted into one of the few remaining spaces, and a big man with a bearded face and shoulder-length curly black hair stepped onto the dock first. He held the boat and extended a hand to help the others. Loukas was still too far away to be certain, but it did look like Atinius. However, it seemed that half the men in this city had curly black hair and a bushy beard.

Loukas shook his head, disgusted that the man had gone weak-kneed and become an ascetic. During the time they had served together in the century, Atinius had been a devotee of the Roman goddess Spes, the god-dess of hope. In fact, he had carried with him a small figurine of Spes. Loukas had seen it once, when the centurion was in prayer on the battle-field. The figurine had shown Spes carrying an opening flower and holding up her long skirt as if about to run away. It had been a beautiful thing. Of course, that was before Atinius was promoted and became the personal guard of Emperor Constantine, and six months before the crucial battle at Milvian Bridge.

What a glorious triumph that had been. They had just stormed Italy and were moving against Maxentius' army, which was fortified in Rome. The men were tired, demoralized, they'd suffered many desertions. Worse, Maxentius would be fighting on his home ground. They were all scared. Then, the night before the battle, the emperor had seen a cross in the sky, and heard the words *In hoc signo vinces,* "In this sign you will conquer." When the news of his vision spread through the troops, many of whom were Christian, the men rallied. Even the wild Teutons and Celts had rallied, for, to them, the cross evoked not the image of Iesous Christos, but the ancestral totem of the sacred tree. The next day they went into battle on the wings of angels, fighting with all their hearts. They'd won, of course. As a result, the emperor had become a Christian, as had much of his army.

Many soldiers, most bearing the burden of some shame—Loukas among them—had been chosen by the emperor himself to join the Militia Templi, where they had vowed to forever consecrate their swords, arms, strength, and lives to the defense of the mysteries of the Chistian faith.

Few had run off to become monks.

They were, after all, soldiers.

Loukas examined the newcomers again. All four of the people had stepped out of the boat and stood on the dock, talking. The old man, gray-haired, with deeply sunken eyes and a long, hooked nose, clutched a leather bag to his chest. The big man, possibly Atinius, was pointing to the boat and talking with a fisherman. After a time of arm waving and head nodding, the fisherman handed "Atinius" what looked like drachmas.

Loukas focused on the woman, as did every other man on the dock. What a stunning beauty. Tall, with flowing red hair and the heart-shaped face of a deity, she wore her black cape thrown back over her shoulders, revealing the tan linen dress that clung damply to her perfect curves. Men would pay a fortune to own her. Perhaps, when this was done, Pappas Meridias would reward Loukas by giving him the woman as his slave. In the past two years, he had discovered that the masters of the Militia Templi could be very generous when they approved of his work.

He smiled at the thought. It was something to look forward to.

Loukas lifted a hand to his men, made a chopping gesture, and they began to drift toward the prey. Best not to accost them on the dock. Better to follow them into the crowd where they could take them from behind, one by one.

Flavius went first, ambling toward the dock, just far enough away that he could keep them in sight. A short time later, Janneus positioned himself on the opposite side of the dock.

Loukas remained at the edge of merchant's row, waiting to confirm Atinius' identity.

SIXTEEN

Kalay stood on the dock and surveyed the crowd. The odors of sun-warm fish, dank water, rot, and sewage mingled with that of unwashed humanity. Relief came in the intermittent scents of wood smoke, roasting meat, and fresh baked bread. The place was a cacophony of noise, vendors hawking to each other, children shrieking and calling, and the barking of dogs. Color was everywhere, in people's clothing, in the bright canvas of the stands. It all hearkened to her memories of other times. How long had it been since she'd been here? Four years? Five? She smiled, feeling comfortably back in her element. Challenge was in the very air.

As she threw her long red hair back, men openly stared at her; given her looks, she had grown used to it over the years. She had found it a useful tool for assessing her situation. As her gaze met each of the men's, they glanced shyly aside . . . except for one man. His gaze burned into her, trying to capture her soul. He had a lion's face, the nose broad, eyes slightly slanted, with red-gold hair. In addition, he moved like a Roman—all authority and no sense.

Brother Barnabas had retrieved his book bag and already started down the dock. Zarathan followed just behind the old priest, blissfully innocent as they talked to each other.

From right behind her ear, Cyrus' deep voice said, "Do you see him?"

"The Roman?" she said without turning. "He stands out like a whore among the vestals. You think he's waiting for us?"

"I think he could be. I also think the two men in the clean robes standing on either side of the landing are with him."

Subtly, Kalay located the men in question. She should have spotted them herself. "You'd think killers would have better sense than to appear in a place like Leontopolis looking clean. What do you think they're planning?"

"They'll probably wait for us to enter the crowd. Then they can pick us off one by one. Except for you, of course."

She suppressed the prickle that climbed her spine. "Yes, I'm sure they'll want to keep me for a time. I'd just as soon they didn't have the chance, Cyrus."

She turned partway around and pretended to be straightening her leather belt. Their gazes touched. His green eyes had gone fierce, and he had his right hand curled tightly around one of the bone stilettos on his belt. He drew it out and handed it to her. "Strike first. Don't hesitate."

Kalay took it. "I haven't hesitated since I was fourteen." She tested the balance of the bone weapon. The sharp tip gleamed in the sunlight. "What do you want me to do?"

His voice dropped to a whisper. "Catch up with my brothers. Stay right behind them. The sicarii, the 'dagger men,' will fall into line a few people back, but they'll be right behind you."

"Should I warn your brothers?"

"Their fear would complicate matters."

"I'm to block the killers, is that the idea?"

He hesitated only a heartbeat. "You are. Can you do it?"

"Can I cut a few Roman purses if I've the chance? To help support our Godly mission, of course."

Despite himself, he smiled. "Be discreet."

"I'm always discreet."

She twirled the dagger and started down the dock at a fast walk, hurrying to catch up with Zarathan and Barnabas before they stepped off onto the sand.

"Zarathan?" she called.

He turned and scowled at her. Sharply, he said, "Didn't I tell you not to talk to me?"

Kalay pulled up her skirts so that her tanned calves showed and trotted toward him as she shook out her flowing red hair. As she'd known, all eyes were upon her. The two men stationed on either side of the dock were leering. As she grasped Zarathan's arm and began elbowing through the press around the landing, they began to close in. She watched from the corner of her eye as they followed.

Kalay pointed, shouting, "Look! A booth that sells roasted sow's genitals. I'm starved. Are you?"

The horrified look on Zarathan's face made her laugh out loud. He was shaking his arm, trying to loosen her hold. A violent blush of red stained his cheeks.

Barnabas said, "Bread would be enough, Kalay. Do you see any loaves?"

"I do, brother." She pointed to the packed alleyway that veered to the right. "Walk straight up there. Follow your nose. You'll find it."

Zarathan disdainfully pried Kalay's hand loose, shot a wild glance behind them, and asked, "Where's Brother Cyrus? He has the money. We won't be able to eat without it."

Barnabas, clutching his book bag, said, "Pray to your Lord, and you shall receive."

Zarathan reached down to touch the prayer rope tied to his belt and began mumbling, but his voice sounded pained, as though he felt put-upon having to pray, instead of just receiving a handout from his Lord.

Kalay took a position two paces behind them. As they entered the bread-makers' alley, her pulse began to pound in her ears. She longed to turn around to see where the sicarii were. Instead, she forced herself to look straight ahead.

The crowd moved in a swaying herd, banging shoulders as they passed the merchants' booths, and her skin crawled. She could almost feel the point of a dagger pricking her back.

Where are you, Cyrus?

Janneus turned sideways to slide between two laughing brigands who openly carried their gold-hilted daggers like badges of courage, and picked up his pace.

The woman and the two monks were four steps ahead of him as they entered the narrow shop-lined street. Neither of the monks seemed the slightest bit concerned. If everything was going according to plan, Flavius would be five steps behind him. That way, if Janneus was attacked by the crowd and couldn't jump the second monk in time, Flavius would take him. Decurion Loukas would be bringing up the rear, following closely behind Atinius. Loukas had claimed the former centurion as his own. Apparently there was something between them.

Janneus managed to slip between two old women who were gawking at a silversmith's wares, and gained two paces.

He propped his hand on the hilt of his dagger, unsure what to do about the woman. He had no orders regarding her. Loukas had said only that she was "of no consequence." He simply needed to get around her, quietly kill the monks, and escape before she started screaming her head off.

Janneus' brows lifted admiringly when he saw her neatly untie and pocket a Roman man's purse while he was studying a goldsmith's wares. The victim remained totally unaware.

As they approached the gallery of food booths, the sweet, yeasty fragrance of bread swirled down the alleyway, accented by the scents of cooked vegetables and camel steaks being fried in fat.

Janneus sidestepped a group of children and gained another pace. The woman's hips swayed in an enticing manner. He tried not to think about it. He had to concentrate now. As he rudely pushed past her, he could smell her scent, a mixture of soap and sun-dried clothing. He pulled his dagger, stepping close behind the old priest's back. He drew his arm back . . .

The pain came as a shock, the thrust quick and clean, barely requiring half a heartbeat. Janneus felt the weapon puncture his back and slide between his ribs. His heart started to flutter, pounding desperately.

He spun around with his dagger up, ready to strike at his enemy, but saw no one, nothing. Only the woman staring at him with burning eyes.

Where's Flavius? Is he already dead?

When the crowd erupted in shouts and cries, he fought to get away, but only made it twenty paces before he stumbled into a leather booth, knocked over the table, and toppled to the ground.

People huddled over him, shouting questions, shoving each other to get a better look.

Janneus stared up at the thin slit of blue sky visible between the canvas roofs of the booths. He knew this kind of wound very well, having inflicted it often enough. He tried to breathe deeply, to make his heart pump harder, and hasten the end. Still, it would take another four or five hundred heartbeats before . . .

Almost as though he were not real, Decurion Loukas appeared in the crowd, and then vanished without even a glance at Janneus.

A white-haired crone bent over Janneus and stabbed her finger into the blood pooling beneath his back. She examined it, and her wrinkles tensed. She turned and said something to a man leaning down beside her, but Janneus could no longer hear voices.

Just as his vision began to gray, he saw a big man with curly black hair moving through the crowd silent as a ghost . . . following Loukas.

SEVENTEEN

When he heard the commotion, Zarathan spun around and saw a man collapse sideways into a leather booth, a huge bloodstain spreading across his robe. For a heartbeat, he could only gape.

He started to speak, but Kalay pressed a hand into his chest, hissing, "Don't say a word. Keep walking as though it's none of your concern."

Barnabas froze for an instant, apparently stunned by the tone in her voice, but quickly ordered, "Do as she says."

Blood surged in Zarathan's veins. He felt so light-headed he feared he might faint. *What's happening back there? Is that man on the ground dying? Where's Brother Cyrus?*

Kalay whispered, "Turn right at the next booth, go up the street swiftly, but not so fast that you attract attention."

"What does that mean?" Zarathan hissed back in panic.

"Keep pace with me." Barnabas slipped his arm through Zarathan's in an apparently brotherly gesture. Zarathan feared it was less a display of affection than to keep him from bolting and running.

They strode past a booth selling live goats, and a corral of horses. The acrid stench of urine and manure made his stomach churn. Bleating goats almost covered the loud voices around the leather shop, and that made his anxiety worse.

Kalay said, "Walk straight ahead. There's a church at the end of the street. You'll see it when we pass the last booth."

Zarathan walked so fast he practically dragged Barnabas over the foul-smelling cobblestones. The smells of night earth and standing water burned in his nose. How did people live in a place like this? He pawed anxiously at the flies that swirled around his face.

The church, a magnificent stone cathedral with enormous cylindrical pillars and thick walls, thrust its golden dome into the sere blue sky. The soaring arches and sculpted gargoyles perched on the eaves drew him like a bee to honey.

"Hurry," Zarathan whispered. "If we can make it there, we'll be safe."

"Safe?" Kalay said with her usual irreverence. "Only if they've replaced the eucharist with a big pile of spears. We're going to run past it into that open field just beyond."

"Are you insane?" Zarathan stared at her in shock. "If we're out in the open they'll see us and kill us!"

"I can't believe you've survived this long being so stupid. Just follow me." Kalay veered around both men to lead the way.

Zarathan slowed. Did he dare run in the opposite direction and leave his companions to face their attackers alone? Desperately, he turned . . .

Barnabas' claw-like old hand gripped Zarathan's arm, and he ordered, "Follow her. Do as she says. Just don't think about it!"

Barnabas, overbalanced by the book bag, pulled Zarathan along the path that led through the cool shadow of the church wall and out into the freshly planted field. The place was a small garden where seedlings had just begun to sprout. A rather well-to-do house stood to the south. A wall blocked off the north, and dilapidated sheds and a barn blocked the east.

The recently watered green sprigs of wheat smelled fragrant. From this low rise, Zarathan could see across the river to several villages that dotted the lush delta. The dock was still crowded, and people packed the alleys between the merchants' booths.

Kalay whispered, "There he is."

"Who?" Zarathan asked.

A muscular man dressed in a tan robe stopped at the last booth. He *did* look out of place. He had short red-gold hair and a broad nose with slanted eyes. His carefully shaven face was distinctly Roman. For a few heartbeats, the man frowned at them, as though he didn't understand what they were doing; then he turned to casually examine the harnesses spread out on the table in the last booth.

Zarathan studied the sword belted around the man's waist and panic stung his chest. "Why are we just standing here? We should be trying to escape!"

Kalay said, "If you move, I'll kill you myself," and drew a bone stiletto from her belt. She held it with the ease of a person long familiar with such weapons. He blinked at the sticky red sheen on the bone tip, and went weak-kneed.

As though to taunt the man in the tan robe, Kalay waved to him.

The man turned slightly to stare at her. . . .

Then he jerked, and stood as if frozen. Someone's hand reached around and pulled the short sword from his scabbard. Finally, the Roman spread his arms and started walking up the trail toward the wheat field, with Brother Cyrus close behind him.

Had Kalay seen Cyrus and distracted the Roman with her wave? He stared at her in horror and amazement.

Kalay said, "Now let's get into the shade behind the church where we're out of sight of the merchants' booths."

Barnabas quickly strode into the shadows where he set his book bag down, leaned against the cool stone wall, and wiped his brow with a shaking hand. "I saw that man when we first stepped off the dock. Who is he?"

Kalay's blue eyes had turned hard as stones. "He's one of Pappas Meridias' killers."

Barnabas' bushy gray brows drew down over his long hooked nose. All the world's sadness seemed suddenly to be concentrated in the tight lines of his elderly face. "Was he one of the men who—"

"Who poisoned your brothers at the monastery? Yes."

Cyrus was whispering to the Roman. Zarathan saw the man nod. As they strode into the shadows, Cyrus took in the garden and the nearby farmer's house. Then he considered the outbuildings hunched across the field. Inside the barn, a horse whickered.

To the killer, Cyrus hissed, "Drop to your knees."

The Roman slowly lowered himself, but kept his arms up. He had strange lime-green eyes, like a cat's, cold and inhuman. When the man looked at Zarathan his soul left his body for an instant. Death lived and breathed in those depths.

Cyrus, sword at the ready, said, "Kalay, please unbuckle his sword belt and check him for other weapons."

She started to hand her stiletto to Barnabas, who shook his head vehemently. Rolling her eyes, she angrily shoved it into Zarathan's resisting hands. Though he held it at arm's length, he swore the grisly thing was ready to fly through the air and lodge itself just beneath his breastbone.

Kalay knelt behind the man. As she unbuckled his sword belt, the man turned and his hungry gaze fixed on her body, and a small, cruel smile came to his lips. He whispered, *"Soon, beauty."*

Kalay didn't answer. She set the belt aside, and patted him down, pulling out a beautiful silver dagger with a long, curved blade. Next she found a thin bronze stiletto. She tucked both into her own belt. When she'd finished searching him, she picked up a broken fist-sized piece of brick and rose. With all the strength she could muster, she bashed the killer in the head with the brick and sent him sprawling across the dirt. Zarathan and Barnabas had to leap to get out of the way.

Zarathan cried, "Why did you *do* that?"

Kalay smiled at the sight of the blood trickling down the man's face, tossed the brick aside, and answered, "He wanted a taste of me. I gave him one."

Sweat beaded Cyrus' flushed face, as he belted on the sword.

Kalay gave Cyrus a curious look. "I assume you want to wring some answers out of this piece of filth, or you would have killed him in the crowd like you did the other one."

Zarathan stared at Cyrus and his face slackened. *Cyrus killed the man at the leather booth? Dear Lord, help me. I'm traveling with demons incarnate.*

Unless . . . Zarathan glanced at the blood-smeared bone stiletto Kalay had given him. He felt suddenly faint. Somewhere back there, lay two dead men.

Cyrus nodded to Kalay. "Let's get him to that horse shed."

EIGHTEEN

At dark, the oil lamps of Leontopolis glittered to life and a pale, fluttering gleam danced over the surface of the river.

Zarathan studied it from where he huddled in the shadow of the broken-down barn with his hands clasped over his ears, trying not to hear what was happening inside. Hours ago, when Cyrus and Kalay had first taken the Roman inside, the sound of blows and grunts had filled the air. Zarathan had quaked at Cyrus' demands that the killer tell him why he'd had to murder everyone in the monastery. Who had given the order? The pain in Cyrus' voice had been more agonizing than the groans of the killer. Now there were no sounds except soft voices, and horses chewing hay.

"We should leave," Zarathan said. "Isn't it dangerous to stay here so long? Eventually, someone will hear us, or come to check on the horses."

Barnabas, who knelt in prayer five cubits away, his book bag by his side, did not respond. He'd been praying unceasingly since they'd arrived. In the amber glow of the city, Barnabas' long, narrow face seemed carved of alabaster. Though his deeply sunken eyes remained in shadow, his short gray hair and beard had a faint yellow hue.

Several times, Zarathan would have sworn the old man was weeping. And why wouldn't he? All of this was madness.

Zarathan rose to his feet and walked away. In the distance he could see the empty merchant booths and the dock that jutted out into the water. People still milled around the boats, probably fishermen coming in late from their labors.

A gust of wind blew across the river and flapped the hem of his white robe. He barely noticed. He felt empty. Like a gutted fish, his insides were raw and bleeding. This whole monk idea had been a mistake. He longed for nothing more than to go home and hide in his room. If God would let him do that, he would spend all day, every day on his knees in prayer.

They wouldn't have hurt my parents, would they? Surely they didn't burn our home?

His teachers at the monastery had always taught him that the Lord put people in places where they could learn the things necessary to help usher in the Kingdom of God. But what was he supposed to learn from this? Or from the senseless slaughter of his brothers?

He whispered, "Blessed Iesous Christos, why are you punishing me? What have I done?"

Across the garden, near the church, a dog barked and began to howl. Other dogs joined in, filling the night with an eerie chorus.

Tears rose in Zarathan's eyes. The golden dome of the church shone as though drenched in liquid amber. "We should have gone in. Someone there would have protected us. If Barnabas hadn't listened to that woman, we'd be far away by now."

He folded his arms and hugged himself. The massive stones of the church were perfectly hewn and beautifully laid. Zarathan's father had been a *tekton,* a stoneworker, just like his Lord, Iesous Christos, so he knew quality work when he saw it.

Zarathan missed his family more than he'd ever thought possible. He had the overwhelming urge to run all the way home and throw himself into his father's arms. If he could only lie down knowing that his father stood by the door with a setting mallet in his hand, perhaps he could sleep for days. Then he would wake to find that all this had been a terrible nightmare. He yearned to—

"What?" Barnabas said.

Zarathan turned and saw Cyrus and Kalay exiting the barn leading two skinny horses. The poor animals' ribs stuck out like thin iron bars.

He tramped back across the soft garden soil. Barnabas had risen to his feet and was staring up at Cyrus like a lost soul. "What else did he tell you?"

"He told us that Pappas Meridias is on his way to Caesarea in Palestine," Cyrus said and wiped his right hand on his robe.

Though Zarathan couldn't be certain in the darkness, the stain that coated Cyrus' white linen robe looked like fresh blood. Kalay stood beside him with her red hair tied back and her enticing face gleaming in the moonlight. One of the horses shook its head and it reins clinked.

In a panicked voice, Barnabas asked, "Did he tell you why? Are they going after Pappas Eusebios?"

"I know only that Meridias is desperately trying to find something called the Gate of Yeshua. Do you know what that is?"

Barnabas tilted his head as though reluctant to answer, but whispered, "Yes, I—I've heard of it."

"What is it?"

Barnabas swallowed hard and lowered his voice even further. "It was a question asked of our Lord's brother, Yakob, just before they killed him. But I—I don't know what it is," he said and gestured to the barn, as though saying, *Please, let's speak no more here.*

Zarathan said, "I don't understand how you got the killer to talk. When I looked into his eyes, I got the impression he would rather die than—"

"Oh, you'd be surprised what a man will do"—Kalay tucked the silver dagger into her belt—"when you slit open his sack and start shaving off thin slices of his testicle in front of his eyes."

Zarathan felt light-headed.

Cyrus opened his mouth to say something, then closed it, nodded, and pointed to the horses. "Let's go."

Cyrus literally lifted Barnabas onto the back of the horse. He looked at Zarathan. "Brother, there are only two horses. You will need to ride behind Barnabas. I'll carry Kalay behind me."

Zarathan weakly asked, "Are we stealing horses as well as torturing human beings?"

Cyrus gave him a look that froze Zarathan's heart. He had the feeling that in another place and time, Cyrus would have cut out his heart for that comment.

"I left the farmer half the drachmas we received from the sale of the boat," Cyrus answered. "It should be more than enough to pay for these miserable beasts."

"Then why don't we leave more drachmas and take four, one for each of us?" Zarathan asked.

It was Barnabas who answered. "We may need the rest of that money, and with two horses the farmer can still work his field. Brother Cyrus made the right choice: half the money for two horses. Now, climb up behind me. We need to leave here."

Zarathan handed up the book bag and took three tries to climb up behind Barnabas. The horse tramped and tossed its head in irritation.

"What about the killer?" Barnabas asked.

Cyrus said, "I'll take care of him."

But as he turned back to the dilapidated barn, shouts rang out: *"Stop! Horse thieves! Stop them!"*

Rounding the house, three men—probably the farmer and his sons— were racing across the field toward them.

Kalay said, "Cyrus, get inside and take care of him, or—"

"There's no time." Cyrus mounted the horse and extended a hand to help her climb on behind him. The animal almost buckled under their weight.

As Kalay slipped her arms around his waist, she said, "This is a mistake. If you let him live, he'll—"

"Come on!" Zarathan cried. "They're coming fast!"

Cyrus kicked the horse into a fast trot, and Barnabas and Zarathan, bouncing like sacks of wheat, followed.

NINETEEN

The crowing of a cock woke Loukas.

I'm alive. . . .

He opened his eyes and blinked at the dilapidated barn. Through the gaps in the sagging roof, stars gleamed against an ebony background.

His naked body felt as though it were on fire. Some day, when he had the luxury of time, he would use that torture method on one of his victims. It was singularly excruciating. On the floor around him bloody handfuls of oat straw lay. Atinius had first beaten him into submission with his fists, then he'd walked to the straw bunk and pulled out a handful of the long, golden stems. When he walked back, he'd slapped Loukas across the face with the straw. It hadn't hurt at first. But after an hour the chaff in his eyes had felt like crushed glass, and the minute irregularities in the straw had left thousands of tiny cuts. Two hours later he'd felt as though he'd been flayed alive. His face hurt the worst. He'd been forced to keep his eyes closed to protect them, and his eyelids, the object of constant abuse, had swollen to twice their normal size. Every breath of wind that blew across the bloody pulp was agony.

Through it all, the magnificent woman had smiled at him. Toward the end, she'd been the interrogator. Atinius had told her what to ask, and she'd done it in a cooing voice, like a cat's purr just before it leaps for your throat. Over and over again, the same questions: "Where is Pappas Meridias? What's he looking for? Who's giving the orders?"

He'd refused to speak despite the agony. In the end, the woman had smiled seductively at him, and drawn his own knife from her belt. She'd waved it in front of his eyes with the same flair as a courtesan sensually waving a recently removed piece of clothing.

At the touch of the blade to his scrotum, he'd shrieked into his gag until his throat had gone raw.

Wait until I get my hands on you, beauty.

Just before he'd passed out, he'd seen the farmer charge into the barn, find the money Atinius had left for him, then calmly go about forking more hay to the remaining horses. The man hadn't seen Loukas lying curled in the dark corner . . . but when morning came, he would.

Loukas tested the ropes that bound his hands and feet. Centurion Atinius was a master of knots.

As the night moved toward dawn, the sky brightened, becoming more blue than black, and Loukas saw the glint of iron on the wall near the horses.

He clenched his teeth as he dragged himself across the floor toward the stalls. The big black horse watched Loukas with jet eyes, not sure what to make of him. The smaller bay, more concerned with filling his belly, paid him no attention at all, choosing instead to eat hay.

When he reached the wall, Loukas sagged against it for a few moments, resting, before he awkwardly levered himself to his feet and hopped toward the tool hanging on a peg above the bay's shoulder. The horse shied away from him, prancing in his stall and flaring his nostrils at the scent of Loukas' blood.

Using his head, Loukas shoved the rusty sickle off the wall onto the dirt floor, then he sank down beside it. The bay went back to eating, but his gaze kept darting to Loukas.

Loukas twisted around and placed the ropes against the metal blade. Despite the discomfort, he began patiently sawing.

Then I'll be off to Alexandria.

He'd revealed more than he should have, and loathed himself for it. A shiver wracked him when he remembered the sight of that cold metal slicing through his soft pink tissue. *The Gate of Yeshua. I told them about it. . . .*

Loukas had first heard the phrase whispered in the deepest circles of the Militia Templi. No one knew what it meant, but it carried a strange ring of Truth. Like the "Kingdom of God," anyone who heard "the Gate of Yeshua" stopped for a moment. He could not say why, but the words seemed to resonate in the chambers of the heart, as though the soul heard and understood them, even if the mind did not.

The first strand of rope broke with a dull pop. Loukas shifted to reposition his bound hands.

He would be late for his prearranged meeting with Pappas Meridias, but Meridias depended upon him. The man could not proceed without first hearing Loukas' report.

Loukas inhaled around his gag as best he could and went back to work. While he sawed, he let his thoughts drift, but they always returned to the magnificent woman. Her ethereally beautiful face had carved its own shrine inside him.

Kalay. Her name is Kalay. Oh, you shall pay for what you did to me, beauty.

TWENTY

In the moonlight, the endless desert sands glimmered as though alive. But looks deceived. This was a sere land, wind-scoured and bitter. Outcrops of rock that had once jutted defiantly against the sky were now rounded, veined and ridged from the blowing sand. Here and there dunes lay in hollow crescents on the stony, deflated soil. Above it all, the pewter sky bore down with a relentless weight.

They followed an old caravan trail that headed north toward the city of Bersabe in Idumea. The horses' hooves cracked and popped on the desert pavement. Along the route, decaying bits of old wagons and broken harnesses lay strewn, as well as the refuse of many camps: charcoal, broken pot sherds, torn baskets, fragments of oil lamps. They'd even found three mostly whole clay cups.

Travel, however, was slow. The thin horses, half starved and stable-weak, struggled to carry double. Cyrus had been the first to drop off and start leading his animal, leaving only Kalay in the saddle. Next, Barnabas had dismounted. As he walked, Zarathan bobbed, half asleep, on the horse's back, the book bag cradled like a pillow in his arms.

Walking helped to clear Barnabas' head, though not the overwhelming guilt that tormented his soul. The dead faces of his brothers kept haunting him. And now others were dead at their hands. He had knelt, head bent in prayer, as a man was gruesomely tortured within earshot—and done nothing to stop it.

Dear Lord, forgive me.

Cyrus matched his pace with Barnabas. "I'd like to hear about the Gate of Yeshua now, brother."

Barnabas shot him a sidelong glance. Cyrus' voice had changed since that terrible night in the monastery. It was drifting back to a soldier's voice, growing harder, more demanding. Even his eyes had changed. They were no longer happy and half amused. They'd become green fireballs that burned anyone they gazed at.

Barnabas was deathly tired. His old body just didn't have the strength it had once had. He feared he wouldn't be able to relate the details in a coherent fashion, but he drew in a breath and began. "Around one hundred years after the death of our Lord, a church historian named Hegesippus began writing a history of the True Church. In his book, he recorded the details of the horrible death of *Iakobos,* or *Yakob* in Hebrew, the brother of Yeshua."

Zarathan murmured groggily, "He was killed in the year 62, wasn't he?"

Barnabas shifted to look back at the youth. Zarathan's blond hair and wispy beard had a silver sheen. "Yes. Very good, brother."

"What does Yakob's martyrdom have to do with the Gate of Yeshua?" Cyrus asked.

"This is a complicated story," Barnabas sighed, "bear with me through the first part."

"Of course, brother."

Barnabas rubbed his eyes. They felt as though they'd been blasted by dust storms for days. "There had always been a dangerous rivalry between the family of High Priest Annas, or *Hanan* in Hebrew, and the family of Yeshua. Many books report that it was Annas who discovered Miriam was pregnant and ran back to the Temple to report that she had committed a great sin."[68]

"Annas was high priest during our Lord's trial, too, wasn't he?" Zarathan, proud of his knowledge, asked and lifted his head.

"No, though you are correct that there are references in the gospels to his being high priest during the trial, but those references are not correct.

Annas was appointed high priest by Praefectus Quirinius in the year 6, and removed from his office by the order of Valerius Gratus in the year 15. However, he remained a powerful adviser to Kaiaphas, and was still referred to as 'High Priest,' though the title was clearly honorary. What I mean is that Annas remained very influential. In fact, all of his five sons served as high priest after Kaiaphas."

Impatiently, Kalay said, "I want to hear about the Gate of Yeshua. What is it?"

"I'm getting there, Kalay," Barnabas replied. "Ioannes reports that Yeshua was taken to the high priest's home by Roman and Jewish forces and interrogated. Also, the third and fourth chapters of Acts describe Annas' participation in the interrogation, a decade later, of Petros and Ioannes, who were arrested for healing a lame man at the Beautiful Gate of the Temple."

When Kalay started to interrupt, Barnabas hurried to add, "Here's where the Gate of Yeshua comes into the story. It is Annas' son, also named Annas, who ordered the arrest of our Lord's brother, Yakob. The younger Annas had been high priest for only three months. One of the puzzling elements of Hegesippus' history is his assertion that Annas kept demanding that Yakob tell him 'what is the Gate of Yeshua.' "

Cyrus seemed to be thinking about that. He cocked his head, and his eyes reflected the moonlight. "Did Yakob respond?"

"Yakob said, 'Why do you ask me concerning the Son of Man? He will come in the clouds of heaven.' "

Zarathan blurted, "That doesn't make any sense! Annas asked him what the 'Gate' was and Iakobos answered that the 'Son of Man would come in the clouds of heaven'?"

"It makes sense," Barnabas said, "if you recall that our Lord told Kaiaphas practically the same thing just before his crucifixion: 'You will see the Son of Man sitting on the right hand of power and coming with the clouds of heaven.' "

"But our Lord was quoting from the Book of Daniel. How does that answer the question about the Gate?"

Cyrus shifted the horse's reins to his other hand and frowned at Barnabas. "You mean that by quoting his brother, Yakob was refusing to answer the question. Just as his brother had refused to answer Kaiaphas' questions?"

"Yes, I think Yakob was, in effect, saying 'I will no more answer your questions than my brother did.'" Barnabas paused. "They killed him for it."

"*If* that's what he meant," Kalay said.

"Yes, of course, we can't be certain, but that's my best guess," Barnabas replied. "And I truly—"

"I have another guess," Kalay said.

The men turned to stare at her.

She continued. "Iesous' name in Hebrew was Yeshua, and the Hebrew word for salvation is *yeshuah*. They're pronounced slightly different, but they might look similar when written down. Maybe Hegesippus couldn't tell the difference."

Barnabas stroked his gray beard thoughtfully. "Then you think it's possible High Priest Annas was asking Yakob about the gate of salvation? Perhaps, though I find it hard to believe a Jewish high priest would ask such a thing. Surely, he believed he knew the path to salvation—and it did not involve Yakob's brother Yeshua."

"Surely," Kalay replied, "but I don't find it hard to believe that later Christians would put such words into a Jewish high priest's mouth."

"Ah. Very true." Barnabas nodded agreeably. He had noted many occasions in the ancient texts where that very thing had happened, particularly in relation to the gospels. "Yes, that's possible."

Zarathan's face screwed up as though he found it unconscionable that Barnabas would actually agree with Kalay about something so odious, but he asked, "How did Yakob die?"

As he had many times, Barnabas imagined the scene in his mind. He could hear the screams of Yakob's followers as they watched from far below the Temple. "The Second Apocalypse of Iakobos[69] says that they cast him down from the pinnacle of the Temple and then seized him, clubbed him, and dragged him on the ground. For a time, while they reviled him, they placed a huge stone on his stomach. After that, they forced him to get up, dig a hole, and stand in it while they filled the hole up to his waist. Finally, they stoned him to death. Legend says he was buried in his family tomb somewhere near Jerusalem."

For a long time, only the sound of the horses' hooves softly striking stone echoed through the night.

Cyrus asked, "Is that all we know about the Gate? Surely the Occultum Lapidem must have researched this over and over."

"Oh, yes, many times. But to little avail."

"The Hebrew word for 'gate,' *sha'ar,* can mean many things other than gate," Kalay pointed out.

"Yes," Barnabas replied. "But "gate" seems to fit the best."

Kalay gave him a disgusted look. "*Sha'ar* can also mean opening, doorway, entry, enclosure, passage."

"The Yeshua Passage?" Cyrus whispered.

"Possibly," Kalay said.

"As in a passage in a book?" Zarathan wondered.

"Or the Doorway to Yeshua," Barnabas replied through a long exhalation. "It could be a theological reference. But I've always wondered if the reference isn't to one of the gates of the Temple."

"Like the Beautiful Gate?" Zarathan asked.

Barnabas nodded. "Perhaps the Gate of Yeshua is the gate where our Lord entered the city the day he threw the money changers from the Temple."

"What gate was that?"

"He entered through the eastern gate, then walked south and approached the Temple Mount through the Hulda Gate. But I know of no tradition that suggests either of those gates ever acquired the name the Gate of Yeshua."

Donkeys brayed in the distance and they all tensed and looked to the west. The faint outline of trees whiskered the horizon. It was probably an oasis. Sounds carried very far on still desert nights.

Cyrus said, "Why would Pappas Meridias be hunting for this gate?"

"I do not know." Barnabas rubbed his eyes again. His legs ached. It had been years since he'd been on a horse. "Church scholars have been trying to decipher the meaning for centuries, but have made little sense of it."

"Yakob was the leader of the Jerusalem Church after the death of Yeshua," Cyrus said. "After Yakob was murdered, who followed him?"

"The apostles selected Yeshua's brother Shimon to lead them."

"That's curious," Zarathan murmured from behind Barnabas.

"What is?"

"Petros was still alive when Yakob died. Why wasn't he selected as the new leader? In the Gospel of Maththaios our Lord says that Petros will be given the 'keys of the Kingdom,' and none of the surviving apostles wanted him to lead them?"

"I suspect that our Lord did not mean political power when he said the 'keys of the Kingdom.' He meant that Petros would be given the spiritual knowledge to find the Kingdom inside himself. Don't forget that our Lord says in the Gospel of Thomas, verse three, 'The Kingdom is inside you and it is outside you. When you learn to know yourselves, then you will be known, and you will understand that you are the sons of the living Father.'"

"So our Lord never intended for Petros to lead the Church?"

Barnabas shrugged. "It is well documented that after Shimon was crucified by Emperor Trajan in the year 106, leadership of the movement passed to the Lord's last surviving brother, Yudas, who was in his nineties."

"So, four brothers in succession led the movement?" Cyrus asked.

"Yes, and his sisters, Mariam and Salome, probably played significant roles as well, unless they were hunted down and killed by the highest levels of the Roman government in Palestine, but we have no record of that."

They continued for a time in silence, but Barnabas could see Cyrus' lips moving, repeating the words: *the Gate of Yeshua, the Gate of Yeshua . . .*

Barnabas said, "If we keep this pace until tomorrow evening, we will reach the village of Gaza. There is a man near there who may be able to help us."

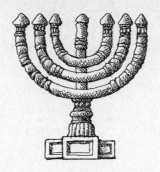

TWENTY-ONE

Manahat

Careful not to wake the man who sleeps beside her, Maryam wraps herself in her worn himation, and takes her time stepping around the dark forms of the others who lie on the floor.

When she pads outside into the cool night air, I follow her, fearing for her safety.

The lamps of Bet Ani glimmer across the rolling hills. The city is so beautiful tonight, I fear it may stop my heart. Flute music, accompanied by the sounds of two different bells, drifts on the cool wind.

As I walk down the hill behind her, the cobblestones feel like smooth ice beneath my feet.

Maryam stares into the windows of the houses, and I suspect she is silently reciting the names of every child and dog, even most of the goats who live here. She has spent her entire life on this street,[70] except for a few years spent in Taricheae working as a renowned hairdresser to the wealthy, which is why many people still refer to her as the Megaddela, the hairdresser.[71]

Maryam turns down another street, and walks with her head down, lost in some inner world.

I follow.

She prospered in Taricheae, but most of her money is gone, poured into supporting Yeshua's ministry, though I suspect this does not matter to her. Yeshua has told us that the Kingdom is almost upon us. Soon, no one will need money or status. God will return to Zion to vindicate his people, to redeem Yisrael, and renew the creation. The exile will end.

When she stops dead in her tracks, and her shoulders heave, I call, "Maryam?"

She spins around breathlessly, trying to make out my face in the gloom. Tears dot her cheeks. "Yosef Haramati?"[72]

"Yes. I saw you rise. I was worried."

She wipes her eyes on her sleeve. "I thought a walk might ease my belly."

"You shouldn't be outside alone. Let me escort you."

I trot to catch up with her, and she says, "Thank you for protecting Yeshu tonight. If someone in the crowds had recognized him, and reported his whereabouts to the Temple, he could have been killed, as he almost was last Chanukah."

Maryam shivers at the memory.

They'd made a clandestine trip to Yerushalaim so that Yeshua could pray in Herod's Temple. He'd been caught by Temple authorities in the Portico of Solomon, and they'd demanded that he state plainly whether or not he was the mashiah. *It was obviously a plot to arrest him. Had Yeshua said yes, he would have been declaring himself king, and they would have arrested him for sedition. Instead, he'd told them that they couldn't believe because they were not among his sheep, whereupon they'd picked up rocks to stone him. Yeshua had fled back across the Jordan to their hiding place at Wadi el-Yabis, barely escaping with his life.*

We stand for a time, side-by-side, gazing out at the golden city lights.

As night deepens, the lamps in the houses begin to go out and the starlight seems brighter, reflecting from the cobblestone streets, turning them into a tangled necklace of silver beads.

With tears in her voice, she says, "He wasn't supposed to have to do this alone. All of the prophecies said there would be two. 'For the Lord will raise up from Levi someone as high priest and from Judah someone as king,'" she quotes from the Testament of the Twelve Patriarchs, *and puts a hand to her mouth to still the cries that climb her throat.*

I give her a few moments to gather herself, before saying, "Yes, I know, two 'sons of oil,' two mashiahs *to usher in the Kingdom."*[73]

She whispers, "The murder of Yohanan was so unexpected."[74]

"There is still time," I remind her. "If the calculations of the Essenes are correct the Kingdom will not arrive for another three years. Perhaps, before then, another mashiah will appear, and there will indeed be 'two sons of oil' to bring about the End."

"I pray it is so," she murmured. "But what of the next few days, Yosef? Have you heard more?"

I let out a breath and nod. "Kaiaphas has sent word telling every Council member to be prepared to attend a meeting of utmost urgency. I suspect it regards Yeshua, but no one has said this. If it does, I will, of course, try to exert some influence on the course of events. No Council member wants to see him harmed, Maryam. If Rome tries to take action against him, the Council will do everything it can to keep him from disaster. The last thing we need with Pesach approaching is for one of the people's most beloved teachers to be arrested. If Rome wants a riot, that's the way to start it."

She folds her arms tightly across her breast. "I don't know, Yosef. The Law forbids us to leave our homes on the holy days. If they did try to harm Yeshu on Pesach or on the Sabbath, who among us would be brave enough to violate the Law and go outside to object?"

"I would."

She gives me a tearful smile. In a shaky voice, she says, "Yosef . . . can't you speak with Yeshu? Try to convince him to run away?" Her inner struggle is plain on her face. It makes my heart ache. "Just for a short time, Yosef. Convince him to return to the Galil where he's safe. Tell him whatever you must . . . perhaps you have a sick relative there who needs healing? He would run to help, you know he would." With effort she steadies her voice. "I haven't much money left, but if there's someone you need to pay, to pretend to be sick, I can borrow from Yoanna—"

"Maryam." She lifts her dark eyes to me. "I have already tried. Many times. He refuses to even consider it. He says he must be here. Now."

"Yes, yes, I know. But I'm just—"

I fill in the rest. "Desperate. I understand, but perhaps he's right. Have you thought of that? Maybe he does need to be here for this Pesach. He's very wise. Have confidence in his judgment."

A sudden chill leaves her trembling. She rubs her cold arms. "He's trapped, Yosef. Don't you see that? If he runs away, it proves he is not the Annointed One. His flock will accuse him of being a false mashiah."

"There are other choices."

"What choices?" Anxiety lines her face, as if she is haunted by a gnawing dread that will not leave her alone.

"He can stand up to Rome and explain that his kingdom is not of this earth. Rome is only threatened by earthly kings with human armies. He has neither."

Somewhere a goat bleats, followed by the barking of a dog.

Maryam whispers, "Yosef, there's something I must discuss with you."

"What is it?"

"I have one final favor—" Maryam turns sharply.

I jerk around to follow her gaze, and glimpse a man in the shadows to our right. He moves swiftly around the corner of the house and is gone.

"Do you think that was Kepha?" she whispers.

Her fear seems to shiver the very air we breathe.

"He was very tall. That's all I could tell. It might have been Cleopas, or even a Roman soldier. What makes you think it was Kepha?"

In a whisper, she answers, "Because he's always spying. Always listening."

I take her by the arm and start back up the hill, not willing to wait to find out. "Let's return to our room, Maryam. It's too dangerous to stand out here alone in the darkness."

TWENTY-TWO

Pappas Meridias stood beside the long table with his arms crossed. His black robe almost blended with the deep hues of the walnut and stood out in stark contrast to the gray stone walls. All around him, dusty shelves filled with scrolls and codices rose to twice his height—the weight relieved only by tiny windows high up on the walls. The church library in Alexandria was quiet, which seemed to magnify his voice.

"Did you follow our plan?"

Loukas nodded. "You said if we were captured we should tell them you were headed to Caesarea. I did."

Meridias ran his hand over the table. Though it had recently been polished with oil, dust coated his fingertips. He longed to return to Rome, where cleanliness prevailed. Out here, everything was filthy, all the time. He didn't know how people lived in such squalor. But, of course, they were peasants, common laborers. Perhaps they did not notice.

He wiped his hand on his robe and said, "Do you think they believed you?"

"Yes, Pappas. I heard them talking. The old man, Barnabas, was worried about his friend Eusebios."

"As we knew he would be. They may not, however, head straight for the library.

"Why not?"

"Pappas Athanasios, the patriarch here, has no love for Eusebios. He tells me that two of Eusebios' former library assistants live between here and Caesarea."

"And you think Barnabas may try to contact them?"

"It's possible. One lives near Agrippias, the other in Apollonia."

"Do you wish me to seek out these men?"

"I haven't decided. The man near Agrippias is said to be an old hermit. No one here knows exactly where he might be found. He apparently roams from one cave to another, constantly moving. The other, in Apollonia, would be easier to locate. He's a local hero, a street preacher of some renown."

Loukas waited for instructions.

Meridias examined him. The man's tan, coarsely woven robe was torn in several places, and his face looked raw. Red and hideously swollen, he might have been caught in a sandstorm far from home and his face scoured to a bloody pulp. He also walked stiffly, and stood as though tender.

"Atinius had a reputation for being able to make men talk."

Loukas stared dully at Meridias. "Centurion Atinius knows the frailties of men."

"Yes, I'm sure our many wars taught him well."

"The woman, she was the worst. She . . ."

His voice trailed away, and Meridias frowned. "Did you tell them anything else?"

Anger stirred the icy depths of Loukas' eyes, but he calmly answered, "They already know you are behind the attack on their monastery. There was nothing else I could tell them. You have given me no information as to what we are searching for."

That was, of course, true, at least about the critical information—of which Meridias knew precious little himself. Meridias had been carefully instructed to tell the Militia Templi only what was necessary for them to accomplish their holy missions. Loukas had just demonstrated the wisdom of that.

"I have outlined the new plan. Pappas Athanasios has offered to send some of his best men to accompany you. Do you have any objections?"

"Not if they are truly skilled."

"Good. I have arranged for transport to Jerusalem. I leave at noon today. Pappas Athanasios has graciously supplied you with clean clothing and supplies for your journey. I'll have them delivered to your cell. You may go and ready yourself. As to the hermit and the preacher, I'll let you know when I've decided their fates."

Loukas shifted, clearly wanting to say something.

"What is it?"

"Pappas, when this is over, if you choose to reward me, as you so often and generously do, I would like to own the washerwoman, Kalay."

Meridias made an airy gesture with his hand. "So long as she remains ignorant of that which we seek, you may do with her as you wish."

A tiny, frightening smile touched the man's lips.

"What of your wounds, Loukas? Can you ride?"

"I can ride."

Loukas bowed at the waist, winced, and stiffly headed for the massive door. As he swung it open, a cool breeze blew into the room, fluttering the ancient pages that cluttered the shelves.

Meridias watched the dust swirl up from the table and glitter as it re-settled over his shoulders. Irritated, he brushed at it and turned his attention to the library. Heresy was everywhere. One by one, he removed books from the shelves, and placed them on the table.

Before this day was through, each would be burned.

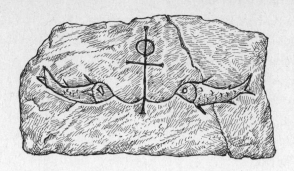

TWENTY-THREE

Kalay gazed up at the stars that glittered across the heavens as she dipped a cup of water from the still pool beneath the palms. Though Cyrus, not knowing this part of the country, had advised against stopping, they were all bitterly tired. If the horses didn't rest, the poor beasts would collapse.

Barnabas slept curled on the sand five paces away, his head pillowed on the book bag. To his right, Zarathan looked like nothing more than a knot of bunched cloth. The star gleam had bleached their faces a ghostly white.

Cyrus sat beside the pool with his prayer rope in his hands, his sword within easy reach. He was struggling mightily with himself. She could see it in every tight line of his face, plus he kept knotting and unknotting his prayer rope. In the past hour, he'd filled it with knots ten times, untied them all, and started the process over again. Just now, it rested on his drawn-up knee. He tied a knot, lowered the rope to the sand, grimaced at it, tied another knot. Finally, he gripped the prayer rope in hard fists.

As she walked back, she said, "Planning on using that to hang yourself?"

"Hmm?" He looked up her as though he'd forgotten she was there.

She sat down beside him and pointed to his hands. "I'm talking about the way you're wringing the life out of your prayer rope."

He relaxed his grip.

"Cyrus, you didn't have any choice. Except you could have quickly slipped a dagger between the ribs of that worm-ridden, cold-eyed *mamzer*, before we got scared off. In fact, you should have, but you didn't. I don't understand why you're lashing yourself so."

His shoulder-length black curly hair hung around his handsome face in sweat-soaked locks, tangling with his beard and mustache. "You wouldn't understand."

In the distance, their horses placidly nipped the grasses at the edge of the pool. The bony beasts needed every scrap of nourishment they could find.

"Try me."

He tied another knot. "I don't want to talk about it."

"When a man says that it means he's ashamed of something."

The desperation in his gaze made her feel as though she were being impaled. "Go away."

A gust of wind blew through the oasis, tousling the palm fronds and fluttering red hair over her eyes. Kalay caught the strands with one hand and held them until the gust passed on. "Well, if you want my opinion, you're being a fool. You had two choices. You could have let those foul sicarii kill your brothers and me, or you could have killed them first. Do you truly think your God would rather have us dead and Loukas and his boys drinking and whoring?"

The lines at the corners of his eyes deepened. "What worries me"—he paused and tied another knot—"is that I fell back into my old life as easily as though I'd never taken vows, never dedicated my life to following my Lord's teachings."

"Ah. I see."

"Do you? My Lord would have preferred that I avoid the situation altogether. That was my failure."

"So you should have run away?"

"No, I . . ." He heaved a deep sigh. "I don't know what I should have done. I only know that what I did was wrong."

It was clear that he keenly felt the weight of the lives he'd taken, despite the fact that he'd saved four in the process. It was unfathomable to her, but she said, "You didn't start this, Cyrus. Your church did. You protected your friends the only way you knew how. And, I might add, did it with remarkable skill."

He twisted his prayer rope and gazed out at the starlight glimmering from the pool. "You're not helping much."

"Well, talking a man out of his guilt takes a while. I need more time."

As he lifted his eyes to the trail they had ridden in on, he said, "I swear I've seen him before."

"Who?"

" 'Loukas,' if that was his name."

Kalay frowned. "Where have you seen him?"

"I'm not sure. Maybe in the army."

"Did you serve with him?"

Cyrus cocked his head, as though trying to recall. "I remember the face of every man in my century, as well as every name. If I did serve with him his appearance is much changed, and he's using a different name."

"Why would that be?"

He tied his prayer rope to his belt, as though finished for the night. "He may have been very young when I knew him. Or he could be a member of a secret military or religious order that requires such changes. Altering one's appearance and undergoing a name change is symbolic of giving up your old life and accepting your new duties and responsibilities."

She pondered that for a moment, considering how similar it was to Christian baptism. "What secret military orders?"

He dropped his head into his hands and massaged his temples. "All I can tell you is that there are many, and they share a common belief that paradise lies in the shadow of swords."

"Do you think Loukas is some sort of grand master?"

His gaze shot in her direction as though even that knowledge was reserved to a select few.

Kalay took a drink of water. It had a clean, earthy taste that pleased her. "Men love to strut and preen when they're attempting to impress a woman, Cyrus. They drink too much. They brag about their importance. Most mistake divulging a secret with intimacy." She let him digest what that meant and took another drink of the cool water. "Do you think the man in charge is Roman?"

"Almost certainly. There has always been discord between Egypt and Rome, which makes me wonder if this doesn't go all the way to Bishop Silvester of Rome."[75]

"Who is he?"

"The right hand of Emperor Constantine."

"You mean he's the emperor's lackey?"

"Yes."

He rose and walked to the pool to fill his water cup. For a big man, he moved with the silence and grace of a leopard. Dust coated his black hair and white robe, and she could see his powerful shoulder muscles flexing beneath the dirty fabric as he lowered his cup to the pool.

Kalay stretched out on her side and propped her head on her hand. Zarathan had started to snore. In response, Barnabas flopped to his opposite side.

Kalay tipped her head toward Barnabas. "I found it curious that the old monk did not try to stop us when we were questioning 'Loukas.'"

Cyrus walked back and sat down beside her. "As did I. I expected him to intervene."

"To spare you?" she asked bluntly.

Cyrus closed his eyes as if at a sudden stab of pain. "Did no one ever teach you subtlety?"

She shrugged. "It's easier on people in the long run if you're just frank."

Cyrus swallowed a gulp of water, before he said, "I wouldn't know. It's something I've never tried."

"Well, you're probably afraid of hurting other people's feelings. I'm a beast."

"That hasn't been my impression."

As they stared at each other, conflicting emotions danced across his face. The longing in his gaze touched her. Irritated with himself, he looked away.

Softly, he said, "Forgive me."

"For what?"

"I know you don't like to be stared at."

"It's all right. You can't help it. I'm the most beautiful woman you've ever seen." She the repeated words she'd heard a thousand times.

The lines at the corners of his eyes crinkled with amusement. "Actually, you're not."

She pulled back as though shocked and dismayed, then said, "Does that mean I won't have to worry about you creeping into my blankets some night?"

He smiled.

Kalay drained her water cup and set it aside. The more time she and Cyrus spent together, the more the attraction between them grew, though it was a reluctant attraction on his part. As for her part . . .

As the silence lengthened, Cyrus' smile faded and he frowned down at the chipped clay cup in his hands. "I wish it were that simple. You and I know it's not. May I tell you something? It may make things easier between us."

"Of course. I can stand rejection."

It seemed to take a long time before he decided which words to use. "I had a wife once, a long time ago. I still miss her. When I'm truly tormented, she comes to me in my dreams. We talk. We laugh. I cannot tell you how very much I crave the tenderness of her touch." His jaw clenched. "There are times when I look at you . . ."

He stopped.

Kalay carefully asked, "What was her name?"

"Spes."

"Like the Roman goddess?"

"Yes."

"Is she the woman more beautiful than me?"

Old pain tightened his eyes. "She was."

The agony in his voice went straight to her heart. "Did she have red hair, like mine?"

He nodded.

She had heard this story many times. *"You remind me of my lost childhood love . . . my dead wife . . . the woman I could never have . . ."* The words always came out in a tormented voice.

Sympathetically, she said, "Then it's natural that I remind you of her. But I'm not her. And no man on earth would describe me as 'tender,' Cyrus. Now that you realize your heart is just hoping too hard, let it go."

"I *am* trying."

"I know you are, and you're a valiant warrior." She reached over to playfully slap his cheek. "You'll get over me."

She rose to her feet. "I'm going to bed now. Don't follow me."

As she walked away, he laughed and shook his head.

Kalay curled up on the sand at the base of a palm tree, and used her arm as a pillow. The fragrance of the water and sound of the wind rustling the fronds was soothing.

Cyrus sat for a time, staring at the pool, before he got to his feet, picked up his sword, and belted it on. As he walked past her, he halted briefly to say, "That was an unexpected kindness. Thank you."

"Get some rest, Cyrus."

"I will. Later."

He continued up the trail to the top of the dune where he could watch the approaches that led to the oasis. They made dark, sinuous lines through the sand.

When she woke in the middle of the night, he was still standing there like a soldier on duty, staring out at the starlit desert.

Forget it, the last thing you need is a man.

But when she rolled over and closed her eyes again, he was smiling in her dreams.

THE TEACHING ON THE BEAST

"All of our lives we tiptoe around him, afraid lest he wake. I tell you now, brother, it is absolutely necessary to awaken the Beast, for it is only when we are crouching in that dark pit of terror, shivering and lost, that we clearly hear God calling and run toward the resurrection."

TWENTY-FOUR

Sand blew across the dusk-shadowed trail in glittering veils. They'd alternately ridden and walked all day and were bone-weary, but their horses were in much worse condition. When the lathered animals had started to stumble at sunset, they'd gotten off and started leading them. As she walked, Kalay stroked her horse's flank, speaking gently to the animal to keep it going, but the trick would not work forever.

She smiled at herself. She was more weary than she'd ever been in her life. The long, exhausting days of washing and drying at the monastery now seemed laughable. At least there, when she'd fallen into bed at night, she'd gone right to sleep, and slept straight through with few worries.

Far in the distance, a thread of deep blue painted the horizon, marking the location of the ocean. Already a salty scent pervaded the air.

"Cyrus," she said, "we should find water and camp for the night."

"Yes. Soon."

The trail dove off the edge of a dune. As Cyrus cautiously led the horse down, she walked out front.

Brother Barnabas tugged on his horse's lead rope, pulling the animal closer to Cyrus. His gray hair, soiled with dust and sweat, appeared darker, which gave his deeply sunken eyes a haunted look. She feared that if they did not find a place to rest for a few days, and soon, he would be ill, or worse.

"My old friend, Libni, lives just south of Agrippias," Barnabas said to Cyrus.

"How far south?"

Barnabas pointed a gnarled finger. "There. Somewhere."

Cyrus shifted to study the broken distance, a terrain of dark jutting rock, stony flats, and occasional dunes. Twisted lines of wadis, drainages, carved their way toward the west. "You don't know exactly where he lives?"

"No, but I have a good general idea. Once or twice a year, he sends me letters through traders."

"Have you ever written him back?" Zarathan called from where he walked in the rear.

"Three times in the past twenty years traders have been able to deliver letters for me."

Zarathan scratched at the blond fuzz that he called a beard. "You've only written him three times in twenty years?"

"No. I write him every month, but Libni is very hard to find."

"Then what makes you think we can do it?"

"Libni described the area for me," Barnabas said. "When we reach the branch in the road just west of Gaza, I'll lead."

Cyrus nodded.

The horses panted and licked at their lips, as though desperately thirsty.

"Brother Barnabas," she said, "you clearly know these roads. How long before we reach water?"

"Not long. Around the first hour of night, we'll pass by a pool outside of Gaza. We can let our horses drink there, and drink our fill ourselves."

Eagerly Zarathan asked, "Will we camp there? I'm starving."

Barnabas turned to Cyrus, the question in his eyes.

Cyrus said, "I don't know. I'll have to scout it first. If it's too close to the town, I think we should move on."

"It is close to town, or at least it was when I last passed through Gaza over twenty years ago."

The dune flattened out, and Barnabas fell into line behind them again. Kalay could hear him talking softly to Zarathan.

She gently stroked her horse's flank, apologizing for the fact that he would have to walk for another hour without a drink. At the feel of her hand, the bay swiveled his head to look at her.

"It's all right," she soothed. "It won't be long now."

The horse shook his head, and she wondered if it wasn't his way of re-marking, *That's what you said an hour ago.*

Cyrus patted the horse's neck. "Kalay, I have a question for you. It's about the papyrus. Did you notice that the word *Selah* breaks the pattern?"

"I did. All of the other names, with the exception of the name for God, begin with the letter *m.*"

"I don't think that's a coincidence. Do you?" He swiveled to look at her as best he could.

"No. I suspect every letter means something."

"Do you have any idea why that word breaks the pattern?"

"Well, for one thing, it's the seventh word."

"The seventh word? Why is that important?"

She frowned at the back of his head. "Have you ever studied the He-brew prophecies?"

"Some. Why?"

"The number seven is a sort of divine cipher. For example, along with the break, I also noticed that if you total all the letters through Selah, there are forty-three, which, when added together, four plus three, equal seven."

"So? What does it mean?"

"Will you just listen for a moment? There are another twenty-eight let-ters after Selah, which equals ten. Two plus eight."

Cyrus didn't say anything, but she could see he was thinking about it. "Are the numbers seven and ten important?"

"Well, yes," Kalay answered, a little taken aback. "Because seven times ten is seventy."

She gave him time to consider the implications while she watched a whirlwind spin across the road ahead of them. It was small, without much strength, and faded to a gust of sand a short time later.

"Seventy," he repeated as though he had no idea what she was talking about.

Kalay sighed. "Think of the Book of Daniel."

Cyrus paused. "Ah. You mean the Seventy Weeks prophecy about the appointed End of Time?"

"Yes. Daniel prophesied that there would follow seventy weeks of years after the destruction of Jerusalem by the Babylonians before the messiah came. Jerusalem was destroyed in the Jewish year 3284. One Sabbatical year equaled one 'week,' or seven ordinary years. The total period then, seventy times seven, was four hundred and ninety years. The final Sabbatical year, that is the *last seven years of the world,* began around the year, on your calendar, of twenty-six or twenty-seven. Your Lord and his followers believed the world was going to end in the year thirty-three or thirty-four."[76]

Cyrus pulled the horse to a sudden stop. "I didn't know that."

"You would if you were Jewish. As your Lord was."

That seemed to stun him.

Barnabas pulled his horse forward, glanced between them, and his elderly face tensed. "What's wrong?"

"Kalay and I were talking about the papyrus. The seventh word, Selah, breaks the pattern, and if you total all the letters through Selah it equals forty-three. Which—"

"When added together," Barnabas interrupted, "totals seven. What else?"

"Kalay also noticed that there are twenty-eight letters after Selah, which—"

"Equals ten, and ten times seven is seventy."

Cyrus' mouth hung ajar. "You knew?"

"That the papyrus might refer to the Seventy Weeks prophecy in Daniel, yes. But keep in mind that Selah could also be a simple musical stop. There are many *selahs* in the Psalms, for example, and that is what they are. When poems were sung, there had to be musical stops."

Cyrus' gaze fixed on the horizon, as though it was a centering point for his thoughts. "But, it could also mean the papyrus is about the End of the World."

"Or the appearance of the messiah, who is supposed to herald the End," Barnabas said.

Zarathan peered around Barnabas' shoulder. It amazed Kalay that his blue eyes retained their perpetual look of surprise. You'd think, after what they'd been through, he'd have gotten over that.

In a grave voice, Zarathan said, "The papyrus map leads to the End of the World? I'm not sure I like that."

Cyrus said, "I thought you longed for the coming of the Kingdom?"

"Well, yes, of course, I do. It's just that the End of the World sounds so final."

Barnabas wiped his sweating forehead on his dirty sleeve. "Don't worry, Zarathan. We don't even know that it is a map."

Cyrus whispered, "The year 27. Isn't that the year our Lord began his ministry?"

Barnabas nodded. "Probably, although it might have been the year 28, or even 29, depending upon which gospel you believe."[77]

The last gleam of dusk faded, and as twilight settled over the desert, the shadows of the dunes took on a faintly purple hue.

Cyrus said, "It's no wonder our Lord says his own generation would live to see the Apocalypse, and Petros wrote that the end of all things was at hand. They truly believed that they had accurately calculated the Seventy Weeks prophecy."

"And I'm sure they did," Kalay noted, perhaps a little too gleefully. "Unfortunately, the prophecy was bunk, and you monkish fools have wasted three centuries waiting for the End, instead of living fruitful lives the way God intended."

The tone in her voice must have frightened the horses. They both stamped and shook their heads, jingling their reins, which sounded loud in the desert quiet.

Barnabas patted his horse's neck. He whispered something Kalay couldn't hear, but the animal calmed down.

As night descended, the wind became a soft purl, and she could smell the ocean again.

Zarathan glared at Kalay. "You are so hateful! At every opportunity you demean our religion. Why is that?"

Kalay's brows arched. "Because it's a well-known fact that he whom the gods wish to destroy they first make Believers."

"What?" Zarathan glanced at his brothers, hoping they would explain the comment.

Instead, Barnabas said, "We're all tired. Let's get to Gaza."

It took another half hour before they reached the pool that Barnabas had recalled. It turned out to be inside the city walls. As they rode their horses through the gate, they smelled the sweet fragrances of boiled goat and fresh bread. The spring had been rocked in, creating a tank of crystal-clear water.

They dismounted and let their horses drink while they dipped up water with their cupped hands. Drinking his fill, Barnabas sighed and patted his book bag, as if the gazelle leather were the cherished hide of an old friend.

The sounds of the city carried: dogs barking, supper dishes clacking and rattling. Somewhere a man let out a big, throaty laugh and, when a baby cried, a woman scolded him.

Kalay sat on the lip of the tank and let her gaze drift over the softly lit flat-topped houses. At some point, probably soon, she imagined they would close the city gates, but for now, people seemed occupied with feeding their families.

"They were thirsty," Barnabas noted as he watched the horses drinking. "But we shouldn't stay long. It's too risky."

"We'll find food first, though, won't we?" Zarathan's voice was a whine. He looked from man to man.

Kalay studied them. Their faces had changed dramatically since that deadly night in the monastery. All of the serenity and faith that had softened their features were gone. Barnabas' wrinkles had frozen into determined lines, as though he'd been given a sacred mission and would not fail to accomplish it. Zarathan's eyes darted about like a scared cat's. If he'd had a tail it would be switching as he ran for cover. And Cyrus . . . Cyrus was simply the man in charge. Their safety depended upon him and he knew it, and would do whatever was necessary to keep them from harm. They had, she supposed, returned to their former selves, before their lives in the monastery.

"Brothers?" Zarathan pressed. "We *are* going to eat here, aren't we?"

"There's no time," Cyrus said. "Just get your fill of water so that we can leave."

Zarathan let out a pained groan and cupped another handful of water.

"Don't worry," Barnabas said. "I'm sure Libni will feed us when we arrive. He was always very generous—if a bit odd."

"What do you mean, "odd"?" Zarathan asked suspiciously.

"Oh, he's a very spiritual man . . . not often in contact with this world, that's all."

Kalay took the opportunity to wash her face and throat. The horses were still drinking, but their eyes were half closed, as though in relief. The pungent smell of the animals' sweat comforted her, bringing back memories of her childhood and her family's barn. Memories of a happiness that seemed unreal now.

"Are you finished?" Cyrus said, rushing them. His eyes had narrowed as they scanned the dirt streets, moving from house to house, lingering on every unusual shadow.

"Yes," Barnabas said with a deep sigh. "I just—"

A man came out a doorway with a jug and headed for the well. He had a mass of curly brown hair and a full beard that obscured most of his face. But his eyes crinkled at the corners, as though he were contemplating something pleasant or amusing. He didn't even look startled when he saw them, just dipped his jug into the water, and said, "May the peace of Iesous be with you."

Barnabas replied, "And with you, also."

The man turned and started back for his house, but stopped when Barnabas called, "Forgive me, sir. We could use your help."

Water splashed from his jug when he turned to face Barnabas. "What is it you require?"

Zarathan hissed, "Ask about food."

Barnabas pulled a rolled scroll from his book bag and walked forward. "I have a letter that I must get to Jerusalem. Would you mind giving it to someone who is headed there? Perhaps a caravan? This is very important."

The man took the scroll, read the name written on it, and said, "They'll want payment."

"Forgive me, I have no money. We—"

"Here's a tetradrachma," Kalay said as she pulled the coin from the purse tied to her belt and tossed it to him. He caught it awkwardly in the same hand that held the scroll.

The man nodded. "I'll see what I can do."

"We're deeply grateful," Barnabas said. "Also, if you have a moment more, we're looking for an old friend of ours. He's a wandering hermit who lives somewhere near here. His name is Libni and he—"

"Ah, Old Scary. Yes, I know of him. Is he in some kind of trouble? You're the second person today who's asked where he lives."

Barnabas stiffened. His head trembled on the stem of his neck, but he forced strength into his voice. "No, no trouble. We're just worried about him. I heard he was ill. Do you know where he lives these days? He roams about, I know, but—"

"He used to roam about, but not any longer." The man hesitated, and his gaze went over each of them, as though evaluating whether or not he believed them. Apparently three travel-grubby monks and a woman were no threat, for he said, "He lives two or three hours south of here, depending upon how fast you want to ride. There's a pillar of rock and two humps of stone nearby. A most male-appearing formation, if you catch my meaning. You'll know them when you see them. His caves are obvious."

The man turned back for his house, and Barnabas called, "Thank you, sir. May our Lord's blessings fall upon you."

The man lifted a hand, opened his door, and disappeared into a warm yellow glow and the laughter of children.

"What was in that scroll?" Zarathan asked.

"A pleasantry to an old friend. Never mind. We must hurry." Barnabas threw the book bag up and tugged on his horse's lead rope. "If we're the second people today to ask about him, he may be in danger." Barnabas tugged again, trying to pull his horse away from the well, but the animal lingered a time longer, getting in a few more gulps, before it surrendered.

Cyrus took his horse and followed Barnabas out the gate. Zarathan rushed out on his heels.

Kalay took one last look at the brightly lit houses, and tried to remember what it was like to be part of a family. From a locked chamber deep inside her, she heard her little brother's voice, and her mother's laughter. . . .

"Kalay?" Cyrus called. "We're leaving."

"Yes," she said as she got to her feet. "I'm coming."

TWENTY-FIVE

Magdiel

"Master? Master, forgive me, you must wake."

I feel the hand on my shoulder and groggily open my eyes to see Titus. There is a brief moment of elation. . . .

I'm dreaming. I must be dreaming.

"What's wrong?" I throw off my blankets and get to my feet, breathing hard.

"A messenger arrived moments ago. High Priest Kaiaphas summons you to his house for an emergency meeting of the Council of Seventy-one."

Only one other such emergency meeting has ever been held. One hundred years ago, High Priest Shimon ben Shetah held an emergency meeting that resulted in the hangings of eighty witches in a single day. That meeting had been a matter of national urgency and convened only to save the people of Yisrael.[78]

"Why? What happened?"

"The Rab has been arrested."

As I pull my sleeping shirt over my head and hurry to tug on my finest blue linen robe, I'm panting, on the verge of trembling. "Who arrested Yeshua? The Council or the Romans?"

"The Romans. Apparently the Rab sent Yudah Sicarius to tell the praefectus

where to find him. The praefectus then dispatched a tribune with a decuria to arrest the Rab for treason, but before—"

"Treason!" I shout in disbelief. "That's impossible. Sedition, yes, but not treason."

"The charge is treason, Master. Kaiaphas was notified of the warrant just before the soldiers left, and begged the praefectus to allow several members of the Temple police to accompany the Romans. The messenger said Kaiaphas also gained permission to bring the Rab back to his house for the night. I don't know why Pilatos agreed."

"The praefectus prefers for us to hold our own prisoners overnight to avoid the many dietary and other complications of looking after Jewish prisoners. Has the praefectus set the trial time?"

"The first hour of the morning."

As I'm shoving my feet into my sandals, Titus calmly walks to pull my himation from its peg by the doorway to my bedchamber, and holds it open for me.

I tie my sandal laces, and say, "Was anyone else arrested? Maryam?"

If Yeshua was arrested because he was accused of treason, surely his disciples, his confessed followers, had also been arrested on the same charge. The praefectus would never allow such men to go free to continue conspiring against Rome.

Titus shakes his head. "There were no warrants for anyone else. But the arrest was not without complications."

"What do you mean?"

"Apparently, Kepha panicked when a member of the Temple police tried to lay a hand upon the Rab, and he used his sword to cut off the man's ear."

"So they arrested Kepha." I hurry across the room and slip my himation over my shoulders.

"No. He was not arrested."

I shake my head as though I didn't hear him right. "Your information must be wrong. He assaulted an officer in the conduct of his official Temple duties. They must have arrested him."

"The messenger said the police and the decuria were both under strict orders to arrest no one but the Rab. They let Kepha go free."

"They didn't even detain him for questioning?"

"No."

This astounds me. If they truly fear Yeshua is plotting against Rome, nothing can be accomplished by arresting him alone. His disciples have been instructed to continue his teachings even if—especially if—Yeshua dies.

"Then . . ." I stare at Titus dumbly, still half asleep. "It is Yeshua alone who will stand trial before the praefectus in the morning?"

"That's what the messenger told me."

"It doesn't make any sense," I whisper as I rush past Titus to grab my brush and attempt to make myself presentable. "Saddle my horse. I'll be right out."

Titus bows and leaves.

By the time I have splashed water on my face, and brushed my hair, I am shaking. The charge of treason is totally unexpected. Rome may have seen the Rab's recent activities as stirring up dissent, but then the charge would be sedition. What evidence could the praefectus possibly have that would support a charge of treason? Not only that, it had to be new information. The Romans could have arrested Yeshua at any time in the past few days when he was openly preaching in the Temple. They didn't. Something else is going on, something I don't understand.

I run through my house and out my door to my horse.[79]

TWENTY-SIX

El

My home is all the way across the city from the high priest's grand palace on Mount Zion. I have to ride hard through the twisting streets of Yerushalaim to get there. As I round the last bend, I see the fine bastions and heavy stonework. The entire palace is aglow. There must be hundreds of oil lamps burning.

I slow Lightning to a trot and ride through the gate into the vast, cobble-stoned courtyard where I dismount in a flurry, tie my horse to the hitching rail beside dozens of other horses, and stride for the massive front doors of the palace.

Ahead of me, several men sit around a fire in the middle of the courtyard, talking, laughing. All wear the uniforms of the Temple police, except one very tall man.

I stumble when I recognize Kepha sitting with the police as though nothing at all has happened this terrible night.[80]

I do not stop to speak with him, nor does he glance my way as I run up the steps toward the massive oak doors where two guards stand beneath flaring torches.

But I wonder.

Less than one hour ago, Kepha sliced off the ear of one of the officers sent to arrest Yeshua, but here he sits, totally unafraid of retribution, smiling, talking with the man's fellows.

I hurry by a servant girl carrying a jug of water and lift my hand to the guard standing outside the doors.

"Councilor," the man greets, "please enter."

"Thank you, Alexander," I say as I walk through the doors into the palace.

One of Kaiaphas' servants—I don't know his name—an elderly man of regal bearing, immediately intercepts my path. He wears a pale green linen tunic belted at the waist with a braided leather cord. "They are in the Council chamber, sir. Please, this way."

I allow myself to be led, though I know the way as well as any other member of the Seventy-one. The opulence of the palace always stuns me. Everywhere I look there are smaller versions of the artworks that fill the Temple: stunning mosaics depicting endless flowing patterns interspersed with extensive series of faunal and floral motifs: lions, oxen, cherubim, palm trees, and wreaths. At regular intervals stand costly carved wooden panels, jewel-inlaid, and ten cubits tall, bearing the names of the twelve tribes of Yisrael, and beside them cluster olive-wood lamp stands overlaid with pure gold. The lamp stands glitter with a fiery intensity when the lamps flicker. Just outside the Council door, on the southeast corner of the chamber, stands an enormous basin called the "molten sea." It is filled with water. The basin rests upon four sets of bronze oxen, each facing a different direction.

I kneel before the basin, and softly recite, "Shema Yisrael, the Lord our God, the Lord is One, and I love the Lord my God with all my heart, and with all my soul, and with all my mind, and with all my strength," then I dip my hands and wash them before I rise and pick up one of the towels to dry them.

The slave bows at the waist and backs away.

When I open the door to the Council chamber, dozens of voices flood over me. Men turn to look, then go back to their conversations. I pull my himation up over my head and enter the chamber.

This chamber is thirty cubits square. Four rows of stepped benches line three walls, facing the center. The benches are filled with men, though many still stand. They, too, look as though they hastily rose from their beds and hurried here. Eyes are puffy with sleep. Many yawn. There are five massive lamp stands on the north side of the chamber and five on the south, each filled with multispouted oil lamps. The fragrance of myrrh is intoxicating.

As I work my way through the crowd toward my seat I glimpse the raised altar to the east upon which the sacred golden table sits. Resting on the table is the "bread of the Presence of God." I start when I see a man dressed in white kneeling before the table. His himation is pulled over his head, as is proper and respectful, so I can't see his face, but I know it is Yeshua. Four guards surround him.

"Councilmen," I say as I take my seat between the esteemed Pharisaic scholar, Gamliel, and the brash Sadducean merchant, Shimon ben Yehudah.

Gamliel responds, "You are the last man we require, I believe. We can begin as soon as Kaiaphas receives the count."

I jerk a nod. "Yes, good."

Gamliel is forty-two, but his gray hair and thick beard make him look older. His dark eyes are always serious, thoughtful. The man rarely smiles. He is regarded by all as one of the greatest scholars of the Law who has ever lived. Not only that, he is a kind man. He frequently visits criminals in the prison cells below this palace, just to make certain they are well fed and being treated properly. There are those, myself among them, who firmly believe that when Gamliel dies the glory of the Law and the purity of the Way will die with him.

I turn to nod at Shimon. He yawns and nods back.

Shimon is barely thirty, very wealthy, and so ignorant of the Torah that I suspect he got his position by buying it. Not only that, he is extremely handsome, with a sculpted face, large blue eyes, and wavy brown hair. No matter where he goes, women's eyes follow him.

My gaze focuses on Yeshua, and the ache in my heart grows suffocating. What is he thinking? What is he feeling? He knew his arrest was likely, surely he prepared himself for this hour, but I cannot imagine how.

Shimon leans back so he can see Gamliel, and says, "This is highly irregular, eh, Gamliel? We're supposed to start our sessions in the morning and determine them before sunset. Kaiaphas had better have a good reason for pulling me away from family on the eve of a feast day."[81]

With his eyes on Yeshua, Gamliel replies, "I'm sure he has."

"Are you? I've heard rumors that we are about to hold a secret trial to—"

Gamliel interrupts, "It is unlawful for us to try a man at night, or on the *eve of a feast day. This cannot be a* krima. *We cannot hold court. This can only be a* sumboulion, *a Council session. That's all."*

Shimon looks irritated. "Yes, well, I hope you're right, but if so, who are they?" He points to two people who stand almost hidden behind guards across the room.

Gamliel answers, "The Law requires that there be at least two witnesses who can give evidence of a man's guilt or innocence."

"Then it is a trial."

"A man may give evidence outside a trial, Shimon."

"Really? We're just going to interrogate them out of curiosity?"

Gamliel's gray brows draw down over his hooked nose. He turns to look at Shimon, and Shimon's smirk instantly dissolves. "Perhaps you should save your conjecture until you have facts. It would seem a better use of your time."

Shimon flips his hand arrogantly. "Oh, admit it, Gamliel, this is just as much a quandary for you as for me. According to our laws, we cannot interrogate the accused until we've questioned the witnesses, and there is actual evidence against him. On the other hand, according to Roman law it is a crime to question witnesses before the accused has been interrogated. Of course, the Romans hope they can beat a confession out of the accused, which renders witnesses unnecessary. So, if we interrogate these witnesses tonight, can their testimony be used in Yeshua ben Pantera's trial before the praefectus in the morning? Or are we wasting hours we could be spending with our families?"[82]

Voices suddenly rise and men head for their seats as High Priest Yosef Kaiaphas enters the chamber and strides across the floor toward the altar. While he has not worn the sacred breastplate adorned with the twelve precious stones inscribed with the names of the twelve tribes, he is wearing part of the traditional ritual garb of the high priest—a clear sign of the seriousness of this meeting. The ephod is a long garment with shoulder straps composed of fine linen and gold leaf, woven with woolen threads dyed in brilliant shades of blue, purple, and scarlet. Each strap bears an onyx stone inscribed with six of the twelve tribes' names. Under the ephod he wears a blue woolen robe sewn with red linen pomegranates. Golden bells jingle on the fringe. His indigo himation is pulled over his head. For a tall, powerfully built man, he moves gracefully, with dignity. His hair and beard are still coal black. Rumor has it that he is betrothed to the beautiful daughter of Hanan, the former high priest, but no official announcement has been made.

Kaiaphas steps onto the altar and his voice rings out. "Hear, O Lord our God, the voice of our prayers, and have compassion upon us, for you are a gracious and compassionate God. Blessed are you, O Lord, who hears prayers."

Yeshua does not move, but appears to be praying along with the high priest.

When Kaiaphas turns, the chamber goes quiet. He searches each face with his gaze, before saying, "Guards, bring forward Yehoshua ben Pantera."

The guards grip Yeshua's arms, lift him to his feet, and walk him to stand before Kaiaphas. Yeshua's expression is fierce.

Kaiaphas meets his gaze squarely. "Yehoshua ben Pantera, I have received news from Praefectus Pilatos that you stand accused of treason and there will be a trial in the morning." He pauses to let the charge sink in. "Are you guilty of this crime?"

Yeshua doesn't answer.

It is an ancient Jewish rule of ethics that when a man is insulted or demeaned, he should not reply, and that even while being abused, he should keep silent.[83]

Kaiaphas gives him several more moments. When Yeshua still does not respond, Kaiaphas addresses the Council. "I realize that this meeting is an imposition, but I fear that the outcome of ben Pantera's appearance before Pilatos may be fatal, and that could be disastrous for our nation. Therefore, we are here tonight for one reason: to determine on what possible grounds this man could be charged with treason and to find a way to counter those charges."

"Why?" Yohanan ben Yakob shouts in surprise. A bald-headed old man with a deeply wrinkled face, he rises across the chamber. Speaking without first being recognized by the high priest is a breach of protocol. A few men grumble. Yohanan pays them no attention. "Ben Pantera has been insulting us for many years: he neglects fasts, violates Shabbat, and scorns our purity rules. He caused the riot in the Temple precinct just a few days ago that resulted in the arrest of several Zealots, all good men. This morning, two of those men were convicted of treason by Pilatos and condemned to die! Why should we trouble ourselves to save a man who flaunts our authority and spends his time with sinners?"

"Whom he chooses to dine with is not at issue, Councilor," Kaiaphas sternly says. "We must put our personal squabbles with him aside. Ben Pantera has been accused of treason against Rome. That is the issue. We must discover why."

Shimon whispers to me, "Why is Kaiaphas being so generous? He has been one of ben Pantera's most vocal opponents."

"Perhaps he is wiser than you know," I reply.

Hanan, the former high priest who sits beside Yohanan ben Yakob, glowers at Yeshua. Everyone here knows that Hanan's family business is selling lambs and doves for sacrifices,[84] and it was Hanan's five sons who set up their booths on the Temple porches. When Yeshua overturned the tables and occupied the Temple it significantly diminished Hanan's profits. Hanan has been pushing for Yeshua's arrest ever since, but the Council has refused.

Despite his shriveled features, Hanan is a stately man, tall, with thin white hair and a long white beard. His purple robe is belted with a bright blood-red sash.

Shimon leans sideways and says, "Look at Hanan's face. He's such a greedy serpent. He must be biding his time for the best moment to strike."

Kaiaphas quiets the room with one uplifted hand. "Councilors, it is absolutely indispensable that we do everything possible to prevent his execution. Yehoshua ben Pantera is a very popular figure. If he is executed it may well spark the revolt we have feared for many years. If that happens, you can be certain that Rome will respond with catastrophic force. Do you begin to understand? Yerushalaim is filled with festival attendees. Many innocent people will die."

Fabric rustles as men shift positions or hiss to those nearby.

Yeshua has still not raised his head.

Gamliel stands and every eye moves to watch him. "I would ask a question, High Priest."

Kaiaphas nods. "I recognize the esteemed scholar Gamliel."

"There are many rumors flying. Let us clarify our goals here tonight. I assume, from what you have said, that we are here to conduct the preliminary inquiry necessary for establishing the facts of the case for ben Pantera's defense. Is that correct?"

"It is."

Gamliel exhales. "Very well, I'm sure we all have households filled with family who have come from great distances to celebrate the holy days and want to get home. Let us hear the witnesses."

Kaiaphas turns to the guards. "Bring forward Hanoch ben Bani."

The guards lead forward a grisly little man with rotted teeth. His brown robe is filthy, as is the brown himation that covers his greasy black hair. They must have picked him up off the streets. He kneels before Kaiaphas. "I didn't do nothing, High Priest. I swear!"

Kaiaphas says, "You are not here to defend yourself, ben Bani. You are here to give testimony regarding Yehoshua ben Pantera. You told the Temple police that you had spent the past few days listening to ben Pantera preach in the Temple. Did you ever hear him say he wished to overthrow Rome?"

The little man turns wide eyes upon Yeshua. "No, High Priest. He never said nothing of the kind. He said he would destroy the Temple and rebuild it in three days, and there were those who sat with me that thought he meant to use force to do it—the Zealots especially—but that's not what he said."

Old Yohanan lifts his hand and stands again.

Kaiaphas nod. "I recognize Yohanan ben Yakob."

Yohanan says, "Did you ever hear him say he had kingly blood, that he was descended from the House of David?"

Hanoch shakes his head nervously. "No, he never said that. I did hear him arguing with the Pharisees about the mashiah, though."

Kaiaphas asks, "What did he say?"

"He asked the Pharisees if they supposed that the mashiah was the son of David, and when they told him yes, he said that didn't make no sense because David calls the mashiah 'Lord' in the holy books, which meant the mashiah couldn't be his son."[85]

A hushed discussion rises in the chamber.

Above the noise, Yohanan calls out, "Did he ever preach violence? Especially on the day he caused the riot? Was he preaching Zealot doctrines in the Temple?"

In a trembling voice, Hanoch answers, "He told us that a man must love his enemies, and bless them that curse him. I didn't hear nothing about violence."

"Did you see him meeting with any Zealots?"

Ben Bani blinks. "He talked to anyone who came to him. Some were Zealots. But half of everybody here this week is either a Zealot or has sympathies for the Zealots."

While the Councilmen quietly discuss what he'd said, Kaiaphas calls, "Who else has a question for this witness?"

"I do," Shimon says, and stands. His blue eyes narrow. "Did ben Pantera ever say he was the chosen of God prophesied in the holy books?"

Hanoch turns glowing eyes on Yeshua. His voice grows soft and reverent. "No, but I believe it. I was a follower of Yohanan Baptistoi. When they killed him, I knew that Yeshua ben Pantera was the Annointed One of Yisrael that we've been waiting for."

"The one who will overthrow our enemies and reign forever as king?" Shimon asks.

"Yes."

Shimon's mouth curls into an unpleasant smile. "That, I believe, is the source of the treason charge. He does not have to claim to be from the kingly line of David. He only has to say he is the Annointed One and the rest follows. Pilatos will assume he plans to overthrow Rome and set himself up as our king."

My heart flutters, because I know Shimon is right. Treason against Rome is a slippery charge. It can mean many things, from insulting a centurion to rallying an army to charge Rome itself . . . and setting oneself up as a king challenges the divine rule of Tiberias Caesar.

Shimon sits back down and Kaiaphas says, "Yehoshua ben Pantera, would you like to rebut or cross-examine the witness?"

Yeshua remains silent.

"Guards, you may take this witness back and bring forward the Sidonian, Delos," Kaiaphas orders.

The man walks forward without waiting for the guards, which they do not seem happy about as they follow closely on his heels. Delos is perhaps twenty-five, with a long, slender face and pale golden hair. He wears a tan Roman tunic and a white himation over his head.

"I am Delos," he announces when he stands before Kaiaphas. "Ask me your questions."

Kaiaphas gestures for the guards to back away slightly. "You told the police that you came here from Sidon with your sick daughter. Is that—"

"I did," he says. "My daughter had three demons. I came to beg Yeshua ben Pantera to cast them out."

Yohanan lifts his hand, and Kaiaphas nods to recognize him. Yohanan says, "Did you ever see him speaking with Zealots?"

"No."

Kaiaphas continues this line of questioning. "Did he cast the demons from your daughter?"

"Yes, High Priest. My six-year-old daughter is well for the first time in her life."

"Have you ever heard him preach that Rome, or Roman officials, should be overthrown through violent means?"

The Sidonian opens his mouth to respond, but stops. He seems to be thinking about the question.

"I urge you to answer the question truthfully," Kaiaphas instructs.

Clearly uncomfortable, Delos says, "I heard him say that he had come not to bring peace but a sword, but I took that to mean—"

From across the room, Hanan quietly interrupts, "I think we all know what that means."

Delos desperately turns to Yeshua. "This man works miracles through the power of God! He is one of the sacred 'sons of oil' promised to us by our ancient prophets. If you were wise, you would release him and sneak him out of the city before the Romans can get their filthy hands upon him!"

Hanan says, "High Priest, may I comment?"

Kaiaphas nods.

Hanan stands. "There are those who say he heals through the power of Beelzebub, that he casts out demons by demons. How does Pantera respond to these charges?"

"Ben Pantera," Kaiaphas says, "do you do your magic through the power of evil or good?"

Yeshua stands quietly with his head down.

One of the Temple policemen strikes him with the palm of his hand. "Answer the high priest."

Yeshua clenches his jaw for a long moment. Finally, he says, "If I have done things through evil, show me the evidence of the evil. If you have no evidence, why do you let him strike me?"

"Look at his manner!" Hanan calls in a loud voice. "He believes he is the Annointed One and expects us to bow down to his authority. In the eyes of the people, as well as the praefectus, such an act will confirm the very charges of which he may stand accused: that he claims to be a king!"

Conversations break out across the room.

Kaiaphas holds up a hand to bring silence, and says, "What sword were you speaking of, ben Pantera? The forces of the Zealots?"

This question is more critical than perhaps Yeshua realizes. Tomorrow he will be questioned by a Roman praefectus whose authority to execute a man is said to flow from the ius gladii, the "right of the sword." If Yeshua is seen as claiming this same right, it could very well be seen as a challenge to the authority of the praefectus.

Yeshua inhales a breath and lets it out slowly. "I have said nothing in secret. I speak openly to the world, and daily in the Temple. Why do you ask me of my teachings? Ask those who heard me. They know what I have said."

Impatiently Kaiaphas urges, "I ask you again to explain your teaching."

As though to point out their error, Yeshua gently says, "I teach that a man should do good to them that hate him, and pray for them who use and persecute him. I teach that—"

"Enough," Hanan says. "He is avoiding the question."

Gamliel stands and when Kaiaphas nods to him, he says, "Perhaps the question should be avoided."

I swivel on the bench to stare up at Gamliel.

"What do you mean?" Hanan says gruffly. "We are here to decide the fate—"

"Regardless of the nature of this man's teachings, if they are the work of a man, they will come to naught, but if they are of God, neither we nor Rome can overthrow them. God's way is unfathomable to men, therefore Yehoshua ben Pantera's teachings may indeed be divinely inspired by the one living God.[86] What is at issue here, as our high priest has aptly pointed out, is how we may help him avoid execution. I believe we have lost sight of that."

I rise to be recognized, and when Kaiaphas nods, I say, "I agree. If our goal tonight is truly to prepare a defense for this man, let us get to it."

Kaiaphas looks at Yeshua. "Ben Pantera, would you like to rebut or cross-examine Delos the Sidonian?"

Yeshua pulls his white himation down to cover more of his face.

Kaiaphas waits, then says, "Guards, you may take the Sidonian away."

Delos gives Yeshua an aching look of apology as he is forced to walk by.

Gamliel says, "High Priest, I believe at this point that we must look carefully at what the witnesses have said."

"Go on."

"Their testimonies are clear. One claims he has seen ben Pantera speaking with Zealots, the other says he has not. One says ben Pantera preaches violence, the other says he does not. The witnesses do not agree.[87] If testimony like this is the source of the treason charge, then we must heartily recommend to the praefectus that ben Pantera be released for lack of evidence."

Hanan rises again. "Before we make such a recommendation, ben Pantera must recant his statements that he is the mashiah."

Yeshua turns to frown at him.

I leap to my feet. "High Priest, I object! Yehoshua ben Pantera has never said he is the mashiah, nor did either of our witnesses claim he'd ever said such a thing."

Hanan gives me a small smile. "Perhaps, but his followers preach it loudly. The one known as Kepha has been spreading the story everywhere he heals. Let us be under no illusions. No matter what these witnesses have said, if we cannot provide documentation that ben Pantera has solemnly and formally recanted his pretensions to be the Annointed One, he will be convicted of a capital crime under Roman law."

Kaiaphas surveys the chamber, waiting for other comments, before he says, "Yehoshua ben Pantera, are you the mashiah? The Annointed One?"

Yeshua smiles sadly and whispers, "If I asked you the same question, you would not answer me, and no matter what I say, you will not believe me, or let me go." He extends his hands helplessly. "From now on this Ben Adam will sit at the right hand of the power of God."

"He refuses to deny it! He makes no attempt to recant!" Hanan cries, and waves his skinny elderly arms.

In a ringing voice, Gamliel says, "Calling himself the 'son of Adam' is a clear repudiation of any claims to being the Annointed One! In the holy books the term Ben Adam, literally 'son of man,' is the common way God addresses ordinary human beings."[88]

Hanan, upset, stutters, "He c-claims he is going to sit at the r-right hand of God! What else could he—"

"I assume he is merely making a reference to Psalms one hundred ten, verse one. He is saying that he will not fight; he will wait at God's side until God makes his enemies his footstool."

I lift my hand, and Kaiaphas says, "Yes?"

In a loud voice I call out, "Councilors, please! However mistaken this man's teachings may be, he has broken no law and his persistent and unfailing dependence upon God attest to his piety and devotion. Surely we all see that. He has committed no crime . . . certainly not treason against Rome! When we are forced to send him to Pilatos in the morning, one of us must accompany him to relay the Council's judgments."

The timbre in the room changes. Many men agree with me. The few who do not, scowl in my direction.

Kaiaphas says, "I assume the Council may call upon you to carry out that duty if it so decides."

"It can, High Priest." My legs have started to shake. I sit down.

Yeshua turns and gives me a faint, grateful smile, and I long to weep.

"Then let us next discuss the arguments that have been put forth," Kaiaphas calls. "Yosef and Gamliel, you are both, of course, correct, but so are Yohanan and Shimon. Yehoshua ben Pantera may be a holy man inspired by God, but if he does not openly proclaim that he is not *the* mashiah, *Pilatos will assume he claims the title, even if covertly. If at all possible, we must bring ben Pantera to reason. He must recant." Again, Kaiaphas asks, "Yehoshua ben Pantera, are you one of the 'sons of oil,' the promised Annointed One?"*

Yeshua lifts his head, gazes around the chamber at each Councilor, then returns his eyes to Kaiaphas and replies, "You say that I am, but I tell you now that you will *see the Ben Adam coming in the clouds of heaven."*[89]

"He dares to quote the passage in Daniel about the mashiah!" *Hanan cries. "There is no longer any possibility of saving him!" As a sign of his utter despair he takes hold of his robe and rips it.*

A hush falls over the chamber. Every man stares at Yeshua as though struck mute by his words.

Kaiaphas straightens, peers out at the gathering, and says, "If ben Pantera will not openly deny that he is the mashiah . . . *we may all be doomed."*

Shimon stands up. "Please, High Priest. Ben Pantera may be doomed, but we can still save ourselves. If there is a revolt, we must suppress it before the Romans do. How does this Council plan to accomplish that?"

Several men stand at once and begin calling out in loud voices: Shimon wants to organize the general populace to put down the revolt; Hanan says the Temple police will be enough; Yohanan says we should work with the Zealots to make certain it doesn't happen in the first place. . . .

In the chaos, Gamliel suddenly straightens and his brows draw together over his hooked nose, as though he's just thought of something.

"What is it?" I ask.

The elderly scholar leans toward me and softly says, "I may know how to prevent the violence."

"How?"

"Speak with me later, outside the Council. If we do this, it must not be seen as a conciliar decision."

I stare at him. "Do you mean you want me to take the blame if it goes poorly?"

"You have sympathies for his movement. Everyone knows it. If you agree to do this, they will arrest you to protect the Council."

As a hollow sensation begins to expand in my chest, I sit back on the bench, and try to imagine what he could possibly be considering. I know only that it might leave me in prison.

Gamliel gives me one last look, rises, and quietly walks across the chamber. Few people seem to notice when he walks out the door and disappears.

My heart is racing. I long to stay, to see what conclusions the Council arrives at, perhaps to speak with Yeshua, but I rise, shoulder through the throng, and unobtrusively follow Gamliel.

TWENTY-SEVEN

As they rode over the last hill, the dark moonlit ocean came into view, and Zarathan heaved a sigh of relief. Seagulls squealed and soared on the cool sea breezes.

"How far now?" he asked.

Barnabas pulled up on the reins and came to a stop. "I'm not certain. None of this looks familiar."

"But we're about the right distance from Agrippias, aren't we?"

"Yes, but I don't see the pillar of rock and two humps of stone that the man spoke of, do you?"

Zarathan scanned the terrain. The outlines of the hills were clearly visible. Unfortunately, the vista resembled a vast plain of camelbacks dissected by rocky wadis. The line of white surf divided the worlds of land and water. Wave-washed beach gleamed in the evening light, but off to the east, behind the sullen line of cliffs, ridge after rocky ridge, each limned by crescent dunes, marched off into infinity.

"Perhaps we should camp on the beach and look in the morning when it's light," Barnabas suggested.

"Yes, good idea," Zarathan agreed. "If nothing else, we can dig clams and eat them raw."

Cyrus and Kalay rode up beside them. Cyrus had his curly black hair tucked behind his ears, which made his bearded face seem all the more hard and dangerous. He said, "Camping on the beach in the open makes me uneasy. Let's search for a better place."

Barnabas nodded. "Very well. You lead, Cyrus."

Cyrus kicked his horse into a slow walk and Barnabas and Zarathan plodded up the trail behind.

Occasional farmers and fishermen passed them, going home to Agrippias after a long day of labor. Some made the sign against evil in the dusk as they hurried by.

Zarathan didn't know what to make of it. "Why do they do that?"

"They are simple, uneducated people, Zarathan. Perhaps they believe that three monks in filthy robes are apostates."

"Three monks in filthy robes, traveling with a woman," he said in a low voice. "That's our problem."

Barnabas didn't respond, but surely he knew that Kalay's presence didn't help matters. What would a decent woman be doing traveling with three monks in good standing? The more Zarathan thought about it, they did resemble a band of outcasts, even brigands. If he'd had the strength, he would have scowled at her, for all the good it would have done. She'd probably just give him another of her licentious winks, and then he'd be suffering in more than just his belly.

"It's chilly tonight." Barnabas shivered, and let out a shaky breath.

Zarathan frowned. It was a cool night, but not that cool. For days, they'd been sleeping out beneath the stars in just their thin robes. Had a chill settled in the old man's bones? It wouldn't be surprising. Every time he'd awakened in the past few days, he'd seen Cyrus standing guard and Barnabas kneeling in prayer. The only one who seemed to sleep truly well was Kalay, but then she had her long black cape to comfort her.

"Why did that man at the village call Libni 'Old Scary'?" Zarathan asked.

"Very holy people are always scary, Zarathan. The light of God shines from their eyes like fiery pokers. Ordinary people find it unsettling," Barnabas replied, looking at the empty ocean. The water stretched westward, flowing to the edges of the earth, and the monsters that inhabited the eternal depths.

"I've always thought hermits were an odd lot," Zarathan said. "I can't imagine living most or all of my life without other people close by. What's Libni like?"

Barnabas turned and, in the blue-gray darkness, Zarathan saw the old monk's gray brows pull down. He stared at the seagulls for a long time, before he whispered, "When I knew him he was a laughing youth, always tripping over his own feet, but very studious and devoted to the words of our Lord. Of course, that was before the murder of his wife."

"His wife was murdered?"

Zarathan's voice had risen and attracted Cyrus' attention. He slowed his horse to ride alongside them. "Whose wife was murdered?"

"Libni's," Barnabas said. "It was an ugly crime. He was never the same after that. At least, that's what I heard. I left Caesarea right after it happened."

Kalay asked, "Did they ever catch the murderer?"

"Oh, yes. We found him. He'd fled to the church and was hiding there."

They rode past a wave-smoothed boulder and out onto a plain of glimmering seashells that crunched beneath their horses' hooves. Far ahead, a wall of starlit cliffs glowed.

Fascinated, Zarathan said, "What did you do?"

"I and the other library assistants surrounded the church. We whispered our prayers into the stones, begging God to reveal him to us. Then we fashioned talismans with the sign of the dove and the lamb, and carried them before us into the dark nave. He laughed at us, threw things. We captured him in the bell tower. From there, he was dragged to his death."

"You killed him?" Zarathan blurted, astonished. "You killed a man?"

"No, I didn't," Barnabas said softly. "Libni did. He dragged him out of the church and beat him to death with his bare hands. Though we tried, there was nothing we could do to stop him."

Zarathan exchanged a grave look with Cyrus, but before either of them could speak, Kalay commented with her usual aplomb, "He sounds like my sort. I like him already."

Zarathan looked at her as if she were a half-wit, but the she-demon didn't seem to notice.

A breath of wind blew in off the ocean, whispered across the sand at the level of the horses' hooves, and brought the watery scents of fish and seaweed.

"Brothers, do you see that?" Cyrus asked and pointed. "There. Is that the pillar?"

Zarathan leaned sideways to peer around Barnabas. Standing between two humps of rock, the pillar resembled a finger lifted in warning.

"I've seen that before," Kalay mused. "Men usually greet me that way."

Zarathan cringed in shocked humiliation. "You are so vile! They're just rocks!"

She nonchalantly lifted a shoulder. "A rock by any other name—"

Barnabas called, "Look! Perhaps those are Libni's caves!"

As they rode closer to the black holes that pocked the surface of the cliffs, Zarathan kept shooting disgruntled glances at Kalay, but she was ignoring him. It was infuriating.

Cyrus said, "There must be hundreds of them. How will we find Libni's?"

"We'll search every one, if necessary."

"But that could take forever, and we're almost certainly being followed. If we don't find him quickly, shouldn't we just move on?" When Barnabas didn't answer, Zarathan turned to Cyrus. "Brother, surely you see the wisdom of losing ourselves in a city where it's more difficult to track us?"

Cyrus was examining the rimrock and the tumbled boulders that clustered at the base of the cliffs. Without so much as glancing at Zarathan, he said, "We can hide in a cave as easily as a city. If, as Barnabas believes, Libni can help us understand the papyrus, it's worth the risk."

"Zarathan, our brothers died because of it," Barnabas said with reverence. "We owe it to them to find out why."

As they rode closer to the cliff, a tiny thread of light glinted in one of the caves, then vanished as though it had never been.

Cyrus said, "Did you—"

"I saw it," Barnabas answered, and kicked the horse into a shambling trot. "Let's find out."

TWENTY-EIGHT

A young man, perhaps sixteen, met them at the cave entrance. He was short and ugly, with black, vulnerable eyes. His head had been shaved, probably in penance for some affront. As he stepped toward them, the coarse fabric of his brown robe molded to each hard muscle.

He said, "I am Tiras, assistant to the blessed hermit. How may I help you?"

Barnabas carefully took hold of his book bag, dismounted, and handed the reins to Zarathan. A tattered curtain covered the cave entrance. Through the rips, warm golden light streamed. "I am Brother Barnabas, here to see my old friend Libni, if this is where he lives."

The youth's eyes flew wide. "Oh! He said you were coming!" He swiftly ducked beneath the curtain and a golden glow of firelight flashed across the sand. Soft voices rose inside.

Barnabas turned to the others and said, "You may dismount. All is well."

"Really?" Kalay said suspiciously. "How did he know you were coming?"

"Libni probably foresaw it. He's always had visions."

In the early days, Barnabas had been jealous, wondering why God had chosen to reveal himself to Libni and not to him. Barnabas had studied harder, prayed harder, and worked harder. But over the decade they'd been together, his jealousy had mutated into deep reverence. Libni *had* been chosen, and he was grateful to know a man favored by God.

"That's not a very good answer, brother." Kalay's mouth quirked. "Especially not after what we heard in the last village . . . that someone else had been asking about Libni. I'd say it's likely the sicarii got here before we did and are waiting to greet us."

Barnabas turned in irritation. "Kalay, if that were the case, don't you think Libni would have ordered his assistants to warn us?"

"Not if a dagger is poised over Libni's heart."

"You have so little faith. Please, trust me. All is well. You may dismount." His clutched his bag to his chest.

Despite her misgivings, Kalay dismounted, followed by Zarathan, leaving Cyrus alone on his horse.

"Cyrus," Barnabas said. "Come, join us."

His horse tossed its head and the reins clinked. "I need to scout the area. I'll leave as soon as I know that you are safe here."

"Very well." Barnabas sighed, realizing that arguing would be fruitless. "I'll send Kalay back as soon as we've met Libni."

"Good."

Tiras ducked beneath the door curtain again, followed by another young man, perhaps thirteen, with wavy red hair, green eyes, and freckles. Clearly of Celtic descent.

Tiras said, "My master bids you enter," and thrust out a hand to the entrance.

Barnabas shoved aside the curtain and ducked inside. Tiras and the other youth followed him.

The interior, lit by distant candlelight, was much larger than he'd suspected. The roof of this particular cave rose twenty cubits over his head, but there were tunnels going off in every direction from this main chamber. The faint warmth penetrated his thin robe and made Barnabas shiver in relief.

Zarathan and Kalay entered and stood behind him.

Kalay adjusted her weapons belt and asked, "Where's the murderer? Out on a jaunt?"

Tiras frowned at her as though mystified by the comment, but vaguely aware that he ought to be insulted by it.

Barnabas turned. "I've seen no one since I entered. Perhaps he's in another chamber."

He took two steps forward, but Tiras said, "No, not that way, brother. Please, follow me." He held out a hand to the tunnel on the right, showing them the way.

As Barnabas and Kalay followed the two young monks into the dark tunnel, Zarathan called shrilly, "I'll stay here to keep watch!"

Kalay turned and acidly said, "Cyrus will feel so much better with you at his back."

At the end of the passageway was a large, smoky chamber. The candles on the long table cast a flickering gleam over the stone wall. Over thirty cubits across, the rounded chamber rose another ten cubits over their heads. Holes of every size and shape honeycombed the walls, and each was stuffed with books, scrolls, writing instruments, and ink.

Barnabas smiled. Even in the middle of the desert, a librarian could not survive without books. He set his precious book bag on the table and turned to Kalay. "Please go and tell Cyrus that all is well."

Kalay's thin red brows lifted. "You're a gullible soul, Barnabas. I've seen nothing to suggest safety, let alone—"

The curtain on the far side of the chamber was thrown back and Libni—older, more grizzled—rushed into the chamber in a whirl of threadbare brown rags that fluttered around him like an ancient shroud.

"Tiras! Uzziah! Fetch us down some wine and food," Libni ordered, passing between the startled youths. Libni almost flew across the floor and embraced Barnabas in a bear hug that nearly cracked his ribs. "Barnabas, my dear old friend! How good of you to come see me! It's been what, twenty years? Twenty-one? Did you ever find the village of Asthemo?"

He was a massive man, tall, with the meaty shoulders of an ox, and hands twice the size of Barnabas'. A loose mane of graying brown hair framed his bearded face.

Barnabas pulled away from his strong arms and laughed. "Not yet. I'm still looking."

"I always thought it was in the region of Eleutheropolis."

"As I do. I just haven't found any evidence to support that suspicion." He held out a hand to Kalay, and introduced her. "Libni, this is my friend Kalay."

At some point in the past twenty heartbeats, Kalay had drawn her knife and fallen into a she-wolf's crouch.

Libni turned and went still, looking at her with wide gray eyes. In a tender voice, he said, "At first I thought you were an angel. Now I am genuinely delighted to discover you are flesh and blood. Please, both of you be seated. My brothers will arrive shortly with refreshments."

Kalay nonchalantly kept her knife at the ready. "I'll stand."

"But you must be tired, please sit."

"No."

Libni frowned. "You're going to stand all night, after you've been riding hard for days?"

"Possibly."

Libni's mad eyes flared a little wider. "You don't say much, do you?"

Kalay tilted her head. "Well, if you leave out all the pig shit in life, you don't need many words."

A slow smile came to Libni's lips, and he let out a belly laugh that boomed from the cave walls. "A beautiful woman with a sense of humor! I've been blessed by God."

Kalay squinted at him, straightened, and shoved her dagger into its sheath. "You've a curious way of looking at things, brother."

"Yes, but don't let that worry you. I'm harmless."

Under her breath, she said, "That's not what I've heard." Then louder, added, "Forgive me, but I must go tell my companions that it's safe."

"Well, of course, it's safe," Libni said, a bit indignantly.

Kalay gave him an incredulous glance, and left.

Libni watched her duck into the tunnel, and affection melted his face. "Her eyes remind me of Sousanna's. Do you remember how blue they were? Like pieces of the sky fallen to earth."

"I do remember. I think it is Kalay's misfortune that she reminds every man of a woman he's lost."

A pained smile turned Libni's lips. "Yes," he replied softly, "I can see how that might lead a girl's soul astray. How does she come to be in your company?"

"She was the washerwoman at the monastery."

Libni arched an eyebrow. "What did you do to make our Lord so eager to test the chastity of your monks?"

Barnabas suppressed a smile. "Nothing I'm aware of."

Libni thoughtfully smoothed a hand over his unkempt beard. "And before she was a washerwoman? What did she do?"

"I don't know how she earned her way in life. None of that matters to me."

A sad reverie filled Libni's eyes. "Has she repented?"

"No, and I wouldn't bring it up if I were you. I overheard her say that most of her family was killed during the Persecution. She blames the Church." Barnabas remembered the conversation he'd inadvertently overheard between Cyrus and Kalay that morning on the shore of the Nile. He had wondered then if he shouldn't speak with her, but had decided to wait.

"That is unfortunate. When the time is right, I'm sure you will discuss our Lord's teachings with her."

"I'll ponder the risk of a dagger between my ribs if we survive our current dilemma."

Libni gestured to the dark high-backed chairs around the table. "Sit. Tell me what brings you here."

Barnabas eased into one of the chairs and exhaled hard. "You're looking better than I would have thought."

Libni seated himself at the end of the table. As he leaned forward to brace his elbows on the dark wood, his shoulder-length hair fell forward. His sparkling eyes were half insane, and filled with tears. "I dreamed you were coming. God told me to prepare for your arrival. I am so glad to see you."

"God told you?" Awe filled Barnabas, just like in the old days.

"Oh, yes." Libni looked around the cave. "Every stone here breathes the Word of God. What He did not tell me is why you were coming."

Barnabas leaned across the table to touch Libni's hand. For several moments they just stared at each other. "I need your help."

"With what? Something in that old gazelle leather bag?" He gestured to the book bag resting on the far end of the table.

"Partly. We are on a mission of great importance." He lowered his voice to a whisper. "Do you remember the papyrus?"

Libni's smile faded. Despite the fact that they had translated hundreds of scrolls, codices, and fragments of papyri in their lives, there was only one that deserved a whisper. Libni took Barnabas' hand in both of his and crushed his fingers. "You found it! Tell me you *found* it!"

"No, no, I'm sorry to get your hopes up. That's why I'm here."

Disappointment slackened Libni's features, and his gray eyes flared as though in sudden understanding. "You're in danger, aren't you? Because of the papyrus?"

"More danger than I can tell you. Some days ago a bishop from Rome came to our monastery to deliver the edicts of the Council of Nicea. That night, the monastery was attacked. The supper was poisoned. Everyone was killed, murdered because of the books. Two brothers and I—and Kalay— escaped down the Nile in her boat. I'm certain we're still being followed."

"By whom?"

Barnabas shook his head. "The name of the bishop from Rome was Meridias. Libni, if they're terrified enough to kill dozens of innocent monks, they'll do anything. After we leave, you should take precautions."

Libni cocked his head and gave Barnabas a singularly gentle smile. "I've been trying to die for more than twenty years, my friend, and God has not allowed it. I will, however, take precautions. Not for myself, but for the young men who have chosen to study with me."

"I was surprised to see the youths here. I thought you were a hermit?"

"I was." Libni shrugged helplessly. "Now I'm a teacher."

It must have been many years since anyone had visited Libni, let alone come to "study" with him, and the fact seemed to bring him great joy.

He said, "I truly appreciate the lengthy conversations and even more lengthy scriptural readings my brothers and I share. I had forgotten the serenity of—"

Uzziah and Tiras returned, carrying two plates heaped with bread, cheese, and jugs of wine surrounded by chipped ceramic cups. As they set them on the table between Barnabas and Libni, Tiras said, "Brother Barnabas, your companions are on their way. Is there anything else I might bring you?"

"No, Tiras. Thank you very much."

Kalay and Zarathan emerged from the tunnel, and Zarathan's nose started to wiggle. He almost ran across the room to plop himself down in the chair closest to the plates of food. Fortunately, he did not grab for anything, but peered at the feast like a predator about to pounce.

Libni said, *"Kairos,"* and bowed his head.

Barnabas and Zarathan joined him in praying. "Glory be to the Father and to the Son and to the Holy Spirit, as it was in the beginning, is now, and ever shall be, world without end. Amayne."

When he lifted his head, Barnabas found Kalay staring at him with a distasteful squint to her eyes.

Libni said, "Here, allow me to pour the wine while you help yourselves to the bread and cheese."

Zarathan's hand moved faster than a serpent striking. He had a slice of cheese in his mouth before Libni had even fully risen to his feet, and with his other hand was in the process of snatching a chunk of bread.

Kalay, sounding a little bored, said, "I think you missed your calling, Zarathan. You should have been a pickpocket."

Around a mouthful of food, Zarathan slurred something unpleasant that sounded vaguely like "You ought to know."

Libni poured four cups of wine and handed them around the table, before he seated himself again, and noted, "I think that was an attempt to asperse your character, my dear."

"Oh, yes, sitting over there all the way across the table, he's very brave. Unlike me. I won't insult someone unless they're close enough to knife."

That silenced the chamber. Every man stared at her as she nonchalantly ripped off a piece of bread, ate it, and washed it down with a long drink of wine.

Once she'd swallowed, she said, "I hope Brother Barnabas told you that we're being followed by crazed killers, and you might want to boot us out at first chance."

"Yes. He told me." Libni nodded. "But who are these men? Surely, you have some notion?"

Barnabas began, "They may be—"

Kalay interrupted, "Devout men—probably spend their lives with their knees stuck to a floor—but they're well-trained in the military arts. Likely they're members of some secret organization mustered to protect the mysteries of your faith."

Surprised, Libni said, "Which organization?"

"I suspect—," Barnabas tried.

Kalay interrupted again. "My guess is they're Militia Templi. But they might be—"

"Kalay, would you mind if I answer some of Libni's questions?" Barnabas scowled at her.

"Not a bit, brother." She extended a hand, telling him to go on. "Assuming you don't mince words in an effort to protect your holy brethren."

Barnabas sighed in irritation. "The one thing we know for certain is that they came from Rome with orders to burn all the documents recently declared heretical, and to kill anyone who's ever read them."

Libni stared down into his cup, watching the candlelight reflect from the rich red liquid. "Strange."

"What is?" Zarathan took another bite of cheese. "That they came to burn the documents? Or kill anyone who'd read them?"

"Well, I should think both. But that would suggest that they . . ."

His voice faded, and Barnabas frowned. "That would suggest that they what?"

"Hmm?" Libni gazed at him as though he had no idea what he was talking about.

"You said that the fact that they would burn the documents, and kill anyone who'd read them, would suggest something. . . . What?"

A breath of wind penetrated the cave and the flickering candles cast odd shadows over Libni's intent face. In a voice just above a whisper, he said, "Did you know that I once killed a man?"

Kalay and Zarathan both stopped eating and were regarding Libni with wide eyes. His devoted students, Uzziah and Tiras, appeared frozen with shock.

"Libni," Barnabas said soothingly. His old friend's tormented expression broke his heart. "I was there. Of course, I know."

Libni wet his lips. "Were you?"

"Yes, my friend. Don't you remember? We sat for the longest time staring at the stars, talking about forgiveness."

Tears drained down Libni's cheeks. "Oh, yes. Yes, now I recall." He smiled his love at Barnabas. "How could I have forgotten? You helped me that terrible night."

Barnabas reached out to put his fingers on Libni's threadbare sleeve. "God forgave you long ago, my friend. You don't need to keep punishing yourself for it. Let it go."

As though he'd suddenly come back, Libni pulled himself up straight in his chair. "Since that day, I have believed that murder is grief taken to the extreme. It is a desperate act of bereavement. If these truly are Church-sanctioned killers, then what is the source of the bereavement? What loss does our Church fear so much it would resort to murder?"

In a hoarse whisper, Barnabas said, "Have you heard about the declarations of the Nicean synod?"

"We get very little news out here. What declarations?"

"Libni, a synod of bishops just met in Nicea. They cast out the gospels of Maryam, Philippon, Thomas, and many other books, even the Shepherd of Hermas."

"But that's *absurd*!" Libni exploded, half rising out of his chair. Just as suddenly he went absolutely quiet, and a foreboding stillness filled the cave, broken only by the spluttering of the candles. As he sank back down to his seat, he murmured, "Oh. Of course."

Zarathan glanced around at each person in the room, before he asked, "Why?"

Libni stared straight at Barnabas. "It's the fleshly resurrection and the virgin birth, isn't it?"

Barnabas replied, "They just decreed both to be fact and apparently consider them to be the two doctrines that will bind Christianity together."

Libni's mouth quivered with rage or disgust. "You mean they think they need a few miracles for the masses, or they won't believe our Lord's teachings?"

"I think so."

Libni squeezed his eyes closed.

Uzziah and Tiras looked stunned that two old monks would dare to speak such heresy aloud. As they had during their time together in Caesarea, Libni probably said the Creed four times a day, and instructed his brothers to do the same. The youths had to be completely confused by the discussion.

Libni opened his eyes and stared, unblinking, at the dark tabletop. "They have cast aside our Lord's own words." In a very small voice, he recited, "Truth is a life-eater."[90]

"They fear the Truth more than anything." After several taut heartbeats,

Barnabas continued, "That's why they want to destroy the papyrus and anyone who has ever read it."

Candlelight glinted in Libni's eyes as his gaze bored into Barnabas'. "If the fools think we understand it, they obviously give us more credit than we are due."

"We must try harder. Before it's too late."

Libni took a long drink of his wine, set his empty cup down with a thud, and in a forlorn voice asked, "Do you really think they would destroy the Pearl?"

"They must. You know it as well as I do."

Kalay sat forward. "You mean you know what the Pearl is?"

Barnabas remained mute, staring at Libni.

Libni's gaze drifted over the arching stone ceiling, and moved silently from one overstuffed hole in the wall to the next. Finally, he grunted softly and rose to his feet, answering, "Well, let's say we have a good guess."

"A guess? Killers are hunting you down over a 'guess'?"

Barnabas ran a hand through his dirty gray hair and sighed. "They don't realize all we have is a guess, Kalay. I'm sure they think we know everything."

In an innocent voice, Kalay said, "Well, then, why don't you just tell them you don't know anything? Maybe they'll stop trying to kill you. Did you ever think of that?"

Barnabas gave her an annoyed look. "We don't want them to know we're as ignorant as we are. The more time we have, the more likely we are to decipher the papyrus."

She gruffly folded her arms. "You two have bishop potential."

Libni walked to a stash of scrolls. As though touching a frail and beloved child, he lifted one and brought it back to the table.

He rested his hand protectively on top of it as he spoke. "There is a passage I've been meaning to write you about."

Barnabas could tell from the grave tone of his voice that it might refer to the papyrus. In a subtle gesture, he tipped his head toward Tiras and Uzziah. "What do you think?"

Libni studied his students with moist eyes. "Tiras? Why don't you take Uzziah and lay out blankets for our guests. After that, please retire to the reading cave and study the Acts of John. Pay particular attention to the passages regarding our Lord's suffering. We will discuss them tomorrow."

"Yes, Abba Libni," Tiras said, and turned to the table. "Peace be with you, brothers and sister."

"And peace be with you, Tiras and Uzziah," Barnabas responded. Between chews, Zarathan echoed his words. Kalay gave them a saucy wink.

Both youths looked horrified, and left.

Barnabas and Libni next turned and peered at Kalay. She understood immediately and pursed her lips as though she'd just eaten something sour. "Well enough. I didn't want to hear your prattle anyway. I'll go and wait for Brother Cyrus to return."

She rose and strode into the tunnel that led outside.

Barnabas looked back at Libni, who softly added, "I think perhaps we should talk alone, just the two of us."

Zarathan, who had a mouthful of bread, choked it down. "But I know all about the papyrus! I helped translate some of the words."

Barnabas nodded obligingly. "Yes, you did, and I was grateful; but Libni and I have many things to discuss. The papyrus is only one of them. Perhaps it would be better if you waited outside with Kalay. That way, when Cyrus returns, you can lead him here to this chamber and we'll all discuss the papyrus together."

"Kalay could do that just as well as me." Zarathan angrily shoved back his chair, grabbed another chunk of bread, and stalked from the room.

Libni watched the retreat with kind eyes. "Pride is his greatest obstacle."

"As I've told him many times."

"How long has he been a monk?"

"Three months."

Barnabas lifted his cup and took a sip of wine. He could feel Libni's eyes upon him, heavy with the weight of their next words.

Libni waited until the voices in the outer cave had faded before he whispered, "How many of the Occultum Lapidem are left?"

"The two of us, and I pray that Symeon is still alive in Apollonia."

Libni petted the scroll that lay upon the table. "Barnabas, I believe I may have found the answer in the Gospel of Nikodemos."

"Nikodemos? But I've read it a thousand times. Where? What verses?"

"The story of Yosef Haramati." He used the man's Hebrew name, rather than the more familiar Greek, Ioses of Arimathaia. "Do you remember? After he placed our Lord's body in his garden tomb, Annas and Kaiaphas were enraged. They ordered him arrested. While they discussed his fate, they imprisoned Yosef for a week in a room without a window."

"A room with one door, to which Kaiaphas had the only key."[91]

"Yes." Libni's voice was a hiss in the stillness.

For a few brief moments, Barnabas could hear the ocean. Waves crashed upon the shore, and he wondered if a storm had arisen.

"What else, Libni?"

"When Kaiaphas unlocked the door on the first day of the week, the room was empty. Yosef was gone."

"Yes, yes. I know all that. What does the story have to do with—"

"Don't you see? The priests went searching for Yosef after Phinees, Adas, and Angaeus came from the Galilaian to Jerusalem, and told the high priests, 'We saw Yeshua and his disciples sitting upon the mountain of Mamlich.' They thought he was alive! They said, 'Give us Yosef Haramati and he will give you Yeshua.' They truly believed that Yosef knew where our Lord was and would betray him. But they found Yosef's prison empty!"

Libni's face was alight. He was relating the story as though it had just happened days ago, rather than centuries.

Patiently, Barnabas inquired, "What does that have to do with the papyrus?"

Libni leaned forward until his nose was less than a cubit from Barnabas' face. In a wine-scented whisper, he said, "Yosef had spent that entire week on the run, he—"

"Libni, I've read the Gospel of Nikodemos. Papias reports this same story, with a few variations, in his *Logia*. What does it have to do with the papyrus?"

"Oh, Barnabas," he said with true amusement and joy. "You're going to be so surprised when I tell you—"

Voices rose in the next chamber, followed by footsteps in the tunnel. Kalay ducked into the chamber, then Zarathan and Cyrus followed.

The wind must have picked up, for Cyrus' black curly hair had been blown back from his bearded face, making his straight nose seem longer, his eyes more like hard, shimmering emeralds.

"Cyrus," Barnabas introduced, "this is my friend Libni. He is a great scholar of the ancient texts."

Cyrus came around the table and bowed to Libni. His once white robe, torn and streaked with dirt, old blood, and soot, clung to his tall body. "Brother, thank you for sheltering us tonight. I promise we will be gone before dawn."

Libni placed a gentle hand on Cyrus' bowed head. "You must sit and eat to restore your strength for the long journey ahead. Please, let me pour you some wine."

Cyrus cast a glance at Barnabas, as though he could shed light on the "long journey" comment.

Barnabas merely said, "Sit down, Cyrus. I'll explain soon. What did you find outside?"

Cyrus took a chair and reached for the loaf. As he tore off a chunk, he said, "I scouted the area. While I saw no one, there are tracks everywhere. I could make no sense of them, which means I have no idea if we are safe or not."

Libni spilled some wine on the table beside Cyrus' cup and, as he wiped it up with his sleeve, said, "Of course there are tracks everywhere. The coastline is a major thoroughfare. Fishermen, traders, merchants, even whole caravans move up and down the length of it."

Libni finished filling every cup on the table, including his own, and eased back down to his chair. When he looked again at Barnabas his gray eyes had a curious glitter.

Barnabas, exasperated, said, "Libni, just quickly give me a clue. Then we'll open the discussion to everyone else."

Libni sat back in his chair. "Do you know what *mahanayim* means?"

Every gaze fixed on Libni.

Annoyed at the game, Barnabas said, "There are many possibilities. What do you think it means?"

Libni smiled his love at Barnabas, which defused some of his frustration. "I think it means 'two camps.'"

"Two camps?"

"Yes. It's so simple, isn't it? It's hard to believe we missed it all these years."

There were three or four heartbeats of incomprehension in the room, before Kalay gasped, "Blessed Mother! And "Mehebel" means 'from the coast'!"

A tingling rush of heat flushed Barnabas' veins. " 'Two camps from the coast.' " His hand shook as he reached out to touch Libni's wrist. "Dear God, then it *is* a map."

TWENTY-NINE

Kalay sat in the high-backed chair with her knees drawn up, sipping wine while she watched the two old men who stood leaning over the ancient maps on the table. Brittle and yellowed, dotted here and there with drips of candle wax, Libni would allow no one but himself and Barnabas to touch the maps. The four other men had to stand back, watching from one or two paces away as their elders pondered the meaning of the faint, archaic symbols.

"That's the problem," Libni murmured, frowning. "We don't know where to start. There were eight major cities on the coast at the time of our Lord. Which one is the papyrus referring to?"

Candlelight lay like a thick amber resin on the surface of the tabletop. It seemed to catch in glowing lines on the edges of the maps.

"If the beginning point is a city at all," Cyrus countered as he paced behind Libni and Barnabas, his arms folded across his broad chest. "It could be a cove, a standing stone, a ruin, anything. There's no way to know."

Barnabas placed a hand on one curled map corner, carefully flattening it out so that he could read it. "If we are correct that the man who wrote the papyrus was Ioses of Arimathaia, then perhaps we should look at sites closest to Jerusalem."

"Why?" Cyrus asked skeptically.

"No reason really, except that's where he lived, and it gives us a starting place."

Libni's finger was moving through the air above the parchment. "The choices, in that case, would be Apollonia, Ioppe, and Ashkelon. Pick one."

Barnabas waved a hand uncertainly. "The one in the middle."

"Ioppe, or do you say *Yapo*?"

"Ioppe."

They both leaned over the table, staring at the map like scavenger birds waiting for their prey to die.

Kalay sighed. Though she had traveled much of Palestine and Egypt, she did not believe she had seen any place as desolate as the honeycomb of caves that Libni and his students called home. The chambers were virtually empty, except for a blanket folded in the corner where someone slept, or a prayer rug and a candle sitting in the middle of a swept dirt floor. Elsewhere in the region, people might live in caves, but the chambers had color. The walls were painted or contained colorful objects and bright fabrics, beads or polished stones. Except for the library where she sat, this place was barren, the walls hollowed and smoothed by eons of wind and water. There was little here to break the monotony. Fortunately, the wine was tasty. She took another drink.

The faint creak of Cyrus' sword belt broke the silence as he shifted to prop one hand on the hilt. "How many stadia is it from Ioppe to Jerusalem?"

Libni rubbed his bearded chin. "Perhaps three hundred fifty or a little more. Why?"

"Because that means Jerusalem is 'two camps from the coast.'"

"Not if you're traveling on foot, it's at least three camps."

Cyrus lifted his chin and Kalay could see the thoughts flashing behind his emerald eyes. "If Ioses of Arimathaia is the writer, he was a powerful and renowned leader of the Temple. He must have had friends all over Palestine, people who would have helped him. I suspect he was on horseback."

Libni and Barnabas looked at each other, as though to see what the other thought. Finally Barnabas said, "Let's assume he's right."

"I agree. Does that mean then that Jerusalem is the place that is 'two camps from the coast'?"

"That's circular logic. That's where we started from." Barnabas grimaced. "If we assume that Ioppe is the starting place, it is just as likely that Mount Gerizim is the place 'two camps from the coast.'"

Kalay hugged her knees to her chest and said, "Well, if those are the choices, I'm of a mind to agree with Cyrus."

Zarathan scowled at her as though upset she'd spoken. He looked from man to man, clearly waiting for someone to reprimand her.

"Go on," Libni said. "Why?"

"Because the next word is *mahray*. David's champion was from the hill country of Judah, southwest of Bet Lehem, which is close to Jerusalem."

Libni's bushy gray brows lifted in admiration. "And what of *manahat*?"

She sat up straight and lowered her bare feet to the cold floor. "Well, if I'm following you, and going for a literal translation, I'd say it means 'resting place.'"

A warm, half-demented grin brightened Libni's face. "You are such a surprise. Where did you learn Hebrew?"

"My grandmother was Jewish. She read me the scriptures in Hebrew every night."

Libni's smile widened. "Then you should know what *magdi*—"

Zarathan piped up, "Magdiel was an Edomite chief." He was obviously pleased with himself for remembering. An arrogant smile tugged at the corners of his lips.

Libni said, "Yes, but not in this case."

Zarathan's smile drooped. "What do you mean? We all agreed that it was an Edomite chief!"

Libni's fond gaze fixed on Kalay. "Do you know, my dear?"

"I know that the translation of the word is God's gift, or the gift of God."

Cyrus' eyes widened. He propped his hand on the table and murmured, "Two camps from the coast . . . David's champion . . . lay to rest? . . . God's gift?"

Barnabas' knees seemed to go weak. He gingerly lowered himself to a chair and said, "God's gift, God."

"What does that mean?" Zarathan's mouth puckered into a pout. "It's gibberish."

Wind whipped around the chamber, fluttering the maps on the table, and Libni carefully reached out to hold down the corners.

Ignoring Zarathan, Kalay said, "After that, we've a problem."

"Because *selah* breaks the pattern," Zarathan said a little too loudly and thrust out his blond-fuzzed chin.

It truly amazed Kalay that he *had* been listening. She'd thought his head filled with nothing but bawdy paintings.

"Yes, it does," Libni agreed and the wrinkles in his forehead deepened. "You have all clearly been considering this. What conclusions did you come to regarding *selah*?"

Barnabas braced his elbows on the table and answered, "We thought it might refer to the Edomite rock city, or perhaps the place in Moab."

"But," Kalay pointed out, "it literally means 'rock'."

The men shifted, apparently waiting for someone to say something.

"God's gift, God, rock?" Zarathan asked, as though annoyed. "That's ridiculous."

"Maybe not." When Cyrus began pacing again, the flickering candlelight gilded his sword with a heartbeat of fire. "Is it possible that *Selah* could be a hidden reference to Saint Petros? His name also means 'rock'."

"Yes, and in Hebrew "rock" is *kepha*," Kalay said.

Libni steepled his fingers and propped his chin upon the point. "I hadn't thought of that one," he praised. "That's exactly the sort of twist Ioses of Arimathaia would throw in to confuse the idle reader. What do you think, Barnabas?"

Barnabas ran a hand through his gray hair. In the muted light his deeply sunken eyes turned glassy. "It is possible, but . . . it doesn't feel right."

"Well enough," Libni said, picked up the jug, and poured himself another cup of wine. "Let's move on to *massa, massa*. Cyrus? Your thoughts?"

"I thought it might be a reference to the son of Ishmael mentioned in the Book of Genesis."

Without being asked, Kalay offered, "I'm fairly sure it's from the *massa umeriba*, which literally means 'proof and strife,' or maybe 'testing and contention.'"

Barnabas said, "It could just as easily refer to the 'oracle' taught to

King Lemuel. The problem is the papyrus is not written in Hebrew, it's written in Latin, which was surely designed to lead the reader on a merry chase, for, without the Hebraic letters, we've no idea how each word might truly be translated."

"Um, yes. Quite correct," Libni said. "*Massa* as it appears in Latin may be an exact transliteration from the Hebrew, but in Hebrew the word may have been pronounced *massha,* or *massah,* each with a different meaning. Without seeing the context in which the words occur, we cannot pretend to know their exact meaning."

Since Kalay had never learned to read, such distinctions had little impact on her, but Zarathan looked truly perplexed.

His blond brows pinched. "Two camps from the coast, David's champion lay to rest God's gift, God, rock, proof, proof? It's nonsense."

"Perhaps if we could decipher *selah* it would all be perfectly clear." Barnabas sighed.

The stone floor was cold. Kalay drew her feet into the chair again and propped her cup of wine on her knees, wondering about *selah*. It was an Edomite fortress city conquered by Amaziah, King of Judah. Could it refer to a fortress made of stone? If the papyrus was, truly, a clever map, finding the fortress would be essential.

She leaned her head against the chair's back and let her gaze drift over the rounded candlelit ceiling. The men had lowered their voices, and begun talking softly among themselves.

Maybe Zarathan was right. It was all nonsense. She picked up the jug and refilled her cup again. A pleasant warmth was filtering through her veins, making all of this seem somehow less deadly than it was. She liked the few moments of respite.

In a nasty voice, Zarathan commented, "Soon, you're going to be slurring your words, then what will we do with you?"

She deliberately slurred, "I don't shink I want to answer that queshtion. It might give you ideas, and you've already got plenty in that young head of yoursh."

Red crept into his cheeks. He clamped his jaw, and glowered at her. As though it would upset her, he announced, "I'm leaving. Where am I supposed to sleep?"

Libni looked up. "Tiras and Uzziah placed blankets in the entry cave for you, and they will be standing guard tonight so that you all can sleep without worry. Please try to rest."

Cyrus replied, "That will be a welcome relief. Thank you, brother."

Zarathan marched from the chamber, and Libni and Barnabas returned to the map. They whispered and pointed at different squiggly lines, lost in their own private conversation.

Cyrus gestured to Kalay to get her attention, then tilted his head toward the tunnel, silently asking her join him outside.

Kalay rose to her feet and followed him.

In the entry cave, they found Zarathan rolled up in a blanket. Three other blankets lay folded in the rear. As they passed, Zarathan flopped to his opposite side, showing them his back, before they ducked outside.

Fog spun out of the sea, ghost white in the moonlight. Cyrus walked a few paces down the cliff face, taking them out of earshot of anyone who might be listening.

She walked along behind him, pondering why he needed to leave the caves to talk to her.

Finally, he stopped in a pool of cold shadows and leaned back against the cliff. Shreds of mist blew about him.

"What is your opinion of Libni?"

Kalay shrugged. "He's a curious one. I was unsure at first, but I like him."

"And his two assistants?"

"They're boys, Cyrus. They're no danger to us."

The world shimmered in the mist. His black hair and beard had already picked up an opalescent sheen.

"Do you believe Libni?" Cyrus cocked his head.

"If you're asking if I think the papyrus should be translated literally, it makes more sense than anything else we've tried."

"But Zarathan is right, it's gibberish."

"Everything is gibberish until you understand it, Cyrus."

She looked out at the oddly shaped boulders that thrust up from the surf. Moonlight streamed between them, bleaching the foamy water a stark silver color, and casting the rocks' inky shadows across the sand. As the fog floated over the dark sand toward them, she had the urge to try and summon the voices of the air and sea, as she'd been taught to do in the ancient mystery religion she followed. But she feared it might curdle Cyrus' Christian soul.

"What is 'God's gift'? Do you have any ideas?" he asked.

"Life. At least that's how I would answer that question. How would you?"

He gave her an uncertain half-shrug and shake of his head, but she could see the strange, somber expression on his handsome face.

"What's wrong, Cyrus?"

His gaze slid to her, but he paused for several moments before he said, "I think it's the Pearl."

"Which is . . . what?"

In the long silence that followed, Kalay heard one of their horses blow softly, and then the faint crunching of sand beneath hooves as the animals meandered along the beach, nipping every edible plant they could find. She kept her eyes on Cyrus. The lines at the corners of his eyes tightened. Finally, he answered, "You've heard us talk about Papias' book?"

"The *Lord's Logia*? Yes, what of it?"

While his gaze moved along the shoreline, he said, "The passage I read went something like this: 'The Son of Panthera will again put on his robe of glory, and call up the headless demon whom the winds obey when the Pearl is in hand.'"

"That's interesting. Or confusing."

"Yes," he said softly, "and that could be my fault, because I'm not skilled at Hebrew. I had to guess at many of the words." As though angry with himself, he slapped the grit from his sleeve.

They had taken refuge in the shadows of a tumbled pile of boulders that had cracked off the cliff some time in the distant past and begun to sprout tiny wind-tortured trees. As the fog moved through, the branches sighed and shook water droplets onto the rocks. The blend of surf and dripping trees calmed her after the long days on the desert trail.

She braced her shoulder against the cliff and faced him. His gaze, however, was not on her, but on the fog, staring at it hard, as though trying to read their dire fortunes in the shifting patterns.

She asked, "What if the map leads nowhere and we're just chasing ghosts?"

"I believe in ghosts. Don't you?"

She hugged herself against the misty chill. "No."

"No? Really?" He sounded truly astounded. "What about angels and demons?"

"Ah." She waggled a finger at him. "I believe in demons, yes, I do. But I've seen them walking the streets, looked into their eyes, and seen evil looking back. Trust me, the world is filled with demons. Remember Loukas?"

He paused. "But no angels?"

"I've never seen one. Simple as that. When one appears, I'll reconsider."

In a deeply reverent voice, Cyrus said, "They exist, Kalay, believe me. They've saved me many times on the battlefield."

"I've seen you fight, Cyrus. I suspect it's a good deal more likely that you saved yourself. You're handy with a sword and dagger. Not only that, you're smart. You probably made the most of the few pieces of luck that turned your way." She shrugged. "But if you want to believe that angels whispered in your ears, that's your affair."

Cyrus smiled. She saw his teeth glint in the moonlight. "Perhaps that is a guardian angel's strength. There's never proof of his handiwork, which means that people must have faith."

"Faith that they're being watched over?" Her mouth tightened with disbelief. "Seems like a waste of effort to me."

"But you have faith," he pointed out. "You told me you're a Goddess worshipper. Surely that requires as much faith as believing in angels."

She moved away from the cliff, straightened, and let her gaze roam the shadowed boulders. The mist had grown thicker, obscuring the gnarled trees, and she had a curious feeling that all was not as it seemed. She tried to shove the premonition away.

"The Goddess doesn't demand as much in return as your angels do," she replied. "My Goddess is happy with a prayer now and then, maybe a sacrifice on high holy days. She doesn't demand celibacy, or poverty, or any of the other unnatural things that your God does. The Goddess, as a result, is a whole lot easier to have faith in."

In a conspiratorial whisper, he said, "I think you're the most devout person I know. You just don't like to show it."

"And why would that be?"

"Because you're afraid it makes you look weak." He took a breath, and through a long exhalation said, "And weakness is something you of all people cannot afford."

Kalay considered him for several moments, watching the moonlight waver over his lips and flash in his eyes, surprised that he understood her so well. "Nor can you, I think. Though I suspect you believe your Lord would prefer it."

He shifted his back against the damp cliff, and fabric grated against stone. "There is not a night that passes that I don't feel Him seeking me in my dreams, calling to me to put away my sword and pick up His cross."

"Are you truly so deep a believer, Cyrus? I know you're a monk, but you don't seem to share their cowardly failings. At least, I haven't seen it."

"Haven't you?" His mouth curled into what could only be called a smile of self-loathing. "I'm afraid that what you see as my strengths I see as cowardice."

"Really? I'm surprised."

His gaze lowered, as though he didn't want to look at her when he said, "My Lord taught me to 'turn the other cheek,' to seek peace and love my neighbor. I believe those teachings with all my heart." His voice grew pained. "But I don't have the courage to follow them when people I care about have been murdered and others are in danger. But I should, Kalay, I should have the courage."

She opened her mouth to blurt something unpleasant, but his tormented expression stopped her. He had lifted his eyes and was gazing at her as though for reassurance. Perhaps he just wanted a few kind words? Someone to tell him she believed in him and was grateful for all he'd done to protect them?

Instead, she said, "That's the problem with your Lord. He's always forcing people to give up everything they know, everything they are, and for what? Nothing."

He straightened at her hard tone. "I wouldn't call salvation 'nothing.' I'd much rather be saved than eternally damned."

"Is that what you fear? Damnation? Well, stop it. Your tradition teaches you that no matter what you do your Lord will forgive you, doesn't it?"

"No, there are certain sins that God cannot forgive, but—"

"I trust you're not planning on committing any of those, are you?"

He regarded her suspiciously. "No."

"Then what are you worried about? When all this is done, your Lord will forgive you your trespasses, and you can go back to following His teachings as though nothing happened."

He squinted at her. "You have a truly unbalanced way of looking at things."

She grinned. "That sounded like a backhanded compliment. Are you trying to be romantic?"

His mouth opened, but he couldn't seem to find the correct response.

"Good," she said, taking his arm. "Now that you're speechless, let's talk of more important things."

"What could possibly be more important than the salvation of my immortal soul?"

She guided him away from the boulders toward the beach. "You told Libni we'd be gone before dawn. Where are we going?"

"I haven't the slightest idea. I assume that Libni and Barnabas will work out our route tonight."

"But we've only two choices, haven't we? Mount Gerizim or Jerusalem."

"Jerusalem," he said softly, as though feeling the names on his tongue. "It's so strange to call it that. For almost two hundred years it has been called by the name Emperor Hadrian gave it in the year 130: Aelia Capitolina. All my life, that's what I've called it."

"Well, Emperor Constantine just changed it back. It may be the one good thing he's done in his entire reign. Though Jews are still banned from entering the city, except on the ninth of the Hebrew month of Av."

"The ninth of Av? Why?"

She sucked in a breath, stunned by his ignorance. "That's the anniversary of the destruction of the Temple in the year 70. Jews are allowed to return to mourn the loss, and are tormented by Christians who circulate through the mourners berating them for continuing to weep and wait for the messiah. They shout that he's already come . . . that all the prophecies have been fulfilled, and Jews are just too stubborn to admit it."[92]

Cyrus' face tensed at the angry tone in her voice. "Have you visited Jerusalem on the ninth of Av?"

"My grandmother took me to the anniversary commemoration when I was five years old. I'll never forget how I felt. My parents were Christians, but I cannot tell you how very much I hated Christians that day."

Softly, Cyrus said, "I'm sorry."

Like most devout Christians, Cyrus believed Iesous was the messiah, and the destruction of the Temple was irrefutable proof that Iesous' prophecies had come true. It was enough to make her feel slightly ill.

She took a breath and let it out in a rush. "If we go there, we'll be riding into the lion's den, won't we?"

"Almost certainly. Bishop Macarios of Jerusalem is a close ally of Bishop Silvester's."

"Emperor Constantine's lackey?" she recalled. "Do you think he might be handing out daggers to our sicarii?"

"I think it's possible."

"Then I'd best get used to this fear that's been eating my belly for days."

As she released his arm and started to walk out onto the beach, he said, "Kalay?"

Even pitched low, his deep voice carried on the wind. She turned to find him gazing at her with pained eyes.

"Despite my beliefs, I will do everything I can to make certain we do not come to harm." He had his fists clenched at his sides, as though fighting the overwhelming urge to touch her.

"I've never doubted that, Cyrus."

"I know that you think I—" Cyrus went suddenly still and his gaze fastened on the sand at their feet. He cocked his head, as though listening.

After several moments of holding her breath, she whispered, "What is it?"

He pointed. The constant sea breezes had nearly covered them, but the dark spots of shadow that marred the sand could only be tracks.

She knelt to examine them, trying to decide if they'd been made by men or animals. "They're badly washed out, Cyrus."

She started to walk along them, and he reached out and took her hand with an unthinking intimacy. She flinched at his touch, as though her soul were warning her to run.

"No, don't follow them," he ordered.

The warmth of his flesh against her cold fingers made her shiver. "Why not?"

"They're hoofprints."

"So? Libni told you, this coast is a thoroughfare. Fishermen, traders, merchants, even whole caravans move up and down the length of it."

"This was one man on a horse, riding very close to the surf, as close as he could."

"A scout hoping his tracks would be washed away quickly?"

"Maybe."

Looking across the sand, Kalay saw how the tracks curved with the line of the water, veering around a narrow spit of land, and disappearing into the unknown night beyond.

"Do you think it's one of our pursuers?" she asked.

Cyrus propped his hand on the hilt of his belted sword and his fingers tightened around the grip, as if ready to draw it against things unseen. "I always assume the worst. If it doesn't come about, I'm pleasantly surprised."

"You and I have learned the same lessons."

He turned to survey the white ribbon of foam that marked the waves. "I swear I—" He stopped and clamped his jaw.

A strange undercurrent filtered through the words. She reached up and turned his face to look into his eyes. They were overflowing with guilt. He was holding something back, drowning in secrets that were eating him alive. "There's something you haven't told me, isn't there? Something you haven't told anyone. What is it?"

"I—I can't tell you."

She let her hand drop. "Is it about Loukas?"

He just stared at her. "You're too perceptive for your own good."

"I've been told that before. Best to tell me now, Cyrus."

He braced his feet. As though the words were being ripped from his chest by a hook, he croaked, "I—I remember where I've seen him."

"Where?"

"The day my wife died."

He spun around to walk away, but Kalay grabbed his hand and jerked him back. Agony lined his face. As though he was expecting the question, his fingers crushed hers.

"When was that?"

He seemed to be struggling with himself, deciding which words to use.

"It was right after the Milvian Bridge battle. I—I just couldn't stand the hypocrisy." A hushed violence strained the words. "I deserted the army. The emperor sent men to bring me back—or maybe to kill me. They broke into my home in the middle of the night. I told Spes to run while I fought them off. . . ." His shoulders hunched and he seemed to fold in upon himself. "They killed her first."

"Right in front of you? You saw it?" His expression told her everything. She exhaled hard and nodded. For a brief moment, the mist parted and she saw the horses galloping along the beach in the moonlight, their manes and tails flying. Playful whinnies carried on the wind. "Was it Loukas who killed her?"

"No. He was the reason I got away."

"I don't understand."

He gripped his sword again, as though to comfort himself. "He was young. Inexperienced. I surprised and overpowered him, then ran. I doubt he ever completely lived down the humiliation. He was supposed to be guarding my door."

Kalay shivered and started back toward the caves. Cyrus walked behind her. Every so often she caught the jangle of the weapons on his belt, or heard his soft footsteps.

Just before they reached the entry cave, she turned. "Cyrus, what did you mean by 'the hypocrisy'? Not that I'm an admirer of Rome or the emperor, but you don't seem like the sort who would desert."

He stood perfectly still. The wind blew his curly black hair straight back, showing the smooth curves of his cheekbones and brow. "I was there that day."

"What day?"

"*The* day. The day before the battle."

She searched her memory, trying to figure out what he meant. "The day the emperor saw the cross in the sky?"

He snorted in disgust. "He'd been sitting in his tent all morning drinking wine. He called me in just after noon. I was his trusted adviser, and he needed my advice. He told me he had decided how to motivate our men to attack the bridge. The only part he couldn't decide was the exact form the myth should take."

"The myth?"

"Oh, yes. He was a master mythmaker. He knew exactly what he was doing. But he couldn't decide if he should see a cross of light or the letters *chi-rho*. You know, a kind of divine monogram? Or maybe he should simply hear angels singing 'By this conquer.'[93] He asked me which I liked better. I said I thought it was a foolish idea that would alienate many of our devoted Roman soldiers."

"And how did the emperor respond?"

"He threw me out of his tent."

The fog shifted, swirling around them in the glittering haze, and the shadows turned slippery and liquid.

"I think that's when it began to worry him."

"That you knew it was not a miraculous vision but a political ploy?"

"Yes."

Kalay folded her arms tightly over her chest. "I can't believe you're still alive."

"Nor can I."

"Have the Romans hunted you ever since?"

He rubbed his scabbard, as though smoothing away the drops of moisture that glistened on the leather. "I don't know."

She slowly lowered her arms. "I think that's the first lie you've told me."

He squeezed his eyes closed for a long moment, before saying, "They probably have. I do not know for certain, but I've often feared it."

Kalay put a hand on his broad shoulder. It was a friendly gesture, nothing more, but he uncertainly reached up, took her hand, and pulled her toward him. His arms shook as he wrapped them around her. "Don't say anything. Just let me hold you for a few moments."

Stunned, she just stood there. A strange sensation of relief possessed her. Not desire, not love, just . . . relief. Which was totally foolish. They were being stalked by dedicated killers who might be watching them at this very instant. Though to see through this fog, they would have to be very close by.

Tenderly, she said, "I'm starting to hope you're right."

"About what?"

"About there being angels watching over us."

His grip relaxed slightly. He looked down at her. Something about the softness in his eyes touched her, building a warmth in her heart.

"Why?" he asked.

"Because both our guards are down. If I were a murderer, this is the moment I would strike."

He backed away and his gaze quickly searched the beach and the cliff. "You're right. Let's get back inside. If God is very good to us, tonight we'll get some sleep."

She let him walk past her, and followed a pace behind.

A half hour later, Kalay pulled the worn softness of the blanket up around her throat and stared at the dark ceiling high above. Cyrus and Zarathan were sound asleep. She'd been trying, but thoughts of Cyrus kept waking her. A sharp ache invaded her chest. She couldn't shake the sensation of his arms around her. . . . It was as powerful as a polished golden calf in the searing deserts of old.

THE TEACHING ON THE SHADOW

"Are you still there, brother?"

You roll over at his whisper and inhale a breath of the warm night air. Stars glisten overhead, and the breeze is redolent with the scents of damp earth and trees. He lies rolled in his blanket two cubits away with his head propped on his laced hands, staring up at the darkness. Every time he blinks, his eyes catch the starlight and hold it for an instant.

"Of course I'm still here. Where else would I be?"

"I can't find you."

You prop yourself up on one elbow. "I'm right here. Turn and look at me."

You see his mouth curl in a smile. "I've been looking at you for months. I still can't find you."

Ah, now, you understand. He's being profound. You say, "Well, it's not my fault that you won't open your eyes. I'm so close to you that I could be your shadow, yet you are blind to me."

His smile fades as though it never existed. For several instants he does not speak. Finally, he says, "Shadows need light to live. They die in the darkness. I fear that's where you are, and why I can't find you."

You study his silhouette. . . . He's the one who is the shadow to-night. The shadow of the darkness itself. "Yeshu, I am not in the dark. I am a shadow in love with the sun who hides out of self-preservation. That's why you can't find me."

He somberly turns to me. "What do you mean?"

"I mean I know what you're planning, and when the sun dies, all of the shadows it casts die just as completely. How can you be so heartless, so careless of those who love you?"

He takes a breath and exhales very slowly, as though cherishing the sensation of air moving in his lungs. "Are you afraid?"

You stare up at the stars again, at the way they silver the heavenly vault.

"Yes," you say. "I am afraid."

In a voice almost too soft to hear, he answers, "Then perhaps I have finally found you."

THIRTY

In the depths of the night, when only one candle continued to burn in Libni's library, Barnabas gently shoved the map aside and reached for a slice of goat cheese. As he took a bite, the rich flavor filled his mouth. They had been tossing ideas back and forth since he'd arrived, just as they used to at the library in Caesarea. Both of them were happy.

Libni broke off a piece of bread and, as he ate, his gaze filled with far-away places, memories that Barnabas could only guess at. After a long while, he reverently touched the corner of the papyrus. "Have you ever figured out why there is a large cross at the bottom of the papyrus, surrounded by three small crosses?"

"I'm not sure they are crosses."

"The central feature is a cross. It just has other symbols attached to it."

"Which means it may not be a Christian symbol at all. And if it is, it was almost certainly added decades later, probably by some pious monk. Not only that, the small crosses were definitely written in a different ink."

Prior to Constantine's vision, the cross had been viewed as the instrument of Iesous' execution, of his shame. As Saint Paul noted, it was a huge "stumbling block" to conversion. The cross was not revered in and of itself, nor were Iesous and the cross seen as identical. One did not signify the other. There were many symbols revered by early Christians: the palm branch, the olive branch, the dove and the lamb, the anchor, the baptismal waters, the blood of Christ, the fish, or *ichthys*—because it was an acrostic of Iesous Christos, Son of God, Savior. But not the cross.

Then, thirteen years ago, Constantine's vision had changed all that. The cross had become the black blossom of the Church's imagination. It was painted on armor, shields, military standards, weapons of every variety, even gallows and prisons. It had become a symbol that Barnabas strongly suspected the savior himself would have abhorred. To Iesous and his disciples, the cross had not represented salvation, but absolute injustice and humiliation.

"I think you're right on both counts," Libni agreed. "It is not a Christian cross, and it was added by a very pious man: Ioses of Arimathaia, a devout Jew. The cross does not symbolize the crucifixion; it symbolizes something else. As do the small crosses."

Barnabas took another bite of the exquisitely aromatic cheese. "It sounds like you have an idea what that might be?"

Libni's mouth curled into a faint smile. He reached out, gripped the corner of the oldest, most frail map, and carefully dragged it across the table. His movements made the candle splutter. He positioned the map between them, then lifted and let his finger hover over a specific area. "Do you recall what's located here?"

Barnabas leaned forward to study the brown lines that indicated the old walled city of Jerusalem. "What's the date of this map?"

"As best I can determine, somewhere between the years zero and seventy. At any rate, before the destruction of the Temple." His finger was still hovering.

Barnabas said, "You have a big finger. Is it over the Garden Tomb, or the Damascus Gate?"

Libni's smile widened. "The gate."

Frustrated, Barnabas said, "I'm tired of guessing. Just tell me."

Libni's gaze scanned the shadows before he murmured, "The Square of the Column."

Barnabas blinked. Just inside the Damascus Gate there had been a broad plaza. In the middle of that plaza had stood a tall column that served as a reference point for the measurement of road distances.[94] Many groups of laborers had devised plays on that column. The one that particularly interested Libni was the form used by the stoneworkers, the *tektons,* which appeared as a builder's square tented over a circle, or column.

234 KATHLEEN O'NEAL GEAR & W. MICHAEL GEAR

"And how," Barnabas inquired, "does the Square of the Column relate to . . ." His voice faded as the answer became obvious, and a hollow floating sensation of elation possessed him.

Libni leaned back in his chair and chuckled.

In a hushed voice, Barnabas said, "The Square of the Column marked the crossroads of the sacred city, so you think . . ." He paused to consider before he finished. "You think the cross on the papyrus might refer to the Crossroads?"

Libni made an airy gesture with his hand. "It explains the extra 'arms' on the basic symbol: they're roads. And it's as good a hypothesis as anything else I've come up with over the years, and not nearly as wild as some of my ideas."

For the first time in months, Barnabas saw a tiny pinprick of light shining through the dark veil of the papyrus, and he could feel his soul take another silent, measured step into the dark Chamber of Hewn Stone.

He leaned forward, slapped Libni's shoulders, and laughed, "Oh, my dear friend, how I've missed you."

THIRTY-ONE

Kalay jerked awake in the darkness, and glimpsed Tiras and Uzziah standing guard just inside the rounded cave entry. Their presence, however, did little to soothe her. They didn't have any weapons. What were they supposed to do if attacked? Scream? She gripped the long, curved knife in her hand all the more tightly.

The wind had dwindled to a distant whimper and the night air was thick with the smell of the sea. She inhaled deeply, but the waves of shakiness wrought by the nightmares did not go away. She couldn't shove the frightening images from her mind. Finally, she looked over at Cyrus.

He lay within reach, flat on his back, his hand on his sword. His chest rose and fell in the deep rhythms of sleep, and she was glad for him. Across the room, Zarathan slept like a child, with his straggly blond hair hanging in his eyes. His snores resembled the troubled breathing of an infant. He appeared to be in a cocoon, so tightly was he rolled in his blanket.

Kalay shook her head. If they had to rise quickly, he would still be wallowing on the floor trying to disentangle himself from his blanket when the killer cut his throat with one clean stroke. Didn't he ever think of such things?

She pondered that, and decided the answer was "probably not." He'd led a soft, warm life with caring parents, always safe and well fed. A life she envied with all her heart.

As she closed her eyes and tried to force herself to sleep, a queer dread filtered through her. Once again, she found herself back in Caesarea—her parents freshly dead, fighting for garbage against fierce stray dogs whose eyes were as hungry as her own, dodging cart wheels as wagons thundered down the dirty streets, running from the smiles of men . . . and looking, always looking, for her brother. No matter where she went in the city, she expected to see him walking around a corner with his new family. Or maybe he'd escaped and was hiding as she was, struggling to eat. If only she could find him, they could be a family again, and—

She jerked awake when a gentle hand touched her hair.

"Are you all right?" Cyrus whispered.

"I was asleep. Why did you wake me?" she asked, her heart pounding in her throat.

He stared at her with kind eyes. "You were crying. I thought you might be having a bad dream."

Kalay blinked and discovered that tears had wet her cheeks. She hastily wiped them away. "I'm fine."

"What were you dreaming?"

"Nothing. I—I don't recall."

He softly said, "Sleep, Kalay. Uzziah and Tiras will warn us if anything is amiss. We must sleep."

"I know."

She laid her head down and discovered that he had not moved his hand; it still rested comfortingly against her hair. She didn't roll away, just focused on the moon-silvered edge of his sword where it rested between them. With a light touch, Cyrus stroked her hair.

And she longed for nothing more than to lie in his arms and sleep for a month.

Her fear was more than just the nightmares, more than the utter terror of their situation, of being on the run, chased by a man who might capture and keep her alive for months or years, or until she managed to hang herself. She had begun to fear solving the riddle of the papyrus.

In a bare whisper, she asked, "Cyrus, are you afraid of what we'll find when we reach the end of this journey?"

His hand went still.

Tiras turned to look at them with wide, unblinking eyes, as though he'd heard and was as interested in the answer as she was.

Cyrus murmured, "No. But I fear what we will have to do afterward."

Kalay stared at the dark ceiling.

Afterward?

The very idea struck her as strange beyond belief. Cyrus was worried about what they would say and do after they recovered the Pearl . . . or failed to recover it. For her, only one question mattered: Would they live or die?

She tucked her knife beneath the edge of her blanket and listened to the night. Outside, waves washed the shore, as they had since the beginning of time, totally unconcerned with the fears of men.

THIRTY-TWO

Massa

I wait in the dark courtyard just outside the high priest's palace. Less than a half hour ago, Kaiaphas summoned me and charged me with relaying the Council's decisions to the praefectus. I feel sick to my stomach. More than anything, I long to rush into the palace, free Yeshua, and make a mad dash to escape.

Laughter rises, and I glance to my right where the Roman decuria stands. It will escort Yeshua to the Praetorium where he will stand before Praefectus Pontios Pilatos. The ten soldiers talk and smile, apparently oblivious to the danger of the duty they are about to perform. To them he is just another Ioudaios, just another Jew.

My gaze drifts to the thirty Temple police officers who are stationed around the courtyard. Kaiaphas, clearly, is taking no chances.

The sound of feet upon stone echoes from inside the palace.

The massive doors swing open and two guards bring Yeshua out. He has his hands bound in front of him. Dark curly hair sticks out around the edges of the white himation pulled over his head. His eyes resemble black bonfires.

I start to go to him, but the Roman decurion, in charge of his decuria, shouts in Greek, "Stay back. No one is allowed to speak with the prisoner."

I back up, and Yeshua sucks in a breath as though to fortify himself for what is ahead.

The soldiers surround him and the decurion orders, "March to the Praetorium."

I follow along behind, escorted by two officers of the Temple police.

Pilatos' Praetorium is a magnificent structure situated on the crest of the western hill in the upper city. From the rooftop, he has a view of the sacrificial altar in the Temple compound. This pleases him. He takes every opportunity to remind the priests that he literally has his eye on them. As well, he loves the fact that one hundred years ago, his Praetorium served as the ancient royal palace for the Jewish Hasmonean kings.[95]

As I walk due east along the road, I can see the Praetorium. Built in a huge square with a massive tower at each corner, it resembles nothing so much as a luxurious fortress.

The soldiers have gone quiet, but the sound of their boots on the cobblestones echoes from the low, flat-topped houses of the poor that line the road. Here and there dogs sleep before doors. Some growl or bark at us as we pass. People are just beginning to rise, and the scent of wood smoke from breakfast fires rides the wind. Lamps gleam in many windows. Often, I see a face staring out at us.

As we climb the western hill, my breathing grows deeper. Seven years ago, because of my language skills, the Council appointed me as liaison with the praefectus. That means I have known Lucius Pontios Pilatos since he was first appointed as praefectus of Judea, three years ago. He calls me his friend, and insists we address each other by our first names. I think it amuses him. But I know him for what he is: a brutal, shrewd man, capable of extreme cruelty. He can smell weakness and eats weak men alive. And he has contempt for all Jews. No matter what I'm feeling, I must appear to be strong.

We climb the steps to the gate and the Praetorian Guards gesture for the decuria to enter the courtyard. Broad and filled with palms and olive trees, it is a beautiful and fragrant place, especially at this tranquil hour of night.

The decuria continues walking, but my legs freeze when I see men moving in nearly every lamp-lit window. And there are more soldiers standing in the shadows against the walls of the courtyard. Panic seizes me. If I had to guess, I'd say that there are five hundred men or more here—an entire Roman cohort. There are already three cohorts stationed around the city. Did Pilatos call in this additional cohort because he feared rioting over the holy days? Why wasn't the Council informed?

I hurry to catch up with the decuria as it continues across the courtyard to the hall of judgment where two soldiers stand guard outside the door.

Before we enter, I say to the Temple officers, "Remain outside in case I have reports I wish you to carry back to the high priest."

"Yes, Councilor."

I follow the decurion through the doors and into the hall of judgment. Despite the gleam of dozens of lamps, it is a stark place, very white, filled with white limestone, white marble, and white plastered porticos. Even Lucius Pontios Pilatos is dressed in a white toga. He stands near the Secretarium, the secret chamber where hearings and trials are held. Two of his apparitores, *clerks, stand nearby. Pilatos is tall, muscular, with a swarthy complexion and hard black eyes. His closely trimmed black hair makes his clean-shaven face seem severely triangular. He has a cup of wine in one hand, and a report of some kind in the other. He's reading.*

"Salve, Praefectus," *I greet and bow.*

"Ioses of Arimathaia, a pleasant morning to you," he says without taking his eyes from the scroll. "Are you well?"

I straighten. "Well enough. Do you know why I am here?"

He lowers the scroll and looks at me. "Yes. I was surprised when Kaiaphas sent word that you would relay the Council's decisions. Knowing, as they must, that you are a devoted follower of the accused." He holds out a hand to Yeshua.

For a moment, I cannot speak or even move. While the Council does not know it, I should not be surprised that Pilatos does.

I say, "You pay your spies far too much, Lucius. Surely they have better things to do than follow me around."

Lucius smiles. "You? Why would I follow you? My spies follow subversives and malcontents. You're not one of those, are you?"

I gruffly fold my arms. "What if I am? Would it scare you very much?"

He laughs. "Only if I see you riding into the city tomorrow on an ugly little ass with a filthy, screaming throng behind you. Then, yes, of course, that would tremble the very foundations of Rome." He gives me a mock tremble for effect. He's enjoying himself.

I return to the issue at hand. "Lucius, being his follower does not, I believe, disqualify me from relaying the Council's decisions."

"No, of course not. I didn't mean to suggest that it did, only that they must trust you very much. Were I in their situation, I would fear that you might not relay my words accurately. Would you like a cup of wine?"

"You're very gracious, but no."

"Water, perhaps?"

"I am fine for the moment."

Pilatos shrugs and sips his wine. The cup is a work of art. Around the lip is a row of red Roman soldiers carrying shields and wearing bronze helmets. The detail is stunning. I can see the individual designs on each of the shields.

Pilatos casually asks, "It is true, is it not, that your people are forbidden to leave their houses beginning at sundown tonight?"

"When two witnesses have counted three stars, yes, Praefectus."

"And it is a grave crime if they disobey this law?"

"It is."

Pilatos smiles deprecatingly. "Then surely all will be quiet tonight. After the excessive noise, and all the shoving and pushing in the markets, I shall look forward to that."

He stares at me, smiles, then signals for his clerk to refill his cup of wine. As the clerk obliges, I wonder what he's up to. He never asks a question idly, and he knows Jewish laws for Pesach almost as well as I do. He's been here for three Pesach feasts.

Suspiciously, I say, "It will be quiet. Unless you are planning to stir up trouble. Is that why you have an entire cohort living in your palace?"

"Me? Cause trouble? You mean by executing your pathetic little bastard friend over there? Would that cause a riot? Or should I say, another riot?"

The guards have backed away, leaving Yeshua standing alone in the amber gleam of lamplight. He seems to be staring into some faraway kingdom, and not much liking what he sees.

My stomach muscles clench. "Yeshua ben Pantera is greatly beloved by almost everyone, as was evidenced by his rapturous welcome a few days ago when he rode into the city on his, as you say, 'ugly little ass.' And Rome, as you know, is hated by almost everyone. Surely you don't want to risk provoking a revolt."

"And surely you are not suggesting that I ignore treason."

I lift my chin. "Praefectus, the Council of Seventy-one met for most of the night. We interrogated Yeshua ben Pantera and examined witnesses. We found no evidence of treason. In fact, the witnesses agreed on almost nothing.

If you have other evidence, we would very much appreciate the chance to review it."

Straightforwardly, Pilatos says, *"I have two witnesses who, in separate interrogations, implicated him in acts of treason against Rome."*

"Honorable men?"

"Despicable men. Zealots. They killed three of my soldiers earlier this week in the riot that occurred near the Temple. I condemned them to death, of course, but during their lengthy floggings they named ben Pantera as one of their supporters. Indeed, I suspect he caused the disturbance to provide a distraction that allowed the Zealots to attack my men."

I am stunned by this accusation. *"What are the names of these Zealots?"*

"Dysmas and Gestas. Both are from the Galilaian . . . as I believe your friend is."

I do not even blink. *"Being from the same region is hardly a crime, Lucius. Did these Zealots say that Yeshua ben Pantera was a member of their movement, or that he agreed to help them—"*

"Am I mistaken that one of his disciples is called 'Shimon the Zealot'? My sources tell me that's his name. But perhaps that's inaccurate." He waits for me to answer, knowing what I must say.

"You are not mistaken, Praefectus, but—"

"And what about the one called Yudah Sicarius? Is he not called by that name because he is a member of the dagger-wielding group known as the sicarii?"

My heart is thundering, but I lift my brows in exaggerated surprise. *"You've become quite a scholar, Lucius. What's your point?"*

He grins. *"My point is that ben Pantera openly welcomes the enemies of Rome into his ranks."*

"That says very little. He also welcomes lepers, tax collectors, and women. It doesn't matter who they are or what they believe so long as—"

"Ioses, did you know there is a large Zealot camp hiding out in the Kidron valley, only a few steps from where your friend ben Pantera has been living with his pitiful disciples? You might as well say they've been living together."

Blood drains from my face and I feel suddenly cold. Naturally, I know. The Council makes a point of knowing such things. *"I heard something, yes. Why?"*

"I just found it interesting. But I'm sure that despite their loud cries for the

overthrow of Rome, the Zealots are only here to celebrate the holy days, or you, my good friend, would have warned me." He sips his wine, watching me over the rim of his cup.

The soldiers around the room whisper to each other and stare hard at me. Several lower their hands to their belted daggers.

I say, "Do you have information that they plan an attack?"

He thrusts his scroll out for his clerk to take, then exhales hard. "You asked what evidence I have of ben Pantera's treason. During their floggings, the two Zealots told me that ben Pantera likened conquering Rome to a very valuable 'Pearl,' and said they should forsake even their families to obtain it. He told them he would welcome their help." Pilatos makes an airy gesture with his wine. "I call that treason. What do you call it?"

Faint tendrils of understanding are twining around my heart, crushing it. Pilatos is a clever politician. Surely he has been considering for some time the best way to be rid of the Zealots.

"I call it lies."

Pilatos' smile fades. "You admire him. I know that, but try to see this through my eyes. When a man stands so accused, three courses of action are open to me: I can find him guilty and sentence him, I can find him not guilty and acquit him, or I can decide the case has not been proven and ask that further evidence be produced. Of course, if the accused confesses, that solves the matter. So, let us proceed and see which way these proceedings go. Decurion, bring Yeshua ben Pantera into the Secretarium."

"Yes, Praefectus."

Pilatos turns his back to me and strides into the small, curtained room where hearings and trials are conducted. I see him sit upon his sella, *his seat of judgment. His white toga falls in sculpted folds around his sandaled feet. When Yeshua is brought forward into the Secretarium, the clerks pull the curtain closed for privacy and station themselves outside. The decurion backs away, and to my surprise, Pilatos' hand appears and shoves the curtain open, so that I can see him—or perhaps so he can see me.*

This mystifies me. I know the rules. Once these proceedings begin, no one outside the Secretarium is allowed to speak. It's called a Secretarium *because the proceedings are supposed to be secret. Surely he can't be planning on carrying on a conversation with me. Roman law is clear:* vanae voces populi non sunt audiendae, *the vain voices of the people may not be listened to.*[96]

"Come forward," he orders Yeshua.

Yeshua kneels at Pilatos' feet.

Pilatos' brows lift, as though he suspects the gesture is an obsequious appeal for leniency. I know it is not, since I've seen Yeshua kneel before his own disciples, as well as the lame, the sick.

"They call you Rab, *do they not?" Pilatos asks.*[97]

Yeshua closes his eyes again and his lips move with a silent prayer.

"Shall I call you that? Rab?*" Pilatos presses. "Are you a teacher? A great chief? A wise man?"*

Yeshua whispers, "Everyone that is of the Truth hears my voice."

Pilatos glances at me, and hisses, "His voice, not the emperor's." He turns back to Yeshua. "I have heard many of the Ioudaiosoi say that you are the son of David. Are you a king? The king of the Jews?"

Almost forlornly Yeshua exhales the words, "You say so."

"Is that a yes or a no? And take care in answering me, for pretending to be a king is treasonable under the Lex Julia, *the Laws of Rome."*

Perhaps suspecting he's walking into a trap, Yeshua wisely says nothing.

Pilatos heaves an annoyed breath. "Let me clarify so that I am sure you understand the charge. It is a capital offense known as crimen laesae maiestatis *to claim to be the king of a province under Roman rule, unless the emperor has nominated you as the king of that province, as the emperor did for your King Herod. But I do not believe you have been so nominated. Have you?"*

Yeshua replies, "My kingdom is not of this world. If it were, wouldn't my followers be fighting for my release right now? I came into this world to bear witness to the Truth."

"I didn't ask about the bravery of your so-called followers, I asked if you were a king. I assume if you have a kingdom—wherever it is—then you claim to be a king. Is that correct?"

Yeshua stays silent.

Pilatos' dark brows plunge down. "Perhaps I have misunderstood your answer. Are you telling me that you are not a king in a political sense, but rather in a theological, moral sense?"

Yeshua's mouth tightens.[98]

Pilatos turns to me. "Ioses, surely you see that pretensions such as this make his offense all the more grave. He claims that his kingdom is not comprised of this puny little remote province, but is divine and universal. He has set himself and his kingdom up against the divinity of the emperor and Rome. Only the kingdom of the immortal Tiberias Caesar is divine and universal."

This sends a flood of red, hot blood surging through my veins. Now I understand why he left the curtain open. I am his witness. He wants me to report what I have seen to the Council.

I open my mouth to object, despite the consequences, but Pilatos says, "Ioses, even if I did not have the testimonies of the Zealots regarding his treasonous words, I could not allow such contempt of the emperor to go unpunished. Surely you see that." He rises to his feet and passes sentence: "Yeshua ben Pantera, in accordance with Roman law, I find you guilty of treason against the holy Roman Empire. I sentence you to be crucified on this day, along with your conspirators Dysmas and Gestas."

Then he turns to me and smiles as he says, "Decurion, take him to his cell, and as a favor to my good friend Ioses of Arimathaia, I order you to scourge ben Pantera until he's half dead. That should hasten his death on the cross. He won't suffer so long. I'm a generous man, aren't I, Ioses?"[99]

The decurion waves his soldiers forward and they surround Yeshua and march him away.[100]

A stinging sensation filters through my body. I feel light-headed. Somewhere deep inside me a voice keeps saying, no,no,no . . .

Pilatos glances at me and starts to walk away.

"Praefectus, please give me a few moments to speak with you."

"You are my friend, Ioses. Of course."

I can barely stand, and he smiles as though the morning has been a trifling matter.

"By Jewish law and custom, we must bury our dead before nightfall on a feast day. I humbly request the right to take down and bury each man who dies today."

The God of Yisrael demands that I show the same generosity of spirit for the other two criminals that I do for Yeshua. And Yeshua . . . Yeshua would expect that what I do for the man whom I love, I also do for the strangers whom I know not.[101]

"But Ioses, you know it is Roman law that a crucified man may not be buried. Such bodies are to be left on the cross until beasts and birds of prey devour them. We even post guards to make certain that friends or family members

cannot take down a corpse. In fact, unauthorized burial of a crucified criminal is a crime."[102]

"Yes, I—I know that. But we both also know that the emperor or his officers may grant special authorization to bury such a convict. You yourself have given such permission on occasion. I'm asking that you, once again, grant a special dispensation to allow me to bury them."

An expression of annoyance creases his lean, dark face. "If these Zealots had been convicted by the Council of Seventy-one, what would happen to their corpses?"

I wonder why he's asking. He couldn't care less what happens to Jews. "It is against the law for any person to bury or mourn a criminal executed by a Jewish court. Such convicts are buried by the court in the court's graveyard, outside the city walls."[103]

Pilatos frowns, as though thinking. "Then if I grant you a special burial permit, I will appear particularly generous, won't I?"

"Oh, yes, very generous. And I assure you the Council will be deeply grateful."

Pilatos signals to his dark-haired clerk and as the young man rushes across the room, he says, "Write out a burial permit for Ioses of Arimathaia."[104]

"For all three convicts?" the clerk asks.

"Yes, all three, providing they die today. But—," Pilatos adds, "bring me the nails."

"Yes, Praefectus."

Pilatos gives him a cold smile, says, "Valete, Ioses," then turns and walks away.

The clerk says, "If you will wait a few moments—"

"I'll wait."

The clerk leaves.

My thoughts are disjointed, flashing from one image to the next, as though I've been struck in the head and can no longer piece together even the simplest of puzzles.

There is only one thing I know for certain: Pilatos has no idea what he's about to do. A holy man who perishes at the hands of the oppressors of Yisrael will join the ranks of heroes who, throughout history, have sacrificed their lives for the faith and paved the way for the ultimate liberation of Yisrael. He's about to turn Yeshua into a holy martyr, a man whose name other men will *fight and die for. A man who, by the end of the day, every Zealot in the city will be ready to die for.*

I suddenly go numb.

A breath of cool wind eddies through the hall, and causes the lamps to waver and spit. Yellow light flutters over the walls.

Dear God.

A riot is just the excuse he needs to attack the Zealot camp and wipe out every last man. With the streets clear because people must remain in their houses, his legions will be able to move unheeded, to slaughter at will.

And, for the first time, I know Gamliel is right.[105]

THIRTY-THREE

Loukas flattened his body against the shadowed cliff, and watched the horses on the beach. They walked with their heads down, as though too tired to place one hoof in front of the other. He'd watched as Atinius and Kalay had disappeared into the cave, leaving the two inexperienced youths to guard the entrance. He'd been working his way from shadow to shadow since that time, and the young monks had not even glanced his way. Now and then they spoke to each other, but he couldn't understand their words.

He let his gaze wander to the boulders that lined the shore. From this vantage, they resembled a curving mouth filled with broken, rotting teeth.

It had taken meager effort to find this place, ten well-placed questions in the local villages. Everyone knew of Libni the Hermit, or Old Scary, though only a few knew the exact location of his caves.

Loukas motioned to his accomplices. The four men slid forward, and one by one, ghosted past him. Loukas watched with narrowed eyes. Why on earth Pappas Athanasios had chosen these men from all of the defenders of the faith stationed in Alexandria, Loukas did not know. They were too old to be given such responsibilities. Gray shot through their short hair and eyebrows, glinting in the moonlight. And, despite their muscular frames, Loukas doubted they had the agility to respond to a well-timed assault. At least they wore black togas that blended with the darkness. That would give them a small edge.

Not that it mattered. They had one purpose here tonight. To Loukas it seemed ludicrous. All the more so since his second humiliation at the hands of Atinius in Leontopolis. He needed but reach down to remind himself of the wound to his manhood and pride.

I just hope this new plan of yours works, Meridias.

For a long time, Loukas' world consisted of standing with his back pressed against the damp, cold stone, watching the Egyptians' slow advance, and straining to hear.

Despite his desperate need to watch Atinius bleed, and to wring terror from that she-devil of a woman, he would follow orders.

He always had.

THIRTY-FOUR

It was still the middle of the night when Kalay awoke, stirred, and combed tangled hair out of her eyes. For a blank moment, she couldn't remember where she was; this was *not* her washing hut. Where the dank, muddy odor of the Nile should have been, the scent of the sea confused her . . . then a flurry of hushed voices sent her scrambling for her knife. In a flash, she'd thrown off her blanket and rolled against the wall, Loukas' long, curving blade clutched in her fist.

The unearthly glow of starlight through thick fog turned the world murky, and she saw the dark shapes of three men near the cave mouth. The tallest, Cyrus, was little more than a black ghost, moving along the wall toward the entrance. One of the shapes—Tiras, she thought—edged into the tunnel that led to the library and vanished.

Near the entrance, there was the startled snort of a horse, and a flurry of pounding hooves.

Kalay felt her insides shrivel. She pulled herself to a squat and held her breath.

She could no longer see Cyrus. He had blended into the darkness. Was he by the entrance?

From somewhere outside a man said, "Centurion? You can't escape. Give up now. Surrender the papyrus, and you'll save the lives of your companions. Trying to stand against us is useless. I have a full garrison out here."

Not Loukas. Nonetheless, a thousand years from now, her moldering bones would recognize that cold, insidious voice.

A black shadow wavered near the entrance.

Cyrus said, "I don't think so. If you did, twenty men would have already rushed this cave and dragged us out. Since they didn't, I assume you're either alone, or have but a few men with you."

Turning her head slightly, she looked across the room and made out Zarathan, still fast asleep.

Dear Iesous Christos, the stupidest killer in the world could creep up on him and crush his skull.

The man outside moved . . . and she saw him. He stood with his back pressed against the stone just beyond the lip of the cave. There was another man behind him, shorter, with a wealth of gray hair that glimmered in the starlight.

Kalay gestured to Cyrus, held up two fingers, then pointed to where they stood. She had no idea if he could see her or not, but his black shadow moved another step closer to the entrance. He slid his hand into the light, lifted one finger, and pointed to her side of the entrance.

The fear pumping in her veins almost made her sick. She rose to a crouch and moved into position.

From this perspective, she could see the men clearly. Both were dressed in black, but their swords glinted wetly, appearing and disappearing in the windblown shreds of fog.

The cave suddenly felt stifling; fear sweat matted her dress to her body. Fighting to keep her breathing even, she leaned her shoulder against the stone wall.

"I have been authorized to make you an offer," the tall man called.

"What offer?"

"The Church is willing to pardon all of you. You need only surrender the papyrus and take vows of silence."

She saw Cyrus shake his head as though incredulous and heard his low laugh. "Tell Pappas Meridias that there is no 'papyrus.' And of what use is such a guarantee? On the Church's orders, Meridias murdered an entire monastery . . . almost one hundred monks who had devoted their lives to God. What are seven more lives?"

The men skulked closer, close enough that Kalay could see their pale faces.

"Centurion, we know that you are the only one in there with fighting skills. If you don't surrender, all of your friends will die because of you. Is that what you want?"

Despite her best efforts, her breathing had gone low and ragged, hissing through her nostrils.

On the far side of the cave, three quiet shadows emerged from the tunnel and took up positions around the walls. The sound of their footsteps was barely audible. They might have been soldiers rather than monks.

Kalay heard fabric grate on stone outside, and knew they were moving in for the kill.

She gripped her knife in her right hand and held it low, ready to lunge and rip upward. By the age of fifteen she'd learned you never raised a knife over your head. A man could grab your wrist, twist, and take it away from you with little effort. It was harder to block a knife if it was held low and close. Problem was, if they came in with swords swinging, she'd lose her hands long before she had a chance to attack.

Cyrus looked directly at Kalay. He mouthed the word, "Ready?"

She jerked a nod.

Just as Cyrus lifted his sword . . .

A wild, inhuman shriek rose from the rear of the cave, congealing the blood in Kalay's veins. Before she could force her shaking legs to move, a mountainous vision of fluttering brown rags rushed past her and out into the thick fog.

Barnabas cried, "Libni, no!"

After a heartbeat's hesitation, Cyrus, Barnabas, Tiras, and Uzziah charged out behind Libni. The metallic clashings of swords erupted . . . along with screams.

Kalay girded herself and eased out into the moonlit mist, trying to see what was happening. She glimpsed swirling figures, flashes of swords, and saw that the battle was moving south, down the beach.

She took two running steps to follow . . .

A big black-gloved hand thrust out of the mist, caught her sleeve, and wrenched her off her feet. She hit the ground hard, kicking and flailing, roaring in anger, until she saw the sword blade drop through the fog and stop just above her heart.

"Move and you're dead," the harsh voice ordered. She could hear the tension, nearly panic, behind it.

Kalay subtly tucked her knife beneath her skirt and stared up at him.

"Lie still, you little *scorta,* or I'll forego my orders and cut you in half." The man was muscular, stalky, with gray-streaked black hair.

"What do you want with me? I don't know anything!"

A shout rose down the shore and he glanced in that direction, smiled, and boldly knelt beside her. His gaze traveled over her throat and the swell of her breasts. With one swift jerk he undid her belt. Ripping away the bronze dagger and purse, he tossed them aside. Then he grabbed her jaw in his gloved hand and wrenched her face to look at it. "Now I see why he wants you alive. You're a pretty thing."

"Who? Who wants me?" A fiery rush flushed her veins.

If he would just drop his guard for a moment. . . .

"Get on your feet, and let's go. He's waiting for you." He stood up and loomed over her, his sword clutched in both hands.

Shaking and terrified, she did her best to conceal the knife as she struggled to stand up, but he must have seen a glint of silver, for he shouted, "Throw it down!" and sprang at her. His mistake was raising his sword for a strike.

In one smooth motion, Kalay stepped inside the reach of his sword, and slashed with all her strength. Her blade cut a diagonal across his chest. His tunic parted under the keen edge and she watched his flesh part in the blade's wake, could feel it vibrating across bone.

The man jerked back, bellowed in rage, and stared down at the blood welling on his chest. When he glanced up, a dazed disbelief filled his eyes. He began to circle; his sword gleamed with an unnatural fire as, bleeding badly, he raised it to strike her. She tried to fling herself aside, but didn't have time. . . .

A hollow thunk rang out, and the killer staggered, stared at her in surprise, then toppled to the sand in a black heap. Rolling on the ground, his arms flailing, he managed to get to his hands and knees, almost stood, and dropped back to all fours.

Kalay leaped, grasped his hair, and drew her blade across his throat. His frantic exhalation blew a spray of night-dark blood across the churned sand.

The entire time, Zarathan stood shaking, clutching a driftwood club in his hand. His chalky face was sweat-drenched. When the killer finally stopped spasming and lay still, Zarathan's legs failed him. He crumpled.

"Zarathan? Are you all right?"

He hunched over and held his belly, while he rocked back and forth, sobbing like a child. "I—I didn't know wh-what else to do."

The assailant kicked one last time. Kalay glanced at him, watched for a moment, then looked back at Zarathan. "Stop crying," she said unsympathetically. "You should be happy. You just accomplished the impossible."

Confused, he looked up at her with huge tear-filled eyes. "What are you talking about? I just *killed* a man!"

"Yes, and because of that, no one will ever again say that you resemble a circumcised cat." She paused to wipe her face on her sleeve. "And, actually, I killed him, but you certainly stunned him. You're braver than I thought. I'm grateful. You saved my life."

"Brave?" he wailed. "I'm a coward! I sneaked up and struck him from behind! And now I—I can't stop crying!"

"Yes, well, the first time I killed a man, I couldn't stop throwing up."

He buried his face in his hands and made sounds like he was suffocating.

To give him time to collect himself, Kalay walked over and retrieved her belt, knotted it back around her waist, and went about picking up the Roman purse and bronze dagger. Finally, she lifted the dead man's sword. When Zarathan still hadn't stopped crying, Kalay marched over, grabbed him by the arm, forcibly dragged him to the ocean, and flung him face-first into the surf.

He came up spluttering, looking like a drowned weasel, and cried, "Are you insane? Why did you do that?"

"I thought another good baptism would clear your head. You . . ."

Twenty paces down the shoreline she thought she glimpsed a figure, a shape moving silently in the bottomless fog. Her heart almost leaped out of her chest.

"Zarathan, stand up!" she ordered as she tested the sword's balance. "Come on!"

He got to his feet and staggered out of the water with his saturated robe clinging to his skinny frame. "What's wrong?"

The ominous figure had vanished in the fog, but she could feel him, slipping closer. The hair on her neck began to prickle.

"Quickly. Grab your club, we—"

From near the cliff, Cyrus shouted, "Kalay? Zarathan?"

"Here! We're over here!"

Footsteps pounded the sand. Kalay turned back, scanning the fog, the tip of the sword swinging in small circles as she prepared to defend herself.

But the figure was gone.

If he'd ever really been there.

Cyrus appeared out of the mist, covered in blood, hauling Libni with one hand and carrying his dripping sword with the other. "Libni is wounded. Hurry!"

THIRTY-FIVE

"Find candles," Barnabas ordered Tiras. "Bring them to the library immediately."

"Yes, brother."

Tiras ran ahead of them through the dark tunnel.

Barnabas trailed along behind Cyrus. The warrior monk was virtually carrying Libni, though his old friend was making an effort to put one foot in front of the other. When they entered the library cave, Tiras had one candle lit and was placing it on the far end of the table.

Cyrus propped his sword against the wall, and bodily lifted Libni onto the tabletop.

A long sword gash sliced diagonally from his collarbone to the base of his ribs. The amount of blood was disconcerting; it ran from the gaping flesh, soaked his clothing, and pooled on the table. Spatters had patterned Libni's face and throat.

Tiras, as though totally disoriented, gaped in shock, swallowing and licking his lips.

"Tiras, bring the candle down here, please?"

The dazed youth blinked, picked up the candle, and brought it to Barnabas, who took it from his shivering hand. The boy had just seen his best friend, Uzziah, killed, and was watching his mentor bleed to death in front of him.

"Tiras," Barnabas said gently. "Fetch a jug of water and bandages. Oh, and I will need a needle and heavy thread. I assume you have these things?"

"Yes, b-brother." Tiras turned and shouldered between Zarathan and Kalay, who'd just entered the chamber.

"Oh, dear God." Zarathan's voice was a thin wail. He put a hand to his mouth and stared wide-eyed at Libni's unstaunched blood.

Cyrus didn't waste a moment. "I must go and guard the entrance. Kalay, can you gather our horses and bring them here?"

"Of course." She vanished down the tunnel at a run.

"Our horses?" Barnabas said, "Cyrus, you're not planning on leaving? Libni needs our help!"

"I know that, brother, but as soon as we've done what we can, we have to go."

"But—"

"Brother Barnabas! We killed two of our attackers. At least two ran, and it is prudent to believe that the leader was watching from a distance. Someone must carry the tale back to his superiors. By dawn, they will be on their way back here in force. We can't stay." He gestured to the gazelle leather bag sitting almost invisible on the floor in the rear of the cave. "Unless you want the papyrus to fall into the Church's hands."

"No, of course not, but—"

Libni reached out and gripped Barnabas' sleeve. "He's right. You have to go. Tiras will care for me."

"Libni, you and Tiras must come with us. It's not safe here."

Libni smiled and through a long, pained exhalation, he replied, "There are . . . many other caves. Near here. Very difficult to negotiate. No one knows the maze but me. We will hide there."

"No, Libni, please. You must leave. You don't know these men, they'll—"

"We will trust our fate to God and our Lord Iesous Christos. But . . ." He winced as he sucked in a breath. "Promise me that if you succeed you will return and tell me what you saw?" Libni's eyes shone with hope.

Barnabas took his hand in a hard grip. "You know I will."

Tiras rushed back into the cave with an armload of bandages, herbs, and a jug of water, which he deposited on the table beside Barnabas. Then he laid out a long iron needle and a ball of dark brown thread.

Cyrus collected his blood-darkened sword, adding, "Call out if you need me."

Zarathan, sodden, stood with his shoulders hunched and a puddle forming at his feet. Wet blond hair straggled around his face. Zarathan . . . half drowned? Barnabas didn't have time to ask.

"Zarathan," Barnabas said, "please hold the candle for me while Tiras and I tend to the wound."

Zarathan, looking as if about to faint, took the candle and held it close. Barnabas carefully peeled back the blood-slick fabric. Without realizing it, his eyes tightened, and Libni said, "Am I dying? Finally?"

"Don't be ridiculous. God still needs you. If for no other reason than to irritate me with guessing games." Turning just slightly, he said, "Tiras, hand me the needle and thread. Once we get the bleeding stopped, I will need to sew the cut closed."

"Yes, brother."

Zarathan swallowed hard. "How do we stop the bleeding?"

"Set the candle down and press both your hands on the wound, here and here," he pointed. "Press the cut edges together. Don't let up on the pressure until I tell you to." Barnabas unwound the thread and slipped it through the eye of the needle. "Tiras, help him."

Zarathan did as instructed and Tiras pressed his hands on the other most critical gaps. Libni gritted his teeth in pain, but barely a moan escaped his lips.

It seemed to take an eternity before the blood flow began to ebb. Cautiously, Barnabas drove the needle into Libni's flesh. Not even the years of tailoring his own clothing had prepared him for this. Stitch by stitch he closed the wound. "Let go now, Zarathan, and move down some. We'll wash it after we sew it closed."

Libni uttered a rasping groan.

"Forgive me." Barnabas continued to sew, attempting to copy the neat stitches he'd seen Roman surgeons make.

Libni vented a low laugh. His bloody face appeared ghoulish in the candlelight, especially surrounded by that mop of gore-clotted hair. "Barnabas?"

"What is it?"

Libni's voice changed. "I have a favor to ask. Can you take some of my books with you? I know they're cumbersome, but Tiras and I, we'll have to leave quickly. I don't think we'll have time to carry all of them to our hiding place."

"Yes, of course. But just the most important documents, Libni. One bag full. I'll tie it as a counterweight to the gazelle leather bag."

"Thank you, thank you . . ." Libni winced at a sudden stab of pain and focused on the arching cave ceiling where candlelit shadows danced. Tears were leaking down the side of his blood-spattered face. "I have . . . have copies of the gospels of Markos, Thomas, and Maththaios in Hebrew and Aramaic. Very rare. The only copies I've ever seen."

"The only copies I've ever heard of," Barnabas said in awe. *Dear God, the implications.* Softly, he asked, "Does Markos have the longer ending?"

"No, of course not. It ends at chapter sixteen, verse eight. As it should."

Barnabas glanced up at Zarathan and Tiras. Both were obviously running verses through their minds, trying to decipher the meaning.

Libni followed his gaze, saw their expressions, and said, "The oldest versions of the Gospel of Markos end at chapter sixteen, verse seven or eight. There is no resurrection."

"But," Zarathan said, "don't both Irenaeus and Hippolytus mention verse nine? They lived in the second and third centuries. Surely that proves—"

"It proves that even then men were using their pens to mutilate the original gospels," Libni said gruffly. "Mythmaking at the cost of history. It's disgraceful. My Hebrew and Aramaic gospels date to the latter half of the first century. They were written only a few decades after our Lord was crucified. And my Hebrew Gospel of Thomas dates to around the year 40, maybe 50 at the latest. I think it was written before the letters of Paulos. Take them with you, Barnabas. Don't let the Church editors get their grubby nibs near them."

"I won't. I swear it." But he wondered how, if they were captured, he would be able to keep that promise.

As he worked his way across the wound, the blood ceased to flow, but he could see Libni's face going more and more pale, probably a combination of shock and loss of blood. He took his last stitch, tied it off, and said, "Tiras, find every blanket here. We need to keep Libni warm while he sleeps."

Tiras hurried from the room.

"But aren't we leaving soon?" Zarathan asked hopefully.

Barnabas smiled down into Libni's pained eyes. "As soon as we've gathered whatever books Libni tells us to."

Libni gave him a weak smile, sealing a bargain that the protection of the original gospels was passing from one trusted friend to another. What was at stake was no more, and no less, than the Truth.

Libni lifted a shaking hand and pointed to the small hole in the wall on the right side of the cave. "Thomas is there, and Markos . . ." His finger moved through the air to a large, squarish hole. "Markos and Maththaios are there. But there are others. An early version of Hebrews and the second volume of Papias' *Logia* . . ."

Tiras returned and began piling blankets atop Libni while he continued with his list.

For nearly an hour, Barnabas and Zarathan collected and carefully packed the ancient papyri, scrolls, and codices into a cracked leather bag Tiras had found.

Finally, Libni allowed himself to fall into a deep, exhausted sleep.

Barnabas backed away from the table and motioned for Tiras to follow them out.

When they stood on the sand, Barnabas said, "Zarathan, please take both bags to our horse and tie them over the withers."

"Yes, brother."

Barnabas turned to Tiras. The youth gazed up at him with terrified eyes, as though he longed for nothing more than to run away and hide from all this.

"Tiras, remember that 'there is light within a man of light, and he lights the whole world. If that man does not shine, he is the darkness,'[106] and he will not find the Kingdom." He put his hand on the youth's shoulder. "Shine, Tiras. Be a man of light, as he taught you."

Tears welled in Tiras' eyes. He nodded and reverently said, "I will try, brother. Don't worry. I'll take care of him."

"I know you will."

Barnabas turned and strode for the horses.

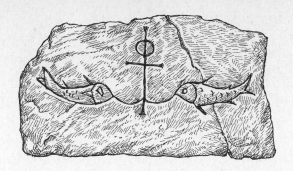

THIRTY-SIX

Zarathan helped Cyrus adjust the book bags over the horse's withers, while he cast occasional glances at Kalay. The woman knelt by the dead assassin, going through his pockets. She'd rinsed her bloody face and hair in the sea, but there were still dark splotches on her dress.

Solemnly, Cyrus said, "Kalay told me you saved her life. Thank you, brother. I know it was a hard thing to do."

Zarathan's gaze pulled back, and he anxiously toyed with the ropes on the bags. What could he say? His wrists ached from the panicked strength of the blow he'd wielded, but it was nothing compared to the pain that seemed to live and breathe in his heart.

Despite what Kalay said, I killed him. Without my blow, he would be alive.

In a soft, confidential voice, Cyrus asked, "Are you all right?"

He had never known why, but he found it difficult to share grief, even with his family.

Cautiously, he said, "Cyrus, you—you're a soldier. You probably think I'm a weak fool. And I—I am." He hated the frail timbre of the words. "But I've never been in a fight before, not even with my fists. Every time I got into a situation that looked like it might turn ugly, I walked away—as I believe my Lord wants me to do."

"I believe he does, too, brother." Cyrus adjusted the bags for a final time, and the smell of the sea seemed to grow sharper, more intense.

Zarathan wiped his nose on his wet sleeve. "I acted like a coward. I didn't even fight the man face-to-face. I sneaked up on him and clubbed him from behind!"

Cyrus rested his arms across the horse's back. His thick black brows drew down over his straight nose. "Zarathan, these men are trying to kill us. Always, whenever possible, attack from behind. The goal is for you to come out alive. Use whatever tactics you must to accomplish that."

"Including acting like a coward?"

Cyrus considered him. "Had you called him out, faced him man-to-man, what would have happened?"

"He . . . would have killed me."

"That's right. He was skilled in arms, you are not. He would have lopped your head off with one stroke, and then turned and finished Kalay. You would both be dead, and he would have been there to turn the odds against me and in our attackers' favor. Which means that Brother Barnabas, Libni, Tiras, and I would be dead, too. And, at this moment, the papyrus and all the books would be burning."

"But . . ." He suppressed a sob. "If what I did was right, why do I feel so horrible?"

A bitter smile turned Cyrus' lips. "I executed my first man when I was your age, Zarathan. Sixteen. They called it 'military training.' My commander brought me an enemy soldier who'd been taken prisoner in battle. He was a barbarian, filthy—and he was trussed up like a hog ready for roasting. It certainly wasn't a fair fight."

Zarathan managed to get a shaky breath into his lungs. "What did you do?"

"I was ordered to slice off his head, and I really tried to obey. I lifted my sword several times. But each time I looked into his pleading eyes, and I couldn't do it. When I broke down in tears, my commander ordered the other recruits to beat me until I either begged to go home to my mother, or until I begged to kill the prisoner."

There was a long silence while Cyrus patted the horse's mane; his eyes were lost in distant memories. Barnabas ducked out of the cave, and walked toward them with his head bowed, as though beneath a great weight.

"Did you kill the prisoner?" Zarathan asked.

"Oh, yes."

"And af-afterward? Did you feel weak all over? As though your muscles had been boiled until they felt like they would fall apart?"

"I still feel that way when I kill a man. I don't think good soldiers ever get over it. Killing is wrong. We all know it. I don't know God's reason for it, but there are times, my brother, when it simply cannot be avoided. Like today."

Zarathan chewed his lip while he looked out at the frothy surf.

Cyrus softly said, "You weren't a coward tonight. You were braver than I was when I first killed a man. You knew what you had to do, and did it without thinking, without hesitating. From now on, I know I can rely upon you when the time comes."

Several hollow thuds echoed down the beach, and they both turned to see Kalay level yet another brutal kick at the dead man's privates.

Baffled and annoyed, Zarathan said, "I still think she's a demon."

Cyrus studied Kalay. "Don't forget that our Lord sent her into the dining hall that night at the monastery. Then he placed her in the boat with us. And tonight he had you pick up that piece of driftwood to save her life." His eyes softened. "There must be a reason."

THIRTY-SEVEN

Massa

Yosef slipped the bit into his horse's mouth and patted the animal's silken neck as he secured the bridle. The horse blew and looked at him with big, trusting eyes.

"Just two more days, Adolphus," he said gently. "Then you'll be able to spend the rest of your life grazing in fields of green grass. I promise."

All around him, the Essenes were busy, packing their horses, cleaning up camp, speaking in low voices. He looked out across the silent, dove-colored hills to the highlands in the distance. As sunlight broke over the horizon, a tawny gleam haloed the place where the holy city of Yerushalaim nestled. He thought of his home, the home he suspected he could never again return to, and a pained yearning struck his heart. He so wanted to sleep in his own bed, and to see his ailing father one last time. Perhaps, if Petronius . . .

No, you can't let yourself believe that. It will weaken your resolve. You have one duty left to perform, then you must flee.

He patted the horse again, gripped the reins, and led Adolphus toward the other horses; his hooves clip-clopped across the stone in a slow, patient rhythm.

Mattias called, "We're ready if you are."

"Good. Let's ride."

Either they would find Titus waiting for them tonight at the pre-arranged place, or they would not, which meant he'd been captured and the Pearl stolen.

Regardless, someone would be waiting for them.

He prayed it wasn't an entire Roman century.

THIRTY-EIGHT

Melekiel

By the time they neared the city of Emmaus,[107] the sun had long ago dipped below the western horizon, and the brightest stars glittered to life.

Yosef galloped his horse in the lead, following the twisting path through the fruit orchard. The fragrance of green leaves and last year's rotting pomegranates carried on the breeze.

When he saw the dilapidated house ahead, his heart ached, for he did not see Titus.

Mattias galloped up beside him and hissed, "Where is he?" Sweat-soaked black hair clung to his cheeks.

"I don't know, but I pray he's alive. Where are your brothers?"

"They're watching the main road."

Yosef said, "Stay here. I'm going in alone."

"But why? You may need me."

"If this is a trap, someone must ride back and warn your brothers, or they too will be caught and executed."

Mattias stared at him, then nodded. "You're right. I'll wait here."

Yosef reined his horse to within twenty paces of the house and cautiously dismounted. "Titus?" he called. Then a little more loudly, "Titus? Are you here?"

The only sound was the breeze whistling through the gaps in the collapsed roof.

He impatiently tied Adolphus to an overgrown bush, and walked toward the dark house. From the smell, the building had recently been used as a barn. The scents of manure and moldering hay were strong.

As he peered in one of the windows, his nerves stretched to the breaking point. He couldn't keep his hands still.

He walked to the door. Inside, he could see fallen roof beams, broken pots, and piles of windblown debris. "Titus?"

Wind shoved a loose board, and when it creaked mournfully, Yosef jerked his knife from the sheath and froze. Along the wall to his right, tiny, glistening eyes flashed as mice scurried for cover.

He listened for any other sound.

Then he stepped into the house, edged around a pile of sheep manure, and tiptoed toward the closed door in the rear. "Titus?"

He pushed the door open and entered. Blackness. When he and Titus had last been here three years ago, this had been a storage room. The faint fragrances of dried fruits and herbs temporarily overpowered that of the manure and mildew.

As Yosef groped along the wall to his left, he bumped against an old crate. Then his hand touched another wall and he felt his way toward the wall niche he remembered—the curtained niche where the farmer had stored his family's most precious items. When his hand brushed a rotted piece of cloth, then sank into the wall, he knew he'd found it.

For five rapid heartbeats, he just stood there, praying. Then he stuck his hand deeper into the niche and felt around. Nothing. Just thick dust and spiderwebs.

Yosef pulled his hand out and sank against the wall. There was no message. Titus had not been here. At least not yet, and if he hadn't already arrived, there was a good chance he never would. Though Titus must have been forced to hide out for hours or even a day, he would not have lingered anywhere, knowing as he did that time was of the essence.

Yosef's despair was so overpowering, he barely noticed the tiny creak in the outer room. As the night cooled, wood contracted and the small animals began to emerge from their hiding places in search of food....

The next time he heard it, he looked up and focused on the ajar door.

The third time, he crouched down behind a toppled cupboard and gripped his knife in a hard fist.

Just above a whisper, a man called, "Master?"

"Titus!"

Yosef lunged for the door, threw it open, and ran straight into the arms of four Roman soldiers. Dressed in common brown robes, they had clean-shaven faces and carried the *gladii,* the short swords, of the Legion. Two of them held Titus by the arms. He was filthy and sweating profusely. His face and brown curly hair were covered with dust and streaks of soot.

"Throw down your knife!" the tall blond man said and aimed his sword at Yosef. He had an almost feminine oval face with long lashes, but the muscles that bulged through his robe spoke of many battles.

Yosef tossed the knife to the floor and held up his hands.

"Forgive me, Master," Titus said in a shaking voice. "I arrived only moments before you and found them waiting for me."

"Then . . ."

Neither of them had to say it.

They have the Pearl.

Titus' chest heaved with silent sobs.

The officer said, "I am Centurion Lutatius Crassus, here by order of Praefectus Pontios Pilatos. You are under arrest."

"On what charge?" Yosef asked.

"Come with us." The officer led the way out the door and the men holding Titus forced him to follow. The remaining soldier used his sword to gesture for Yosef to follow Titus.

With his hands up, he stepped out into the dusk, where four more soldiers stood guard.

The surrounding orchards had turned dark and foreboding, but the sky continued to gleam with a faint purplish hue.

Centurion Crassus strode out into the trees and, as Yosef fell into line behind Titus, he saw eight horses grazing placidly amid the fruit trees . . . and the packhorse tied to a low branch with the linen-wrapped bundle still on its back; it looked intact.

Hope rose up to choke him.

Perhaps, if one of them could create a diversion, the other could . . .

The centurion walked straight to the horse, used his knife to cut the straps, and shoved the heavy linen bundle to the ground. Yosef let out a small cry of shock, and tried to run forward, but his guard shouted, "Stop or I'll kill you!"

Yosef's steps faltered. He stood trembling as tears filled his eyes.

"What is this?" the officer asked pointing at the bundle with his sword.

Titus and Yosef glanced at each other, but neither answered.

Grumbling, the officer bent down and ripped at the linen with his sword, shredding it. He ripped again, only to stop when a human arm flopped out. The sword had cut a wide gash across the wrist. Bloodless, it gaped open like a ragged violet mouth.

For a moment, Yosef was so stunned, he couldn't speak. He could clearly see the man's right hand. What had happened to his ring? His grandfather's ring? He'd placed it on the index finger himself, he knew for certain. . . .

"Are you aware," the centurion said, "that it is a crime to steal the body of a crucified criminal?"

Yosef's eyes blurred. The world took on a blinding shimmer.

The centurion kicked the bundle over and tugged hard to unwrap the linen. When the body rolled out, Yosef couldn't help it, a sob choked him and tears traced warm lines down his cheeks. If he lived to be a thousand, he would never forget this terrible, wrenching moment. He felt like his heart had been ripped out.

The centurion stared down, then straightened. "You"—he gestured to Yosef—"come forward and identify this man."

Guards escorted Yosef to the body. He looked down, and his knees went weak.

In stunned confusion, he stammered, "It—it's Dysmas. D-Dysmas the Zealot."

"That's what I thought. I was sent to arrest you for the theft of the body of the criminal known as Yeshua ben Pantera, but this is not his body."

Yosef glanced at Titus, silently asking what he'd done, but Titus violently shook his head.

The centurion appeared perturbed. "Where is the body of ben Pantera?"

Yosef shrugged. "I do not know, Centurion. That's the truth."

The officer scowled at Titus. "Where is the body?"

"I don't know what you're talking about! We promised that when the holy days were over, we would get Dysmas' body to his family in Ioppe. My master received a special permit from the praefectus himself to bury this man! Now . . ." He swallowed his tears and waved to the body. "Now, his body has been violated, mutilated! I can't face his mother."

Yosef longed to kiss him.

Crassus sheathed his sword and propped his hands on his hips as he glared at Yosef. "You are Ioses of Arimathaia, yes?"

"I am."

"High Priest Kaiaphas told the praefectus that after you'd placed ben Pantera's body in your tomb, he'd had you imprisoned to prevent you from doing something foolish, like stealing the body and proclaiming your friend had fulfilled Jewish prophecies. Were you imprisoned?"

It was against the law for Romans to interfere in the actions of the Council of Seventy-one, unless the Council requested their assistance. Yosef was praying it had not.

Yosef wiped his eyes on his sleeve. "I was not imprisoned by Roman order, Centurion, therefore you have no jurisdiction over my escape. Do you? Are you here to enforce the orders of the Council of Seventy-one?"

Crassus' mouth pursed disdainfully. "I do not enforce Jewish orders."

"Then we'll be on our way. Good evening to you." Yosef started to walk away.

"Wait." Crassus frowned angrily. "How did you escape?"

"I have *good* friends."

Crassus did not need to know that Gamliel, who routinely used Kaiaphas' key to visit prisoners in the dungeon cells, had secretly released him.

Yosef sucked in a halting breath and shifted his weight, waiting for the final hammer's fall.

The centurion said, "My orders are to arrest you for stealing the body of ben Pantera, and to return the body to the praefectus, but—"

"But we do not have the body. There is also no evidence that we are guilty of the theft of his body. Were you ordered to arrest us without evidence?"

If Pilatos had followed his own procedures, the body would have been the condemning evidence required to justify the arrest. Without it . . .

The centurion gazed at him with stony eyes. As night deepened, the horses began to wander into the shadows. Two of the soldiers went in search of them, and Yosef heard reins jingling as the men gathered the animals and led them back.

Upset, the centurion ordered, "We have no proof that any crime has been committed. Let's return to Jerusalem and report our findings to the praefectus."

A little resentfully, Yosef said, "Please give Lucius Pontios my regards."

The centurion glared at him, then waved his men forward. They mounted their horses and galloped up the twisting trail toward the main road. A gossamer haze of dust rose in their wake.

When they'd ridden out of sight, Yosef's legs failed him. He sat down hard. Titus knelt in front of him, his eyes wide and filled with questions that Yosef did not know how to answer.

Yosef said, "The soldiers were waiting for you here?"

"Yes."

"How is that possible?"

Titus shifted uneasily. "I'm not sure. But . . . Master, on the way here, just outside of Emmaus, I passed two of the Rab's followers."[108]

"Which two?"

"Cleopas and Kepha."[109]

Yosef's gaze drifted over the dark orchard, the packhorse tied to the tree, and the body on the ground. "Did you see them speaking with the Romans?"

"No, but why else would they be out here?"

Yosef concentrated on his heartbeat, which continued to slam against his ribs as though unaware that the danger had passed. "I don't know," he murmured.

This morning, Nisan the seventeenth, had been the first morning people were allowed to leave their homes. Maryam would have found the tomb empty and run to tell the disciples. Why weren't Kepha and Cleopas in Yerushalaim consoling their heartbroken, grieving flock, which numbered over one hundred people?

"Perhaps there was rioting and they needed to get away," he said.

But he didn't believe it.

Titus surveyed the darkness. "Where is the Dawn Bather? I didn't see you ride in with him."

"I left him a good distance back. I suspect that when he saw the soldiers, he assumed the worst. He and his brothers must have fled."

Titus' lips pressed together in disdain, as though he'd always known Mattias was a coward, but was restraining himself from voicing that opinion.

Yosef forced himself to breathe, hoping it would relieve some of his anxiety. His gaze returned to the body of Dysmas. The sense of utter astonishment had not diminished.

Bewildered, Titus said, "I don't understand. I thought we—"

"As did I."

Titus exhaled hard. "Well, now we have another problem. What shall we do with Dysmas? We can't just leave him out here for the wild animals."

"Let's bury him and be on our way."

"To where?"

Yosef ran a hand through his dirty hair. "Maryam wrapped the bodies in linen. She's the only one who knows the truth."

THIRTY-NINE

Following behind a young monk named Albion, Pappas Meridias tramped across the once beautiful city of Jerusalem. The boy was around fifteen years old, with soft brown eyes and short, sandy hair. His tattered brown robe looked as though it had recently been plucked from a trash heap. Meridias eyed it distastefully. Surely Pappas Macarios of Jerusalem could do better. Was he teaching the youth some lesson in poverty? Or perhaps self-denial? Regardless, such dress did not project the image of the Faith that Rome wished to cultivate. Who would convert if he thought he had to look like a derelict?

As they strode up the flagstone-paved street toward the hilltop, Meridias got a good view of the city. Remarkable. The devastation caused by the Tenth Legion during the Jewish wars of 66 and 132 was still evident. The Temple Mount, at the emperor's orders, had been left in ruins, and everywhere he looked he saw the remains of Roman camps, as well as the infamous pagan temples built by Emperor Hadrian: the Temple honoring Jupiter built on the Temple Mount, and the Temple to Aphrodite built over the site of the crucifixion. From this angle, he could just see the top of Aphrodite's Temple.

After the defeat of Shimeon Bar Koseva and his rabble in 135, the Tenth Legion had remained in Jerusalem for almost two hundred years. Their main occupation had been the production of clay bricks baked in fireproof kilns. The demand for bricks was great, and each brick was marked with the Tenth Legion's emblem and trademark: LEG X.

As Meridias and the youth crested the hill and walked into a thick cloud of dust, Meridias drew a scarf from his pocket and placed it over his nose. Then he carefully scrutinized the huge excavation.[110]

Only the might of Rome could have orchestrated and engineered the filling and leveling of an entire valley. And now, only the might of Rome could have initiated the massive effort to restore an entire valley to its original condition.

Meridias might have stood atop some unnatural human hive. Hundreds of men carried baskets of dirt on their backs or shoveled it into carts to be hauled away. The mountains of refuse, stones, artifacts, and earth that had been dug up, were growing by the instant. As well, another group of laborers worked to tear down the magnificent Temple to Aphrodite. Meridias shook his head. In his opinion it was unfortunate that they couldn't have saved the structure and reconsecrated it to the Virgin Miriam, or to the Magdalen. But perhaps the emperor was right; it had been irreparably tainted by idolatry. Not only that, they had to remove the massive landfill if there was any hope of locating the actual remains of the crucifixion and tomb of Iesous. Unfortunately, the Temple to Aphrodite sat on part of the landfill.

"There he is," Albion said with a big, boyish smile. "Down there."

Meridias squinted against the dust and saw a man dressed in a long black robe apparently directing the excavation. He was short and ugly, with heavy jowls and wispy brown hair. "He's not very impressive, is he?" Meridias said.

Albion's smile dissolved in horror. "But . . . he's a very holy man."

"Yes, well, perhaps he is. Let's go meet him."

Albion led the descent into the yawning excavation, picking his way down through the gray haze. As they descended, the banging of hammers against chisels, of shovels striking hard-packed dirt and cart sides, along with the sharp ringing of picks on rocks, became almost unbearable.

Macarios saw him coming, detached himself from a group of engineers, and walked to meet Meridias with a smile on his ugly, dust-coated face. He had a large gap between his two front teeth.

"Pappas Meridias?" he greeted. "May the peace of our Lord be with you. I hope your arrival here has been—"

"Pappas Macarios," he interrupted with a dismal sigh. "I am happy to find you busy obeying the emperor's orders. What have you found?"

Macarios, clearly taken aback by the lack of polite opening conversation, said, "Uh, well, many things. Firstly, how was your journey?"

"Long and dirty. *What* have you found?"

Macarios blinked. "To b-begin, let me explain that when Emperor Hadrian built the Temple to the god—"

"To the pagan deity Aphrodite," he corrected.

"Yes, of—of course. Anyway, in order to build the Temple, the emperor had to fill in the garden and the rocky escarpments to raise the level of the garden to the level of the remaining saddle of the mountain. We're talking tens of thousands of square cubits of—"

"I know all that. What have you found?"

Macarios' jowls jiggled as he rushed to say, "Just today we uncovered the rocky spur of Golgotha itself. That's it there." He pointed.

Through the dust, Meridias studied what looked like a small nondescript hump of rock. It was little more than a ridge of *malaky,* or "royal stone." "What else?"

Macarios' expression drooped. "Well, on the west side, the escarpments of the saddle contain at least two tombs."

"Our Lord's tomb?"

"I don't know yet. Not for certain. We've only just begun our excavations. As we proceed, we will be able to answer your questions more reliably."

"That will be a welcome change. The emperor wants answers now."

Something on the ground caught his eye. Meridias reached down and pulled a small clay lamp from the soft earth. As he brushed it off, the image of a naked woman suspended with her legs spread over an erect male became clear. He roughly tossed it to the ground again.

Macarios glanced at it and said, "Appalling, aren't they? We've uncovered a number of pornographic oil lamps in the vicinity of the Tenth Legion's camps. Apparently they amused the soldiers."[111]

Meridias lifted his scarf and, again, covered his nose. Already his clean robe was coated with a fine powder, and he imagined that his blond hair looked the same.

Macarios studied his expression for several moments before bravely asking, "Meridias, can you tell me what this is all about? Pappas Silvester sent a series of questions regarding biblical place names that he wished me to answer. He seems to believe they are a map, but I could make no sense of them. Do you know what he's talking about?"

Gruffly, Meridias pulled a small roll of papyrus from his cape pocket. He'd written down every word he'd gleaned from the library assistants he'd questioned. He shoved it at Macarios. "Are these the names he sent you?"

Macarios took the papyrus and unrolled it. "Yes."

"I'm the one who provided Pappas Silvester with the list."

Macarios handed it back. "And where did you get it? It's very interesting, but I don't see how it could be important. We should focus—"

"That list has existed for almost three centuries, Macarios. I suspect it was written by Ioses of Arimathaia, at least that's what my sources suggest. It *is* important. Didn't you have any significant observations to report to Pappas Silvester after you reviewed it?"

Macarios flinched at his tone. For a time, he just stared at Meridias as though in a futile effort to peer past his eyes to locate a soul. Finally, he said, "I noted one thing."

"What was it?"

Macarios reached out gently and tapped a word in the middle of the papyrus. "This word intrigues me."

"*Selah?* What of it?"

"Well, the papyrus is written in Latin, but I wonder if the original Hebrew word wasn't really *Shelah,* from Nehemiah, chapter three, verse fifteen."

Irritated, Meridias demanded, "What difference would that make?"

Macarios drew himself to his full height and squared his shoulders. Apparently, knowledge had bolstered his courage. "A good deal, my brother. Since Shelah is located right there." He thrust his arm out, pointing to the south.

A strange, fiery sensation swelled around Meridias' heart. He took a step forward and tried to see what Macarios was pointing at. "I can't see anything through this haze. What's down there?"

"We call it the Pool of Siloam. Actually, there are two pools, an upper and a lower pool. They're fed by the Gihon Spring mentioned in First Kings, chapter one, verse thirty-three."

"What would it have to do with the word *Shelah?*"

"The pool has two names in the Hebrew holy books. In Isaiah it's called *Siloah,* but that same pool is referred to as *Shelah,* in Nehemiah. The terms also clearly referred to the area around the reservoirs as, for example, Luke says, in thirteen-four, that there was a tower in the place called 'the Siloam.'"

"So, you mean"—he paused while he considered the implications—"the entire area near the pools may have been called Siloam or Shelah?"

"Yes."

A gust of wind blew over the excavation and peppered Meridias' face with sand. He turned away until it passed, then stared in the direction of the pool again. "Why would the area around the pools have been important?"

Macarios opened his mouth to answer, but from behind Meridias, young Albion suggested, "Perhaps because of the tombs?"

"What tombs?" Meridias swung around to peer at the boy. He'd forgotten he was there. Albion was biting his lower lip as though expecting a reprimand for speaking up.

Albion looked to Macarios and softly said, "Forgive me, Pappas. I didn't mean to—"

"It's quite all right, Albion," Macarios said gently. "Go ahead and tell Pappas Meridias about the tombs."

As though excited, Albion broke into a silly grin. "They are everywhere, Pappas! The tombs fill every hole in the limestone, and we suspect there are many you can't even see because Emperor Hadrian covered over so many when he was filling the Kraniou Topon. But we—"

"Show me these tombs." Meridias took off without further discussion, striding down the hill toward the Siloam.

FORTY

Melekiel

I am standing in my home, sipping a cup of wine, surrounded by my four sis-ters and their families. The sun has set, but it is not yet Pesach. The Temple priests have not yet blown the horn to announce the arrival of the holy day. We are all waiting.

My eight nieces and nephews are running about, playing. But for the rest of us, this is a somber gathering. I couldn't bear to watch him die, to see the sa-cred light go out of his eyes, but as my sisters were preparing the Pesach meal, I watched the crucifixions from afar. Only Yeshua's female disciples were brave enough to follow him to the cross: Maryam, and Yeshua's two sisters, Mariam and Salome. They made certain that he did not die alone, but surrounded by people who loved him. They remained there, praying, through the entire terri-ble ordeal. It is perhaps curious that in Aramaic there is no feminine form of the word "disciple," talmida, but through their deeds, Yeshua's female follow-ers have proven themselves disciples nonetheless, especially in light of the fact that his male disciples betrayed, denied, and abandoned him.

Shortly after the ninth hour, Centurion Petronius sent word that I could remove two of the bodies. Dysmas and Yeshua were dead. Gestas was still alive, still suffering.

A tremor goes through me. I only heard his voice once. At the end, he shouted, "My God, my God, why have you abandoned me?"[112] While the Romans in the crowd, who didn't understand Hebrew, began taunting him, saying that he was calling for Elijah to save him, I lifted my eyes to the heavens expecting to see a legion of angels descending, clothed in garments of pure light, or perhaps a pillar of fire, even a dove fluttering down to settle upon his head. A simple sign from God that he had not died in vain would have been enough.

I saw nothing but clear blue sky.[113]

I open my right palm and stare at it. I pulled out the nails myself, then lowered Yeshua's limp body into the arms of Titus, who carried him to the horse-drawn cart where he gently laid him down. Then we repeated the process with Dysmas. Because of the crowds of pagans and Greeks on the streets, it took almost an hour to get the bodies back here and placed in the newly hewn tomb in my garden.

Involuntarily, my eyes drift to the nails that rest in a pot upon my table. Nails removed from crucified victims are believed to have great medicinal value. They reduce swellings, inflammations, and fevers. Even the Romans hold that blood-soaked nails from victims of crucifixion cure epilepsy, and halt the spread of epidemics. Perhaps that's why the only mode of crucifixion practiced by the Romans in Judea is crucifixion by nailing, not binding, the victim to the cross.[114] If I were wise, I would carry one of the nails with me, to protect me from illness . . . but I cannot bear to touch them. Besides, I have already made arrangements to return them to Pilatos in fulfillment of our agreement. He will count them carefully, and hold me to blame if one is missing.

My gaze moves to the window where a charcoal veil is settling over the land. In my mind's eye, I imagine Maryam and Mariam in the tomb, preparing the bodies, annointing them with spices and oils, wrapping them in the finest linen I could afford. . . .

"Yosef." My sister Yuan touches my sleeve. "The woman, Mariam, is at the door. She requests to speak with you. I told her you were grieving and that she should come back after the holy days, but she said it was urgent."

As though waking from a terrible nightmare, I blink at her pretty face, actually seeing it for the first time today, and say, "Thank you."

I stride past her, through the middle of my confused family, and duck out my doorway into the gray gleam of dusk. Mariam is standing quietly, wringing her hands. She is Yeshua's youngest sister, thirty-two, married to Clopas. They have two sons. The rest of her family is home celebrating, as best they can, the holy day. But she is here. She has her white himation pulled over her head and it accentuates the oval shape of her face and the size of her large, dark eyes. She looks very much like a female version of Yeshua.

"What is it, Mariam?"

"Forgive me for disturbing you, elder, but you must come. It—it's Maryam. I swear she has lost her mind!"

"What do you mean? What's happened?" *I close the door behind me, blocking out the sounds of the sacred evening, of children's voices, and the smell of food.* "Is she ill?"

When we arrived with the bodies at the tenth hour, we'd found Maryam standing by the tomb with a basket of spices. Her beautiful face had gone as pale as death. She hadn't wept, or railed. She'd just watched us carry the bodies into the tomb as though her soul had long ago left her body and flown away. Mariam had arrived shortly thereafter with an amphora of oil.

"Maryam asked me to go and fetch her himation. She'd left it near the cross today. She was getting cold. Even though I knew it was a long walk, I did it. It had been so hard to watch her, I actually welcomed the trip."

"Why was it hard to watch her?"

Tears fill her eyes. She uses the hem of her himation to wipe them. "For the longest time, she wouldn't let me near my brother's body. She was h-holding him, crying against his shoulder, sobbing, 'the light in the darkness shines, the light in the darkness shines.' She kept repeating those words. She wouldn't even let me wash the wounds in his hands and feet. Honestly, I didn't know what to do to comfort her."

"What happened when you returned with her himation?"

"She shouted at me to go away!" *Mariam clutches Maryam's himation to her chest.* "I called to her several times, but she told me to keep out or she'd kill me! When I tried to force my way in, she ran at me with a dagger! I don't know where she got it, but her eyes blazed as though her demons had returned."

"She's overwhelmed by grief, Mariam. That's all. I'm sure she isn't possessed—"

"You have to come and talk to her," she pleads and tugs at my sleeve. "She'll listen to you. She always has."

"I'll help any way I can."

I lead the way across the courtyard toward the tomb where faint lamplight etches a golden line around the stone that, when Maryam is finished preparing the dead, will be rolled over the entry to seal it until the holy days are over. Then we can finish preparing the bodies in our traditional ways.

Nearby, in the stable, lamplight also gleams. I try not to look at it, try not to draw Mariam's attention to it. I know Titus is in there saddling our horses, readying our packs. We will leave just after supper, after the city has quieted— but Mariam does not know this—nor does my family. Our conspiracy is small, consisting of only myself, Maryam, two Essene brothers, and three of Yeshua's most trusted apostles. Even Titus does not know the whole truth, just the necessary facts.

The agonizing sound of muffled weeping reaches me long before I get to the tomb. She has always been brave. I am stricken to the heart by her cries. Not only that, the thought of arguing with a woman as grief-crazed as the one Mariam describes makes my soul shrivel. What can I do or say to ease her pain when my own is strangling me?

I stop by the stone outside, and call, "Maryam? It's Yosef. May I enter?"

The weeping stops. Sandals scrape the stone floor.

I stand irresolutely, wishing I could avoid this, then I brace myself and call again, "Maryam, please let me see him. I need to see him."

She appears, and stares at me with wide, burning eyes. Insane eyes. Without a word, she grabs my hand and pulls me into the tomb. The two bodies are already wrapped in white linen, and the intoxicating fragrances of myrrh and aloe are almost staggering.

Maryam stands as though frozen, looking up at me with those wild eyes. "Yosef, please, I beg you. The savior himself must be saved. You understand that, don't you?"

I nod, endeavoring to appear calm. "That's what we're trying to do, Maryam. Tonight, we—"

"If you love them that love you, what reward have you?"

They are his words. I know, as well as she does, that Yeshua meant we must love our enemies. I stare into her strange eyes for a long moment. "Who are you talking about?"

She steps forward, very close to me, and whispers, "He would want us to save him, don't you see? And by saving him, we can save the savior."

I am totally confused now. "Maryam, please, slow down. I don't understand anything you're telling me. Yeshua would want us to save . . ."

Outside, down the lane, I hear hooves pounding. In only heartbeats it becomes clear that the horses have turned onto the path to my home. Several men dismount.

"Yosef Haramati?" an authoritative voice calls.

"Here! I'm here." I hurry across the floor and duck outside into the dusk.

Four members of the Temple police stand holding their horses' reins. The captain of the guard says, "You are under arrest by the order of High Priest Kaiaphas."

Gamliel was right. They are deeply afraid. They mean to stop me.

All of my family rushes out of my house. My sisters begin shouting questions while my nieces and nephews bawl. My brothers-in-law tug their wives back as I am led away.

I mount the horse they've brought for me, and as we ride down the path toward the Damascus Gate, the horn blows. The sound echoes from the walls of the city and floods out over the surrounding hills.

The holy day has begun . . . it is Nisan the fifteenth.

FORTY-ONE

Following behind Albion and Macarios, Meridias tramped by the beautiful rocked-in Pool of Siloam with its intricate mosaic floor, and out of the city through the Dung Gate.

Macarios extended his hand to the steep valley that dropped away in front of them. In the late afternoon light, the upthrust rocks and brush cast long, dark shadows over the limestone slopes now tawny with sparse grasses. What he could see of the far slope was dotted with small black holes, some in flats carved from the valley stone. Faint trails crisscrossed the slope as though woven between the features.

Macarios spoke reverently. "This is the Hinnom valley."

Meridias studied the narrow gorge. The length of it curved along the west and south sides of Jerusalem like a V-shaped moat. "What is the name of the valley that the gorge intersects at the bottom?"

"The Kidron valley."

Both the Hinnom and Kidron valleys were areas of exposed limestone ridges and wind-smoothed barren hillocks. If there ever had been any trees here, they'd all been cut down and used by the soldiers of the Tenth Legion to warm themselves, cook their food, and bake their bricks. Now only scrub brush and grass filled the spaces between the rocks.

"Here, Pappas, let me show you some of the most interesting tombs," Albion said, and started off down the slope at a fast walk.

Meridias, careful of the footing, fell into line behind him. As they made their way along the precarious trail, he noted the numerous fragments of incised limestone slabs that had been scattered down the slope. Some of the stonework was extraordinary. "Macarios? What are these?"

Macarios strode up beside him and looked at where Meridias pointed. "I'm afraid those are pieces of broken ossuaries, bone boxes. Grave robbers always come out after dark to plunder the tombs."

"Grave robbers?"

"Yes, we post guards, of course, but it does little good. We don't have enough people. They raid the tombs looking for precious jewels, gold, anything they can sell."

"They break into the tombs and drag out the ossuaries?"

"Or crush them inside the tombs. But I suppose it's easier to see the contents if you drag the ossuaries outside into the light."

The path down curved into a gorge where the walls of limestone rose three or four times their height. They passed several rock-hewn tombs with rectangular and T-shaped doorways blocked by stones.

"How old are these ossuaries?" Meridias asked.

"Ossuaries were used for burials for only a very short time—we suspect from about thirty years before the birth of our Lord, until the destruction of the Temple in the year seventy."

"So they date to the time of our Lord?"

"Approximately, yes."

Albion called, "Here! Pappas Meridias, come and look at this one!"

Meridias hurried to the place where the youth stood. The tomb facade was magnificent. The stoneworker had hacked a man-sized square at least three fathoms back into the face of the limestone wall, flattened it, and cut a T-shaped doorway, which had been sealed with a stone. Above the doorway three elaborate interconnected circles had been carved. Each circle had an incised border of triangles, and what appeared to be a large six-petaled flower in the middle.

Meridias said, "It's beautiful. I had no idea the Ioudaiosoi were such skilled stoneworkers."

Albion smiled, pleased by his response. "This is my favorite, but there are thousands of tombs here. Would you like to see more of the special ones?"

"No. Not today. I'm tired. But perhaps tomorrow."

Albion said, "Yes, Pappas."

Macarios gave Albion a proud nod. "Thank you, brother, for your help today. Can you take Pappas Meridias back to the cell we prepared for him in the monastery?"

"Of course. Please follow me."

Albion started back up the gorge trail and Meridias followed close behind Macarios. The sun had set, and dusk was descending over the city.

The climb was strenuous. They were both breathing hard when they climbed out of the gorge and started up the slope for the city.

Meridias stopped to catch his breath. While Albion continued up the hill, he turned to Macarios. "Tomorrow, first thing, I want to see the two tombs you found near Golgotha."

Macarios used his sleeve to wipe the sweat from his jowls and nodded. "Of course. Our workers should have more cleared by then. Perhaps we will be able—"

"Pappas Macarios!" Albion cried.

Macarios jerked his head up, strode past Meridias, and climbed the rocky slope toward the young monk who was standing bent over with his hands propped on his knees.

As Meridias followed in Macarios' footsteps, he saw the soft dirt pile before the freshly opened tomb. Broken fragments of ossuaries littered the ground in front, and he could clearly see the doorway, measuring about one fathom square.

Macarios knelt and peered into the tomb, as though hoping to find one of the grave robbers still at work so he could arrest them.

Meridias stood a few paces back. "Do you see anyone?"

"No, but it's very dark in there . . . and the tomb is larger than I would have thought given its unimpressive facade."

Meridias went to kneel beside Macarios and look inside. A damp, musty scent breathed from the tomb, which sent a chill up Meridias' spine. "Let's see what's in there."

"You're going in?" Macarios asked in surprise. "What if the thieves are hiding in one of the inner chambers?"

"Surely we scared them away," he answered as he got on his hands and knees and crawled into the darkness.

Once through the opening, the tomb yawned around him, soaring twice his height and spreading ten fathoms across. Despite his brave words, Meridias reached for the long-bladed dagger he kept under his robes. Stairs led downward. He took them one at a time, dagger ready, fingertips tracing the close wall on his left. In ten heartbeats his eyes began to adjust and objects crystallized. There were at least twenty ossuaries resting on stone shelves. He called up, "It's safe. You can enter."

Macarios and Albion crawled in, and climbed down the steps. As their eyes adjusted, Meridias walked to the stone shelf on the left where two ossuaries nestled side-by-side. There were words written on them. He could see them in the faint light that penetrated through the doorway.

"Macarios, when you can see, come over here. You read Hebrew, don't you?"

"Yes." Macarios walked toward him, blinking his eyes.

Albion stood as though frozen to the floor, looking around wide-eyed.

Macarios bent to study the words scratched into the ossuaries. "Hmm. This one says *Salome*."

Meridias dusted off the word on the other ossuary. "And this one?"

Macarios squinted at it. "It's not very clear, but it may be *Mari,* or *Mariam*."

Albion sucked in a sudden breath. His eyes had adjusted, and he lifted a shaking arm to point at something in the rear of the tomb. "It—it's a skeleton!"

"Where?" Meridias spun around to look.

"Back there, lying on that rock shelf."

Meridias edged around the broken chunks of ossuaries that had been destroyed by the thieves in their haste, and made his way toward the rear. "Dear God, Albion's right."

A skeleton lay on its back, a burial shroud covering the collapsed ribs, arms, and legs. The fabric had been drawn back to expose the skull. It gleamed as though sculpted of polished brown marble.[115]

Macarios came up beside him. "I wonder why his bones were never collected and placed in an ossuary as was customary."

"His family must have brought him here, sealed the tomb, and never returned to finish the work," Meridias suggested. "Maybe he was one of the last ones, left behind when the Temple was destroyed?"

"That's possible. According to the ancient texts, a corpse was prepared with oil and spices, then wrapped in white linen and placed on a shelf in a tomb. After which, the tomb was closed up with a blocking stone. In a year or so, the stone was rolled aside and the bones of the dead were collected and placed in a box, usually made of limestone—though those in the Galilaian seem to have been made of clay."

"Why didn't they just bury them and be done with it?" Meridias asked.

"Some people did, but the Pharisees believed—as we do—in the physical resurrection of the body. The decomposition of the flesh supposedly cleansed the body of sin and left the bones in a pure state, ready for the resurrection."

"Then the tradition of ossuaries was strictly a Pharisaic one?"

"I believe it was primarily practiced by the Pharisees, but that's all I can say."

Meridias cautiously walked toward the skeleton. As he neared the shelf, he noticed a darker patch to his left, and could make out at least two steps. "There's another chamber," he said. "It looks like it goes down to a lower level."

Albion's young voice had gone shrill with fear. "We n-need a torch, or a lamp. Perhaps we should return tomorrow with the proper equipment to search the rest of the tomb."

"I agree. It's getting dark outside," Macarios said. "When we return to the monastery, I'll dispatch monks to guard this tomb until we can reseal it."

"Reseal it?" Meridias said.

"Well, yes. Out of respect for the dead, we should—"

"We should probably reseat the blocking stone, and then bury it beneath as much earth as we can," Meridias said, "or the thieves will certainly return."

Macarios tilted his head in reluctant agreement. "That is a good suggestion, brother. I'll pull some workers off our excavation and send them over here in the morning."

Macarios and Albion climbed up the stairs and when their bodies blocked the light, the tomb went utterly black. Meridias stood with his eyes focused on the place where he knew the shrouded skeleton rested. A strange prickling crept up his spine. He sensed or heard something. *Probably the wind outside.* It grew louder, and sounded oddly like a soft, mournful voice. In mere moments it seemed to fill the chamber.

Meridias backed toward the steps. A fear like nothing he had ever known rose inside him. He was certain now that it was a man's voice.

Finally, both Albion and Macarios crawled out, and light once again streamed into the chamber.

The sound vanished.

Meridias forced a deep breath into his lungs. With the light restored, the tomb was, once again, utterly quiet.

"Are you coming, Pappas Meridias?" Macarios called.

"Yes."

As he made his way out into the dusk, he silently cursed himself for being a fool and strode bravely for the city gate.

FORTY·TWO

Loukas sat his horse atop a hill; his remaining men slouched on their mounts just behind him. On the road below, Atinius, the woman, and the other two monks made their way toward Jerusalem. His eyes focused on the woman.

I'm coming for you, beauty.

"Why are we waiting?" Elicius asked. "They're too far ahead. We should be going."

"In a moment," Loukas answered without looking at the old man.

The holy city draped like a cluttered blanket over a rounded mountaintop. In the distance the massive stone walls gleamed faintly blue with the falling of night. Broken in many places by former sieges, the wall was no longer a defensive structure. Rather, it had become an ancient artifact of toppled stones, interspersed with remnants of standing walls—more a monument to Roman superiority than to the engineering skills of the Ioudaiosoi.

Just outside the Damascus Gate, Loukas could see the massive, partially completed monastery. Meridias should be there. Was he watching, even as Atinius and his companions rode past?

"I thought they would have headed for Apollonia, or perhaps Caesarea. I'm stunned that they came here," Elicius said with a shake of his gray head. "Pappas Meridias was right about spooking them."

The old man had a doglike face with a long snout and fierce brown eyes. After a week on the trail his once-shaven face had again sprouted gray hair. It covered his cheeks and chin, making him seem old beyond belief. Alexander, the second men, sat his horse a few paces away, silent.

Loukas kept his eyes on the prey. Atinius had almost reached the northern gate that led into the city, the Damascus Gate. As part of his training, the Militia Templi had required that he study the holy city. After the death of Iesous Christos, it had been transformed from an earthly city into a celestial one: the heavenly Jerusalem. His gaze took in the legendary Temple Mount and the ruins of what had once been the most extraordinary sacred space on earth, then drifted to the still standing towers of the Citadel to the west, which had served as the royal palace of King Herod. He could see the vast excavation ordered by Emperor Constantine, and the dust pall that trailed off to the east, carried by the breeze.

Jerusalem! Reverence filled him. He was a soldier of the Faith, sworn to protect it, and this place, this broken city, was its heart. Whatever monstrous thing Atinius and his allies were after, he had to stop them from finding it. Or if they did, he was bound to destroy it before anyone knew it had existed.

Loukas remained, squinting in the darkness as Atinius finally passed through the gate, followed by the other horse and riders.

"Are you sure we can find them in there?" Elicius asked.

"Quite sure." Loukas kicked his horse into a trot, and continued his pursuit.

As night deepened, the scent of tilled soil wafted on the breeze, along with the musky odor of animal dung. Tawdry little huts dotted the hillsides leading to the holy city, and he could make out corrals filled with one or two cows, maybe a few sheep or goats. As they passed, hidden horses, lodged in barns, whinnied and their own horses pranced and answered.

Just before they began the final steep climb to the city, Elicius rode up beside him. "Should we find Pappas Meridias and report before we continue our pursuit?"

Loukas gave him a withering look. "We stick as close to our prey as possible. Meridias can wait."

FORTY-THREE

Barnabas guided his horse beneath the massive gray stone arch of the Damascus Gate. Despite his exhaustion and fear, he felt Jerusalem's influence as powerfully now as he had when he'd first visited here thirty years ago. The air was cool and still between the tumbled walls, and a divine loneliness seemed to seep from the very earth itself, as though the city grieved a loss that human beings would never be able to comprehend. Even in the growing darkness, he could make out the ruins on the Temple Mount and the dust rising from the massive excavation they'd noticed as they'd ridden in. The slight breeze had stretched the haze over the city like a gauzy burial shroud, accentuating the smell of ancient destruction.

Cyrus straightened. He raised an arm to point. "Is that the Square of the Column?"

"Yes," Barnabas replied.

As they rode forward, lamps glittered to life behind the small windows. People passed, most dressed in white robes. The smells of evening fires, burning oil, old urine, and cooking food carried on the air.

Barnabas reined his horse to a stop at the base of the Square of the Column. Tall and round, it stood in the middle of a central plaza where the streets branched. Upper Market Street ran off to his right and Lower Market Street to his left.

For a time, Barnabas just stared at the column. He was vaguely aware that Cyrus had tilted his head back to stare up at the square cap on top of the column.

Yes, this is the place. If a man studied it carefully, he could see the symbol of the *tekton*. He had only to turn it into a two-dimensional figure. Cut that square base in half and it appeared to be an inverted *V* tented over a circle: the round column.

Kalay asked, "Which street are we taking?"

"Lower Market Street. We're heading for the Temple Mount. There are a number of pools and fountains there."

Barnabas' horse lifted its nose, sniffed the air, and let out a low whinny, as though scenting other horses, or perhaps a barn with fresh hay. The poor animals were hungry after the past two days when they'd only been able to nibble grass along the road.

As they plodded up the flagstoned street, the painfully sweet strains of reed pipes rose and fell, eddying on the wind. Someone was baking bread, and the smell of boiling spelt sent a quiver through Barnabas' empty stomach.

They passed four monks in brown robes walking back toward the gate. Their hoods were up, so Barnabas never saw their faces, but the monk who walked in front called, "May the Lord's peace be with you."

"And with you, brothers," Barnabas, Cyrus, and Zarathan answered in unison.

They'd ridden by what appeared to be a monastery being constructed north of the Damascus Gate. Perhaps that's the place these monks were headed.

Flat-topped homes crowded together on both sides of the road, their shared gardens adorned by palm and fig trees that swayed in the night breeze.

Several people were still out, walking up and down the street. Barnabas and his friends received quick glances, but little more.

As they continued south, the majesty of the Temple Mount became apparent. The stone retaining walls that supported the Temple platform were still mostly intact and stood eight to ten times the height of a man.

"I've always thought it must have been unbelievable before the revolt in the year 66," Cyrus said in awe.

"It was." Kalay gazed up at the top of the Western Wall and the few stars visible beyond. "The Temple was covered with gold. You could see it shining, like a beacon, from a half day's walk away."

"Yes, it was one of the great wonders of the world, and the house where God's presence resided," Barnabas added. In his mind he could see the massive arches and endless rows of columns, the vaulted ceilings, underground passageways, and ingenious aqueducts—all the things he'd seen or read about. "I suspect no other building in the world has heard as many prayers, or seen as many pilgrimages. Or, perhaps, witnessed as much suffering."

As they neared the Beautiful Gate, Barnabas said, "There's a pool just inside where we can water our horses."

"Yes," Kalay said. "I remember that from when I was here before."

"As do I." Cyrus led his horse through the gate and stopped, his eyes warily on the empty street behind them, as if expecting to see furtive movement. Kalay slid off and winced.

"You may dismount, brother," Barnabas said, aware that Zarathan was staring unabashedly at Kalay as she arched her tired back and her dress pulled tight across her chest.

Zarathan jumped down and stood awkwardly, his gaze darting from one shadow to the next, trying to look in any direction that wasn't toward Kalay. "What are we doing here? Why couldn't we have asked for food and lodging at the monastery outside the city? That's what that was, wasn't it? A monastery?"

"I wasn't sure, brother. I thought it better not to take chances."

Barnabas dismounted, took the reins, and led his horse to the rocked-in pool. Their horse was sucking up water as fast as it could, long swallows running up its neck like mice. Barnabas sat wearily on the edge of the pool while his horse drank, and heaved a heavy sigh. He could feel every muscle in his body. His bones might have been stone, so heavy did they feel.

Have I ever been this fatigued?

Narrow streets radiated off from this plaza, but to the east a broad stone staircase led up to the top of the Temple Mount. The last time he was here, the ruins were little more than massive piles of stones too big to be carted off. Over the centuries, everything that could be taken and sold had been. But not the largest stones. They remained as mute testaments to the extraordinary engineers who'd cut and laid them.

"We're going up to the ruins of the Temple?" Kalay asked between dipping handfuls of water and drinking them.

"Yes."

She dried her fingers on her dirty tan dress. "Why?"

Hesitantly, he answered, "I need to test one of Libni's hypotheses, but please don't ask me to explain it. It's far-fetched."

Kalay exchanged a concerned glance with Cyrus, who said, "I'm willing to help you test whatever you wish, brother; but let us be quick about it. This place stinks of a trap."

Zarathan eagerly added, "For once, I agree. I think the only safe place is the monastery just outside the city. We should go back there and ask for lodging and food."

"You're an imbecile. That monastery is about as safe as your monastery in Egypt was," Kalay said.

Zarathan glowered at her. "You have a poison tongue. Do you know that?"

"At least mine is still in my head. I'm afraid yours is going to end up ripped out of your mouth by one of Meridias' fanatical followers and left lying on a table."

The full moon edged above the Mount and sent a pale flood over the sky. The horses temporarily stopped drinking to look up, then lowered their heads again.

"Why would someone torture me?" Zarathan asked. "I don't know anything."

"The problem is they don't know you're completely ignorant. They probably think you've read a papyrus or two. Even *the* papyrus. And once they find out you have read it they have ways to make sure you never tell anyone about it." She stuck out her tongue and made a sawing motion with her finger.

Zarathan winced and drew back.

Barnabas rose and tugged his horse toward the hitching rail that abutted one of the dark walls near the Beautiful Gate. "Brother," Barnabas said to Zarathan as he tied his horse to it. "Could you help me lift the book bags down?"

"Why?" Zarathan demanded as though greatly aggrieved by the request. "You're not planning on hauling those around with us all night, are you? Why don't we leave them here? I'll be happy to stay with the horses and guard them."

Cyrus said, "No. We stay together." He tied his horse to the rail, and shouldered past Zarathan to get to Barnabas. Together, they lifted the precious bags off, and gently rested them on the ground.

"But I want to stay with the horses!" Zarathan pleaded with such persistence that Barnabas wondered if he might be planning on taking one and riding back to the monastery in search of food.

Cyrus ominously said, "It's too dangerous, brother. This is Jerusalem. From now on, we should never be out of each other's sight."

Zarathan's face twisted into a pout. "But where are we going to sleep? I'm tired!"

As Barnabas separated the two bags, untying them to make them easier to carry, he said, "We'll decide after we've finished our task on the Temple Mount."

Kalay started off in that direction, and Cyrus said, "Brothers, go ahead of me. I'll bring up the rear."

"Thank you, Cyrus."

Barnabas and Zarathan each picked up a book bag and marched after Kalay. As they climbed the stairs, Zarathan started making small, tormented sounds, as though the weight of the bag was far too much for him to carry—or at least for him to carry on an empty stomach. Barnabas decided not to ask; he knew the answer.

At the top of the stairs, they stepped out onto the paved Temple grounds and Barnabas took a few moments to catch his breath.

The sound of Cyrus' footsteps coming up behind him had a feline quality, soft and deliberate, as though stalking an unsuspecting bird.

"Where do we go from here?" Cyrus murmured.

Barnabas turned. "The Western Wall. It has a good view. Follow me."

FORTY-FOUR

Loukas crouched in a shadowed alleyway, gazing up at the Temple Mount and the three people high above who clustered at the edge of the massive retaining wall. In the moonlight, they appeared as black silhouettes. What perfect targets they made for a good archer. It surprised him that Atinius would make such a careless error.

"What are they doing?" Elicius asked from two paces away, where he and Alexander—their gray heads shimmering in the silver light—held the reins of their horses.

Loukas answered, "Just standing there."

"They seem to be looking out at the city," Alexander said. "Why?"

"I don't know."

"The Temple Mount makes a perfect trap. Perhaps we should go up after them?"

Loukas slowly shook his head. He couldn't afford any extravagant motions. Despite their shadowed location, he wasn't certain that they were totally concealed from Atinius' view. "No."

"Why not?" Elicius challenged. "It would be easy to corner them up there."

Alexander added. "We could force them to tell us what they know."

It amazed him that Pappas Athanasios had relied upon and trusted men like Elicius and Alexander. Did Loukas truly have to explain that it was wiser and less time-consuming to let the prey lead them to the "monstrous thing"? Perhaps in their youth these old men had been great soldiers of the Faith, but if so, age had simply dulled their wits.

Or did Pappas Athanasios foist them off on me with the expectation that they'd fail? Perhaps he wants them dead as much as I do.

Loukas said, "Stop asking me ridiculous questions. I don't have the time to keep answering them."

Elicius' eyes narrowed in anger. The old man was accustomed to giving orders, not receiving them. Having to obey Loukas clearly irked him.

"Do you have a plan? I don't think that's a ridiculous question."

Softly, Loukas replied, "We wait for them to move, then we follow from a respectable distance. That's the plan. Do you understand?"

"Of course I understand."

"And you, Alexander? Do you understand?"

The old man gave him a hateful glare. But nodded.

FORTY-FIVE

Cyrus' sword belt jangled as he walked forward, calling, "Brother Barnabas, it's not a good idea to stand at the wall. You're clearly visible from below. If someone wishes—"

"I won't be long, Cyrus. Please give me just a few more moments."

Cyrus stood behind his three friends, watching as they gathered around the papyrus that Barnabas had spread out on the stone wall.

He clenched his jaw, worried.

Cyrus knew—as perhaps none of them did—that they had almost certainly been followed. The man who'd fled the fight at Libni's cave would have reported to his superiors. There weren't that many roads to watch, and three priests and a striking red-haired woman on two horses would be easily spotted. That no one had tried to ambush them on the road meant Meridias and his agents knew where they were headed. Perhaps they had decided it was smarter to allow Barnabas to find the Pearl and simply take it.

Not only that, Cyrus could *feel* eyes upon them, watching them.

He looked back at Barnabas. From up here, they had a clear view of the city that sprawled over the hills in every direction, and Barnabas seemed to be comparing the papyrus to Jerusalem.

Cyrus once again scanned the Temple Mount with its massive toppled stones, then his eyes drifted to the street far below that ran due east-west.

So bright was the moonlight that he could trace the patterns in the flag-stones, see the rosette designs that decorated the doors of houses, and discern even the shadows of fallen palm fronds. There were many people outside, some sitting in their gardens, others walking the streets. In the distance, Upper Market Street gleamed brilliantly silver in contrast to the gaping black hole of the excavation.

The Temple to Aphrodite was half torn down, its foundations about to be devoured by the pit. He wondered what they were looking for. The site of the crucifixion? Perhaps the tomb of Iesous?

Kalay said something soft to Barnabas that he couldn't hear, and tapped the map. Though she'd braided her long red hair, the wind had pried several tendrils loose and draped them in damp ringlets across her forehead and cheeks. She looked achingly beautiful.

Perhaps, when this was all over—No. Not even then.

He'd made his choice years ago. He'd given his sacred vows, promised his soul to his Lord. But as he watched her, he felt a desperate longing growing inside him. No matter what he tried to tell himself, his attraction for this woman was turning to love. And he seemed incapable of stopping the metamorphosis.

When she glanced up and noticed his gaze, she gave him a small smile, and a discouraging shake of the head, as though she'd understood his heart at once.

He spread his feet and forced himself to watch the city.

Finally Barnabas called, "Cyrus, could you come and examine this?"

He walked forward and looked at the papyrus held down by Barnabas' dirty fingers. "What am I looking for?"

"Anything. Libni thinks the cross symbol at the bottom of the papyrus may designate roads. Do you see any resemblance between the symbol and the roads visible in front of us?"

Cyrus bent to examine the symbol. Despite the moonlight, it wasn't easy to see. The smoky scent of Barnabas' clothing mingled with the unmistakable odors of unwashed bodies and horse sweat. Oddly, he found them comforting, for it reminded him of long-ago military camps, of battles won and the smiles of long-lost friends.

Cyrus gazed northward. "The *V* at the top of the symbol is similar to the branching of Upper and Lower Market streets at the Damascus Gate.

After that . . . there are too many hills and houses to be able to see the streets . . . even from up here."

"Yes, but Lower Market Street," Kalay said with her finger hovering over the long right arm of the symbol, "really does look like it matches this part of the symbol."

"And the far north-south line, though we can't trace it out fully, seems to match Upper Market Street," Barnabas said.

"Well"—Cyrus made an airy gesture with his hand—"then I think the street below us, that runs east-west, may match the crossbar of the symbol."

Zarathan's stomach growled loudly. Irritably, he said, "Oh, this is ludicrous. Watch, I can play the game, too. Do you see the small crosses on the map? I'm sure they match those crude stone walls you can see over there, and over there, and over there. And if the long right arm on the papyrus is Lower Market Street, it runs right down into that valley to the south. So who wants to go with me and see if we find buried treasure?" He made a deep-throated sound of disgust. "This is all just useless. You can make anything out of the crosses. We should leave and go beg for—"

Barnabas' sharp gasp silenced everyone.

With trembling hands, he lifted the papyrus and his fingertip touched the small crosses on the papyrus one by one before pointing in turn toward the stone walls Zarathan had indicated. After several moments, a tiny, pitiful cry escaped his throat. "Blessed God . . ."

"What is it?" Cyrus asked. "What do you see?"

Tears streamed down Barnabas' face as he stared unblinking at Jerusalem.

"Brother!" Zarathan said. "Forgive me. I didn't mean to upset you. I was just being frivolous."

Kalay pulled the map from Barnabas' hands and repeated his actions, glancing down at the small crosses, then up to the distant stone walls. It seemed an eternity before she said, "When I came here as a child, I remember those stone walls enclosed Roman camps." She extended her arm to point out each one. "To the south was the Temple Mount camp. To the southwest, the Mount Zion camp, and due west was the Palace camp. Why would someone hundreds of years ago have used crosses to mark Roman camps?"

Though absolutely silent, Barnabas was sobbing uncontrollably.

Cyrus took the papyrus from Kalay's hand. He, too, had made a pilgrimage here when those stone walls had been filled with Roman soldiers. He remembered the colorful flags flying over the gates and the—

It hit him like a blunt beam in the stomach. Suddenly, he couldn't breathe.

He straightened. As full understanding dawned, it seemed to hollow out his insides, leaving behind a black, empty husk that throbbed.

"Do you see it?" Barnabas wept the words, and turned to look up at Cyrus with tear-drenched cheeks.

"Oh, yes," he whispered. "They're not crosses."

Surprised, Zarathan frowned. "They're not? Then what are they?"

Cyrus' gaze fixed on the road that led south into the night-silvered Kidron valley, and quietly answered, "Roman numerals. Tens. For the Tenth Legion. We're standing in the middle of the map."

FORTY-SIX

NISAN THE 18TH, MIDNIGHT

I expected to see a city in the grips of rioting with half the buildings on fire, or perhaps the aftermath of forced suppression with precious belongings strewn, dead bodies lining the streets, and Roman legions crawling all over.

But an eerie quiet possesses Yerushalaim.

The city looks iron gray in the cold grip of night. We trot our horses through the endless wheat and barley fields that encircle the north side of the city and head east toward Bet Ani.

"It's too quiet," Titus whispers from where he rides to my right.

"I know."

"Perhaps the praefectus ordered a curfew."

"Perhaps, but if so, where are the soldiers to enforce it? I count barely a handful of men standing guard in front of the gate east of the Temple Mount."

Titus swivels on his horse to look and frowns. "Where are the other soldiers?"

"Somewhere else."

"Master . . . listen. There are no babies crying, no dogs barking. Not even any drunken laughter. It's as though . . ."

He doesn't finish, and I don't have the courage to do it for him.

It's as though the world has died.

We ride on into the queer leaden light that swaths the fields and the trees that grow on the west side of the Mount of Olives. Was it so long ago that I found Yeshua at the foot of the Mount after he had thrown the merchants from the Temple porches?

Wrenching sadness knots my belly. I inhale the faint green fragrance of recently sprouted wheat. I desperately wish I could go back. . . .

"What if Maryam isn't there, Master?"

"Her family will know where she is."

"She was the Rab's constant companion. She may have been arrested."

"If she was arrested by the Council, they just questioned her and let her go. If she was questioned by the praefectus' skilled interrogators, she told them everything . . . and you and I are both as good as dead."

Titus shifts on his horse and looks straight ahead again, paying attention to the road.

"Titus, if we don't find her tonight, I promise we'll ride on. We'll get as far away from here as we can."

We turn down the street where Maryam's family has lived for generations. Our horses' hooves slip and skid on the cobblestones as we make our way down the row of flat-topped houses and alongside the beautiful gardens filled with fig and date trees. No lamps burn in any of the houses. It is a strange, unearthly sight.

"Stay here," I order and give my reins to Titus to hold. "Be ready to run."

"Yes, Master."

I sprint up the steps to her father's door and knock, lightly at first, then, when no one comes, harder.

Voices hiss inside, asking questions. A single lamp is lit. Through the windows, I see its wavering light moving.

A man opens the door a slit and peers out. When recognition dawns, he flings the door wide open. "Yosef Haramati!" Lazaros, Maryam's brother, cries. "Come in. Quickly!"

I step inside and he closes the door.

"They're looking for you. Do you know that? Everyone is looking for you. The Council, the praefectus, the multitudes—"

"Yes, yes, I know," I say. "Forgive me for endangering your family by coming here, but I must speak with Maryam. Is she here?"

The scent of fresh-baked bread fills the house. It is a large, lovely place, with gorgeous rugs on the floors and many scrolls on shelves. It is too dark to see much else. The small lamp flame is barely enough to allow me to clearly see Lazaros' round face. He is tall and thin, with brown hair and a beard. His dark eyes are wide, as though he's just suffered a fright.

"No, she's not here, she . . ." Lazaros stops as though stunned. "You haven't heard?"

"Heard what?"

He stares at me dumbly for several heartbeats. "The Rab . . . he's risen."

"Risen?"

Excitedly, he says, "Yes! This morning Maryam and the other women went to the tomb and found it empty! The Rab was gone. It's a miracle!" Tears blur his eyes. His voice grows soft and reverent. "Just as the prophecies foretold, elder! He rose and ascended to sit at the right hand of God."

I stammer, "L-Lazaros, what happened this morning when people could first leave their homes? Did the Zealots—"

"Oh, elder, it was terrifying. The Zealots had gathered five thousand strong to remove the body of Gestas from the cross. He'd died some time over the holy days, no one knows when. The Zealots were angry, stamping around whipping up hatred, accusing Rome of murdering three sons of Yisrael—"

"What of Pilatos? What did he do?"

"He dispatched three Roman legions to surround the Zealots. I heard that they had orders to slaughter everyone—man, woman, and child—at the slightest provocation. You could feel the fear in the air. But . . ." He paused and turned glowing eyes on Yosef.

"But?"

"Before dawn, right after she'd visited the tomb, Maryam ordered the women to run in different directions proclaiming the startling news. She herself went to the disciples. Kepha . . . Kepha told her he didn't believe her.[116] *But she didn't stop, she ran to the Zealots. In less than three hours, Maryam and the other women had told everyone that the Rab had risen. I swear the story spread like wildfire."*

"And the Zealots?"

"It was like a flood, a human flood. Thousands of the Zealots ran to your home to see the tomb. Every person wanted to touch the cast-off burial cloths. I think the entire city of Yerushalaim is empty tonight because people are still camped all over the hills around your house, waiting their turns."

I am thinking only, Gamliel . . . thank you, God, for Gamliel.

"One other thing, elder," Lazaros says.

"Yes?"

"There was a man dressed in white in the tomb. He told Maryam that the Rab had given him a message to deliver. He said that the Rab would meet his disciples and Kepha in the Galil."

"His disciples *and* Kepha? Meaning Kepha is no longer one of his disciples?"

Lazaros shrugs uncertainly. "I don't know, the man didn't—"

"Do you have any idea where Maryam might be? I must speak with her."

Lazaros gestures lamely. "Elder, we haven't seen Maryam since before the crucifixions. She sent Yoanna to tell us about the miracle. But I did hear a rumor that someone had seen her in the Kidron valley just after sunset. I don't know why she would be down there when she could come home, but—"

"Thank you," I say and bow. My heart has begun to thunder. "I'll be on my way now. The less time I spend here, the safer you and your family will be." I turn and swiftly walk for the door.

Lazaros rushes ahead to pull it open for me. "Elder, please be careful. If the crowds recognize you, the soldiers—"

"Yes, I know. I will."

Without a good-bye, I step out the door and run for my horse. Titus, probably fearing we've been discovered, kicks our horses around and holds my reins out for me to grab.

I take them, mount my horse, and we ride away down the street at a gallop.

"What's wrong?" Titus asks. "Was Maryam there?"

"No." I shake my head. "But I think I know where she is."

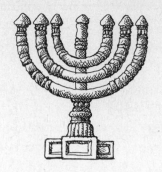

FORTY-SEVEN

The wind picked up the instant they stepped outside the Dung Gate. Zarathan grimaced as another gust whipped his long robe into snapping folds and hurled a trough full of gravel at his eyes. He squinted in defense.

Three paces ahead of him, Cyrus and Barnabas led the horses down the steep trail, apparently unaffected by the gale. He didn't know where Kalay was, probably out in front of the horses or he'd be able to see her.

He started walking again.

In the moonlight, the slope seemed to be littered with massive misshapen beasts, though when he walked up to them they turned out to be limestone outcrops. He sidestepped another one, and plodded onward with his head down.

For over two hours, they'd been examining one squat, ugly tomb after another, and found nothing interesting.

The horses stopped ahead of him, and Cyrus said, "This path is too steep to take our horses down. We'll have to go the rest of the way on foot."

Barnabas stared at the deep, moonlit gorge, then turned to look back at the Dung Gate, tracing out a straight line like the one shown on the papyrus. "Yes, you're right. We don't have the luxury of going around or we may lose our bearings. Let's find a rock or bush to tie our horses to."

Zarathan walked forward and gazed down into the gorge. In the bottom, a narrow, winding path led south into the Kidron valley.

As Cyrus and Barnabas hunted for a good place to tie the horses, Zarathan stood in the background with his arms folded, moping.

Kalay's mouth quirked when she saw him. She walked over and said, "You look like you ate a horse apple."

"As you well know, I haven't eaten anything for two days, let alone a horse apple."

"Why don't you try to be helpful and find a rock to tie the horses to? It will make you forget your hunger, and," she stressed the word, "would be good for your soul."

Tartly, he replied, "How would you know? You're an unchaste, pagan demon-worshipper."

Kalay propped her hands on her hips. "I've been demoted to just a demon-worshipper? I liked it better when I was a full demon." She gave him an evil look, hitched up her dress, and tramped away after Cyrus and Barnabas.

Zarathan took a quick look around, and rapidly followed her. The last thing he wanted was to be left alone out here.

Just after they'd exited the Dung Gate, Barnabas had wanted to turn right, to follow the short leg of the map that branched off to the west of the long straight leg, but they'd seen two men standing in that direction, and decided it would be best to follow out the long leg instead.

"This will do," Barnabas said.

Cyrus tied the horses' lead ropes to an eroded pinnacle of rock that stood as tall as Barnabas, then he turned and said, "What now?"

"We have to find a way down into the gorge."

Barnabas started untying the book bags from the horse, and Cyrus said, "Brother, I suspect that any trails out here are going to be narrow and covered with slippery sand and gravel. Perhaps it is wiser to leave the books tied to the horse."

Barnabas leaned heavily against the bag. "I am tired. Perhaps . . . just this once . . ."

Barnabas hesitantly turned away from the books, and picked his way along the edge of the precipice. After several moments, he said, "There. Is that a trail cut into the side of the gorge?"

Kalay said, "Looks like several trails to me. They seem to crisscross the cliff face. Let's find out if they're passable."

She strode ahead, followed the trail over the rim, and disappeared into the gorge. In less than ten heartbeats the sound of cascading rocks erupted.

"Kalay!" Cyrus called, and hurried over the edge.

Barnabas and Zarathan rushed after Cyrus. When they'd scrambled down the first treacherous gravel-slick incline, the trail leveled out and they saw Kalay and Cyrus ten paces ahead. Kalay was pointing to something on the wall of the gorge.

Barnabas turned to the stone wall beside him. "Oh," he said softly. "Look, Zarathan."

Zarathan walked forward and his mouth dropped open. The entire cliff face was one tomb after another. Some were so old their entries were barely visible. It was as though over time the blocking stones had melded with the limestone cliff, becoming one. Other tombs appeared to be brand-new.

"That's why this trail is here," Barnabas said. "The bottom of the gorge must have been used up first, and people had to start carving their family tombs higher and higher on the cliff."

"How old are these?" Zarathan asked in awe.

"Such tombs only date to the first century, or perhaps a few decades earlier."

"You mean, to around the time of our Lord?"

"Yes." Barnabas smoothed his hand over an elaborate carving that adorned the facade of a small tomb. "This is the Ben Hinnom family tomb."

"Hinnom? Like the valley?"

"I suspect it's the very same, or at least a relative."

Zarathan edged forward to look at the inscription. The moonlight was strong enough that he could see the letters perfectly.

Kalay and Cyrus had started walking down the trail again, and Barnabas said, "Let's not fall behind, brother."

The footing was so uneven that Zarathan often had to grab for one of Barnabas' flailing arms after he'd tripped.

"Forgive me, brother," Barnabas said on the fourth stumble. "My eyes are particularly bad at night."

"Just don't fall. It's a long way down."

Barnabas peered over the edge, nodded, and braced a hand against the cliff to steady himself as he slowly continued down the trail.

It took another half hour to reach the bottom of the gorge. In that time, they must have passed hundreds of tombs. The smallest were barely the length of Zarathan's forearm and he suspected they had been carved for children.

They walked up beside Cyrus and Kalay, and Barnabas said, "Surely there's no one after us at this time of night. Why don't we split up and see what we find down here."

"No," Cyrus ordered sharply. He had his fingers around the hilt of his sword, as though ready at any instant to draw it. "We stay together. Pick a direction and we'll all follow you."

Barnabas flapped his arms helplessly. "Very well, south."

"Zarathan?" Cyrus said. "I'll lead. You bring up the rear."

"Oh, for the sake of the Goddess Mother, let me do it!" Kalay said. "I'm much better with a knife than the bo—than Zarathan."

It intrigued Zarathan that she'd stopped short of calling him a boy. *I should have saved her life sooner.*

Cyrus paused, considering, then pulled a fine silver-handled knife from his belt and held it out to Zarathan, saying, "He'll be all right. Take this, brother."

Zarathan backpedaled. "Didn't that belong to one of the dead sicarii?"

Cyrus stretched his hand out farther. "It doesn't matter who it belonged to, you may need it."

Zarathan plucked it from Cyrus' palm with two fingers and gingerly tucked it into his belt. It looked very strange resting right beside his prayer rope.

Cyrus gave him a soldierly nod and turned around to head south. Barnabas followed behind him. As Kalay passed Zarathan, she gave him an incredulous look, grabbed a handful of her skirt, and held it up as she followed Barnabas down the winding path that led deeper into the gorge.

Seven hours later, when the full moon had traveled all the way across the sky and perched just above the western horizon, Kalay finally grew tired of listening to Zarathan's excessive yawning. He'd been alternately yawning, stumbling, and grumbling since midnight.

She swung around, glared at him, and jerked the knife from his belt. "Walk in front of me," she commanded. "I'm bringing up the rear now."

"That's my knife. Give it back!"

"You're barely awake. You couldn't guard your own backside. Now, go on, walk in front of me."

Cyrus turned at the commotion, saw Kalay with the knife, and looked genuinely relieved. He called, "Brother, could you take Barnabas' arm? I think he's as tired as you are. I don't want him to fall and hurt himself."

Zarathan tramped forward, roughly gripped Barnabas' arm, and said, "Come along. We'll hold each other up."

"Thank you, brother. I admit I can barely seem to put one foot in front of the other. I—"

Barnabas stopped suddenly, looked up, then lunged for the cliff so fast he almost jerked Zarathan off his feet.

"Dear Lord," Zarathan gasped. "Why did you do that?"

Barnabas was panting, his gaze roving the tomb facade. "Cyrus! Please come . . . come and tell me what you see? My eyes . . . I'm n-not certain I—"

"I'm right here," Cyrus said as he strode to Barnabas' side and intently stared at the facade.

Barnabas turned to search Cyrus' face. "Is it? Is—is it what I think it is?"

Cyrus used his finger to trace out the symbol for all to see. "It's an inverted *V* tented over a circle."

Barnabas' knees started shaking. He staggered forward and propped his hands against the cliff to keep standing. Zarathan and Kalay both rushed up to make certain he was all right.

"Brother?" Zarathan examined his face. "Can I help you?"

"You're exhausted. Why don't you sit for a time," Kalay suggested, taking his arm to help steady him.

Barnabas did not even look at them. His eyes were riveted to the tomb. "It's the symbol of the *tekton*. The symbol that's on the map, marking the place where the Square of the Column stands."

A gust of wind swept the gorge and tousled Cyrus' curly black hair around his face. "Does it mean something?"

Barnabas straightened, pulled away from Zarathan and Kalay, and edged closer to the symbol. "It may mean . . . everything."

He gently caressed the lines of the symbol, as though trying to memorize every detail.

Cyrus watched him for a time, before asking, "What do you want me to do?"

"Open it. Hurry, before it gets light and someone can stop us."

Cyrus waved to Zarathan. "Brother, we'll both need to put our shoulders against the blocking stone and push."

Barnabas dropped to his knees to the left of the blocking stone and clasped his hands in prayer, murmuring while Zarathan and Cyrus pushed.

Kalay stood back.

It didn't take long. The blocking stone grated and scraped, and a musty rush of air escaped from the tomb. It sounded like the last breath of a dying man, and smelled similar.

Cyrus said, "It's open, brother. The moonlight is filling it up."

Barnabas struggled to his feet and hobbled forward to look inside. "We're lucky we didn't find it earlier. The moon would have been in a different position, and we'd never have seen the symbol of the *tekton,* let alone have light streaming into the tomb." Without another word, he ducked through the entry and disappeared inside.

Cyrus' gaze sought out Kalay. "I'll stand guard by the entrance. You go with my brothers. If there are inscriptions, they may need you to help translate the Hebrew."

Zarathan backed away. "Brother, I'd rather stay out here with you. I don't—"

"Zarathan," Cyrus said in a stern voice. "Barnabas is frail and tired. He doesn't see well in the dark. If he stumbles and falls, I doubt Kalay has the strength to get him on his feet again. He needs you in there."

Zarathan gulped a swallow, seemed to be mustering his courage, then resolutely walked forward and ducked into the tomb.

A loud gasp sounded, followed by Zarathan's frightened voice: "There are skulls on the floor in here!"

"Well, don't break them!" Kalay called back.

She remained outside for a time, staring at Cyrus. His hair was blowing around his face. Even in the moonlight, his emerald eyes glittered when he looked at her. Softly, she said, "We are probably not alone out here. You know that, don't you? They almost certainly followed us."

A slow, radiant smile turned his lips—the smile of a man who's already given himself up for dead. "Yes. I know."

Annoyed, she snapped, "Get that martyr's smile off your face. You're not going to die unless you start taking reckless chances."

His smile widened. "This entire trip is one big reckless chance."

"Yes, well, there is that, but I order you to call out immediately if you hear or see anything suspicious."

He nodded obediently. "I will. Kalay, can you . . ." He hesitated. "If you find anything important, will you come out and tell me?"

He obviously longed to be one of the chosen to enter the tomb, to see what it contained for himself. But he trusted no one else to protect them from the evils that might lurk in the night.

"Don't worry," she said. "If we find something inscribed with the words THE PEARL, I'll bring it right out to you."

He gave her a mildly irritated look. "Thank you."

She grinned and ducked into the tomb.

FORTY-EIGHT

Loukas, on his belly, slid back from the precipice, and whispered to Elicius, "Pappas Meridias is probably staying in the new monastery being built north of the city. Find him. Tell him we believe they have found it, and he should bring at least ten men to surround the tomb. Twenty would be better."

"Yes," Elicius said, and tossed windblown gray hair out of his eyes. "Just the sight of twenty armed men will take the fight out of Atinius."

When Elicius kept lying there, smiling, Loukas said, "Now. Go now. And pick up those two men we saw guarding that open tomb. We'll need every man."

Elicius' mouth pursed, but he got to his feet and silently trotted away into the darkness.

Alexander glared at Loukas, as though he didn't much like the way he treated his friend Elicius.

Loukas slid forward to the edge of the precipice again, and watched Atinius standing guard in front of the tomb. The gorge was deep and narrow, the rocky footing treacherous. The fool. With one well-placed arrow, an archer could kill him, then block the tomb and trap his friends inside. Even if they escaped, no one could run far or fast in these eroded limestone outcrops. They could be easily hunted down and killed. What was Atinius thinking?

But he's surprised me before.

Loukas turned to Alexander. "Stay here. Signal the soldiers when they come. I'm going to take my horse, go around, and block the mouth of the gorge below, so they can't possibly escape."

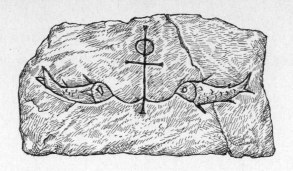

FORTY-NINE

I see her the instant we ride to the edge of the gorge. In the moonlight, the pale limestone cliffs have a liquid silver shine. She sits far below, in front of the tekton's *tomb. Her himation is pulled over her head, and she is rocking back and forth. The breeze carries the faint sound of her mourning cries.*

"Leave the horses to graze," I tell Titus. "Come with me."

We dismount and carefully make our way down the narrow trail that leads to the bottom of the gorge. Along the way, I touch the tombs of people I have known and loved. People I miss.

We reach the trail in the gorge bottom where the footing is better, though still precarious, and I quicken my pace. Ahead, the symbol of the tekton, *carved only a few days ago by Yeshua, reflects the moonlight, glowing as though lit from behind.*

She looks up when we stop before her. Long black hair fringes the edges of her himation, and frames her swollen, ravaged face. In her eyes, I do not see surprise, but utter despair.

I crouch beside her. "Maryam," I softly say. "You did well. I spoke to Lazaros. He told me—"

"You don't know the whole truth, Yosef," she says in a grief-stricken voice. "Forgive me, I—I deceived you."

I reach out to touch her hand. "I know part of it. We were ambushed by Roman soldiers at dusk tonight, just outside of Emmaus. They cut the burial shroud open. We saw the man we carried."

Her wet eyes widen, and tears trace lines down her cheeks. "You saw him?"

"Dysmas, yes."

"Did you"—she wipes her cheeks with the corner of her himation—"did you take care of him?"

It was so like her to worry as much about the soul of a crucified murderer as she would the soul of a saint.

I gently say, "If you love them that love you, what reward have you?"

Her mouth quivers.

I smile. "We did the best we could for him. We buried him in a beautiful pomegranate orchard. I prayed for his soul. The rest is in God's hands."

In a tender, almost lover-like gesture, she reaches out and clasps my hand. "He would be grateful, Yosef, as I am."

I know she means Yeshua, not Dysmas, and her words bring tears to my eyes.

"Yosef, please try to understand. You helped us so much, helped . . . him . . . so much. I couldn't take the chance that if they caught you, you would bear the brunt of the praefectus' wrath. So, I . . ." She lowers her gaze, as though ashamed of her deception.

"You alone took the risk." I expel a breath, and close my eyes for several long moments, letting her bravery sink into my heart before I say, "Maryam, truly, you are the greatest of his disciples. You made his teachings a part of you. He would be very proud."

A sob lodges in her throat. She closes her eyes, trying not to make a sound.

I give her some time. Then I ask, "What will you do now? You mustn't stay in Jerusalem. It's too dangerous."

She swallows hard. "I'm going to the Galil. A friend told me that's where Kepha has gone. I must face him. Yosef, I'm sure he's the one who—"

"As I am." Anger stirs the ashes of my grief. "Do you want me to go with you?"

She shakes her head. "No, I must do it alone. And you must leave, Yosef. Tonight. The Council is looking for you, and the praefectus—"

"Yes, Lazaros told me. If I stay, I fully expect to be arrested."[117]

A cloud passes across the face of the moon, and the gorge is shrouded in utter darkness.

"Master," Titus says. His curly brown hair looks gray tonight, making him seem older. "I know you could not tell me the whole truth when this began, but now—"

"Yes." I exhale the word. "Now it's time you understood. You deserve the truth more than anyone."

He waits, watching me. Occasionally, he glances at Maryam.

"Gamliel . . . he said it would take something monumental to stop the revolt, something so stunning that the shocked crowds would forget their anger and lay down their arms to embrace each other."

Titus appears to be thinking about that, his mind working through the maze of information. A cool breeze blows up the Kidron valley and flattens his robe against his chest. "You mean it had to be the fulfillment of prophecy?"

I glance at Maryam. When she says nothing, I add, "We knew that many people would think he'd escaped, and many more that his body had been stolen, but the faithful, those looking for the coming of the messiah . . ."

In an awed whisper, Titus says, "They would believe."

Maryam breathes, "With all their hearts."

I wait for him to ask more. When he does not, I rise to my feet and look at the tomb.

Maryam begins rocking again, back and forth.

"Is he in there?" I ask. "Is that where you put him?"

Why else would she be here?

She closes her eyes, and her shoulders heave. When she gains control, she says, "It is his family tomb. He carved the facade just days before. . . ." Her hoarse voice trails away.

I lift my gaze to the symbol of the tekton. *His grandfather, and his great-grandfather, and more fathers back into the dark mists of time, were excellent stoneworkers. He would rejoice to be with them. It is a fitting place.*

I just stare at it for a time, remembering the sound of his deep voice. . . .

Finally, I bow my head and pray, "Happy are they who dwell in the Lord's House, they shall be ever praising thee! Happy the people that is so circumstanced, happy the people whose God is the Eternal. I extol thee, my God, my King, and bless thy name evermore."

Maryam, surprised, lifts her head. Together, she and Titus reply in unison, "Let the name of the Eternal be praised, and exalted in his name alone. Amayne."

A trembling smile touches Maryam's lips. She rises unsteadily to her feet and turns, with me, to face the tomb as I begin the Yiskor, the burial service.

The setting is wrong. I cannot do everything I need to. But what little I can offer is better than nothing.

I take a deep breath, and sing in a soft voice, "May God remember the soul of our honored teacher, Yeshua ben Pantera. . . ."

FIFTY

The moonlight shining into the tomb was dazzling. It was as though it had been carved in anticipation of this exact moment.

As Kalay's eyes adjusted, she studied the squarish shape of the main burial chamber. There were three skulls on the floor; each rested before a loculus, or in Hebrew, *kokh,* a tunnel carved into the wall where ossuaries were placed on rock shelves. There were six *kokhim.* Even from here, near the entry, she could count several bone boxes in the recesses.

In a strained voice, Barnabas said, "Kalay, please, let me read this to you."

She walked through the silver wash of light to where Barnabas and Zarathan crouched before a rectangular box carved from limestone. Back in the tunnel, she counted two more ossuaries.

Barnabas said, "I can't see very well, but I believe this one says, *Yuda bar Yeshua.*"

Kalay translated, "Iuda son of Iesous."

Zarathan stared at her aghast. "Our Lord had a son?"

Barnabas shook his head. "It may mean nothing, Zarathan. Let's keep looking."

He crawled deeper into the tunnel, and read aloud: "Here's one marked *Yose* and another, *Maria.*"

"Our Lord's parents!" Zarathan looked like he might faint.

Kalay shook her head. "Those are two of the most common names in the history of the Ioudaiosoi, you idiot. They don't mean anything."

"There's also a *Mariamne* back here," Barnabas called. "The inscription is in Greek, which is a little curious."

Kalay looked straight at Zarathan and hissed, "That's probably one of your Lord's sisters that you don't believe in."

"I didn't say I didn't believe!"

Barnabas crawled out and moved to another tunnel. He reached into it, turned one of the ossuaries, and leaned so close to the inscription his nose almost touched the box. He haltingly read, *"Yakob . . . bar Yosef . . . achui de . . . Yeshua."*

Kalay grinned at Zarathan. "Iakobos, son of Ioses, brother of Iesous."

When Zarathan fell back against the wall with his mouth agape, Kalay said, "Obviously, your Lord's brother—er, cousin."

In a strangled voice, Zarathan said, "I don't believe it!"

Barnabas continued moving around the tomb. "These have no inscriptions," he said after searching three ossuaries.

As he moved to the fourth tunnel, he sucked in a deep breath and placed a hand against the wall, as though to gather his failing strength. They'd been up all night, eaten nothing in two days, and been traveling hard. She was amazed he'd made it this far.

"Brother," Kalay called. "Please sit down and rest for just a few moments. Otherwise, I'm afraid you're going to fall down."

"No, no, I . . . I can't. There's no way of knowing how much time we have."

Zarathan righted himself, blinked as though waking, and marched across the room to take Barnabas' arm. "Forgive me, brother, I should have been helping you all along."

"Thank you, Zarathan," Barnabas said and leaned on his brother as he moved to the next tunnel.

The ossuary in front sat in a particularly bright patch of moonlight. It seemed impossible that such a thing could be an accident. Had the person who'd placed it here done it at night? With moonlight streaming through the entry just like this?

Barnabas got down on his knees to examine it. "There's an inscription," he said, "but it's difficult to make out." He sounded out the letters for a time, then in a shaking voice read, *"Yeshua . . . bar . . . Yosef."*[118]

Zarathan let out a small cry and spun around to stare at Kalay. "I *told* you Ioses was his father! I knew it!"

"Zarathan, do you know how common these names are?"

"B-but all of them!" Zarathan stammered. "All of them in one place? This must have been Iesous' family tomb!"

Kalay folded her arms. "That means you'll have to admit that your Lord had a son. Hmm. Then maybe that Mariamne was the one known as the Magdalen. Yuda's mother?"

It might have been the moonlight, but she swore that Zarathan's young face lost all color. "No," he whispered. "I don't believe it. I *won't* believe it!"

Barnabas said, "There's another inscribed tomb back here."

Kalay asked, "What does it say?"

He squinted hard. "It might be . . . *Matya.*"

"Oh, there's a ringer for you, Zarathan." Kalay's brows lifted. "In Greek that's *Maththaios.* Why would there be a Maththaios in Iesous' family tomb?"

Zarathan wet his lips, and breathed before he said, "Maybe he was the son of Yuda or some other family member who lived later?"

"Now you're thinking," she said, and shoved a lock of long red hair from her eyes. "Maybe all of these are from a later time. Maybe decades, or centuries later. Even yesterday—"

"No," Barnabas corrected as he grabbed Zarathan's wrist to steady himself. "Decades, perhaps, but we know that this burial tradition dates only to the time just before and just after our Lord was alive."

"See, I told you," Zarathan stubbornly insisted. "It's Iesous' family tomb!"

Kalay gestured to Barnabas' hand where it clutched Zarathan's wrist. "Best let go, Barnabas. Your grip's jeopardizing the blood flow to his brain."

Barnabas turned and his face glowed with deep reverence. Softly, he said, "The likelihood that the map would lead us here, and that all these names would occur in one tomb and not be associated with our Lord . . . well, it's virtually impossible."

"Brother Barnabas," she said as though reprimanding a child. "Do you know how many members of my own family have these names?"

He blinked. "No."

"I have a cousin named *Yeshua ben Yosef*. My three aunts are named *Mari, Maryam,* and *Miryam*. My grandfather was *Yakob*"—she took a breath to continue her litany—"I have three second cousins named *Yuda*. And the number of men named *Matya*—well, too many to count."

Zarathan's jaw had locked, and his eyes narrowed like a wild pig's just before it charges. "There are ten ossuaries in this tomb, and five have inscriptions that bear the names of our Lord's family. This is no accident. You're just trying to demean—"

"I surrender," she said and threw up her hands. "You've found the Pearl. Let's go home to Egypt."

Kalay stalked across the chamber and ducked outside into the night.

Cyrus, who stood three paces away, spun breathlessly, waiting for her to tell him what they'd discovered.

"Yes?"

The wind still gusted wildly, flinging sand and gravel in every direction.

She strode to him and said, "Go see for yourself. There's a tomb in there that bears the inscription *Yeshua bar Yosef*."

His anxious expression slackened, and his eyes went wide and wet with faith. For several moments, he was unable to speak. Finally, he whispered, "Truly?"

"Yes, absolutely. Go and see it. I'll stand guard for the few moments it will take you."

Cyrus hesitated. He clearly wanted to go inside, but was uncertain he could leave his post.

"Go on," she ordered and made a shooing motion with her hands.

Cyrus grimaced, then broke. He rushed past her and ducked into the tomb.

Voices rose and carried on the wind, filled with awe and conviction. Several instants later, someone started crying, barely audible. She thought it was Barnabas. Then Zarathan let out a deep-throated sob, and burst into tears.

Kalay drew the knife from her belt and walked a few paces down the gorge. There, in the shadows, she leaned heavily against the cliff. The moon had almost sunk below the western horizon and the first rays of dawn filtered through the sky like pale blue smoke.

She took a deep breath and let it out slowly. What fools men were. A few names scribbled on rocks and they went to pieces.

Though, she had to admit, they were intriguing names.

She tried to imagine what the monks would do if they all agreed the ossuary was the Pearl. Would they pack it up and haul it home to place on the altar of a new monastery? Perhaps they would open it, and each start carrying around finger bones; "relics," they were called. That was such a ghastly thought it made her slightly ill. She took a few more steps down the gorge.

Just ahead of her a cascade of pebbles bounced down the cliff, and Kalay craned her neck to scan the stone wall high above. The ferocious wind had probably scooped it from a ledge . . . but an old and familiar chill crept about her bones. It was like hearing a footfall in a room that's supposed to be empty.

She turned to study the black pool of moon shadow across the gorge where a small sandstorm spun. There was nothing there. Nothing.

Then . . . a whisper of leather and metal, a sudden glint of silver.

Instinctively, she spun with her knife held low, and slashed straight into the downward arc of a sword. The impact knocked her blade to the ground and left her hand stinging. Madly, she grabbed for the bronze dagger that remained in her belt, and fell into a crouch.

Loukas laughed and circled her. "You must have known I'd find you," he said. His reddish-blond hair looked pewter in the moonlight, and his broad nose shone, as though covered with sweat. "I hope you've been preparing yourself for this moment."

Kalay lunged at him with the dagger.

Loukas countered with the flat of his sword, bashing her hand, sending the dagger spinning off into the darkness. A cruel smile turned his lips.

She ran headlong down the narrow gorge, her heart pounding to the sound of his boots crashing on the dry gravel behind her. She fought to think, to—

Just as she started to scream, a hand clamped hard over her mouth, jerked her backward, and a muscular arm tightened against her throat.

In her ear, he whispered, "Be quiet, *beauty*. Don't struggle. Or I'll see that your friends die very slowly."

As he gagged her, bound her hands behind her, and tied her ankles, she shot a frantic glance up the gorge, expecting to see Cyrus stepping outside.

"That's a good girl," Loukas hissed as he pulled the ropes so tight they cut into her flesh like rusty knives.

Then he forced her to walk down the gorge to where a horse stood hidden in the shadows. By the time he finally muscled her onto the horse's back and took off at a fast trot, she could barely breathe.

As they galloped away, she heard horses. Many horses. Coming fast.

She had to twist around to look.

High above, flooding out of the Dung Gate, were at least two decuria, and perhaps another ten men dressed in religious robes.

Loukas quickly reined his horse down into a small shadowed drainage that emptied off to one side.

Kalay wrenched her body and tried to scream, to get someone's attention, maybe she could distract the soldiers long enough for—

Loukas slammed a fist into the back of her neck, almost knocking her unconscious. "Don't try it!" he hissed. "Your friends are doomed. You had better start thinking of yourself, and what you can do to make me forget that shed in Leontopolis."

Kalay shuddered and closed her eyes.

FIFTY-ONE

Zarathan slumped down on the rock shelf in front of one of the uninscribed ossuaries and watched Cyrus and Barnabas where they stood talking and gently touching the box marked YESHUA BAR YOSEF.[119] The last half hour with the three of them together had been like a revelation. That same divine bliss that came over him when he'd prayed all night now filled his heart, but even more powerfully; it was an ineffable radiance, a peace such as he had never known.

He looked around. They'd gone over each ossuary again with Cyrus, and he'd added his own knowledge of the people whose names were written on them. Zarathan felt for the first time as though he truly knew these long-dead saints.

They had decided that the tomb simply marked YOSE may have been their Lord's brother, rather than his adopted father, which conveniently settled a dispute, and that Yuda bar Yeshua was probably a relative from a decade or two later. His ossuary did seem different. It was smaller and more crudely carved. Maria and Mariamne were likely his mother and sister. Matya was still a mystery, one that, even now, Cyrus and Barnabas quietly debated.

"It's possible that he might have been the disciple known as Levi, but if this is our Lord's family tomb, it seems unlikely the former tax collector would be here and none of the other disciples would be."

Cyrus was smoothing his hand over the Yeshua bar Yosef ossuary as though touching a lover. "I agree. Again, it could be a family member from the same time as Yuda. Perhaps even Yuda's brother."

Cyrus' deep voice had a strange resonance, a kindness that left Zarathan trembling.

The wind outside increased to a roar and a fierce gust swept into the tomb and blew around the ossuaries like a ghost, kicking up dust.

As though something had just occurred to Cyrus, he jerked his hand away from the ossuary, whirled toward the entry, and his eyes went huge. "Kalay! I forgot! Brothers, stay here. I'll be right back!"

He ran for the entry and ducked outside into the howling gale.

Barnabas stared after him, then he glanced at Zarathan. "I'm sure she's well."

But in a quarter hour, when neither Cyrus nor Kalay had returned, Barnabas began to grow anxious. He walked to the entry and peered outside. The moonlight had given way to a cerulean hue, heralding the coming of dawn.

Barnabas turned back to Zarathan, took two steps, and opened his mouth to—

A tall body blocked the entry, and Zarathan could see several other men behind, filling the gorge.

"Brother!" Zarathan cried as he leaped off the stone shelf and stared wide-eyed over Barnabas' shoulder.

Barnabas swung around.

Four Roman soldiers ducked into the tomb and took up positions around the chamber, their swords drawn. They wore bronze helmets and held the shields of the legion. The clinking of all the metal sounded loud in the quiet tomb.

Two other men, both dressed in the black robes of bishops, entered after them.

The tall, younger bishop had short blond hair and a clean-shaven face. The older man was short with wispy brown hair and heavy jowls. He looked to be about Barnabas' age.

Barnabas said, "Who are you?"

The blond bishop extended a hand to the other man. "This is Pappas

Macarios of Jerusalem. I believe you remember me, don't you, Brother Barnabas?"

Barnabas stared daggers at Meridias.

Macarios glanced between the two men, then bowed slightly to Barnabas. "Brothers, greetings in the name of our Lord. Do you—"

Meridias interrupted, "What are you two doing here?"

Barnabas folded his hands in front of him and Zarathan wondered if he was thinking about the dead monks in Egypt, many of whom Barnabas had known and loved for twenty years. In a matter-of-fact voice, Barnabas said, "You know very well what we're doing here, Meridias. We're searching for the Pearl."

Macarios frowned as though confused, but he looked excessively nervous. Despite the wind and cold, his forehead glistened with sweat. "I don't know what that is." Macarios turned to Meridias for an explanation.

Meridias didn't look at him. He kept his narrowed gaze on Barnabas. "And did you find it?"

"Of course not. It's a legend. A fantasy created by some cruel prankster three centuries ago." Barnabas pulled the papyrus from his pocket and threw it on the floor. "There's the map, if you want it."

Meridias gestured for Macarios to pick it up. The elderly little bishop stooped, grasped it, and looked at it briefly before he handed it to Meridias.

Zarathan couldn't speak. He stared at the map in Meridias' hand in horror. The man who'd destroyed their monastery, killed their brothers, was now holding the sacred artifact. It was almost too much to bear.

Meridias glanced at Zarathan. "You. Boy. Why are you crying?"

Zarathan planted his feet, swallowed hard, his mind racing. "I—I'm sad because we didn't find the Pearl."

Again Macarios said, "What is the Pearl?"

Impatiently, Meridias said, "No one knows, it's—"

"It was supposed to be the tomb of our Lord, Iesous Christos," Barnabas said to Macarios. "Just foolishness."

A stunned look of reverence came over Macarios' face. "And—and the map led you here?"

"If we followed it correctly, yes. Though I'm still not certain we did. However, the ossuaries in this tomb do make one wonder."

"What do you mean?" Macarios took a step forward.

Barnabas gripped Macarios' arm and led him around the chamber, reading the inscriptions aloud. Macarios' expression grew more awed with each name.

Zarathan knew how he felt, but Pappas Meridias seemed totally unaffected . . . until they came to the tomb inscribed YESHUA BAR YOSEF.

Meridias shouted, "*What?* Is that correct? Macarios, you read it. Is that what it really says?"

Macarios leaned down to study the inscription. After several agonizing moments, he straightened. "Yes, that's what it says."

Meridias spun around to the soldiers and ordered, "Crush every one of these ossuaries and scatter the shards in the desert. Then come back to destroy this tomb! I want it—"

"Why?" Macarios asked in a calm, inquiring voice.

"Don't ask me idiotic questions. I give the orders here. Decurion, arrest these men!"

The decurion marched toward Barnabas and grabbed hold of his sleeve.

"Wait, Rufus," Macarios said almost casually to the decurion, and it occurred to Zarathan that the soldier was, of course, stationed in Jerusalem, and therefore accustomed to obeying Macarios. "There's no reason to arrest these men. These ossuaries are nothing special."

The decurion released Barnabas.

Meridias looked to be on the verge of exploding. He yelled, "What are you *talking* about? If the bones of Iesous Christos are in that box, don't you see what it will do to our Church!"

"Pappas." Macarios sighed. "Your reaction is understandable, but it is misguided. I have two ossuaries in my office at the monastery inscribed in exactly the same way, *Yeshua bar Yosef*. When we return I will be happy to show them to you."

Meridias seemed totally taken aback. He glanced around the chamber, as though he feared he were the butt of some terrible joke. "Two?"

Macarios gave him an indulgent smile. "We have recovered over two thousand ossuaries from the hills around Jerusalem. From the written information as well as the ossuaries we've gleaned, we have determined that perhaps one thousand men in Jerusalem at the time of our Lord were named Yeshua and had fathers named Yosef."

Angrily, Meridias said, "And what about Yakob son of Yosef, brother of Yeshua? Surely there can't have been many men who carried such a name."

"No, that's true. But I estimate perhaps twenty or twenty-five.[120] These names are extremely common. Why, consider the names Maria and Mari-amne in the back loculus. Both are variations of the Hebrew name Miriam, which was the most common female name of the first century. And the names Yakob, Yosef, Yudah, Yeshua, and Matya were so common that we believe perhaps forty percent of all men at the time carried those names."

Zarathan's heart began to sink. Macarios almost had him convinced, and Meridias seemed totally confused. He'd started pacing like a madman.

"Pappas Meridias, think of the holy Roman Empire. How many men are named Gaius, Julius, Marcus, Lucius, or Septus? Thousands in the city of Rome alone."

Meridias gaped at Macarios in disbelief.

The short priest put a hand on the decurion's shoulder and gently said, "Rufus, please take your men and return to the monastery. You're not needed here."

"Yes, Pappas."

As the decurion motioned to his men and they began to file out of the tomb, Meridias cried, "Wait! I haven't dismissed you!"

The soldiers paid him no attention. One by one they ducked outside, and the decurion's voice rose above the wind: "Climb the trail. We're returning to the city!"

Only one man remained guarding the entry. A gray-haired old man that Zarathan recognized as one of the men who'd attacked them at Libni's caves.

A dangerous brew of terror and rage boiled in his veins. If only he could get his hands around the man's throat! Memories flashed of the fight on the beach, of all the fear and pain they'd endured . . . so powerful was the need to hurt in return, that it took all of his control to remain in place.

Barnabas said, "Pappas Macarios, I'm sure we broke some law when we entered this tomb. Whatever penalties you judge appropriate, we will of course submit to without argument."

Macarios thoughtfully fingered his beard. "It is illegal to damage graves, or steal grave goods, but"—he looked around—"I see no evidence that you did either. You opened the tomb, yes, and that showed poor judgment on your part, but you did no harm."

"You're very gracious, Pappas." Barnabas knelt before him and kissed the man's hand. "Forgive us for causing such an unintended uproar."

Meridias stared at them with narrowed eyes. He spun on his heel, stalked out of the tomb, and shouted, "Elicius, we're leaving!"

When the sound of their footsteps died away, Barnabas rose to his feet, faced Macarios, and a slow smile came to his face. Barnabas whispered, "You received the message I sent from Gaza?"

Macarios chuckled softly. "I did."

Macarios spread his arms, and the two men embraced like lifelong friends.

Zarathan gaped. He stumbled in his haste to reach the entry and look outside. When he was certain no one stood close enough to see them, he hissed, "Do you know each other?"

Barnabas said, "Macarios and I were both library assistants in Caesarea—"

"Along with several others," Macarios clarified.

Tears welled in Barnabas' eyes when he looked at his old friend. "When I heard they were hunting us down, I was desperately afraid you would be one of the first they'd find. You are so visible."

"Yes, but I've made a point of supporting Pappas Silvester's every whim. I wasn't worried about me, but you? I was sure they'd kill you. You are known far and wide as Barnabas the Heretic." Macarios chuckled again, then his voice lowered. "Do you know anything of the fates of Libni and Symeon? Are they well?"

Barnabas expelled a breath. "I know nothing of Symeon, but when we left Libni, he was gravely wounded. He—"

"Meridias' work?"

"Almost certainly."

Macarios clamped his jaw and looked away as though considering what to do. After a time, his gaze darted around the tomb, and he whispered, "When I received your warning, and the message about what had happened at your monastery, I began my own search. Of course, I've been at it for years, as you have, but I believe I have uncovered something important."

Barnabas eyed him for several heartbeats, then stepped back. "More important than this tomb?"

"Maybe. I'm not sure yet. I had two of my most loyal monks excavating when Meridias arrived. They had to abandon their work and make it appear as though grave robbers had broken into the tomb, but—"

Barnabas sucked in a sudden breath. "The short leg? On the map? You found what lies at the end of the short leg!"

Macarios held up a hand. "Don't get your hopes up. I *may* have. But we've barely begun to explore the Shroud Tomb. Meridias himself entered it, but the man is too dim-witted to understand what he was seeing." His expression tightened. "He's ordered it resealed. I'll have to stall."

Zarathan ducked out to inspect the gorge outside one more time, then turned. "Brothers, we must find Cyrus and Kalay. They are nowhere to be seen."

Barnabas said, "Macarios, I may need your help again. We—"

"You have it without asking. You know that. Why don't we head for the Shroud Tomb and you can tell me about your friends on the way."

Barnabas nodded, but his eyes drifted around the tomb again, landing on each of the ossuaries, and a soft light shone in his eyes. "Are you sure this isn't it? It—it feels right. Holy."

"It is holy. But as to whether this is our Lord's family tomb . . . I cannot say for certain."

"No," Barnabas whispered. "No, I suppose not."

As they walked toward the entry, Macarios affectionately put his arm around Barnabas' shoulders. "Still, it might be."

FIFTY-TWO

Kalay didn't know how long they'd been riding. It seemed only moments, but when Loukas dragged her off the horse, her legs felt like boiled straw. She could barely stand. He'd struck her harder than she'd thought.

They were on the slope, just at the brow overlooking the gorge. She recognized another of the numerous tombs, this one freshly opened, with loose dirt piled beside the dark opening. She ground her teeth in an effort to chew through the cloth he'd tied tightly around her head to gag her.

Loukas picked her up bodily, and carried her to the tomb. He shoved her through the small entrance, heedless of banging her against the stone. She almost tumbled down the stairs, squirming to keep from knocking her head.

Loukas stepped over her and reached down to drag her across the rough limestone floor. Then he shoved her onto a rock shelf near two ossuaries. He was smiling as he climbed the steps and went outside again.

While he was gone, and she heard him rummaging through the pack on the horse, she rolled to the floor, sat down, and managed to slip her hands beneath her hips, then her feet. When they were in front of her she frantically started trying to untie the knots.

Loukas returned with a burning oil lamp, saw her, and made a disappointed clucking sound. As he calmly set the oil lamp on an ossuary, he said, "I can see you're going to be a problem." With lightning speed, he backhanded her.

Kalay tumbled across the floor.

When she opened her eyes, she caught sight of a shrouded skeleton lying on the shelf above her. *I'll probably be up there with you soon, friend. After what I did to him in Leontopolis, he's not going to keep me for long.*

Loukas carried the oil lamp into another chamber. When he returned, he knelt in front of her, and stroked her hair with a gloved hand. *"Soon, beauty."*

He roughly grabbed her by her bound feet and dragged her into the next chamber, where the oil lamp cast a faint amber glow over another dozen ossuaries.

As he glared down at her, Kalay didn't move. She just stared back, reading his hatred, breathing hard, trying not to think about the future.

The lamplight flickered, and she noticed small things. There was a strange, spicy scent that seemed to ooze from the walls, probably myrrh and aloes, maybe frankincense. And the ossuaries here were elaborately decorated, not like the plain, inscribed boxes in the *tekton*'s tomb. These had domed lids with exquisite carvings around the rims and gorgeous interlinked rosettes cut into the sides. Many were painted. A master stoneworker had carved these. In the far corner, almost hidden by shattered ossuaries, was a sealed doorway, or the top of a doorway. It was as though there had originally been a third, lower level, and this chamber was built over the top of it, forever sealing the lower chamber, except for a maybe one cubit of the old doorway.

Loukas tugged his robe over his head and stood naked before her. His healed scrotum looked lopsided with its missing testicle, but his rising penis left no illusions about his intentions. He had arms as big around as her waist. As he knelt and cut the ropes binding her ankles, she wildly kicked him in the head, rolled to her feet, and made a mad run for the door.

He tackled her, bringing her down hard. She screamed against her gag, kicked him, and as a last act of defiance slammed him in the face with her forehead. When he finally pinned her arms and legs with his heavy body, his face was bleeding, but his eyes . . . his eyes were alight.

"Oh, I look forward to watching you suffer. You took half of me in

Egypt. Before I'm done, there will be nothing left of you but a bloody shell."

Kalay locked her jaw as he viciously jerked her dress up past her waist. A hard slap dazed her enough that he could force her legs apart. He was watching her intently as he drove himself inside her. His thrusts were wild and brutal, designed to hurt her, to make her cry out.

Her entire body screamed at the hurt and outrage, but she bit back the cries that rose in her throat.

Instead, Kalay sought an old refuge, one she hadn't used in many years. It was a dark, quiet place inside her. As a child, she'd built it, brick by brick, creating a sanctuary from men, one she could return to in the worst of times, when she felt utterly hopeless.

She closed her eyes and with all of her strength sought to abandon her body. She sent her soul traveling down into that brilliant darkness, far away from here, from his stinking body, from—

A voice filtered through the chamber. Soft, calling out. A man's voice. She couldn't understand the words, but she knew it was a question.

She opened her eyes. Loukas didn't seem to hear it. He'd started to pant and move faster, and his eyes had that glazed look she'd seen on the faces of so many men.

The voice came again, this time louder, more mournful, as though pleading for someone to hear him.

To her right, a tiny flash of light sparked near the floor.

She jerked her head sideways to try to find the place it had come from.

"Move," Loukas ordered. "Move or I'll tear your heart out."

She moved.

His frenzy built. He buried his face against her shoulder and began grunting and groaning, writhing on top of her.

Footsteps.

She heard footsteps.

. . . and that voice again, this time it was frantic, almost shouting. The words lay just beyond her ability to hear.

Pure terror fired her veins.

Another flash of light to her right. She didn't have time to look. Loukas stiffened and cried out, and a massive shadow crossed in front of the lamplight, hurling down.

Kalay screamed into her gag, and barely jerked aside as Loukas' head smacked face-first into the floor, bounced off the stone, then was pounded down again.

"Get out of the way, Kalay!"

As the heavy ossuary lifted again, she glimpsed Cyrus' face, his eyes wild with rage. She shoved out from under Loukas and rolled away.

Blow after blow, Cyrus pounded Loukas' head until there was little more than pulp remaining. When the ossuary cracked on the final blow, and shards cartwheeled across the floor, Cyrus dropped the chunks he still held and stumbled backward.

For a long while, he stared at the body, waiting until the arms and legs stopped jerking. When he knew the man was dead, his gaze lifted to Kalay.

She made a muffled sound through her gag.

Without a word, Cyrus pulled his knife and went to her, sawing first through her gag, then the ropes tying her hands. When she was free, he said, "Forgive me," pulled her into his arms, and ferociously crushed her body against his. She felt him shaking, as though on the verge of tears.

She sank against him, her relief so great she couldn't seem to think. "I thought you were dead."

"I shouldn't have left you alone out there. I started looking at the ossuaries and I lost track of—"

"Cyrus?" She suddenly remembered the soldiers. "Where are Barnabas and Zarathan?"

He released her. "As soon as I realized you were missing, I ran to the top of the cliff and grabbed one of the horses, then I saw the soldiers riding down the slope and had to hide until they'd passed."

"You left your brothers to face the soldiers alone and came after me?"

His jaw clenched for a moment and she could see the turmoil, the admission he didn't want to make. "It was too late, Kalay. There were too many of them. I wouldn't have been of any use there."

"But how did you find me?"

He cocked his head as though the question were absurd. "I heard you calling me."

"Calling you?"

"Yes."

"What are you talking about?"

His brows pulled together. "You shouted my name. Over and over. I heard you from halfway across the Kidron valley."

"Cyrus, I . . . I was gagged."

His eyes darted to the gag on the floor. He'd cut and pulled it from her mouth only moments ago. He stared at the soggy cloth as though it were impossible. "Then, who called me here?"

Kalay's gaze went to the bricked-up doorway across the room. That's where the flashes of light had come from. She was sure of it.

Cyrus followed her gaze. "What is that? An old doorway?"

Shooting Loukas' corpse an angry glare, she struggled to her feet. "I swear I saw something. . . . Help me open it."

FIFTY-THREE

This is the stone which was not set by you builders, which
has become the cornerstone.
   —Acts 4:11

By the time Macarios had led them to the Shroud Tomb, the wind had almost vanished, and the cloudless morning sky was shot through with pink
lances of light that radiated outward from the golden halo on the rugged
eastern horizon. The sweet scent of freshly sprouted wheat fields carried on
the breeze.

As they rode over a rise, Barnabas saw the open tomb down in the Hinnom valley. He swiveled around on his horse and, in his mind, drew a line
from the Dung Gate to the tomb.

"It's possible," he whispered, but feared to hope.

For the first time in many years, he felt alone. From the moment they'd
left the *tekton*'s tomb, a black emptiness had begun filling him, until now
he feared it would suffocate him. He had failed. The entire Occultum Lapidem had been a farce. There was no hidden stone. But many men—good,
faithful men—had died to help him protect what was hidden at the end of
the papyrus map. How would God ever forgive him? How would he ever
forgive himself?

He kicked his horse into a trot, calling to the bishop who rode the horse in front of him, "Macarios, what is in this Shroud Tomb?"

Macarios slowed his horse so he could ride alongside Barnabas and Zarathan. "The ossuaries are extraordinary, much more elaborate than those in the *tekton*'s tomb. I only got to look at them briefly, but two of the boxes are inscribed with the names Mari and Salome."

"Possibly our Lord's sisters?"

"Possibly, but again, both names were common in the first century."

As they rode down the hill for the tomb, Barnabas asked, "Why do you call it the Shroud Tomb?"

"In the rear of the tomb, there's a body laid out on a shelf, still wrapped in the original burial linens. It's an amazing sight. Though sad."

"Why sad?" Zarathan asked from where he rode behind Barnabas.

"His family laid him out as was customary, but they never returned to finish the ritual burial, to clean his bones and place him in an ossuary. If you believe that the soul rests in the body until the resurrection, he's probably still waiting for his loved ones to come back and care for him."

Macarios rode to a stop in front of the tomb, studied the two horses that wandered through a garden of wind-sculpted boulders in the distance, and gave Barnabas a warning glance. "Do you recognize those animals?"

Barnabas felt as though a huge hand had reached out and squeezed his heart. In a whisper he said, "The horse with the big bags strapped over its withers belongs to Cyrus, the other monk with us."

"Just one of the beasts?"

"Yes, I don't know the second."

Barnabas and Zarathan dismounted and walked to stand beside Macarios near the entry. The tomb was deathly quiet.

Barnabas turned to Zarathan. "Brother, could you go and retrieve the horses? We may need them in a hurry."

"Yes, of course, brother." Zarathan started down the hill at a trot toward where the horses grazed among the standing stones.

"Let me go in first," Barnabas said. "In case Cyrus is hurt. He was once a Roman soldier and sometimes acts on instinct."

Macarios nodded, and Barnabas ducked through the entry into the tomb. The floor was covered with broken shards of ossuaries. Barnabas could see the skeleton lying on the shelf in the rear. In the chamber to the left of the skeleton, lamplight fluttered.

FIFTY-FOUR

So as not to spook them, Zarathan cautiously approached the horses. The animals placidly grazed upon the taller grasses growing at the bases of the head-high boulders. The whole slope seemed to be one highly eroded limestone outcrop. He whistled as Cyrus did when he wanted the horse to come, and the big bay lifted his head and pricked his ears. Zarathan whistled again and the horse trotted toward him. The other horse, seeing his friend leaving, let out a short, startled whinny and followed.

"Good boy," Zarathan praised as he gripped the lead rope on Cyrus' horse. It took two tries to catch the rope dangling from the unknown horse's halter.

The horse leaped and tossed its head. Zarathan caught a glimpse of the sheathed sword that hung from the saddle. The ivory hilt gleamed in the dawn light.

"Shh," he soothed. "You're all right, boy. Everything's fine."

The horse stopped twisting, but pawed the ground, throwing up a gray haze of dirt.

As Zarathan turned, he noticed three men as they rode around the southeastern corner of the Temple Mount. When they started down the mountainside, they were silhouetted against the sunrise. They were just dark riders. Zarathan couldn't make out anything about them, but the way they sat their horses sent a surge of fear through him. They were Romans.

Had they been hiding up there?

Zarathan hesitated, uncertain what to do, then led the horses back into the boulders where they'd been grazing.

The riders were negotiating the steep slope as quickly as they could, and appeared to be heading straight for the Shroud Tomb.

"D-did they follow us?"

He glanced at the horsemen, then whirled around to stare to the north, toward the monastery he'd seen being built outside the Damascus Gate. The brothers there must all love Pappas Macarios. Surely he could convince several to ride back with him? But how long would the trip take? How long . . .

Don't be a fool! Go for help! Now!

Without further consideration, he leaped upon Cyrus' horse, reined it around, and rode flat out for the monastery.

FIFTY-FIVE

Barnabas walked toward the lamp-lit chamber just left of the partially shrouded skeleton. As he neared the doorway, a strange, eerie glow overwhelmed the lamplight. The hair on his arms stood on end, as though lightning were about to strike the tomb.

Just as suddenly, the glow faded.

He took two more steps, and saw the body on the floor. "Cyrus!"

He ran to kneel beside the man. In the frail lamplight, he could tell very little. Blood had soaked the corpse's hair, making it impossible to judge the original color. "It's not black. It's . . . lighter. And shorter."

A queer sensation of panic broke inside him. He longed for nothing more than to turn tail and run.

But he rose and walked deeper into the tomb.

"Cyrus? Kalay?" he called loudly.

"Brother Barnabas?" There was a clatter to his right, then a face appeared in a narrow slot near the floor.

"Cyrus!" Joy flooded Barnabas. "You're alive!" Had he crawled in there to take sanctuary? As the stinging rush of blood began to subside, Barnabas said, "Please tell me Kalay is with you?"

"She is, brother."

"Praise be to God."

"Brother Barnabas?" There was a stunned look in Cyrus' eyes, and his voice . . . his voice had a low, haunted timbre.

"Cyrus, what's wrong?" Barnabas hurried forward to kneel before the opening. He'd thought at first that it was just another loculus. But now that he could see more clearly, it looked oddly as though it were once a door—a door that had been sealed long ago. The scent that escaped from the chamber was something a man never forgets. The same scent they'd just smelled at the *tekton* tomb . . . centuries-old air flavored with a hint of spices and aromatic oils that created a tang at the back of the throat.

Inside the chamber, blinding light suddenly blazed and Barnabas flung himself backward with a short cry as he covered his eyes. Icy-blue radiance filled the tomb. As he lowered his shaking hands, he whispered, "What is this?"

As though his words had triggered a silent clap of thunder, another salvo of light burst forth from the opening and dazzling blue fox fire spattered the walls, flickering, dancing, pouring down in glowing serpentine rivulets to puddle on the floor where they pulsed as though alive.

Barnabas couldn't feel his body. He felt as though he were numbly floating off the floor.

"Barnabas?" Cyrus called. "Barnabas, please come over here. Do you know what this is?"

His voice snapped Barnabas from his trance. He got on his hands and knees and crawled through the fox fire to the narrow opening.

In the frosty splendor, Cyrus' bearded face looked unearthly, like an angel's at the moment of creation, pale and shining.

Cyrus stepped aside so that Barnabas could see into the glowing chamber. Kalay stood to the right, near the source of the light, her face invisible in the blue blaze.

"Wait just a moment," Cyrus said. "The light will die down. Or at least it has since we've been here. It seems to come and go at irregular intervals."

Barnabas closed his eyes and watched the streamers on the backs of his lids. When they began to fade, he opened them again.

Kalay came into view, her female figure haloed in glowing blue. Her hair seemed to dance of its own volition.

Dearest Lord God! She's been an angel the entire time!

And then he fixed on the thing resting on the stone table. . . .

The sensation of awe that raced through Barnabas could have been no greater if God himself had stepped into the chamber.

In a hoarse whisper Cyrus asked, "Is this what I think it is?"

Barnabas got down on his stomach and slid partway through the opening, trying to get a better view. The drop was long. He hesitated to jump down, as they had, for fear that his elderly bones would snap on impact.

The skeleton on the table two fathoms below was fully dressed. A large golden ring encircled its right index finger. Even after centuries, the ephod cloth was miraculous. The glittering gold leaf that mixed with the blue, purple, and scarlet threads might have been woven yesterday. But it was the ancient high priest's breastplate—worn over the ephod—that he could not take his eyes from. The twelve translucent stones, rubies, sapphires, opals, and sardonyxes of many colors, each inscribed with the name of a tribe, were the source of the light.[121]

In a trembling voice, Barnabas said, "God always signaled victory in battle by shining those stones."

Astonished, Cyrus said, "Then it is the *essen*? The lost, sacred breastplate of the Essenes?"

"Yes, it must be. Outside of the Ark of the Covenant, this is the most precious sacred artifact in the history of the Ioudaiosoi." Tears blurred Barnabas' eyes. The Truth was sinking in, and with it awestruck fear. He added, "And he is ours."

Perhaps it was the way Barnabas said *he,* but Cyrus suddenly jerked his head around and stared at the skeleton. He took a small involuntary step forward, then a tortured sound escaped his throat. A heartbeat later, he fell to his knees and clasped his hands in prayer, choking out the words, "Oh, my Lord, my Lord!"

Kalay squinted in disbelief. "It doesn't make sense. Why would Yeshua, an executed criminal, be given the *essen* to wear?"

Barnabas said, "Many saw him as the greatest sage of the time, and hoped he would be the military leader promised in the scriptures. Perhaps the Essenes hoped that by giving him the *essen,* he would return to lead them into battle against Rome and win."

"You mean they hoped he was the messiah?"

"Yes." Barnabas tipped his chin to the large, golden ring that encircled the skeleton's finger. "Kalay, is there a symbol on that ring?"

Kalay, still appearing disgruntled, walked around the table and examined it more closely. "It looks like a pomegranate design."

"Yes, that would make sense. The hem of the high priest's robes was embroidered with pomegranate designs, and they were used as the motif for the capitals of Solomon's Temple. The calyx of the fruit also served as a pattern for the crowns of the Torah."

"The *rimonim*," Kalay explained in Hebrew. "Yes, I remem . . ." Her voice faded, and she frowned.

"What's wrong?"

She gave Barnabas an askance look. "There's a—a scroll. I think. In his hand."

His heart beat louder. "What?"

Kalay gently tugged it from the curled finger bones of the skeleton's left hand. It had been rolled into a tube and tied with what looked like a braid of black hair. "There's something written on the outside of the tube. It's in Hebrew."

Barnabas ordered, "Bring it to me."

When Kalay got to within arm's reach, she handed the narrow papyrus tube up to him.

Barnabas studied the scroll. It was old, fragile beyond belief. Bits of the hair tie cracked off when he touched them and coated his hand. He squinted at the discolored ink. Most of it was impossible to read. Probably the inside was in much better condition. "I can only make out fragments: *Yakob . . . le . . . Yos . . . mati . . .*"

"From Yakob to Yosef Haramati?" Kalay suggested. "Yeshua's brother? Are you sure?"

"No, of course not. I'll look at it more closely later. Right now I'm more concerned with him." He gestured to the skeleton.

"Yes, me, too." Kalay's eyes took on a strange, savage glow. "What are you going to do with him? Turn him into a thousand splinters of holy relics? Or respect his beliefs?"

Taken aback by her tone, Barnabas asked, "What do you mean?"

"I mean, stop thinking about yourself. What if he really did believe in the physical resurrection of the body? If you start carrying off pieces of him—"

"Kalay," Barnabas defended, "what ever made you think that I would—"

The clacking sounds of feet shuffling through broken fragments of ossuaries came from the next chamber. Barnabas drew his head from the opening and called, "Zarathan? Macarios? Forgive me, I should have gone to fetch you. I—"

He froze when Macarios entered the lamp-lit chamber with his hands up, followed by Pappas Meridias and his gray-haired henchman.

Quickly, Barnabas tucked the scroll down the front of his robe.

FIFTY-SIX

The burial chamber went dark. It was as though someone had just blown out a candle—but not before Kalay glimpsed the tall blond bishop she'd first seen in Phoou the morning before the attack on the monastery.

"What happened to the light?" someone gasped.

Barnabas responded, "The wind stirred by your entry must have snuffed the oil lamp."

"Do you take me for a fool?" a man demanded to know. "Lamplight is yellow, not blue! Where did that glow come from?"

Barnabas shifted, and Kalay thought he'd sat up with his back against the entry to conceal as much of it as he could. "Pappas Macarios?" Barnabas called. "Are you well?"

An unknown man answered in a shaky voice, "Yes. They crept up on me outside. I don't know what they—"

"Silence!"

"Pappas Meridias," Barnabas replied, making an effort to sound calm. "Please, tell us what we may do to help you, and we will do everything in our power—"

"I *knew* you were hiding something!" Meridias said. "What's in here? Is the Pearl here?"

Kalay quietly eased away from the opening, felt for the corner of the table, and edged along it until Cyrus' hand touched hers. Barely audible, he said, "How many men entered the chamber?"

She felt for his face and cupped a hand to his ear to whisper, "I saw three."

"Meridias, Macarios, and another man?"

"Yes, an old man. Gray-headed, but he carried a drawn sword."

"Where was Zarathan?"

She hesitated. He was probably lying dead just outside the tomb. "I didn't see him."

"Kalay, I have to get into that chamber."

"If you grab hold of the ledge right behind Barnabas, when the moment is right, I'll boost you up."

Together they silently eased back to the opening, and Kalay lifted his foot and placed it in the basket she'd made of her knitted fingers. He was heavy; it wouldn't be easy to support his weight. But she had to.

Without warning, the *essen* burst to life. The blue flames flashed and grew into a conflagration that consumed the chamber. Kalay couldn't see anything in that blazing core. Terror emptied her bones, leaving her hollow and frail. As she waited for Cyrus to make his move, she gritted her teeth.

"Get away from that opening!" someone outside ordered. "I want to see what's in there!"

Broken ossuary shards clattered as Barnabas seemed to sit forward, saying, "Give me a moment. I need to brace my hands. I can't see—"

"Move or you'll be dead!"

Barnabas stood up, and Cyrus hissed, "Now!"

His weight suddenly depressed her hands, and she heaved with all her might.

FIFTY-SEVEN

As he lurched through the opening, Cyrus shoved Barnabas to the floor, scrambled to his feet, and charged Meridias before the bishop could react. Driving with all the power in his legs, he collided with Meridias, slamming him into the gray-haired guard. The impact toppled both men to the floor.

"It's Atinius! Kill him, you fool!" Meridias shouted and madly crawled away.

Cyrus leaped for the man, grabbed his sword hand, and bashed it into the floor. The man's grip relaxed, and Cyrus wrenched the sword away, rolled, and came up swinging for Pappas Meridias. The bishop managed to leap back just in time, and careened out into the other chamber.

Cyrus lunged after him.

As Cyrus' sword arced toward him, Meridias threw up an arm to protect himself and screamed, "No! Don't!"

The blade gleamed with an edge of pure blue fire as it sliced through Meridias' forearm, hacking off his hand above the wrist; it thudded on the floor, a dead lump of meat.

In shock, Meridias bellowed, "Iesous Christos, save me! Save me!" He grabbed the gushing stump and staggered backward toward the sunlit doorway that led outside, crying, "You'll be damned for eternity for killing me!"

Cyrus hesitated for less than a heartbeat, but it was too long. He felt the keen bite of the dagger piercing his back, and heard a low laugh behind him. Stumbling forward, he lifted the sword and spun in an old military maneuver, but his movements were awkward, off-balance. The sicarii easily stepped inside, and plunged the dagger into Cyrus' chest. Stunned by the fire, Cyrus froze in disbelief.

The hole in his chest sucked air and spewed blood with each breath he took, telling him it had punctured his right lung. Past the sicarii's head, he saw Barnabas pull Kalay from the hidden doorway, and glimpsed her expression as she charged into the room. Roaring like a lion, she leaped on the killer's back just as he drove the dagger into Cyrus again.

"Get off me!" the man shouted, and whirled around, trying to throw her off.

"Cyrus, run!" Kalay clawed her fingers into the killer's eyes. The man shrieked as blood spurted over his face.

In panic, the dagger man whipped his knife wildly, trying to strike her in the face. Cyrus mustered his last ounce of strength to bull forward, slamming into the sicarii and knocking both him and Kalay to the floor.

"Kalay, get out of the way!"

Cyrus jumped on the man and wrestled him for the dagger. He was growing weak. Blood sprayed in a fine mist from his mouth. His body was failing him.

The sicarii ripped the dagger from Cyrus' grip, rolled to his knees, and plunged it once more into Cyrus' chest. The pain was like a bolt of lightning cutting through him. His back arched and he writhed like a fish out of water.

A shadow crossed the chamber outside, and Cyrus glimpsed Zarathan. The boy was shaking so badly he could barely lift the heavy sword in his hands. An incoherent cry ripped from Zarathan's throat as he charged into the chamber.

The stunned guard jerked around and threw up his arm, as though to stop the sharp blade. Zarathan brought it down with all the insane strength in his terrified arms. The keen edge drove through the bone, severing the lower arm, then it cleft the man's skull, and lodged midway through his face. Zarathan wrenched the sword loose and the body flopped on the floor, spasmed violently, and gradually went still.

"Cyrus?" Kalay ran to him. She used her hands in a vain effort to stop the blood spurting from his chest.

"Oh, dear God, dear God," Barnabas sobbed. Macarios took the old monk in his arms.

Blood frothed at Cyrus' lips as he looked up at Zarathan, and whispered, "Good . . . good . . . brother."

Zarathan fixed on his stab wounds. "Oh, forgive me, Cyrus! I—I was afraid to enter the tomb. I rode for the monastery to get help, but turned back. Just . . . not soon enough."

Kalay said, "Where's Meridias? Did you kill him?"

Zarathan wildly shook his head. "No, he—he fled. I killed another man who was standing guard outside. Meridias darted past me and blindly ran for the city."

Cyrus coughed up gouts of blood, steadied himself by bracing one hand on the floor, and whispered, "Thank you . . . brother."

"Cyrus, don't try to speak!" Kalay ordered, but Cyrus wrapped one arm around her and crushed her against him, holding her close, his bloody lips pressed against her red hair. "I love you. I . . . I needed to tell . . . you."

Through the gray haze that was filling the chamber he saw Barnabas and Macarios on their knees, praying . . . Zarathan weeping.

His heart started fluttering as fast as a bird's, pattering against his ribs, and he couldn't seem onto get air into his lungs. He slumped to the floor and rolled onto his back.

His last glimpse was of Kalay. Damp curls of red hair streamed around her beautiful face as she leaned over him. Her cheeks were flushed, and she had a soft, luminous love in her eyes. He kept his gaze on her, fixing on the love . . . if he could just see her . . . her love would keep him safe . . . warm . . . he wouldn't . . .

FIFTY-EIGHT

The sound of the waves brushing the shore filled the cave.

Barnabas toyed with his chipped wine cup, aimlessly moving it around the table. In the candlelight, the crimson liquid appeared to be alive with golden sparks. His gaze drifted over the codices, scrolls, and papyri in the wall niches, then came back to Libni's face. Graying brown hair straggled around his dark, tear-filled eyes.

Libni whispered, "Was it the *essen?*"

Barnabas heaved a sigh and nodded. "Yes, I think so."

Libni closed his eyes. Tears ran down his cheeks and dripped onto the table where they shone like perfect diamonds. "Are you sure it was him?"

Barnabas sighed. "Many things are possible. I only know that it *felt* like him."

Libni nodded and opened his eyes. As he wiped his face on his sleeve, he said, "It's far more likely that it was a former high priest of the Council, or—"

"Yes, it is."

But as they gazed at each other, Barnabas knew that neither one of them believed that.

Libni leaned forward, his eyes aglow. "Barnabas, do you think that he—"

Voices rose from the tunnel.

Barnabas looked up when Kalay ducked into the chamber. She'd left her long red hair loose; it fell about her shoulders in lustrous waves, high-lighting her high cheekbones and full lips. He would always remember her as a blue glowing angel standing beside the long-dead body.

"What is it, Kalay?"

"I just wanted you to know that Zarathan's finally sleeping. Tiras is with him."

Barnabas exhaled a relieved breath. "Thank you."

After they'd fled Jerusalem, Zarathan had taken over Cyrus' role, rid-ing out front, scouting the roads, making certain every place they stopped was safe before they dismounted. He hadn't slept in two days. It was a strange, eerie transformation that Barnabas did not yet understand.

And Kalay . . . she had barely spoken since Cyrus' death. She, too, had changed. As if the sacred feminine had somehow filled her with its power. She was stronger, more a fortress than any man he had ever known.

"Kalay," Barnabas said, "come and sit down with us. Have a cup of wine."

She ran a hand through her hair, glanced back down the tunnel, then came over and sat at the table.

Libni poured and handed her a cup of wine. "Are you hungry, my dear? I can have Tiras bring food."

She shook her head. "I'm not hungry."

Libni studied her for a long moment with kind eyes, then returned his gaze to Barnabas. "I wouldn't have believed it if I hadn't heard the story from your own lips. I still can't imagine how you had the courage."

Barnabas swirled the wine in his cup, watching the candlelit reflec-tions. "I didn't have any courage. It was Cyrus, Zarathan, and Kalay who were heroic. I just followed the path God set before me."

"Did you hear his voice, as Kalay and Cyrus did?"

He gazed into Libni's wet eyes. "No. If you'd been there, I'm sure you would have heard it. But I did not."

Kalay took a long drink of wine and said, "*If* it was his voice."

Libni smiled his love at her, indulging her disbelief. "What will you do now? Where will you go?"

Barnabas inhaled a deep breath and let it out slowly. "Back to Egypt. There are many rare books there that I buried twenty years ago. It's time I made copies of them and buried them in a variety of places to make sure they survive."

After a time, Libni asked, "And what of Meridias?"

"I assume he lived and returned to Rome, though I have no way of knowing for certain."

"Then Pappas Silvester may know about the Pearl. I assume you took precautions?"

Barnabas wiped his damp palm on his dirty robe. It seemed as though it had been an eternity since he'd bathed or changed clothes. "Meridias never looked into the lower chamber. I don't think he had the slightest idea what was causing the unearthly glow."

Libni stared at Barnabas. "But you know, as well as I, that he'll be back. He'll see it, realize what it is, and destroy—"

"No, he won't," Kalay said. "Nor will he find the books we were carrying with us."

Libni's bushy gray brows drew together. "Then you *did* take precautions? You know what the existence of his body means to Constantine's church?"

"I do. They murdered the monks of my monastery to keep the Truth hidden." Barnabas finished his wine and set his empty cup on the table with a thud. The chips around the rim were sharp and ugly. "Libni . . . at the Last Supper he told his disciples he would go before them into the Galilaian."[122]

Libni frowned. "Yes, in Markos. I remember."

For a long while, they just gazed into each other's eyes, and a silent communication passed between them, as powerful as it had been in the old days at the library in Caesarea.

Barnabas tapped the side of his cup with a hard fingernail. "Unlike the Church, I respected his wishes."

Libni smiled. Then he chuckled. "Don't tell me," he said as he wiped his tears on his sleeve. "I don't want to know where it is."

Kalay drew her feet up into her chair and propped her wine cup atop her knees. In a soft voice, she asked, "Did you tell Libni about the scroll?"

Libni's head jerked around. "What scroll?"

Barnabas gave Kalay a sour look, and hesitated. "Are you sure you want to become involved?"

Ignoring Barnabas' stern expression, Kalay said, "I found it in the hand of the skeleton, as though he'd been clutching it when he died."

"More likely," Barnabas corrected, "it had been tucked into his dead hand after his body had been prepared."

Libni blinked and straightened in his chair. In a breathless voice, he said, *"You found a scroll in his hand?"*

EPILOGUE

As Pappas Silvester strode down the brazier-lit palace hall, he nervously tugged at his collar; his neck felt swollen, his collar too tight. His fingers came back slick with sweat. He passed several soldiers on guard. Not one looked at him. He might have been a distant insect to them, barely visible.

The deeper he went into the palace, the more the endless columns below the high-arched vaults resembled cold stalagmites. He swore he felt the touch of evil. He had always felt it here, in Constantine's palace. The air grew cold and sinisterly damp. Behind every shadow there lurked a presence, like a living thing, whispering to itself in the darkness.

Or it could have simply been his own fear. At the moment it was slithering around his belly, making him ill.

He rounded a corner, and stopped. At the end of the hall, in front of Constantine's chamber, stood four centurions. That was . . . odd. There were always sentries, but he almost never saw men of this rank, or at least, not this many, gathered just outside the emperor's door.

As he walked toward them, the centurions turned.

"A pleasant evening to you, Centurion Felix." Silvester dipped his head. "And Pionius, how are you?" The other two officers, he did not know.

Pionius, a tall, dark-haired man with burly shoulders, answered, "I am well, Pappas. He's waiting for you. *Been* waiting for you. For some time."

In a faintly shrill voice, he cried, "I was only just informed he'd requested me! I hope he's not annoyed."

Pionius extended a hand to the door. "See for yourself."

Pionius and the other officers walked away down the hall, talking in low voices.

Silvester squared his shoulders and, in a small voice, called, "Your Excellency? It's Silvester."

"Enter."

The word carried no hint of anger, which relieved Silvester. He pushed open the heavy door and walked into the chamber.

The emperor sat behind his table, heaped with maps, reading some missive. His brow was furrowed distastefully. He wore a dark blue cape—threaded through with silver and gold—over a scarlet robe. His sword belt lay across the back of a nearby chair. Easily within reach.

Silvester patiently waited to be recognized. The fire in the hearth cast a flickering amber gleam over the ornately carved furniture and the vaulted ceiling.

Without looking up, Constantine inquired, "Did they find it?"

"Well . . . er, no. Not exactly."

Constantine's gaze slowly lifted. His eyes were like oiled metal, shiny and hard, capable of ringing eternal darkness. "Answer me."

Silvester flapped his arms against his sides. "Pappas Meridias informed me that they *did* find a tomb with an ossuary marked *Yeshua bar Yosef*, but—"

"And, as I instructed, it was destroyed."

Silvester ran his fingers around his collar again. It was strangling him. "No." He rushed to add, "Because we could not be certain it was *the* ossuary. Pappas Macarios claimed to have *two* more such ossuaries in his office! Apparently the name was extremely common during the time our Lord lived. So, you see, the tomb is no threat to us. We can't prove it is his burial, but *no one else* can prove it either."

Constantine toyed with the missive on his desk, then tossed it aside and stood up. He reached for his sword belt and strapped it on. As he came around the table, Silvester's soul shriveled to nothingness. He had always known that death awaited him here, in this chamber.

Constantine stopped before him, propped his hands on his hips, and said, "I still want the tomb covered over with earth. Bury it deep."

"Yes, Excellency. I'll send word to Pappas Macarios immediately."

Constantine swayed slightly on his feet, as though he'd drunk too much wine while conferring with his centurions.

But when he looked down, there was no hint of drunkenness. The eyes that burned into Silvester were the eyes of an emperor who was at heart also a beast. They were not quite human.

"Silvester, I have spoken with my *strategoi,* my generals, and they agree with me that Christianity, as we have created it, may be the most powerful imperial tool in the history of the empire."

Silvester blinked his confusion. "Excellency?"

"The religion is spreading like a raging forest fire."

"Oh, well, yes, Excellency!" Silvester replied, suddenly excited. "Of course, it is! The Truth is like a rare pearl—"

"If we are careful to control and direct the Faith, it will be very useful." He swayed on his feet again, perhaps from exhaustion. "That shouldn't be too difficult now, should it? Without a body, the resurrection is safe."[123]

"Well . . . we still have enemies. Pappas Eusebios is an advocate of tolerance. He will never willingly submit to our hard-line dogmas. And Pappas Macarios in Jerusalem almost certainly helped the Heretic and his band of thieves. He—"

"There will always be those who oppose us. But when we are finished, only *our* version of the Truth will remain. And, Silvester, I guarantee you, in the end, there will be only *one* pappas of the Church, and he will be in Rome."

The veiled promise that Silvester would one day lead all of Christendom sent a heady rush through him. "But why Rome, Excellency? The other bishops will not be happy."

Constantine turned his back on Silvester and returned to his chair. As he sat down, he extended his hand, palm up, then suddenly closed it to a crushing grip, and hissed, "The Church *will* be mine."

NOTES

1. The gospels contained in our modern New Testament were written decades after the events they describe. The Gospel of Mark, probably written in Rome, is the earliest gospel, dating to around 68–70 c.e. Matthew and Luke clearly relied upon Mark's gospel, incorporating it into their own gospels without substantial changes. Matthew was likely composed in Antioch, the capital of Syria, and dates to around the year 80. The writings of Luke, who authored not only the Gospel of Luke and the Acts of the Apostles, but probably the Pastoral Letters attributed to Paul, date to 80–85. The Gospel of John was the latest to be written, dated to around 100–110 c.e., though some scholars argue for an earlier date, 90–95.

   And let us be clear at this point that the documents themselves are silent as to their authors' identities. During the second century, early Christian scholars attributed the texts to Mark, Matthew, Luke, and John, but nowhere in the texts is the author cited.

   As well, our current New Testament gospels were not the earliest versions of those gospels. The oldest surviving papyrus of any gospel, known as the Rylands Papyrus, is a 3.4-inch-tall Greek fragment of the Gospel of John that dates to around 125–35 c.e. The earliest copies of the other gospels date to the fourth or fifth centuries. We know that over time, the gospels underwent dramatic editing, and there is good evidence that the evangelists invented or interpreted the stories to make them relevant to their place and time. John, for example, originally ended at chapter 20. An early editor clearly didn't like John's ending, so he created a new one. This is made clear by the fact that the additional chapter, which immediately follows, arrives at a completely different conclusion than the original ending. (For more on this see Galambush, pp. 284–86.)

In addition, virtually every scholar agrees that the earliest versions of the Gospel of Mark end at 16:7 or 16:8. Clement of Alexandria and Origen, two of the earliest Church scholars who lived in the 200s, had no knowledge of verses 9–20. In the fourth century, Eusebius and Jerome knew of the existence of this longer ending, but also said it was absent from almost all Greek manuscripts they had seen. In the oldest known Bible, the fourth-century "Sinaiticus" document, the women find the tomb empty and are told by a man in white that he has risen. They run away in terror. The gospel ends, simply, with an empty tomb. There is no resurrection, and no "sightings" of Jesus.

The longer ending of Mark was clearly added in the fourth century, probably by a pious scribe who was copying Mark and decided he needed a more dramatic ending, one akin to the endings of Matthew and Luke. Verses 9–20 were not the only "other" endings of Mark, either. Two more invented endings were also circulated in the early years of the faith. Both were shorter versions.

But do not mistake this historical analysis to mean that early Christians did not believe in the resurrection or the post-crucifixion sightings of Jesus. Some certainly did, as the letters of Paul, dated to the 50s, document—though it's clear Paul believed in a spiritual resurrection, not a bodily resurrection—but there was a great argument about these issues among early Christians.

For a more lengthy discussion of these subjects, please review the entries under the evangelists' names in *The Anchor Bible Dictionary* edited by David Noel Freedman, and also see Tabor, pp. 230–33.

2. The ancient system of weights and measures was not precise, but generally, one cubit equaled about eighteen inches. Four hundred cubits was one furlong. One fathom was the stretch of the arms from fingertip to fingertip. One Roman stadium equaled six hundred

Roman feet. Sixty stadia were about 7.5 miles. One hundred sixty stadia equaled 19.5 miles.

3. The Gospel of Philip II, 59, 1–6: "For it is by a kiss that the perfect conceive and give birth . . . we receive conception from the grace that is in one another."

4. The Gospel of John, 6:15.

5. Luke 22:36; cf. 12:51.

6. The Hebrew term for *Passover*.

7. While we do not know for certain that Judas of Galilee was crucified, it is likely, since his sons, James and Simon (Yakob and Shimon), were crucified by the Romans for revolutionary activities, and Menahem was the leader of the rebellion in Jerusalem just before the war with Rome in 66. Eleazar, probably Judas' grandson, led the defense of the fortress of Masada. For more on this see the *Anchor Bible Dictionary*, the tenth entry, for *Judas*.

8. Although translators throughout time have gone to great lengths to eliminate all references, Jesus was often charged with being a magician, as in Sanhedrin 43a. Also, in John 18:28 ff., he is charged with being "a doer of evil," common parlance under the Roman law codes for being a magician. In addition there is the story in Matthew that after the crucifixion, "the high priests and Pharisees met with Pilate, saying . . . 'That magician said, while he was yet alive, after three days I shall arise.'" Mark 9:38 makes it clear that people used Jesus' name in conjuring spells, though Acts 19:13–16 says it backfired on those who tried it. Jesus' own followers were accused of being magicians. For example, the following was listed by Roman historian Suetonius as one of the praiseworthy reforms of Emperor Nero: "Penalties were imposed on the Christians, a kind of men with a new superstition (that involves) the practice of magic."

Anyone interested in the details of this charge should read Morton Smith's book, *Jesus the Magician*. Also, John Hull's book, *Hellenistic Magic and the Synoptic Tradition*, p. 116 ff., does a good job of showing how the canonical gospel writers, particularly Matthew, assiduously deleted references to Jesus' magical works.

9. The Aramaic term is *Bar Abba*, though New Testament readers will be more familiar with the Greek rendering: *Barabbas*.

10. During Roman times, the high priesthood was limited to the Sadducean aristocracy. This meant that the ordinary person saw the Temple hierarchy as a group of wealthy Jews intimately allied with the hated Roman oppressors. Judge Haim Cohn gives an excellent discussion of this tradition in his book *The Trial and Death of Jesus,* pp. 22–23.

11. The Gospel of Thomas, 40:42.

12. This happened in 135 C.E. See the *Anchor Bible Dictionary* entry for *Golgotha* for more on this.

13. This was a difficult subject in early Christianity. In Asia Minor, Easter was celebrated on the Jewish Passover (*Pesach*), that being the date of the crucifixion in the Gospel of John. But Matthew, Luke, and Mark make the Last Supper the Passover meal, and place the crucifixion a day later. In the 150s Polycarp of Smyrna visited Rome to discuss this issue, but no agreement could be reached. Rome insisted upon celebrating Easter on the Sunday following the full moon after the spring equinox, and nothing was going to change its mind. In the 190s, Bishop Victor of Rome was so upset that the churches in Asia Minor celebrated Easter on the Jewish Passover that he threatened to excommunicate anyone who did not adopt the Roman date. In the mid–third century Bishop Stephen of Rome got into a vehement argument over this subject with Bishop Cyprian of Carthage, who had the support of the Greek East. It was the first occasion on which the Bishop of Rome is known to have invoked Matthew 16:18 to justify the primacy of Rome. This disagreement would be one of the lasting disputes between the Eastern Church and the Western Church. (See the *Oxford Illustrated History of Christianity,* pp. 36–37.)

14. The Secret Book of James, 13:17–19.

15. After the Council of Nicea defined which texts would be included in the New Testament, Constantine ordered that the books of Christian "heretics"—meaning the books that had been excluded—be hunted out and destroyed. Within a few years, to be a Christian heretic became a capital crime: treason. Once both church and state agreed that it was legal, and righteous, to execute Christians who disagreed with the official dogma, everyone was in trouble, particularly pagans and Jews. Pagan worship was formally banned, and the authority of the

Jewish patriarchate was abolished forever. In 388, the bishop of Call-
inicus, on the Euphrates, attacked and burned a synagogue. Bishop
Ambrose of Milan declared himself prepared to burn every synagogue, "that there might not be a place where Christ is denied," and it
was considered an act of treason for anyone to rebuild a burned synagogue. The first pogrom in history occurred in 414 C.E. It was an or-
ganized, violent assault on Alexandria's Jews, which entirely wiped out
the city's Jewish community. (See Carroll, pp. 176, 206–07.)

16. The Greek word used in the New Testament is *adelphos,* meaning
"brother." There is no case in the New Testament where it means
"stepbrother." Also, it is simply not true that *adelphos* can mean
"cousin." There is a Greek term for cousin, *anepsios.* When Mark 6:3
says that Jesus is the son of Mary and brother (*adelphos*) of James,
Joses, Jude, and Simon, his meaning is clear. He does not call any of
these men Jesus' *anepsios.* As well, in both Galatians 1:19, and I
Corinthians 9:5, Paul uses the term *adelphos.* Since he uses the term
anepsios in Col. 4:10, he obviously knew the difference. If Paul had
meant "cousin" he would have used the word *anepsios* in Galatians
and Corinthians. He didn't.

For more on this discussion of Jesus' brothers and sisters, please
see John P. Meier's book *A Marginal Jew: Rethinking the Historical Jesus,* vol. 1, pp. 324–332.

17. A new day began at around 7:00 P.M. at night. That means the date
changed at this time. Hours were calculated based on that date
change, so that Nisan the 15th began at the first hour of night, or
7:00 P.M. The second hour was 8:00 P.M., etc. The first hour of day,
Nisan 15th, was the next morning at 7:00 A.M. This fact is critical for
understanding the dates associated with the crucifixion. If Jesus rose
on Sunday, then, according to the Jewish method of determining
time, Jesus did not rise in three days, but two.

18. For more on the *essen,* see the *Anchor Bible Dictionary* entry for *Essenes.*

19. As was Roman law.

20. The Sanhedrin was composed of seventy members, plus Moses.

21. Though the New Testament uses the term *procurator* for Pontius Pilate, that is not correct. It's an inaccuracy that actually helps us date

the documents. We know from numerous archaeological inscriptions that, during the reigns of emperors Augustus and Tiberias, provincial governors were addressed by the title *Praefectus*. This is certainly true of inscriptions about Pontius Pilate, who is listed as being the *Praefectus Iudaeae,* the Prefect of Judea. Only after the reign of Emperor Claudius began in the year 41 were such governors called *procurators*. (See the *Anchor Bible Dictionary* entry for *Procurator*.)

22. Which he did, in 36 C.E. When a Samaritan prophet proclaimed that he would reveal the vessels of the tabernacle to his people, Pilate sent his troops to intercept the crowd and slaughtered them. Josephus reports this in his *Antiquities,* XVIII:85–89. Also, we know that in the year 70 over 11,600 Samaritans were murdered on the top of Mount Gerizim when the Romans attacked the mountain and surrounded those worshipping there. Even today, the Samaritan community near Nablus celebrates its annual feasts on Mount Gerizim.

23. In I Corinthians 1:18, Paul notes that nonbelievers considered it "sheer folly" to proclaim a crucified man as God's son. A century later Church Father, Justin Martyr, said that calling a crucified man divine was utterly offensive to nonbelievers, and wrote: "They say that our madness consists in the fact that we put a crucified man in second place after the unchangeable and eternal God, the Creator of the World" (1 Apol. 13.4). It is also interesting to note that the original profession of faith established at the Council of Nicea in 325, the Nicene Creed, mentioned neither the death of Jesus nor his crucifixion, probably for this same reason.

24. See 1 John 5:8.

25. Papias wrote between 60 and 130 C.E. We have only fragments of his works, and know of his books, *Exposition of the Lord's Logia,* because they are referenced by later Church historians. Irenaeus, who lived from 140 to 202 C.E., and was bishop of Leon in Gaul, mentions Papias' books in his most important work, the *Adversus Haereses,* literally "Against Heresies." In that work, Irenaeus says that Papias was "a hearer of John and a companion of Polycarp." Polycarp was bishop of Smyrna in Asia Minor and lived from 70 to 156 C.E. Papias' books are mentioned again by Eusebius, "the Father of Church History," who lived from 260 to 339 C.E., and served as bishop of Caesarea, in Roman Palestine.

26. The Gospel of Nicodemus, IX.

27. The Gospel of Nicodemus, X–XII.

28. In the Gospel of Thomas, verse 77, Jesus says, "Split a piece of wood, and I am there. Lift up a stone and you will find me there."

29. Based upon the bindings, and the archaeological context, we know that what we now call the "Nag Hammadi library" was probably the private library of one Egyptian monastery, likely buried to protect the texts from the Church's edicts that all such documents should be burned. The codices are fourth-century Coptic translations of the original Greek documents dating to the second and third centuries.

30. The Gospel of Philip, verse 21.

31. The Gospel of Mark, 16:23. Yakob and Yohanan are, of course, James and John.

32. Josephus estimates that two and a half million Jews came to Jerusalem for Passover (Josephus, *Jewish War*, 6:423–27) and that they slaughtered over 225,000 lambs.

33. The Platonist historian, Celsus, in his book entitled *On The True Doctrine*, VI.75, which was written between about 170 and 180 C.E., reported that "they say" Jesus was "small, ugly and undistinguished." Church Father Origen (185–253 C.E.) found a curious source for "ugly" in Isaiah 53:1–3. Celsus' words, "they say," indicate that he had some source for this description, and it may have come from earlier versions of the gospels of Matthew and Luke, since he is dependent upon them for portions of his book. However, this description remains unverifiable.

34. Second-century pagan and Christian writers include these "tattoos" as part of the Jewish description of Jesus (b. Sabb. 104b; t. Sabb. 11:15; y. Sabb. 12–4), and we know that magicians did write spells on their flesh, because the directions for it are given in the Egyptian magical papyri, PGM VII.222–32 and VIII.65ff. For more on this, read Morton Smith's outstanding book, *Jesus the Magician*, pp. 46–48.

35. The Gospel of Mary, 18:5–10.

36. There is an excellent discussion of Peter's relationship with Mary Magdalen in Elaine Pagels' classic book, *The Gnostic Gospels*, pp. 64–66.

37. The Gospel of Thomas, verse 114.

38. For more on the role of women in Jesus' ministry, see the *Anchor Bible Dictionary* entries for "Susanna" and "Joanna."

39. The Gospel of Thomas, verse 111.

40. Pistis Sophia, 36:71.

41. Dialogue of the Savior, 139:12–13.

42. The Gospel of Philip, 63:32–64:5.

43. John 11:47–48. History demonstrated that Kaiaphas was right. The insurrection against Rome that began in 66 C.E. ended in total disaster, with the Temple burned, the city of Jerusalem left in ruins, the population decimated and scattered.

44. *Hanan* was the Hebrew name of the man New Testament readers know as "Annas."

45. Dead Sea Scrolls' Community Rule (IQS) 9:10–11, also the Damascus Document B20.

46. The Gospel of Thomas, verse 113.

47. There is a good discussion of this name issue in John Meier's book *A Marginal Jew,* vol. 1, pp. 231–233.

48. The Gospel of John 18:31 credits Jews with saying to Pilate, "It is not lawful for us to put any man to death." This could not possibly have been said by any Jew with any authority, because it is simply not true. The Sanhedrin certainly did exercise jurisdiction over capital cases, as is verified by Acts 4:1–22 and 5:17–42, as well as Josephus in his *Jewish Wars,* 6, 2, 4. Also, see Cohn, pp. 30–34.

   The two courts, Jewish and Roman, apparently handled cases associated with violations of their own respective laws. So, for example, the Jewish crimes of idolatry and blasphemy would have been of no interest to a Roman court. They would have been under the exclusive jurisdiction of a Jewish court. On the other hand, the crime of treason against Rome would have never been referred to a Jewish court. Only Rome would have tried a person so accused.

   In any case, Jews never crucified anyone at any time. Crucifixion was not a legal mode of execution according to Jewish law. The modes of execution were: stoning (Deut. 17:5), burning (Lev. 20:14), hanging (Josh. 8:29), and slaying (Deut. 20:13). Mishnaic codifiers later changed "hanging" to "strangling." For more on this see Cohn, pp. 209–12.

49. Pistis Sophia, 36:71.

50. The Gospel of Philip, verses 32, 55.

51. The Gospel of Philip, 61:29–35.

52. In the Gospel of Philip, 63:25, it says, ". . . for Jesus came to crucify the world."

53. Pappas Eusebius, or in Greek, *Eusebios,* was indeed in charge of the thirty-thousand-volume library at Caesarea. For his time, he was truly broad-minded. He believed in religious tolerance and argued for allowing religious pluralism throughout the Roman Empire. He abhorred the persecution of other religious faiths, and proclaimed that, in the end, the gospel Truth would triumph of its own accord.

54. While Eusebios reluctantly agreed with the conciliar decisions at the Council of Nicea, he eventually got back at his opponents. He toppled Eustathios in 330, and Athanasios in 336.

55. The *sicarii* were a group of dagger-wielding assassins, perhaps associated with the Zealot party.

56. The Great Persecution began on February 23, 303, and resulted in eight terrible years of almost constant attacks on Christians, particularly in the East. Eusebios' patron, Pamphilus, was tortured and put in prison in November of 307, where he remained until he was martyred in 310. The bishop of Caesarea at the time denied the faith and left Christians leaderless through the rest of the Great Persecution. Eusebios, who recorded these events, refused to write down even the man's name or what became of him. After the battle of Milvian Bridge in 313, Constantine met with the pagan ruler of the eastern empire, Licinius, and got him to agree to end the persecution. It is at this time that the retiring research scholar, Eusebios, was made bishop of Caesarea.

57. The arguments that follow, presented by Barnabas, are historically accurate. The Jewish and pagan traditions about Jesus' illegitimacy were strong. Celsus' version of this story, written in 178 C.E. in his work titled *On the True Doctrine,* says that Mary was pregnant by a Roman soldier named Panthera and was driven away by her husband for adultery. While much of Celsus' work is clearly polemical, it's unlikely that he made up Panthera's name or occupation. He was probably reporting information he'd heard.

In addition to the sources mentioned by Barnabas, the Toledoth Yeshu, the Jewish story about the life of Jesus that chronicles the ben Pantera story, dates to the 900s, though the Aramaic original may be from the 400s, and the work probably contains fossil remnants of traditions that date to the second century, and were perhaps influenced by Celsus' work. For more on this see the *Encyclopedia Judaica,* vol. 16, the entry by J. Dan, *Toledot Yeshu.*

Also, the canonical gospels themselves provide evidence. In John 8:41, Jesus is sparring with his Jewish critics in Jerusalem and they say "*We* were not born of fornication!" as if to imply *as you were.* As well, in the Gospel of Nicodemus, which dates to the 300s, but probably has origins in the late 100s, there is an interesting reference. In the story, Jesus is on trial before Pilate and one of his enemies charges, "You were born of fornication," which demonstrates the persistence of the illegitimacy stories.

In fact, the ben Pantera tradition was so widespread and persistent that early Christians could not simply dismiss it as a malicious lie propagated by Jewish opponents; they had to find a way to explain it. So, for example, in the fourth century, Epiphanius gave Pantera a place in the holy family, claiming that Joseph's father was known as Jacob Pantera. As late as the eighth century, attempts were still being made to explain it away, as we see when John of Damascus writes that Mary's great-grandfather was named Panthera.

The best synopses of the Pantera evidence can be found in three books: Morton Smith, *Jesus the Magician,* pp. 46–61; Jane Schaberg's book *The Illegitimacy of Jesus,* pp. 156–178; and James D. Tabor's book *The Jesus Dynasty,* pp. 64–72.

58. Tiberius Julius Abdes Pantera was buried in Bingerbruck, Germany. His tombstone is still preserved in the museum of Roman antiquities, the Romerhalle, in the town of Bad Kreuznach, Germany. The tombstone says simply: *Tiberius Julius Abdes Pantera of Sidon, aged 62, a soldier of 40 years of service, of the first cohort of archers, lies here.*

59. *The Essene Odyssey,* by Hugh Schonfield, discusses the Marham-i-Isa in greater detail: p. 121.

60. Psalms 114:3ff; 148:8 and PGM V. 136 f.

61. See the *Anchor Bible Dictionary* entries for "Joses," "Joseph," and "Jehozadak." Also Schonfield, pp. 40–41, for the Suffering ben Joseph tradition.

62. The word *tekton* is generally translated in the New Testament as

"carpenter," but it referred to anyone who worked in stone, wood, horn, or even ivory—and was particularly used for stoneworkers.

63. Which Matthew 28:1 correctly reports. The Greek word for "Sabbaths" is plural in his gospel.

64. The Gospel of Philip, 66:5–20.

65. The Gospel of Philip, 63:1.

66. See the *Anchor Bible Dictionary* entry for "Nazorean."

67. Josephus says (*Antiquities* 18.2.26) the census took place in 6 or 7 C.E. Also, see the *Anchor Bible Dictionary* entry for "Quirinius" for a full discussion of why Luke was mistaken.

68. For both the murder of James and the Annas-Jesus family rivalry, see Tabor, pp. 284–288.

69. The Second Apocalypse of James, 61:9–62:12.

70. In many early writings, for example those of Augustine and Gregory the Great, as well as Gnostic texts like the Secret Gospel of Mark, Mary Magdalen and Mary of Bethany are identified as the same person. Actually, this makes more sense, especially if you think of "Mary of Bethany" as describing where she came from, and "Mary Magdalen" as describing her profession. See the following for more on this.

71. The town Magdala, from which Mary Magdalen is supposed to have come, is not mentioned by this name in the Bible, though the supposed adjectival form, "Magdalene," occurs. However, the town is generally identified with Migdal Nunnaya of the Talmud (b. Pesah. 46a), and the Greek city of Taricheae. The problem is that Migdal Nunnaya was one mile north of the city of Tiberias, but Josephus says that Taricheae was 3.6 Roman miles from Tiberias, which means they can't be the same place. Because of this, Magdala has always been uncertain. The Talmudic documents, b. Sabb. 104b and b. Sanh. 67A, may provide the answer. They refer to "Miriam the hairdresser," or in Hebrew, *megaddela*. This presupposes that the Greek writers of the New Testament just didn't understand the Hebrew term. But if *megaddela* is the correct word, it may explain where Mary got the money to support Jesus' ministry.

72. Each of the four approved gospels mentions this town only once and always in the context of Joseph of Arimathea. Since there is no known town of this name, scholars have assumed it is most likely identical

with either modern Ramathain, which Josephus mentions (*Ant.* 13.4.9),
or Rathamein. However, in the fourth century, Eusebios identified
it as Aramathem-Sophim, near Thamna and Lydda (*Onomasticon,*
144.28). Additional traditions urge Arimathea's location at modern
Rentis, which is fifteen miles east of Jaffa, or er-Ram, or perhaps el-
Birah-Ramallah, near Jerusalem. The simple fact is that the Hebrew
term *haramata,* or *haramati,* is not a town, but a description of an
area, which would have been known at the time as "the highlands,"
and is probably associated with the Shephelah hills area twenty miles
east of Jaffa. More information is available in the *Anchor Bible Dictionary* under the entry "Arimathea." See also Cohn, p. 237.

73. Zechariah 6:13.

74. She's referring, of course, to the murder of John the Baptist.

75. The Greek word *pappas,* became *pappa,* "daddy," in Latin, and "pope"
in English. The term *pappas* was used by early Christians of a bishop to
whom they bore a filial relationship, that is a relationship where they
stood as child to parent. For example, North African Christians called
the bishop of Alexandria *Pappas,* but called the leader of the Roman
church, "the bishop of Rome." There has never been a single pope in
Christianity, and this was especially true of early Christianity where
many bishops oversaw regional churches. Until the fourth century the
bishop of Rome's authority rested in being the "successor of Peter and
Paul," because those evangelists had presumably been martyred in
Rome. The narrow reading of Matthew 16:18, however, led Rome to
drop Paul's name. But it wasn't until the year 1216, and Innocent III,
that the title "successor of Peter" was changed to "vicar of Christ."

76. When Jesus declared that the "kingdom of God is at hand," he was
not being metaphorical. He meant it. The discovery of the Dead Sea
Scrolls has taught us that there was a definite timetable according to
which the events surrounding the End of the World would unfold,
and Jesus was counting them down. He truly believed that his generation would witness the Apocalypse (Mark 13:30). His followers also
understood this literally. In I Corinthians 7:29, Paul wrote that "the
appointed time has grown very short," and James said, "the Judge is
standing at the door" (James 5:9). In I Peter 4:7, it's proclaimed that
"the end of all things in at hand."

77. Mark gives the impression that Jesus' ministry lasted about a year, or perhaps a little longer. The reason for this assessment is that he mentions only one Passover feast, the Passover of Jesus' death. John, however, says Jesus' ministry lasted two or three years. Actually, as Meier points out in *A Marginal Jew,* vol. 1, pp. 403–05, the minimum amount of time necessitated by the events in John is two years plus a month or two. Jesus goes to Jerusalem for the first Passover in his ministry in John 1:35–2:12. At the feeding of the five thousand we are told that the second Passover was near (6:4), and Jesus goes to Jerusalem for his third and last Passover in 11:55; 12:1,12; 13:1; 18:28.

78. M. Sanhedrin VI 4.

79. We did not use the story of Judas' betrayal of Jesus because it is suspect. The embarrassingly meager sum he was paid could not have been a motivation. Not only that, no one *needed* to betray Jesus. While he was in Jerusalem, he was preaching openly in the Temple. He could have been arrested by anyone at any time. There is only one logical reason for Judas to have gone to the authorities that night, and that is if Jesus knew he was going to be arrested and selected Judas to contact the Romans specifically to avoid the riot and bloodshed that might surround his arrest. It is also possible that the story of Judas is a late-first-century attempt to fulfill the prophecies found in Psalms 41:9 and 55:12–14; Isaiah 53; and Zechariah 11:12–13.

80. Luke, 22:54–55.

81. A condemnation (guilty sentence) is found only in Mark 14:64. Matthew 26:66 records that the members of the Sanhedrin "said" he was guilty. Luke 22:71 has the members merely saying, "What need we any further witness?" And John deletes the entire trial, probably because he understood Jewish law better than the other Greek-speaking evangelists. In fact, the ignorance of Jewish law betrayed by Mark, Matthew, and Luke is colossal.

It is simply impossible that there was a trial of Jesus before the Sanhedrin. According to Jewish law, the Sanhedrin could not try a criminal case in a private house, even the high priest's house; it was not allowed to try cases at night, or on festival days, or on the eve of festivals—all of which the gospels say happened. The conclusion, therefore, must be that there was no *trial* before the Sanhedrin. *How-*

ever, it is likely that the Sanhedrin did hold a Council meeting to examine the charges upon which Jesus would be tried by Rome the next morning. Members of the court could and did consult with each other in their private homes at night. This was perfectly lawful (M. Sanhedrin V 5). The question, then, is why would they have bothered? It was the eve of Pesach, or Passover. They all had complicated ritual obligations to attend to, not to mention the burden of preparing for and hosting many family members who had arrived for the festival.

It has been suggested that the Sanhedrin met to gather evidence for Rome. First of all, there was no Roman law requiring such a preliminary hearing, even for a capital offense. And to suggest that Pontius Pilate would have asked a Jewish court to conduct an inquiry about a crime under Roman law is ridiculous. It would have undermined Pilate's supreme authority in such cases—a thing he would never have tolerated.

There is only one reason that men of good conscience would have considered Jesus' arrest to be a matter of utmost urgency that necessitated convening the Council on the eve of a feast day: *There was more at stake than just one man's life.*

Jesus was, according to all sources, beloved by the majority of the people, and certainly some members of the Sanhedrin felt the same way. At least Joseph of Arimathea and Nicodemus could have been counted upon to *defend* a beloved Jewish son against the hated Roman oppressors. But we also know that Pilate had already assembled three legions around Jerusalem specifically because he expected trouble over Passover. Or maybe because he wanted to provoke trouble.

Our conclusion is that the Sanhedrin probably met for the reasons defined in this novel: It must have been trying desperately to find evidence to prevent Jesus' crucifixion, which it greatly feared would spark a revolt that would result in the destruction of Israel.

The finest analysis of this matter is found in Judge Haim Cohn's book, *The Trial and Death of Jesus,* pp. 94–190.

82. Codex Theodosius IX 3,1.
83. B. Shabbat 88b.
84. See the *Anchor Bible Dictionary* entry for "Annas."

85. Matthew 22:41–45.

86. This is exactly the same argument Gamliel uses to defend Peter a decade later (Acts 5:26–39) in his trial before the Sanhedrin. There is no reason to assume Gamliel would have argued differently in Jesus' case.

87. Mark 14:56, 14:59.

88. Psalms 4:2, 57:4; Jeremiah 49:18, 33; Ezekiel 2:1; and Daniel 7:13.

89. Most scholars agree that Matthew's "Son of God," and Mark's "Son of the Blessed" are later interpolations from a time when the dogma of the divine descent of Jesus had already been introduced into Christian belief. Please see the *Anchor Bible Dictionary* for more information on these terms.

90. The Gospel of Philip, 73:22–23.

91. The Gospel of Nicodemus, chapters XII–XIII.

92. While Jews were not allowed to return to Jerusalem after the siege in the year 70, Christians were. Christians were at first expelled along with Jews, but were permitted to return a few years later because they proclaimed they were not part of the Jewish community, and said they welcomed the destruction of the Temple as the fulfillment of Jesus' prophecies. They were allowed to resettle the Mount Zion portion of the city. For more on this, see Meir Ben-Dov's *Historical Atlas of Jerusalem,* pp. 142–52, and the *Anchor Bible Dictionary* entry for "Temple–Jerusalem."

   Jews were finally given permission to return to Jerusalem in the year 362. The new emperor, who would become known as Julian the Apostate, gladly allowed Jews to return to Jerusalem. He hated Christianity. Right after he decreed the end of the Christian empire, he ordered the Jewish Temple rebuilt in Jerusalem. To place "one stone upon another" was—in Julian's mind—to conquer the false messiah. He reigned for less than two years, dying during a failed invasion of Persia. More prophetic to Christians was the fact that Jews excavating the new foundation of the Temple touched off mighty explosions of gaseous deposits, which ended the last attempt to rebuild the Temple. Christians, naturally, saw this as the miraculous intervention of God. (See more on this in Carroll, pp. 205–207.)

93. These are the oral legends that circulated at the time of the Council of Nicea. The best recommendation for all matters pertaining to

Constantine is James Carroll's book *Constantine's Sword.* For more on his political agenda, see pp. 191–93.

94. Yes, the Square of the Column is real. See Meir Ben-Dov, *Historical Atlas of Jerusalem,* p. 120.

95. Most scholars hold that the probable location for Pilate's Praetorium is Herod's Upper Palace along the western wall of the city. We do not agree. There is a total lack of any early Christian tradition regarding that location. The earliest Christian writings say that the Praetorium stood near the western slope of the Tyropoeon valley, opposite the southwest corner of the Temple Mount. In 333 C.E., the Anonymous of Bordeaux, who provides us with the earliest pilgrim account, reported that the crumbling walls of the Praetorium faced the Tyropoeon valley, and in 450 C.E. a church was built on the site. If early Christian tradition is correct, the only thing that could have stood in these locations was the ancient royal palace of the Hasmoneans.

96. Judge Haim Cohn's analysis of Roman law as it applied to the trial of Jesus before Pilate is fascinating reading, pp.142–90.

97. In rabbinic literature the evidence for the term "rabbi" as a mode of address prior to the year 70 is scant. Before 70, men were apparently not referred to by the title "rabbi" (e.g. Hillel, Shammai), but after 70, they were. For example, Rabbi Aquiba. Though Luke does not use the term "rabbi" for Jesus, Matthew does, and it is apparently polemical, since Judas is the only person who calls Jesus "rabbi." Mark and John also call Jesus "rabbi." But these usages are probably anachronistic. After all, the gospels were written just before or after the year 70. We know of one literary reference in the period before 70 C.E. where *rab* is used to designate a teacher (*t. Pesah.* 4.13–14), and there is one ossuary in Jerusalem that also dates to around this time period that is inscribed RAB HANA. We have, as a result, chosen to use the term *Rab* in the same way that one would say "teacher." For a more detailed discussion on this, please see Meier, vol. 1, pp. 119–20.

98. The silence of Jesus before the Sanhedrin and Pilate has been seen as a fulfillment of Isaiah 52:13–53:12. Whether or not Jesus deliberately

intended to play the role of the Isaianic servant by remaining silent "as a sheep before her shearers is dumb, so he openeth not his mouth" (KJV), or whether he was obeying the Jewish custom of proper behavior when insulted, we cannot say. But Jesus undoubtedly knew these passages very well.

99. There is no report of Jesus' trial in the imperial archives of Rome, though Pilate would have been required to make such a report. (See M. Craveri, *The Life of Jesus,* p. 392.)

   Does that mean there was no trial? It may. After all, a "confession" would have made an official trial unnecessary. Also, there is a letter quoted by Philo, a contemporary of Yeshua's, regarding Pilate. In his *De Legatione ad Gaium,* Philo quotes a letter from King Agrippa I to Emperor Caligula, which describes Pilate's government as characterized by "his venality, his violence, his thefts, his assaults, his abusive behavior, his frequent executions of untried prisoners and his endless savage ferocity." Pilate was well known for executing prisoners who had never seen trial. Add to this the fact that the Roman historian Tacitus (c. 55–115 C.E.) writes in his *Annales,* 15:44, only that Pilate had Jesus executed. He mentions no trial.

100. The date was Nisan the 14th, or, by our calendar, April 7, the year 30. See Meier, *A Marginal Jew,* vol. 1, pp. 401–02. Keep in mind that at around 7:00 P.M. that night the date changed to Nisan the 15th, and Passover began. If Jesus "rose" on Sunday, it had technically only been two and a half days.

101. Joseph of Arimathea, a scholar of the law, and a pious Jew, would certainly have requested the bodies of any fellow Jew who died that day—if for no other reason than to obey Jewish law.

102. Digesta, 48,24,1, and Tacitus, *Annales,* 6,29.

103. M Sanhedrin VI 5.

104. While it was Roman law that a crucified man might not be buried, it was Jewish law that convicts executed by order of the Roman prefect had to, eventually, be buried and mourned according to Jewish tradition (Semahot II 7 and 11). As Cohn notes on p. 239, "That it was a Roman court which had sentenced him was enough to entitle him to the benefits of Jewish burial and traditional Jewish mourning."

105. You may be wondering why we did not use the story of Barabbas' release. This tradition, called the *privilegium paschale,* did not exist at
the time of Jesus. Had there been either a Jewish or Roman law establishing such a custom, there would be a record of its application, either before the life of Jesus or after, by some governor, bishop, or
priest, somewhere. There isn't. Not until the year 367 do we find a
Roman law, the *indulgentia criminum,* which establishes a custom for
pardoning criminals on the feast of Easter, except for those "guilty of
sacrilege against the Imperial Majesty, of crimes against the dead, sor-
cerers, magicians, adulterers, ravishers, or homicides." Even in 367,
then, Barabbas, the convicted murderer, would not have been eligible
for release. As well, only the emperor himself could grant a pardon
under the *indulgentia criminum.* Provincial governors did not have the
right to do so. Such an act would have been seen as usurping imperial
prerogative, and tantamount to treason. Lastly, there is no evidence
that the emperor granted "special" dispensation to Pilate to allow him
to grant such pardons to curry the favor of the Jews. Nor, we must
conclude, would Pilate have done so if he'd had the right to. Pilate
was notorious in his contempt for Jews.

This is another example of the gospel writers' attempts to make
Jews appear to be the culprits, rather than Rome. Keep in mind the
political context at the time the gospels were being written. Jerusalem
was about to be, or had just been, attacked and destroyed. Romans
had issued a decree forbidding Jews from even visiting the city, let
alone living there, and left the Tenth Legion in the city to enforce the
decree. Christians had begged the commanders of the legion to allow
them back into the city, claiming they were not part of the Jewish
community, and saying they were happy Rome had destroyed the
Temple. The commanders, who needed civilians to provide services
for their troops, and were probably happy to work with the enemies
of the Jews, agreed. Christians were allowed to return to Jerusalem.
Relations between Jews and Christians became extremely volatile, so
much so that Judaism and Christianity finally split around 85 C.E.—the
exact time when the gospels of Matthew and Luke were being written.
(For more on this see Meir Ben-Dov's *Historical Atlas of Jerusalem,* pp.
136–42, and *The Oxford Illustrated History of Christianity,* edited by

John McManners, pp. 21–26, and especially Brandon, pp. 2–4 and pp. 262–76.)

Also, try to imagine what it must have been like to be a Christian in Rome, as Mark probably was, after the start of the Jewish War in the year 66. When James was murdered in 62, relations with Judaism began to fall apart, then the revolt of 66 cut all communications with the mother church in Jerusalem. Mark and his community were suddenly rudderless. To make matters worse, to the Romans, Christians *were* Jews. There was no such thing as "Christianity." There were Jews who believed the messiah had come, and they called themselves Christians, but the sect was part of Judaism. The persecution must have been unbearable. In part, at least, Mark's gospel was probably a deliberate attempt to shout, "We are not Jews!" Undoubtedly one of the reasons Mark chose to vilify Jews in his gospel was that by shifting the blame for Jesus' death from Rome, where it belonged, to the Jews, it solved a major public relations problem for Christians in Rome. It was like saying, "Yes, the Jews are killing your sons and husbands in Palestine, but they also killed our Lord. We are *not* Jews! In fact, we hate Jews as much as you do!" While the historical legacy of Mark's vilification is wrenching—his words have been used to support the murder of millions—at the time, it was simply self-defense.

S.G.F. Brandon's chapter entitled "The Markan Gospel," in his book *Jesus and the Zealots,* is very valuable for a better understanding of this issue.

Keep in mind, also, that before the end of the first century, Christians were forbidden to enter synagogues. By the close of the fourth century, marriages between Jews and Christians were prohibited, and if such marriages occurred, they were treated as adultery. Legislation was promulgated forbidding Jews to proselytize, or build new synagogues. (Coogan, pp. 582–87.)

The first few centuries were horrifying—for both sides—and it got worse.

106. The Gospel of Thomas, verse 24.
107. The city of Emmaus is another mystery to scholars. In his *Onomastican* (90:16) Eusebios identifies it as the city of Nicopolis. However, in 440 Hesychius of Jerusalem said that Nicopolis was too far from Jerusalem to

be the Emmaus listed in Luke 24. Other sites have been recommended by scholars, including el-Qubeibeh, and Abu Ghosh, Qaloniyeh. In his *Antiquities* (Book XVIII, chapters 2, 3) however, Josephus says that Emmaus is a "little distance" from the city of Tiberias in Galilee.

108. Luke 24:13.

109. There has been great speculation about the identity of the unnamed apostle who accompanied Cleopas that day outside Emmaus (see the *Anchor Bible Dictionary* entry for "Cleopas"). The main scholarly choices include Peter, Nathaniel, Deacon Philip, Nicodemus, Simon, and many others. We leave you to make your own choice, as we have.

110. A good reference here is *The Oxford History of the Biblical World,* edited by Michael Coogan, pp. 567–69.

111. For pictures of these artifacts, see Ben-Dov's *Historical Atlas of Jerusalem,* p. 139.

112. What Jesus actually said on the cross has been a subject of heated debate for almost two thousand years. This saying is found only in Mark and Matthew. The controversy stems from the fact that the words recorded by Mark and Matthew are not Greek, Hebrew, or Aramaic. Mark's version, *Eloi, Eloi, lama sabachthani,* which is written in Greek, is at best a "Hebraized" transliteration of Aramaic that is probably an attempt to make Jesus appear to be quoting Ps. 22:1. Two early manuscripts of Mark read *zaphthani,* rather than *sabachthani,* which is at least closer to the Hebrew. In addition, many of the ancient Latin translators couldn't bring themselves to translate the nonsense word *sabachtani* as "forsaken," so that we find they substituted *exprobasti me* (you have tested me), or *me in opprobrium dedisti* (you have given me over to hatred), and even *meledixisti* (you have wished me ill). The apocryphal Gospel of Peter reads *he dunamis mou* (my Power) for "My God," and *kateleipsas me* (you have left me behind), rather than *egkatelipes me* (you have forsaken me).

   The best discussion of the evidence can be found in *Mark: A New Translation with Introduction and Commentary,* by C. S. Mann, pp. 650–51.

113. Despite what the evangelists record, we know from a wide variety of historical resources that there was no eclipse of the sun during

Passover of the year 30. There was an eclipse of the sun during the month of Nisan in the year 33, but it was utterly invisible from Jerusalem. The only solar eclipse visible from Jerusalem during the time period in question occurred on November 24 of the year 29. The Greek historian Phlegon mentions this event in his *History of the Olympiads,* and notes that it was accompanied by an earthquake. There were, however, eclipses of the moon on the eve of Passover in the years 30 and 33. A good discussion of the astronomical events surrounding the crucifixion can be found in *Glorious Eclipses: Their Past, Present, and Future,* by Serge Brunier and Jean-Pierre Luminet.

114. M Shabbat VI 10; B Shabbat 67a; J Shabbat VI 9; Maimonides, Mishneh Torah, Hilkhot Shabbot 6, 10; Plinius, *Historia Naturalis,* 28, 36. In addition, Haim Cohn's chapter entitled "The Crucifixion," pp. 219–21, is essential reading for anyone interested in the legal and cultural traditions of both the Jews and Romans.

115. This is partly based on the real Tomb of the Shroud located in the Hinnom valley just outside the old city walls of Jerusalem. Ossuaries labeled MARI and SALOME were found there, as well as the shrouded skeleton described in this novel. See Tabor's *The Jesus Dynasty,* pp. 1–21, for more information.

116. The Gospel of Mary, 17 and 18.

117. According to the Gospel of Nicodemus XV, Joseph of Arimathea was questioned by Kaiaphas and Annas. His answers make great reading!

118. This tomb also exists. It's better known as the Talpiot Tomb, also south of the old city walls of Jerusalem in East Talpiot. For more information, see Tabor, pp. 22–33. Anyone familiar with the ossuaries in this tomb will note that we have slipped the famous James ossuary into the Talpiot Tomb. This is not purely artistic license. The Talpiot Tomb was discovered in 1980. When you read Amos Kloner's original archaeological report, it notes that ten ossuaries were recovered during the excavation. The tenth ossuary was given accession number IAA:80.509, which means it was catalogued, along with the other artifacts, by the Israel Antiquities Authority. However, in 1994 the State of Israel published a catalogue of the ossuaries from the Talpiot Tomb and listed only nine. The tenth ossuary was mysteriously

missing. James Tabor recently noted that the dimensions of the missing ossuary, 60 by 26 by 30 centimeters, exactly match those of the James ossuary. This by no means proves that the *James* ossuary was originally found in the Talpiot Tomb—it's just interesting.

119. There are two other *Jesus son of Joseph* ossuaries known in Israel. One was first written about in 1931 by E. L. Sukenin of the Hebrew University (it was purchased by the Palestine Archaeological Museum, 1926). This ossuary is inscribed twice. One inscription says simply *Yeshu,* the other inscription reads *Yeshua bar Yehosef. Yehosef* is another spelling of "Joseph." The other ossuary has one inscription: *Yeshua bar Yehosef.* (See Shanks and Witherington, *The Brother of Jesus,* pp. 58–60.) One of the most interesting references that uses this name is found in the Cave of Letters at Nahal Hever, seven miles north of Masada. The document says that a woman named Babata married Yeshua ben Yosef, and that their son was named Yeshua (Meier, vol. 1, p. 357).

All this proves is that the name "Jesus son of Joseph" was very common.

120. Shanks and Witherington, pp. 56–59.

121. This description comes from "The Hymn of the Pearl," a stunning narrative poem about a savior who must himself be saved, and is probably pre-Christian and pre-Gnostic. It is a beautiful fable of redemption.

122. Mark 14:28. It is, perhaps, not surprising that there is a grave of *Yeshu ha Notzri,* Jesus of Nazareth, found in Galilee, just north of Tsfat (Safed). Few people know about it. Almost no one visits it.

In the sixteenth century, the Kabbalistic rabbi Isaac ben Luria listed this grave along with the graves of other Jewish sages and saints, calling them "the burial places of the righteous."

123. For more information on the issue of the resurrection, we recommend Gregory J. Riley's book *Resurrection Reconsidered: Thomas and John in Controversy.*

SELECTED BIBLIOGRAPHY

Adkins, Roy and Lesley, *Dictionary of Roman Religion.* New York: Facts on File, 1996.

Barnstone, Willis, ed., *The Other Bible.* New York: HarperCollins, 1994.

Barton, John, *The Biblical World,* vols. 1–2. New York: Routledge, 2002.

Brandon, S.G.F., *Jesus and the Zealots.* New York: Charles Scribner's Sons, 1967.

Ben-Dov, Meir, *Historical Atlas of Jerusalem.* New York: Continuum, 2002.

Betteson, Henry, *The Early Christian Fathers.* London: Oxford University Press, 1969.

——— *The Later Christian Fathers.* London: Oxford University Press, 1970.

Boring, M. Eugene, et al., eds., *Hellenistic Commentary to the New Testament.* Nashville: Abingdon Press, 1995.

Borret, M., ed., *Orìgene, Contre Celse. Tome I (Livres I et II)* SC 132; Paris: Cerf, 1967.

Brooten, Bernadette, *Women Leaders in the Ancient Synagogue.* Brown University, Brown Judaic Studies, Number 36. Atlanta: Scholars Press, 1982.

Brown, Raymond E., *An Introduction to the New Testament.* New York: Doubleday, 1997.

Brunier, Serge, and Jean-Pierre Luminet, *Glorious Eclipses: Their Past, Present, and Future.* Cambridge: Cambridge University Press, 2000.

Carroll, James, *Constantine's Sword.* New York: Houghton Mifflin, 2001.

Cohen, Shaye J. D., "Was Timothy Jewish (Acts 16: 1–3)? Patristic Exegesis, Rabbinic Law, and Matrilineal Descent," *Journal of Biblical Literature*, 105 (1986), pp. 251–68.

Cohn, Haim, *The Trial and Death of Jesus*. Old Saybrook, Connecticut: Konecky and Konecky, 1963.

Charlesworth, James H., *Jesus and the Dead Sea Scrolls*. London: Doubleday, 1992.

Codex Justinianus and *Digesta*. English translation (*Corpus Juris Civilis*) by Scott, 1931.

Codex Theodosius. English translation by Pharr, 1952.

Coogan, Michael D., *The Oxford Illustrated History of the Biblical World*. Oxford: Oxford University Press, 1998.

Dart, John, *The Jesus of Heresy and History: The Discovery and Meaning of the Nag Hammadi Gnostic Library*. San Francisco: Harper and Row, 1988.

Doresse, Jean, *The Secret Books of the Egyptian Gnostics*. Rochester, Vermont: Inner Traditions International, 1986.

Dungan, David Laird, *A History of the Synoptic Problem: The Canon, the Text, the Composition, and the Interpretation of the Gospels*. New York: Doubleday, 1999.

Edersheim, Alfred, *The Temple: Its Ministry and Services*. Peabody, Massachusetts: Hendrickson Publishers, 1994.

Ehrman, Bart D., *Lost Scriptures: Books That Did Not Make It into the New Testament*. Oxford: Oxford University Press, 2003.

——— *Lost Christianities: The Battles for Scripture and the Faiths We Never Knew*. Oxford: Oxford University Press, 2003.

——— *Misquoting Jesus: The Story Behind Who Changed the Bible and Why*. New York: HarperCollins, 2005.

——— *Peter, Paul, and Mary: The Followers of Jesus in History and Legend*. Oxford: Oxford University Press, 2006.

Epstein, Isidore, ed., *The Babylonian Talmud: Seder Nezikin in Four Volumes*. English translation by Jacob Shachter. London: Soncino, 1935.

Eusebius, *Historia Ecclesiastica*. New York: Penguin, 1965.

Filoramo, Giovanni, *A History of Gnosticism*. Cambridge: Basil Blackwell, 1991.

Fredriksen, Paula, *From Jesus to Christ: The Origins of the New Testament Images of Jesus*. New Haven: Yale University Press, 1988.

Freedman, David Noel, ed., *The Anchor Bible Dictionary*, vols. 1–6. New York: Doubleday, 1992.

Galambush, Julie, *The Reluctant Parting: How the New Testament's Jewish Writers Created a Christian Book*. New York: HarperCollins, 2005.

Hadas-Lebel, Mireille, *Flavius Josephus: Eyewitness to Rome's First-Century Conquest of Judea*. New York: Macmillan, 1993.

Haskins, Susan, *Mary Magdalen: Myth and Metaphor*. New York: Harcourt Brace, 1993.

Hatch, William Henry Paine, *The Principal Uncial Manuscripts of the New Testament*. Chicago: University of Chicago Press, 1939.

Hull, John M., *Hellenistic Magic and the Synoptic Tradition: Studies in Biblical Theology*, second series, *28*. London: SCM Press, 1974.

James, M. R., *The Apocryphal New Testament*. Oxford: Oxford University Press, 1980.

Jenkins, Philip, *Hidden Gospels: How the Search for Jesus Lost Its Way*. Oxford: Oxford University Press, 2001.

Martin, Raymond A., *Studies in the Life and Ministry of the Historical Jesus*. New York: University Press of America, 1995.

McManners John, ed., *The Oxford Illustrated History of Christianity*. Oxford: Oxford University Press, 1990.

Meier, John P., *A Marginal Jew: Rethinking the Historical Jesus*, vols. 1–3. New York: Doubleday, 1994.

Metzger, Bruce, and Michael Coogan, *The Oxford Companion to the Bible*. Oxford: Oxford University Press, 1993.

Meyer, Marvin, and Richard Smith, *Ancient Christian Magic: Coptic Texts of Ritual Power*. San Francisco: HarperCollins, 1994.

Meyers, Carol, *Discovering Eve: Ancient Israelite Women in Context*. Oxford: Oxford University Press, 1988.

Nestle-Aland, *Novum Testamentum, Graece*. London: United Bible Societies, 1971.

Neusner, Jacob, *Introduction to Rabbinic Literature*. New York: Doubleday, 1994.

Oden, Thomas, ed., *Ancient Christian Commentary on Scripture*, vols. I–IX. Illinois: InterVarsity Press, 2001.

Pagels, Elaine, *The Gnostic Gospels*. New York: Random House, 1989.

Pagels, Elaine, and Karen King, *Reading Judas: The Gospel of Judas and the Shaping of Christianity*. New York: Penguin, 2007.

Philo, Alexandrinus, *Legatio ad Gaium.* Edited by E. Mary Smallwood. Leiden: E. J. Brill, 1961.

Qualls-Corbett, Nancy, *The Sacred Prostitute.* Toronto: Inner City Books, 1988.

Richardson, Peter, *Herod: King of the Jews and Friend the Romans.* Columbia: University of South Carolina Press, 1996.

Riley, Gregory J., *Resurrection Reconsidered: Thomas and John in Controversy.* Minneapolis: Fortress Press, 1995.

Robinson, James M., *The Nag Hammadi Library in English.* San Francisco: Harper and Row, 1988.

Rudolph, Kurt, *Gnosis: The Nature and History of Gnosticism.* San Francisco: Harper and Row, 1987.

Schaberg, Jane, *The Illegitimacy of Jesus.* Sheffield: Sheffield Academic Press, 1995.

Schonfield, Hugh, *The Essene Odyssey: The Mystery of the True Teacher and the Essene Impact on the Shaping of Human Destiny.* Rockport: Element Books, 1993.

Shanks, Hershel, and Ben Witherington, *The Brother of Jesus.* New York: HarperCollins, 2003.

Smith, Morton, *Jesus the Magician.* San Francisco: Harper and Row, 1978.

Suetonius, Gaius, *De Vita Caesarum.* New York: Penguin, 1957.

Tabor, James D., *The Jesus Dynasty.* New York: Simon & Schuster, 2006.

Tacitus, Cornelius, *Annales.* New York: Penguin, 1962.

Thiering, Barbara, *Jesus and the Riddle of the Dead Sea Scrolls: Unlocking the Secrets of His Life History.* San Francisco: HarperCollins, 1992.

Toner, J. P., *Leisure and Ancient Rome.* Oxford: Blackwell Publishers, 1995.

Torjesen, Karen Jo, *When Women Were Priests.* San Francisco: HarperCollins, 1993.

Ulrich, Eugene, *The Community of the Renewed Covenant: The Notre Dame Symposium on the Dead Sea Scrolls.* Notre Dame: University of Notre Dame Press, 1994.

Vermes, Geza, *The Complete Dead Sea Scrolls in English.* New York: Penguin, 1997.

Wainwright, Geoffrey, and Karen B. Westerfield Tucker, *The Oxford History of Christian Worship.* Oxford: Oxford University Press, 2006.

Whiston, William, *The Genuine and Complete Works of Flavius Josephus.* Dublin: Thomas Morton Bates, 1796.

Interview with Kathleen O'Neal Gear and W. Michael Gear on *The Betrayal*

1. You say that there is an alternate story of the life of Jesus, one that has been suppressed for nineteen centuries. How do you justify that claim? Who suppressed the information?

The Church was involved in a battle to rewrite the "facts" of Jesus life practically from the beginning, and we find the evidence for this in the ancient documents themselves. Keep in mind that the first scribes who copied the sacred books got *them* from earlier scribes, who got them from earlier scribes. They were literally copying copies of copies. Mistakes were bound to creep in. A later scribe couldn't read the handwriting of the earlier scribe, so he had to interpret what he thought the letters were. Some scribes were very good, and some were very bad. Later correctors often disagreed with former scribes. In one case, a later scribe, exasperated by changes he found in the fourth-century *Codex Vaticanus,* wrote in the margin, "Fool and knave! Leave the old reading, don't change it!"

The result was that, by the second century, there was a considerable variety of New Testament texts. The manuscripts that are the closest to the original gospels are actually the ones that are the most variable and amateurish. By the time scholars start finding professional, standardized copies, in the fourth and fifth centuries, the gospels had become very different books. Twelve or thirteen verses had been added to the ending of the

Gospel of Mark, and an entire chapter to John. There were two dramatically different versions of Matthew, and many individual verses and parables had either been inserted or deleted.

The conspiracy to suppress the information, however, actually begins at the Council of Nicea in 325 C.E. where the New Testament was officially determined. There were hundreds of different gospels circulating at the time, and the council was convened primarily to throw out controversial books, to accept certain versions of the gospels, and establish official Church doctrine. Once the council had determined the official gospels, the Roman emperor Constantine ordered that the books of "heretics," meaning Christians who held other gospels as sacred, be hunted out and destroyed. He also declared that anyone found copying them would be officially charged with heresy, which was a capital offense punishable by death.

From this point on, the Roman Empire, working with the Church, suppressed the works of anyone who not agree with the "Official Story." We see this in many places. For example, the Edict of 333 C.E., says:

"Constantine, Victor, Greatest Augustus, to bishops and laity: Arius (presbyter of Alexandria who insisted that since Jesus was indisputably 'begotten,' and therefore 'human,' he must be second to God) having imitated wicked and impious men deserves the same loss of privileges as they. Therefore, just as Porphyry [a Platonist who wrote a detailed work against Christianity] that enemy of piety who put together various illegal works against religion, got his just deserts, so that . . . his impious books have been obliterated, thus, too, we now order that Arius and those who agree with him shall be called Porphyrians . . . and if any book written by Arius be found, it is to be consigned to the fire, so that not only his corrupt teachings may vanish, but no memory of him at all may remain."

2. How do you know that twelve or thirteen verses were added to the Gospel of Mark?

We know because of the writings of early Church fathers. For example, Clement of Alexandria and Origen, bishops who lived in the 200s, had no knowledge of verses 9–20 of Mark. By the fourth century, Church historians Eusebius and Jerome wrote that they knew of the longer ending, but also said it was absent from almost all Greek manuscripts they had seen. The earliest Bible, known as the *Codex Sinaiticus,* ends at Mark 16:8. As well, Matthew 16:2, and John 5:4 and 16:24 don't exist. Luke 22:43 is marked as "spurious" by the first of nine correctors who worked on the codex between the fourth and twelfth centuries, but his words were scratched out by the third corrector. The *Sinaiticus* manuscript also includes two books that were sacred to early Christians—the Shepherd of Hermas and the Epistle of Barnabas—that are not in the modern New Testament.

3. So there was a lot of dissention in the early years of Christianity, a lot of disagreements about who Jesus was, and what he taught?

Oh, yes. In the first few decades after his death, April 7th in the year 30, there was a great disagreement about the facts of Jesus' life, and what his teachings were.

New Testament readers are familiar with part of this battle from Galatians, where Paul writes that Galatian Christians were listening to "those who would pervert the Gospel of Christ" (1:7) and believing in a "different gospel" (1:6). That "different" gospel had come from "men of repute in Jerusalem" (2:2) and Paul says that before "certain men came from James" (2:12) Cephas—Peter—had eaten with Gentiles, but after the arrival of "the circumcision party" (2:12), Cephas, Barnabas, and others separated themselves from Gentiles.

Two of the major disagreements of the first and second centuries were over the virgin birth and the bodily resurrection.

4. You claim that Jesus was not born of a virgin. How can you possibly know that?

To start off, remember that only Matthew and Luke use the word "virgin" (*parthenos* in Greek) for Mary, the mother of Jesus. In the case of Matthew 1:23 he was quoting from Isaiah 7:14 where the original Hebrew word was *alma,* which meant simply "young girl." It had none of our modern connotations of being a biological virgin.

Second, if you're searching for the truth, it's very important to ask what people who did not believe in him had to say about Jesus. And it's also important to ask why certain things were left out of the gospels. For example, the Gospel of John never mentions the name of Jesus' mother. Neither do the epistles of Paul. We have to ask, why not?

We know from the writings of ancient Greek, Roman, and Jewish historians that there a very strong tradition that Jesus was an illegitimate child. For example, in 178 C.E. the Platonist historian Celsus wrote that Mary was pregnant by a Roman soldier named Panthera and was driven away by her husband for adultery. In addition, the Jewish story of Jesus' life, the *Toledoth Yeshu,* which contains remnants from the second century, also names Pantera as Jesus' father. And we know from Roman records that Tiberius Julius Abdes Pantera of Sidon served as a Roman archer in Jerusalem from 6 B.C. to 6 C.E.

And the canonical gospels themselves contain references. In John 8:41, when Jesus is sparring with his Jewish critics in Jerusalem they say, "*we* were not born of fornication!" as if to imply that he was. As well, the noncanonical gospels have many references. In the Gospel of Nicodemus, which dates to the 300s, but probably has origins in the 100s, when Jesus is standing before Pilate, his enemy's charge, "you were born of fornication!" In verse 105 of the Gospel of Thomas, Jesus says, "He who knows the father and the mother will be called the son of a whore."

Also, when Jesus goes to preach in the temple at Nazareth the people call him the "son of Mary." The Jewish people didn't trace descent through the female until after the destruction of the Temple in the year 70. At the time our Lord was in Nazareth descent was traced through the male. To refer to a man as being the son of his mother was gravely offensive. It meant that his paternity was uncertain.

And later gospel writers knew this. So the writers of Matthew, Luke, and John go to great efforts to eliminate this reference. For example, Matthew 12:55 replaces Mary with Joseph, as does John 6:42. Later editors change Mark's words to read things like "the son of the carpenter." The gospel of Mark was often "corrected" by later writers to echo the glosses of Matthew and John.

In fact, the Pantera tradition was so widespread and persistent that early Christians could not simply dismiss it as malicious propaganda. They had to find a place for Pantera. So, for example, in the fourth century, Church father Epiphanius gave Pantera a place in the holy family, claiming that Joseph's father was known as Jacob Pantera. As late as the eighth century attempts were still being made to explain it away, as when John of Damascus writes that Mary's great-grandfather was named Pantera.

5. If Jesus was an illegitimate child, where does the story of Joseph come from?

Again, let's look at the gospels. Mark, the earliest gospel, never mentions Joseph, either directly or indirectly. As well, the Infancy Narratives that name Joseph in Matthew and Luke are problematic. First, they tell different stories. For example, Matthew 1:16, says Joseph's father was Jacob, but Luke 3:23 says his father was Heli. And none of the significant information found in the infancy narratives of either gospel is attested clearly elsewhere in the New Testament. In particular, the following items are found only in the infancy narratives:

1. The virginal conception of Jesus.
2. Jesus' birth at Bethlehem.
3. Herodian knowledge of Jesus' birth and the claim that he was the king. Rather, in Matthew 14:1–2, Herod's son seems to know nothing of Jesus.
4. Wide knowledge of Jesus' birth, since all Jerusalem was startled (Matt. 2:3), and the children of Bethlehem were killed in search of him. Rather, in Matthew 13:54–55, no one seems to know of the marvelous origins of Jesus.
5. John the Baptist is a relative of Jesus and recognized him before his birth (Luke 1:41,44.) But later in Luke 7:19 and John 1:33, John the Baptist seems to have no previous knowledge of Jesus and seems puzzled by him.

What this suggests is that the infancy narratives were once separate elements and were added later to the gospels. They are probably based upon an Old Testament pattern of birth annunciations with stereotyped features: the appearance of an angel, fear by the visionary, a divine message, an objection by the visionary, and the giving of a sign. (For example, the birth of Moses in Exod. 3:2–12 and of Gideon in Judges 6:11–32. For a comparison with Matthew's genealogy, see also Ruth 4:18–22 and 1 Chronicles 1:28, 34, and 2:1–15.)

Many scholars see Matthew's version of the story as a "pre-Matthean narrative associating the birth of Jesus, son of Joseph, with the patriarch Joseph and the birth of Moses." Note also that Joseph, Jesus' "father," like the Old Testament Joseph, had a father named Jacob, went to Egypt, had dreams of the future, was chaste, and was disinclined to shame others, which points to the possibility of there being a "Joseph typology" in Luke 1–2. In other words, using the "Joseph" story was not intended to convey fact, but rather to associate Jesus' birth with other mythic events. Both of the Infancy Narratives seem to be largely products of early Christian reflection on the salvific meaning of Jesus Christ in light of Old Testament prophecies.

In other words, the Infancy Narratives tell us practically nothing about the historical Jesus—nor about his father.

As an aside, many of the early Christian churches used versions of these gospels that did *not* include the Infancy Narratives, probably because they knew they were suspect. This is demonstrated when Theodoret, Bishop of Cyrrhus in Syria, writes about the "heretic" Tatian in 450 C.E.:

> "This fellow also composed that gospel called "By the Four," cutting off the genealogies and such other things as show that the Lord was, as for his body, a descendent of David. Not only the adherents of his party used this gospel, but also those who followed the apostolic teaching. . . . I found more than two hundred such books revered in the churches of my own diocese, and collecting them all, I did away with them and introduced instead the gospels of the four evangelists."

6. **I was intrigued by your analysis of the Gospel of Mark. You say that the author of that gospel probably lived in Rome, and that all the ugly things he says about Jews had a political context. What was going on politically?**

When Jesus' brother James was murdered sometime between 62–70 C.E., relations within Judaism began to fall apart, then the Jewish Revolt of 66 cut all communications with the Mother Church in Jerusalem. Mark and his community in Rome were suddenly rudderless. To make matters worse, to the Romans, Christians *were* Jews. Judaism and Christianity did not split until around 85 C.E., at exactly the time when the gospels of Matthew and Luke were being written. To the Romans there were Jews who believed the Messiah had come, and there were Jews who believed the Messiah had not yet come. The persecution must have been unbearable. In part, at least, Mark's gospel was probably a deliberate attempt to shout, "We are not Jews!" Undoubtedly one of the reasons Mark chose to vilify Jews in his gospel was that by shifting the blame for Jesus' death from Rome, where it belonged, to the Jews, it solved a major public relations problem for Christians in Rome. It was like saying, "Yes, the Jews are killing your sons and husbands in Palestine, but they also killed our Lord. We are *not* Jews! In fact, we hate Jews as much as you do!" The historical legacy of Mark's vilification, however, is wrenching. Before the end of the first century, Christians were forbidden to enter synagogues. By the close of the fourth century, marriages between Jews and Christians were prohibited, and if such marriages occurred, they were treated as adultery. Legislation was promulgated forbidding Jews to proselytize, or build new temples, and if a temple had been destroyed, they were forbidden to rebuild it.

His words have, unfortunately, been used to support the murder of millions—though at the time, they were simply self-defense.

7. **You mention that the gospels of Matthew and Luke date to around 85 C.E. What do the other gospels actually date to, and who wrote them? We all know they are attributed to Matthew, Mark, Luke, and John, but you say those are made-up names. Who made them up and when?**

Yes, the documents themselves are silent as to the names of their authors. During the second century, early Christian scholars attributed the books to Mark, Matthew, Luke, and John, but nowhere in any of the texts is the author cited.

Mark dates to between 68–70 C.E., Matthew to around 80 C.E., Luke dates to 85 C.E., and John to around 100 C.E. The earliest written works that record Jesus' life are actually seven letters from Paul, which date to the 50s, and are incorporated in the New Testament. (Scholars generally agree that Romans, 1 and 2 Corinthians, Galatians, Philippians, 1 Thessalonians, and Philemon are genuinely from Paul's hand.) But the first versions of Mark, Matthew, Luke, and John did not appear until after the deaths of James, Peter, and Paul, which occurred just before the destruction of the Temple of 70 C.E.—almost forty years after the death of Jesus.

Incidentally, the oldest surviving New Testament gospel is a 3.4-inch-tall fragment of the Gospel of John that dates to around 125–135 C.E. The earliest copies of the other gospels date to the fourth or fifth centuries.

8. I want to know how you can claim that he did not bodily resurrect from the cross. If he didn't resurrect, what happened to his body?

According to Jewish law, his relatives would have been required to bury him. In the sixteenth century, Rabbi Isaac Luria listed Jesus' burial site in Galilee, just north of Safed, in a graveyard he called, "the burial places of the righteous."

Remember that the earliest version of the earliest gospel, Mark, has no resurrection, nor does the apocryphal Gospel of Thomas. We know that Matthew and Luke, written a decade or two later, include the story of the resurrection. Also, many early Christians did not believe in the resurrection. We know this because early Church leaders like Polycarp, Bishop of Smyrna, 70–156 C.E., wrote an attack against those who "denied the resurrection" by, he says, "perverting the logia of the Lord." Apparently collections of Jesus' sayings and life story that did not include resurrection, probably more than just the gospels of Mark and Thomas, were circulating.

Scholars generally agree that Matthew and Luke used two "gospels" to compose their stories: the Gospel of Mark, which they incorporated almost word for word, and an unknown gospel that scholars refer to as the "Q" document. One of the interesting things about the Q document is that it contains no references to Jesus' miraculous birth or his resurrection. (A good analysis of this can be found in Chapter 3 of Philip Jenkins's book, *Hidden Gospels: How the Search for Jesus Lost Its Way.*)

What seems clear is that there was an early Christian community that saw little significance in the idea of the Virgin Birth or the Resurrection, or had not yet felt the need to invent the stories. They believed that Jesus' significance lay in his words, and his words alone.

9. Give me some examples of undeniable factual errors in the New Testament gospels.

Let's just talk about a few of the obvious errors.

1. Despite what the evangelists record, we know from a wide variety of historical resources that there was no eclipse of the sun during Passover of the year 30. There was an eclipse of the sun during the month of Nisan (April) in the year 33, but it was utterly invisible from Jerusalem. The only solar eclipse visible from Jerusalem during the time period in question occurred on November 24th of the year 29. There were, however, eclipses of the moon on the eve of Passover in the years 30 and 33.

2. The authors of the gospels call Pontius Pilate the "Procurator of Judea." That term is incorrect. Governors were not referred to as Procurators until after the reign of Claudius in 41 c.e. When Jesus was alive, Pilate was called the "Prefect of Judea," which we know not only from Roman records, but from archaeological inscriptions that date to the period of his rule.

3. The story of Barabbas' release invokes a tradition called the *privilegium paschale* that did not exist in the time of Jesus. Had there been either a Jewish or Roman law establishing such a Passover custom there would be a record of its application either before Jesus, or immediately after him, by some governor, bishop, or priest somewhere. There isn't. Not until the year 367 do we find a Roman law which establishes a custom for pardoning criminals on the feast of Easter, "except for those guilty of sacrilege, adulterers, ravishers, or homicides." So, even in

367 C.E., the convicted murderer, Barabbas, would not have been eligible for release.

4. Luke states that "It happened in those days that a decree went out from Caesar Augustus that the whole world be registered for a tax," but the decree first went out while Cyrenius was governor of Syria. This is the census that leads Joseph and Mary to go to Bethlehem where Jesus was supposedly born. However, we know Cyrenius, which is the Greek form of the name Quirinius, was governor of Syria in 6–7 C.E. We know that the census was held in 6–7 C.E., both from an inscription in Aleppo in Syria, as well as from Josephus. There is no other evidence for an empire-wide census during the reign of Augustus . . . so Luke got the date wrong.

Such anachronisms are very important because they help scholars date the documents.

10. You say the gospels are wrong, that the Jews could not possibly have tried Jesus on the eve of Passover, just before the crucifixion. Why not?

It was against Jewish law. The Sanhedrin could not try a criminal case in a private house, even the High Priest's house. It was not allowed to try cases at night, or on festival days, or on the eve of festival days—all of which the gospels say happened.

The ignorance of Jewish Law displayed by the authors of gospels is colossal.

11. You claim that the only reason for the Sanhedrin to have held a council meeting that night was to prepare *a defense* for Jesus when he went to trial before Pontius Pilate the next morning. Why would High Priest Kaiaphas, his enemy, do that?

Because there was more at stake than just one man's life. Jesus was, according to all sources, beloved by the people, and certainly some members of the Sanhedrin felt the same way. We know that Joseph of Arimathea and Nicodemus could have been counted upon to defend a beloved Jewish son from the hated Roman oppressors. Pilate had assembled three Roman legions around Jerusalem for Passover, either because he expected trouble or because he wanted to provoke it. The Sanhedrin must have been terrified that Jesus' death would spark a revolt that would result in the destruction of Israel—as Kaiaphas says in John 11:47–48, and history demonstrated that Kaiaphas was right. The insurrection against Rome that began in 66 C.E. ended with the Temple burned, Jerusalem in ashes, and the population decimated and scattered.

Also, consider what the four gospels say. A condemnation (guilty sentence) is found only in Mark 14:64. Matthew 26:66 records that the Sanhedrin "said" he was guilty. Luke 22:71 has the Sanhedrin saying only "what need we of further witnesses." And John deletes the entire trial, probably because he understood Jewish Law better than the other Greek-speaking evangelists.

If the Sanhedrin met that night, it was not to hold court.

12. So you say Jesus was tried for a crime against Rome: Treason. Is there any evidence of this trial in the Roman archives? Surely if he'd been so tried Pilate would have had to make a report.

Though Pilate would have been required to make such a report, there isn't one in the Roman archives. The logical explanation is that there was no trial. First of all, a confession would have made a trial unnecessary. Also, Pilate was well known for executing prisoners who had never seen trial. Add to this the fact that Roman historian, Tacitus (55–115 C.E.) writes in his *Annales,* 15.44, only that Pilate had Jesus executed. He mentions no trial.

13. You say that the apostle Peter and Mary Magdalen practically hated each other. What's the evidence for that?

We find evidence for it in several noncanonical books, the *Gospel of Philip,* the *Dialogue of the Savior,* the *Gospel of Mary,* and the *Pistis Sophia.* Here are a couple of examples:

1. In the *Gospel of Mary*, after the crucifixion the disciples are terrified and disheartened and ask Mary to tell them what the Savior said to her secretly. When she does, Peter, furious, says: "Did he really speak privately with a woman? . . . Are we to turn about and all listen to her?" Mary, upset by his anger, says, "My brother, Peter, what do you think? Do you think that I thought this up myself in my heart, or that I am lying about the Savior?" At this point Levi breaks in and says, "Peter, you have always been hot-tempered. Now I see you contending against the woman like the adversaries. If the savior made her worthy, who are you to reject her?"

2. In the *Pistis Sophia*, another argument occurs between Mary and Peter. Peter complains that Mary is dominating the conversation with Jesus and displacing the rightful priority of Peter and the other apostles. He urges Jesus to silence her, but Jesus rebukes him and says that "whoever the Spirit inspires to speak is divinely ordained to speak, whether man or woman." Later, Mary says to Jesus, "Peter makes me hesitate: I am afraid of him because he hates the female race."

3. And in the Gospel of Thomas, Peter says, "Let Mary leave us, for women are not worthy of life."

14. **The Gospel of John 18:31 credits Jews with saying to Pilate, "It is not lawful for us to put any man to death. . . ." You say this could not possibly have been said by any Jew with any authority, because it's simply not true. How do you know?**

Because the Sanhedrin *did* exercise jurisdiction over capital cases, as is verified by Acts 4:1–22 and 5:17–42, as well as the historian Josephus in his *Jewish Wars*, 6,2,4.

15. **Most people are going to be surprised to discover that Jesus had four brothers and two sisters. What were their names? How do you know they were real brothers and sisters, and not just stepbrothers, or cousins?**

All of the extant original gospels were written in Greek. The Greek word for "brother" is *adelphos*. While the term was often used symbolically, when it applies directly to Jesus, as in Mark 6:3, when the text says that Jesus is the son of Mary and brother (*adelphos*) of James, Joses, Jude, and Simon, it clearly means a physical relationship, not just a symbolic one. In fact, there is no clear case in the New Testament where *adelphos* means step-brother or cousin. The Greek term for cousin is *anepsios,* and Mark does not call any of these men Jesus' *anepsios.* As well, in both Galatians 1:19, and 1 Corinthians 9:5, Paul uses the term *adelphos,* when he is talking about the brothers of the Lord. Since he uses the term *anepsios* in Col. 4:10, he obviously knew the difference.

We know the probable name of only one of Jesus' sisters, Mary.

This tradition of Jesus having real brothers and sisters was kept alive by at least some Church leaders up until the fourth century, when Mary's perpetual virginity was established as Church dogma.

16. You say that in 135 C.E., Golgotha, the location of the tomb of Jesus, became a landfill, and was covered over by a statue to Aphrodite. Who did that and why? Were they trying to destroy the tomb of Jesus?

After the Bar Kokhba rebellion, which lasted from 132 to 135 C.E., Emperor Hadrian, who was trying to destroy the Jews and everything they cherished, changed the name of Jerusalem to Colonia Aelia Capitolina, and as part of the construction of the city turned the *Kraniou Topon,* the Place of the Skull, into a vast landfill upon which he built a Temple to Aphrodite.

And that was not the only time the sacred Christian sites were assaulted. In the year 303, Emperor Diocletian ordered the destruction of all Christian churches and texts.

17. Disagreements in the New Testament gospels created a big controversy over the date of Easter, didn't they?

Yes, this was a very difficult subject in early Christianity. In Asia Minor, Easter was celebrated on the Jewish Passover (Pesach), that being the date of the crucifixion in the Gospel of John. But Matthew, Luke, and Mark make the Last Supper the Passover meal, and place the crucifixion a day later. In the 150s Polycarp of Smyrna visited Rome to discuss this issue, but no agreement could be reached. Rome insisted upon celebrating Easter on the Sunday following the first full moon after the spring equinox, and nothing was going to change its mind. In the 190s Bishop Victor of Rome was so upset that the churches in Asia Minor celebrated Easter on the Jewish Passover that he threatened to excommunicate anyone who did not adopt the Roman date. In the mid third century Bishop Stephen of Rome got into a vehement argument over this subject with Bishop Cyprian of Carthage, who had the support of the Greek East. It was the first occasion on which the Bishop of Rome is known to have invoked Matthew 16:18 to justify the primacy of Rome. This disagreement would be one of the lasting disputes between the Eastern Church and the Western Church.

18. You footnoted your novel. Isn't that a little unusual? I mean, fiction is fiction, right?

Yes, and no. In all of our books we use the best nonfiction information available to re-create the past. With this book, we felt it was especially important to footnote our sources. People have a right to know where the information comes from.

19. You are both archaeologists. You must have known that this book would stir up a lot of controversy. Why did you want to write *The Betrayal*?

Because over the centuries the myth of Jesus has so obscured the actual facts of his life that his true story has been lost. We wrote *The Betrayal* in the heartfelt belief that people have a right to know who and what Jesus was. They have a right to read his original words, not those put into his mouth by later politicians with a doctrinal agenda.

We genuinely believe that knowledge does not destroy faith. It does not take Jesus away. In fact, we hope *The Betrayal* can give back the profound meaning of his life that has been stolen by centuries of revisionism.